The General

'The exercise of great power is a wonderful feeling, Charlotte . . . There is a problem. You are not a man. You will have to be better, fight harder than any man can. You must overcome the prejudices and use the abilities of men who would otherwise stand in your way. When you have power you may use it to the full, use it to make a better world. But first you must have it.'

'Thank you grandfather. I will think about it all. It does seem simple enough. Even obviously true. But how am I to know I can do it?'

Patrick Coogan was born the son of a labourer in 1950 in Belfast. His background includes both Loyalists and Republicans: he is fiercely independent of either. He was burned out of his home by Loyalists aged eighteen, and has lost relatives to PIRA. After school in the Falls road he won the Director of Studies Prize at the Royal Military Academy, Sandhurst, rising from Private Soldier to Major in fourteen years. He has now left the Army and lives in Essex.

A great many people brought this book to you. They are:

Jennifer Kavanagh, literary agent and real woman, who took a chance on me. She never gave in, over four long years. I am in your hands courtesy of JK.

Major George H. MBE, who believed so hard I could not let him down. If only for him, this is the best I can do right now.

Caroline Upcher, editor. Caroline has 'diamond bullet' perception and a firm grip on reality. Her input and support have been invaluable.

A number of soldiers, male and female: unnameable because they have not yet faded away. All but one, Major Ivor S., (Ret'd), resident expert in small arms ballistics at Bisley, are still serving.

Beth Humphries, copy editor, who read every word and made sure it was right.

To them all, my deepest thanks.

Patrick Coogan

THE GENERAL

Patrick Coogan

Mandarin

To John Keegan, my Sandhurst tutor, who managed to teach me how but not what to think. Fred Shorrock, who taught me how to get within ten feet of an alert, heavily armed Gurkha sentry; and more importantly, how to get away alive. John Corless, that most honest and loyal of men, who publicly declared me to be the finest young officer he had ever met, and privately kicked my arrogant Second Lieutenant's arse, until he judged me ready for command of his beloved soldiers, my first platoon. I hope I have let none of them down.

A Mandarin Paperback
THE GENERAL

First published in Great Britain 1993
by Sinclair-Stevenson
This edition published 1994
by Mandarin Paperbacks
an imprint of Reed Consumer Books Ltd
Michelin House, 81 Fulham Road, London SW3 6RB
and Auckland, Melbourne, Singapore and Toronto

Copyright © Patrick Coogan
The author has asserted his moral rights

A CIP catalogue record for this title
is available from the British Library
ISBN 0 7493 1689 6

Printed and bound in Great Britain
by Cox & Wyman Ltd, Reading, Berkshire

Chapter One

1.45 a.m. 4 June 1993

LISBURN

Charlotte Aitken snapped the worn leather cover over the luminous face of her watch, quickening her pace as she stepped out in the dark, irritated by the rain lashing across the narrow stone path through the heavy, dripping old pines. 'Damn this bloody country,' she muttered. 'Weather like this in June for God's sake!'

A dim blue lamp came on over the black glass door of the block as Charlotte removed her beret, spoke into the entryphone and turned her face to the camera. Inside, behind the lamp, an unseen Royal Pioneer Corps security guard flicked a switch, checking her voice against a tape marked with her name, her face against a computer-generated image of her salient features superimposed on the screen. He had no choices or judgements to make: the computer in an armoured safe did it for him. A green light on his panel indicated a good match to voice and face. The Pioneer moved to the next stage of the block's entry procedures.

'Your hand, please.'

Charlotte watched a thin aluminium panel slide back to expose a convex glass shape set into the wall. She placed her left hand over it, lightly gripping the warm, smooth surface. The guard checked the computer; palm and fingerprints OK. He flicked two switches, one to deactivate the CS riot gas spray directly opposite Charlotte's face, the other to activate an infra-red scanning camera and a set of movement sensors on the door side of the block. All clear. Finally he pressed the door switch. Half a ton of steel slid back into its slot in the wall behind the black glass, allowing Charlotte into the block, a windowless concrete cube with walls eight feet thick, coyly faced with pretty red brick and false windows in a surprisingly effective attempt to make it look like a standard army office building. Down in the bowels of the block, in the Intelligence Centre operations room Corporal Harry Green dropped a pink file marked SECRET over the spread legs of the 'Girl of the Month' and leapt to his feet as his brigadier stalked into the room, taking in everything in a long sweeping glance. *Shit, does that sodding woman never sleep?*

'Good morning Brigadier, what can I do for you Ma'am?'

'Anything from Bravo?'

Green thought the brigadier looked worried, but it was hard to tell what went on behind that beautiful, ruthless face. 'Nothing ma'am. He's due to call in about now.'

'I know that. Anything from the SAS or the Bessbrook operations room?' Charlotte Aitken turned slightly, her weight on one foot, bringing the full force of her personality to bear on the young corporal. Green swallowed hard. 'Nothing much, ma'am. The Heregans are busy setting up a couple of observation posts to keep an eye on some unauthorised crossing points in Tyrone and the grunts are following their usual pattern in the area of concern, nothing anywhere close to our man. Why don't you take a bleeper and get some sleep, ma'am? I'll call you if anything happens.'

The cold blue eyes warmed, seeming to lighten in colour, and the tall slim figure eased visibly as she glanced at the clock. A soft smile cracked the frost. 'Don't let the infantry hear you calling them grunts. And Heregans?'

Green smiled in return. 'SAS. Hereford hooligans, ma'am.'

Again the smile, a little more strained as she checked the clock again. 'Very well, once he's called in I'll take a bleeper. Wake me for his six o'clock call. What's in that file you're reading, anything new?'

Green blanched. 'No, ma'am.'

'Then why are you reading it? Let me see.' She stepped

2

over to the desk and lifted the file, dropping it instantly as she caught sight of the centrefold below it. She turned the magazine to a better angle, to get a better look. Green quailed. Brigadier Aitken was not an officer to be on the wrong side of: better men than he had found themselves booted out on their arses, their careers in tatters, without so much as a goodbye when they had failed to live up to her standards.

The eyes were dark and chilling again, the cut glass voice lashing into him. 'I was not aware of your studies in gynaecology, Corporal. Get rid of this rubbish and concentrate on your duties.'

'Yes, ma'am. I'm sorry.'

'Don't be sorry. Be professional. Anyone can make a mistake. You have had yours. I will not tolerate such dereliction of duty again. Am I understood?'

Green quivered with relief. 'Yes, Brigadier. It won't happen again.' He moved to turn back to his desk but her eyes held him pinned. Her voice softened as her mind seemed to change gear. 'Corporal, there is a very brave man out there in the dark depending on you. You know that. If he needs you he will need you to act very quickly and he will need you to get it right first time. Be ready for him.'

Green felt his cheeks burn with embarrassment, furious with himself, furious at having to see the intensity in her eyes. He picked up the magazine and dropped it into the big, heavy duty shredder beside the desk.

Both soldiers jumped as the voice burst out of the speakers set in the wall. It was exactly two o'clock. 'Zero, this is Bravo. No change, over.'

Corporal Green grabbed the telephone-type handset, depressing the SEND button with his thumb. 'Zero. No change. Ou . . .' Brigadier Aitken grabbed the handset. 'Bravo, this is Zero Nine. I am here if you need me, over.'

Green was shocked by the whiteness of her knuckles on the handset, the worry in her voice, the bend in her body as she seemed to pour the essence of herself into the ether, shocked at the break in procedure and her personal intervention. More than anything he was shocked by her tone. It was the tone he heard in his wife's voice when his job took him into danger, when she was frightened for him.

Again the voice from the wall, softer, less abrupt. 'Bravo. I know. It's enough. Out.'

Charlotte Aitken dropped the handset and covered her face with her hands, her body in its combat suit and boots rigid.

Suddenly, Corporal Green understood. He grabbed his message pad and wrote quickly, then held the pad out to her. He coughed to get her attention. 'My report, ma'am.' His brigadier took the pad and read the latest in the list of radio reports between her headquarters and the man in the field. It was no different from the others, a five-second exchange recording No Change.

Charlotte Aitken relaxed a little, looking carefully at Green. 'This is not a true . . .' Green turned away. 'Beg pardon for interrupting you, Brigadier. That's all I heard. Take the bleeper. Get some sleep. Leave Bravo with me. I'll not let him down.'

Chapter Two

20 March 1953

ALDERSHOT, HAMPSHIRE

'Matron?'

'Speaking.'

'Captain Helleston, Duty Midwife. We have a problem brewing here ma'am. A retired general and his son-in-law, a padre, the father to be. The gentlemen appear to be in some conflict. We need you to grip them before they disturb the mother ... Mother and baby are well ma'am ... A little girl ... No, the gentlemen have not been told ... The general may be difficult; he has been visiting and talking widely about his first grandson ma'am ... I am grateful ma'am, ten minutes then. Goodbye.'

Major-General (Retd.) Alexander Hopkinson crushed the remnants of his cigar into the tall brass ashtray, grimacing at the nervous pacing of his son-in-law. *Twitching about like a bloody ballerina. Weak. No guts. Never had.* 'Sit down, will you, Charles. Have some dignity.' The Reverend Charles Aitken, his normal unhealthy pallor worsened by worry about his wife's protracted labour rounded on the old general. 'Don't tell me how to behave, General. I'm tired of your interference. Bessie is not strong. This could be too much for her.'

Anger and contempt darkened the general's thin, almost ascetic face. 'Rubbish. Elizabeth is as strong as a mule. Producing babies is a perfectly normal female activity. It's what women are for. Faffing about your parish drinking tea with a bunch of middle-aged hypochondriacs whining about the state of their nerves is no good for a daughter of mine. You should get off your arse and get a grip on your career. You're nearly fifty and

5

still a curate. You're a failure, man. What Elizabeth ever saw in you I'll never know.'

'Will you never underst–' Charles Aitken stopped in mid-sentence, jerking as a small, whip-thin lieutenant-colonel in the dawn-grey ward dress and scarlet tippet of the Queen Alexandra's Royal Army Nursing Corps strode sharply into the waiting room. The colonel's head-dress, a huge white linen diamond starched stiff as a breadboard, forced her to turn her whole body to survey the room. Competence and authority no mere man would even consider querying exuded from her every pore, matched and reinforced by a presence far greater than her physical size. 'Reverend Aitken? I am Charlotte Bruce-Adams, matron of this hospital. I am delighted to tell you that you have a lovely daughter, with all her fingers and toes and a powerful pair of lungs. Your daughter is a beautiful baby, strong and healthy. Mother is well, but a little tired. You can see them both tomorrow, when mother is ready to receive you.' She smiled brightly. 'What's your daughter's name to be? My staff will need it for her identification label.'

Charles Aitken slumped into a chair, unable for the moment to speak, praying silently, giving thanks for the safe delivery and dreading the old general's reaction. But the general was already on his feet. 'Daughter? A bloody daughter? I wanted a . . .' He stopped himself and turned on the hunched figure of Charles Aitken. 'I might have expected it, you worthless creeping Jesus. Not enough balls to give my girl a son, damn you. You're despicable, Aitken, a useless God-bothering half excuse for a man. I have a bloody good mind to . . .' The QA colonel, ready for but still horrified at the scene, decided to take command immediately.

'General! You will compose yourself, sir! How dare you behave in this way in my hospital. I must, with respect, remind you that I command here, not you: I will not hesitate to have you removed forthwith if you persist in such unbecoming conduct. I trust that, when calmer, you will be thoroughly ashamed of yourself. Reverend Aitken, you will give your little girl a name, now.'

The Reverend Aitken did not move or utter a sound. General Hopkinson, watching closely, saw his chance for lifetime dominance, be it boy or girl. He fought his fury as he clamped both hands around his ashplant stick and spoke at first through clenched teeth, easing as the words came. 'Thank you, Matron. I forgot myself, please forgive me. This is Queen Charlotte's Hospital. The girl's father is Charles. Your own name is Charlotte. On the other hand you wear Queen Alexandra's Cross and I am Alexander. Charlotte wins three to two. I see no reason to tempt fate. Charlotte it is. I will arrange to have the girl christened as such at the Royal Military Academy, Sandhurst, in due time.'

Lieutenant-Colonel Charlotte Bruce-Adams, appalled at the general's callous indifference to any preference the baby's parents might have switched her attention to the Reverend Aitken, who was still sitting silent, with his head down. She expected some sign of anger or objection from him, why she did not know: the padre had not spoken a word since she had entered the room. *Maybe the general is right. Maybe Aitken is a nonentity.* The soldier in her sided with the general, preferring positive action of some kind to no action of any kind, but her voice was edged with her irritation with both men. 'Very well, General. I will convey to your daughter your joy in baby Charlotte. A warning: I will not tolerate a repeat of this disgraceful scene in Mrs Aitken's hearing. You may visit her of course, but I direct that you and the Reverend Aitken do so separately. I am extremely disappointed in having to issue such a distasteful order, but you should not doubt that I will enforce it. Gentlemen, you should both be proud of the way Mrs Aitken has borne up throughout a long and difficult confinement. She has presented you with a fine, healthy baby. Be thankful for that. Good day to you.'

Chapter Three

4 September 1956

BELFAST

Four small boys stood in the doorway of old Joe Carlin's butcher's shop, round eyed, watching the battle. Jamie Lappin and Gerry Madden, aged six, and Mick and Joe O'Halloran, aged seven, had seen it all before but never so close or with so many people fighting. Nearly every grown man in the district seemed to be there. They were fighting in the grey drizzle of late afternoon rain, fighting in the middle of the Falls Road with wooden staves and flat square spades, fighting the RUC breaking the painted-over window of the little shop that sold sweets and pens and exercise books and flew a green, white and gold flag above the door. There was a lot happening in the confused, noisy battle, but Jamie Lappin had eyes only for one of the fighters, a huge man in denims using the flat of a spade as a club. The big man was his father, Big Jamie Lappin. Beside Jamie his friend Gerry Madden jumped up and down, excited, not really understanding what was happening.

Wee Jamie lost sight of his father, began to get frightened, the tears starting in the corners of his eyes. More Peelers, piling shouting out of Black Marias, charged in from North Howard Street, outflanking the labourers fighting for their flag. It was too much. Sprawling bodies bleeding from the head littered the road and pavement as the long black sticks swung in disciplined arcs.

Suddenly Mick O'Halloran grabbed his twin brother's hand and ran out of the doorway, keeping close to the wall, running up the street and away. Jamie and Gerry stayed on, watching out

8

for Big Jamie. But the big man was nowhere in sight. Behind them old Joe Carlin, who had seen Big Jamie felled by a blow from a Peeler's riot stick and bundled unconscious into one of the Black Marias, crossed himself and offered a prayer for the young men the Peelers had lifted. They would be beaten hard and sore in the cells of Hastings Street and Brown's Square Barracks before being dragged down to the Law Courts in the morning to get six months a skull for rioting.

Old Joe took a quick look round his shop. He had two sides of beef and a couple of pigs hung up on hooks. His counter carried a few steaks, cut thin for grilling with butter on a plate. Chopped bits and pieces bought that way at the abattoir, plus some mince for stews lay on scrubbed wooden boards in his window. Pyramids of smoked pigs' trotters and knuckles, greasy brown cannonballs of skin and gristle, stood on upturned butter boxes near the door as belly fillers for the poor. Grabbing hold of Jamie Lappin he spun the boy round, tearing his eyes from their fascination with every move that occurred on the street. Joe stuck a trotter wrapped in brown paper into his hand.

'Get away home, Jamie, out of this. Share this with himself there on the way. Straight home now boy. I'll see your Ma tomorrow and ask her what time you got in. You'll get your arse tanned the colour of the devil's elbow if you don't heed what I say. Listen to me now. Tell your Ma I said that Big Jamie will be away a while. Tell that back to me.'

Jamie, used to adults giving him messages to run, knew what he had to tell. 'I'm to go straight home and tell my Ma that my Da will be away a while, Mr Carlin.' He paused. 'Where will my Da be?'

'Never mind that now. Away you go.' Jamie, his oversized coat hanging off one shoulder, shifted his schoolbag, an old army small pack, pulling his coat around him.

'OK, Mr Carlin, thanks for the pig's foot. See us, we're away. Come on Gerry.'

Old Joe shut up his shop, muttering to himself. In the sitting room of the house behind the shop he walked into another scene of conflict. Joe's daughter Marion stood in the kitchen doorway, her own two boys hanging on her skirts, all three staring at her husband sprawled drunk and cursing on the floor, unable to get up. Marion's face was streaked with tears, taut with humiliation and anger, a bruise growing under her left eye. Seeing old Joe, she stiffened, half hysterical. 'Look at that pig! I'd like to stick a knife in him. He came in the back door, staggering. I thought he'd been hurt out fighting with the other men. Some hope there. Staggering drunk he was, not a mark on him. He's been slabbering on about his brave deeds. It's all shite, Daddy. He's been drinking all day with that scum in MacLaverty's bar, talking big and hiding in case somebody put a pick handle in his hand and asked him out to fight the peelers. He hit me for telling him. He says he can't risk being lifted in case he's needed by the IRA. There is no IRA any more. He's dirt, that's what he is, dirt. He can lie there. I hope he chokes.' She burst into fresh tears of shame and rage. 'Oh Daddy, what'll I do? My man's a coward. I'll not be able to hold my head up in the street. What'll I do, Daddy?'

Old Joe sighed. This wasn't the first time Marion had collected a black eye for speaking out of turn. But she was right. Eddie McCaillim was dirt, a goodlooking, soft bellied Dublin-born gobshite whose life revolved around avoiding work, chasing silly mill girls, drinking and swaggering about his membership of the IRA. But he was, and would always be Marion's husband. 'Take the wee ones home Marion, before your Mammy gets back and sees your eye. Wash your face. Leave McCaillim here with me. I'll send him on when he's sober.'

Jogging and walking Jamie Lappin and Gerry Madden took turns to gnaw at the trotter old Joe had given them, its smoky pork taste setting their bellies grumbling. They would need a drink when they got home, for the trotter was salty and greasy.

In a mill house in David Street, just off the Falls, beside themselves with worry, sat three women; one old one trying hard to comfort the younger two, but feeling a sick emptiness inside herself. Maria Corbett understood only too well what might have happened and did her best to calm the others. News of the riot had travelled fast. One of the young women, growing fat on a diet of potatoes and fried sausages was in tears, her hair, rat tailed from the rain, hanging over her crumpled face. She had run round from her own house in Conway Street to see if her youngest child was here. He should have been. Jamie and Gerry were always together, even sleeping in the beds they shared with their brothers, five to each big old double bed, head to toe like sardines in a tin. But the boys were not here. Shuddering with panic Josie Lappin told Philomena Madden and Maria Corbett about the riot. Philomena collapsed on to the small two-seater settee her man had bought her in the Markets.

'Jesus, Mary and Joseph. Gerry said they were going to the pet shop from school, to see a parrot.'

Josie cringed. The pet shop was down the Falls, beyond where the riot had been. Philomena was crying now too, sobbing incoherent prayers for wee Gerry's safety. Maria, her own sons grown and gone, one to Dublin, one to England, nodded to Patricia, Philomena's eldest daughter. Patricia moved into the kitchen to put the teapot on the gas. Out there she found two of her brothers, aged nine and eleven.

'Get away out down the road and find Jamie and our Gerry. Bring them straight home.' Patricia wished her father was not always away working in England. Sighing, she tried to reassure her mother.

'They'll be all right, Ma. Somebody will look after them. Tommy and Peter are away to get them home. Don't worry yourself. Here's a cup of tea and a piece.'

Patricia held out a small tin tray, a giveaway from Guinness telling the world 'Guinness is good for you' in worn, almost illegible script. It held three saucerless cups of sweet tea, without milk. Balanced on Patricia's forearm were thick rounds of buttered bread, one for each woman.

'They'll be back soon. Don't worry, Ma.'

11

No sooner had Patricia spoken than a commotion in the tiny hallway between the room door and the street caught the women's attention. The door flew open. Jamie and Gerry burst in, their faces greasy. Their mothers shrieked and pulled them on to their knees, hugging them close and bursting into fresh tears, frightening them. Wee Jamie, knowing something was very wrong, forgot to pass on Old Joe Carlin's message.

The cell Sergeant Billy McNeill of the Royal Ulster Constabulary stared into was oblong in shape, nine feet long and seven feet wide, built of unplastered concrete. The door, just wide enough for one man at a time to walk through, sideways on, was at the end of one of the short walls, so that the entire cell could be seen from the slot. There were no windows in the cell and the ceiling was high, holding a 40-watt bulb inside a wire mesh, controlled by a switch in the corridor. The dark red stone tiles that sloped gently toward a bolted down drainage grille in the middle of the floor barely offered a contrast to the dull brown gloss paint of the walls. The ceiling, apart from a two foot square of white emulsion around the dim bulb, was black.

Deliberately chosen for effect and convenience the cell's colour scheme and textural mix of rough stone tiles and shiny brown concrete, lit dimly from above, had a strong psychological impact on anyone confined in it for more than twenty minutes. It generated a feeling of defeat and despair, debilitating enough in itself without the ever present threat of a severe beating. McNeill liked this cell; even the hardest of the hard men were reduced by it to a state of anxiety in which their beating, when it came, seemed a relief of some sort: they rarely fought back.

The cell had no furniture or fittings. Bloodspots on the shiny gloss paint and stone tiles could be easily washed down, using the fire hose in the corridor. In the cell now were three men, one lying on the floor, the other two whispering together in the corner farthest from the door. They all wore blue denim dungarees, cheap imitations of the Wrangler and Lévi-Strauss jeans flooding the market. The one on the floor, Big Jamie Lappin, had a denim jacket over a heavy cotton work shirt patterned in the dark hunting tartan of the Campbells: the other two wore donkey jackets with CEMENTATION blazoned in yellow across the back: their shirts, bought as seconds from Milliken's in Andersonstown, sported flawed Tattersall checks, no less warm for all their flaws. The men's waterboots had the tops turned down for comfort, showing three inches of scuffed canvas lining against the black of the rubber, and all three were liberally spattered with dried mud. NcNeill hated them. He turned to the big constable waiting in the corridor.

'Know them?'

The constable, well used to NcNcill's ways, answered promptly.

'Taigs, Sergeant. The whole fucking nest of them should be burnt out of their filthy backstreets and chased over the border away from decent Protestants.'

NcNeill nodded, his mouth tightening. 'You're right, Constable. But mind your language; I've been born again and saved. The Lord Jesus Christ knows the truth of what you say but would burn you for your filthy tongue. Let's just say they're not good Protestants and not loyal to the Crown, all right?'

'Yes, Sergeant. I'm sorry. What do you want me to do?'

'You know what to do. I'll be back in a minute. Wait here.' Turning from the slot NcNeill walked quietly, unhurried, down the corridor to the rest room.

The room was crowded with excited policemen reliving the afternoon's fight; it was thick with cigarette smoke and smelt of sweat and Johnson's floor polish. Shouldering his way through the noisy crowd NcNeill beckoned to first one constable, then another; they followed him out, back into the corridor. As the door closed behind them Constable Nat Carson crushed his cigarette into an old tin and reached out to stop a white-faced young constable fresh out of the police college at Enniskillen from following the chosen ones.

'Stay here boy. You'll do no good. Those Taigs have got it

coming and they're going to get it. Bumps and bruises, that's all. They have to be in court tomorrow. Sit down son. They deserve it. Don't trouble yourself.'

Looking into the face of the older man Peter Ewart hesitated. What was happening was wrong, against the law. He wanted to stop it, but could not. Tired, confused and with the realisation of impotence dawning in him he slumped down on the bench.

'Don't worry about it, Peter, you're young yet. I've been on the streets for nearly thirty years, not long after the province was made safe for decent Protestants. A good hiding is all these people understand. You can't reason with them. A mailed fist in a mailed glove is all they know. Remember, Peter, it's us or them. You'll be all right.'

Reaching out he pulled the young man's ear, a gesture of fondness, of seniority, of weariness. Out of a sewn-in pocket of his jacket the elderly constable, his bones feeling the joints between them, drew a metal flask. 'Get a slug of that down you. It'll calm your nerves.'

Nat Carson, three years from retirement, watched with wet pebblestone eyes as the young lad carefully took a pull at the flask, coughing.

'Christ Nat, that's rough stuff.' The young man's eyes were watering and his voice was hoarse, but he felt better, if slightly sick still. He handed back the flask.

'Don't let Sergeant NcNeill hear you taking the Lord's name in vain. You'll be on night duty in the Docks for a month.'

Peter laughed as Carson pulled a face in imitation of the 'good living' NcNeill. The sergeant neither smoked nor drank and spent his Sunday nights bible thumping and handing out religious tracts in the company of others who had been 'saved' outside the City Hall.

Offering a packet of ten unfiltered Park Drive, the old constable took a drink from the flask.

'Have a smoke, Peter. That stuff is half brandy and half best Fermanagh poteen. Puts hairs on your chest and lead in your pencil.' With a grin that never came near his eyes, Carson watched as Peter awkwardly puffed at his cigarette. He handed the flask to the boy.

'Get some down you, Peter. We're finished for the day. When we've knocked off we'll go round to my house. My Dorothy will give us a good Ulster fry and a glass or two of Black Bush. She knows what a man needs after a day out on the street. A good woman, my Dorothy. Married these twenty-eight years and never a cross word. You can have our back bedroom and come in to work with me in the morning – it'll get you out of the barracks for the night.'

Grateful for Carson's hospitality Peter drank a bit more and thought himself lucky. This was, he supposed, the reality of life: he was being given good advice and the hand of friendship. He had not had much of either since he had left home on the outskirts of Ballymena to spend months at the training college, and then on down into the city. He could go with Carson, get a good feed and a drink or two. It would be nice to get out of the barracks. It was all very well to have humanitarian thoughts and impulses – but where was the sense if people with no sense tried to overcome the lawful government? No sense at all. Northern Ireland was British. British it would stay. The muffled shouts and groans from down the corridor proved it. He was on the winning side. Taking another pull at the flask he smiled, all teeth and eyes, at his benefactor. A good fry and a night out of barracks would be welcome.

Chapter Four

2 May 1960

LONDON

'I don't really give a damn what you think, Haightbury. You are the senior partner and the man I hold responsible. Charles Aitken has been dead for a month and nobody in your office has done anything whatsoever about sorting out his affairs. They're bound to be in a shambles. The man was a weakling and a fool, with no money of his own. I want it sorted now. Elizabeth is worse than useless, mooning about at my place in Essex. You will report to me by next week's end or I will transfer my own affairs to a more efficient firm of solicitors. Goodbye.'

The general slammed down the phone and shouted for ex-Sergeant Platt, his manservant. 'Sar'nt Platt, get me a whisky, will you. These bloody solicitors are grossly incompetent. I won't have it. Send the car down to the station to meet Mrs Platt and bring Miss Charlotte to me as soon as she gets in. We'll shut up here and go to Essex in the morning. Thank you.'

General Hopkinson stood stiffly in front of the fire that was burning brightly in the study of his London flat, his irritation exacerbated by twinges of rheumatism and the prospect of the draughty old house in the Essex marshes. But his plans were advancing well, helped by the sudden death of Charles Aitken. Aitken had tried ineffectually, in bursts, to oppose his monopolisation of Charlotte, but Elizabeth did not have the strength to oppose him at all. What was it the Jesuits said? Give me the boy until he is seven and I will give you the man. Damned right. Ever since she could remember the child had thought of him as her father and not her grandfather; she saw the Reverend Aitken

16

rarely. *The seed is planted, I will see to its growth.* The general smiled thinly, content for the moment. *With that bloody padre out of the way there is no limit.* A thought struck him. School. Aitken had wanted and booked a place at day school near the family home. Not acceptable. Time to go to work. 'Sar'nt Platt. Get me the headmaster of Elliott's on the telephone. And get Colonel Jacobson after that. He's never got over Elizabeth marrying that bloody padre. I want her off my hands. She'll take Jacobson now, if only to put a roof over her head. Thank you.'

9 September 1962
BELFAST

Old Joe Carlin sat in the living room of his daughter's house, puffing on a pipe, throwing clouds of Old Holborn into the air. His wife Geraldine came clattering down the stairs, carrying a bloodstained sheet, her face red and hot. 'It's you, is it? Put that thing out, Joe. You'll choke the child the minute it's born. The nurse is annoyed enough already. Don't start her on you. Put it out, Joe.' She pulled the sheet round behind her, out of his sight.

'What's the matter up there? Is everything all right? The nurse has been here all day. Is Marion all right? I heard her groaning. I'm worried, Geraldine. Will I get the doctor?'

His wife looked shocked. 'You heard her? You never mind hearing. Marion's all right. There's no need for the doctor, the baby's just taking its time. It's none of a man's business, hearing. You get out down to the bar. Marion would be scarlet if she knew you were hanging about here listening. It's not decent. Go and get a pint and try to keep McCaillim half sober. I'll send for the both of you when the baby's here. Get away out now.'

Joe was well into his fourth pint when a big, hefty woman, a neighbour of Marion's, poked her head out of the women's snug and called him. He looked at Eddie McCaillim. No use.

17

Very drunk. Joe went to the snug door. 'It's a wee girl, Joe. She's lovely. Marion's fine. Where's Eddie, or need I ask?'

'Thanks Elsie. I'll come straight over. I'll leave himself here. He's well cut. Thanks Elsie.'

Marion was sitting up talking to her mother, the baby at her breast when he got there. She pulled a quilt up to cover her, flushing as he burst in. 'Daddy! I'm feeding the baby.' Joe laughed at her. 'And didn't I help your Ma feed you and change your nappies? Let me see the wee girl.'

'Where's my man? Still in the pub, I suppose. Here, look.' Marion eased the quilt down.

'Oh! She's ginger! A real carrot top. She's a wee smasher, Marion.'

Marion sat up straighter. 'She's not ginger. She's got red hair, like some of Eddie's people. Her name's Siobhan, Daddy.'

'Siobhan, is it? That's nice. She should be Maeve too, with that hair. You know, Maeve the flame-haired Warrior Queen of Eire? Eddie would love that . . .' There was a pounding on the front door. Old Joe jumped, but his wife was quicker, up and running down the stairs ready to light on a drunken McCaillim as he came in. But it wasn't Eddie at the door. A policeman stood there. Flustered, Geraldine shut the door in his face, and called to her husband. 'Joe, Joe, it's the peelers. There's a peeler at the door.' Joe Carlin rushed down and pulled the door open. A grave-faced RUC sergeant walked in. Peter Ewart, newly promoted, new to bringing bad news, was relieved he had a man to bring it to.

'I'm glad it's yourself, Joe. Put your wife out.' Joe motioned Geraldine back upstairs, wondering what was wrong. Geraldine ran upstairs and crept down again, quietly, to listen from behind the partition wall. Before the policeman was out of the house or her husband could come upstairs she was back with an ashen-faced Marion.

'What is it, Mammy? Is it Eddie causing trouble?'

Her mother eased baby Siobhan into her own arms and

18

put her into her crib. She took Marion's hands in her own, afraid of showing her joy to a wife with a newborn child. 'It is McCaillim, daughter. But he won't be troubling anybody. He was staggering across the Falls, shouting. He fell in front of one of Wordie's lorries. He's killed, Marion. Your man's killed.' She hesitated. 'I'm sorry, daughter,' she said, watching the shock register. Marion covered her face, pulling her hands free, bursting into tears, talking incoherently. It took a few moments for her mother to realise what she was saying through the sobbing that wracked her. It was, 'God, Oh God, thank God thank God thank God. He's dead, dead. Thank God oh thank God . . .'

19 April 1964
TOLLESBURY, ESSEX

Charlotte Aitken eased her stride a little to avoid embarrassing her grandfather: at his age it was a miracle he could walk at all, but here he was, stepping briskly along a narrow path through high, thick-based tussocks of dune grass scattered over the Tollesbury saltings; the flat, sharp-edged planes of his face challenging and cutting at the wind rather than allowing it to cut at him. Even so, the general looked very old and frail, his ancient, dried-out brown Barbour jacket hanging on him, made years ago for a man much deeper in the chest and heavier in the shoulders. Still, the general soldiered on, one big-knuckled fist around the stout old ashplant he had once used to find the solid ground beneath the mud and blood on the stinking battlefields of Flanders, now used for support when the ground rose more steeply under his feet.

He seemed even slighter than Charlotte remembered, but maybe that was because she was growing at an alarming rate. Still, he was there and ready as always to answer her questions, advise and guide her. But Charlotte sensed a tiredness growing in the old general, dreaded the day he would not be there, was sometimes but not always reassured when he promised he would not leave her until she was ready.

'Let's rest here for a while, grandfather. There's something I need to talk to you about.'

'No. We'll carry on for a bit. We'll sit down out of the wind behind the pillbox. Get on with you, girl.' Charlotte smiled to herself. *Gruff old beggar, won't admit he's tired.* 'Very well, grandfather. I'll race you.' She turned and ran, reaching cleanly over the tussocks, her heavy wool skirt lifted to clear her knees, enjoying the wind and exercise.

Sitting back against the concrete base of the wartime pillbox she waited, going over her problem in her mind, scanning the monochrome greys of sky and seascape in front of her, feeling it, feeling the dune grass bend and the waves break before the wind from the east. *Like a TV picture, all shades of grey. This is grandfather's land, so it's mine, all mine, one day. I love it. Not many boats out.* The sea was cutting up a bit, pushing down from the North Sea into the Essex estuaries, flooding up to fill the Blackwater river saltings. Across the water she could see Mersea Island, imagine the coast road in West Mersea and the Strood, the causeway linking the island to Essex, already under water. *High tide. We'll have to go back by the road. Grandfather will be cross. I'll make him stop at the Horse for a glass of whisky to warm him.*

As the general hove into view Charlotte checked that her skirt covered her knees. 'There you are, grandfather! I could hear you a mile away.' Charlotte's grin warmed the general as he cut round the last of the tussocks and got out of the wind. Gruff as ever he barked at her, though his tone had fondness buried in it.

'Rubbish, girl. That's enough of that! Stuff and nonsense. How dare you insult your old grandfather. What are they teaching you at that school I pay a fortune for? I'll have Platt take a Sam Browne to you to teach you some respect for your elders and betters. Platt did it to his son's girl. Did her a power of good. Take that urchin grin off your face. Make room.'

Charlotte smiled, and moved six inches along a thirty foot wall. 'I know you love me, grandfather. Stop threatening me. Sarn't Platt hasn't got a granddaughter. And the last time he took a belt to anyone was when he polished yours for Remembrance Sunday. You can't fool me with your stiff old soldier act. But I need to talk to you. I need some advice.'

General Hopkinson settled against the wall, surreptitiously sliding a hand under his right leg to support it as he settled. 'All right then, let's have it.'

'Well, I'm growing up, in case you hadn't noticed. I wanted to talk about the way the others at school look at me now.'

The general paused for thought. The headmaster of Charlotte's school had buttonheld him on last visitors' day, worried that Charlotte had an 'old head on young shoulders'. *True enough. She is growing up. Quicker than I had expected. Good thing. Quicker the better. See what Elliott was on about. Only eleven after all, talks like she's twenty.* 'I see. What exactly is the problem? Are the other girls nasty to you? Have the boys stopped being rough with you?'

'No, grandfather. It's this Duke of Edinburgh's Award thing that started it. We were all out on Dartmoor. It was foggy and cold. Some of the girls were tired and crying. Some of the boys were crying too. They thought we were lost. Mr Chalmers, our house master, clearly *was* lost. I was tired too but I was all right. I knew where we were because I'd been using the Silva compass you gave me and following the rules you had Sar'nt Platt teach me. So I said so. I said we could get to where we wanted to go if everybody stopped talking about it and got on with it. Mr Chalmers told me to stop showing off. I was furious. I told him I knew he was lost. I told him I was tired and I was going home, on my own if I had to. I told him where we were and which way to go. It was easy. We were standing by Lints Tor. Mr Chalmers believed me and off we went. I didn't think any more about it.

But after we got back to school the girls started cutting me dead and the boys will brag on about how they knew where we were all the time and were only trying to embarrass Mr Chalmers. The boys call me the Explorer and try to bully me. The girls egg them on. Mr Chalmers avoids me. I don't know what to do.'

The general closed his eyes, thinking. *So soon! Thank God in His heaven. Give me the boy until he is seven* . . . 'Don't worry about it, Charlotte. You are very young but you are already learning about the way of the world. Get comfortable and listen to me. Don't interrupt and don't think too hard. Think about what I've said after you get back to school and can look at the other girls and boys – and your teachers – in the light of what I've said. You will be surprised at what you see. All right so far?'

'Yes, grandfather.'

'Good. You did very well on Dartmoor and I am proud of you; I had not expected you to reach this point for a year or two yet. Well done. Now listen carefully.' The general reached out, took Charlotte's hand, and squeezed. She nestled down against him, feeling calm and reassured. He would know what she had to do. Ever since she could remember, it had always been so.

'I'm ready, grandfather.'

'Good girl. Charlotte, this is not easy, but it is probably the most important lesson you must learn. It is very simple, but it is the one that will see you through life. The great religions of the Earth say that the meek and humble of spirit shall inherit the Earth. As a Christian soldier I accept that and believe it to be a fundamental truth. It will be so. The Talmud of the Jews says so. The New Testament says so. The Muslim Q'Ran and the Hindu Vedas say so. Throughout history the great visionaries are agreed. The meek shall inherit the Earth. It would be wonderful if it were so now. Unfortunately it is not, and we have a long way to go before it happens. Today we must live with what we have, in the hope that our efforts help bring about a better world. It is not ideal, but it is reality.

So it is important that you know how the world of today is run.

'Today there are four kinds, four groups if you like, of people: the first three comprise the Leaders, the Followers and the Mob. The mob are like sheep, an unthinking, directionless mass, ready to line up behind anyone strong enough to grip and lead them. The followers are worthy people, possessed of ability, intelligence and integrity. The followers manage and drive the mob. Then there are the leaders, those possessed of real leadership qualities, those who wield real power, carry real responsibility. The leaders exercise command and control over the followers. But among the leaders there is a fourth group, the gifted few, those destined to command the commanders. I am one of those, one who has held and wielded great power. You are beginning to realise that you are also one of the smallest group of all. Do you understand?'

Charlotte felt a rush of exhilaration, a plummet of self-doubt. *Could this be true?* 'I think so. I'm not sure. Please tell me more.'

'Charlotte, you are one of the few. I am deeply proud of you and I envy you. My years are nearly done but yours are yet to come. You are destined to be a leader among leaders, and you are staking your claim already. High command is your birthright, your inheritance if you like. It is also a responsibility you have to shoulder, something you cannot shirk or deny. There will be times when you will wish it otherwise, but you have no real choice. You will command.

'As you grow older you will notice that every time things begin to go wrong people will turn their eyes to you, asking "What shall we do?". You will tell them. They will obey. They will be grateful for your presence. But when the danger is over you will see the same people try to assert themselves over you, to save their faces, trying to pretend they did not really need you, like the girls and boys at school, like Mr Chalmers. It will never be easy for you Charlotte, but remember this: in life you must lead, follow or be part of the mob. You have great gifts growing in you: you must face up to that; you must accept responsibility for your own actions, and also accept responsibility for the actions of those of lesser gifts. To do anything less would be moral cowardice. Following is for those who see the truth of life and are ready to work within their abilities, those who can find and believe in a leader.

'There are leaders in abundance, but high command, leadership of the leaders, is for the few, the very few who have the gifts, the will and the moral courage to seek and take command. There is a catch: no one will give you high command. You must take it, then hold it. You must seek your way forward and fight for it, because lesser people will try to hold you back, put obstacles in your way. They will try to undermine you to further their own careers or to make themselves feel better about following your lead. Do not fight with or ignore these people. Identify and use them. Take command of them from the earliest possible moment, grip them and make them work for you. Never forget your aim: to gain high command. Seek and get it, use it and enjoy it.

'The exercise of great power is a wonderful feeling, Charlotte. It is the most wonderful feeling in the world. One clear order from you could see thousands, perhaps tens of thousands, fighting to obey. One rebuke could break a bad officer's career. One nod could set a good man on his way. It will be lonely, but only as lonely as you allow it to be. There is a problem. You are not a man. You will have to be better, fight harder than any man can. You must overcome the prejudices and use the abilities of men who would otherwise stand in your way. When you have power you may use it to the full, use it to make a better world. But first you must have it.'

A glow grew in Charlotte, as she felt the first glimmerings of the certainty that would rule her life and was not afraid: she had never heard of Adolf Hitler's *Manifest Destiny* or his claim to '... *move with the certainty of a sleepwalker*'. 'Thank you, grandfather. I will think about it all. It does seem simple enough. Even obviously true. But how am I to know I can do it?'

'I'm tired, Charlotte. I'm old and my bones hurt. I do not know everything. But I know that a labourer coming to look for a job on the estate worries about whether he has a back strong enough to dig out the drains. I know that the farm tenants worry about whether they can beat the weather this year. I know that Mr Backus, the estate manager, worries about whether he can enter my study and tell me the estate is producing enough to pay the wages of our people, preserve our villages and make provision for their future. Sometimes Mr Backus looks to me to make decisions that affect all of our lives. Sometimes I doubt that I can do that, because I could get it wrong and throw hundreds of decent people out of job, house and home. I still have to make those decisions and hope that I am right. I cannot dig drains. I do not know how to run a farm. I do not know how to run an estate. I do know how to make decisions based on the best information available, if I know I have done my best to get and evaluate that information. That is all I can do. That is all you can do. You can only do your best, always. It is your duty to yourself and those around you. Divine Providence will see to the rest. You must trust in yourself and your destiny.'

Charlotte's certainty grew, just a little more. 'I will, grandfather. I will always do my best.'

'Excellent. I'll make a general of you yet, Charlotte. Get up. We'll walk on now.'

1 March 1966
BELFAST

Jamie looked at Gerry's boiler suit, brand new, dark blue, with detachable black buttons. It seemed to him to be very fine, but more cumbersome than his own choice. Together they had gone to Smithfield market, to the shop that sold all kinds of workmen's clothing, plus surplus army boots and second hand

25

webbing packs, khaki canvas bags of the kind they had used all their lives as schoolbags and which would serve to carry their lunch boxes and flasks of tea. Gerry bought the boiler suit. Jamie opted for a bib and brace overall, also dark blue, with brass buttons; he liked the freedom it gave to his shoulders and arms.

'Right, Gerry, let's go. We don't want to be late.'

Together as always, the fifteen-year-old boys embarked on their working lives, striding confidently up Conway Street, turning left into David Street then right into Cupar Street, heading for the huge factory on the Springfield Road. James Mackie and Sons, manufacturers of textile machinery, famous the world over wherever cloth was made, had offered them apprenticeships, as fitters.

The boys felt proud that they had jobs. But not just jobs: they were to be apprentices. As men with a trade they would be looked up to on the Falls Road, almost as much as teachers. They would be in work year in year out, while most of their friends spent their teens as junior barmen or van boys for the Pearl Laundry, to be replaced when it came time for them to draw men's wages. The boys felt they had done well for themselves. And there was the chance of going to the technical college, on day release, one day a week to study for exams that could turn them into qualified engineers, people who sat in offices and told others what to do. It was all heady stuff.

As big Jamie Lappin watched the boys step out he was happy for them and proud of them. He kept his deeper thoughts to himself. Now was not the time. Maybe later, when they were older.

He recalled the bad times, when there had been no work for him. He had spent a lot of time in the Carnegie Library on the Falls, fascinated by the rows of books on their polished oak shelves, secretly loving the atmosphere of men thinking. Sometimes he had managed to get into discussions of politics and economics with teachers who used the library. He had felt proud when the educated men had come to respect him, a big rough labourer with hands like shovels, and he delighted in the diversion from sitting hunched over the books he read as ravenously as a starving dog eats meat, but with as little discrimination. He had tried to read everything, with a dictionary always to hand, absorbing the written word, until one day an elderly priest, a retired Monsignor, engaged him in discussion, countered his arguments with ease and wagged a knowing finger.

'You're a far from stupid man, Big Jamie Lappin. Stop parroting the opinions of the authors of your books. Read them, compare them and think for yourself. Maybe then you'll be worth arguing with.' Big Jamie thought the old Monsignor's rebuke the best piece of advice he had ever had.

Now, years later, watching his son's receding back, Big Jamie regretted that he could not have given him more of a start in life. *He's not aware of the depth of his poverty. He doesn't know that a man cannot reach for the stars if he has never even seen the moon.*

Ten days later, at six o'clock in the evening, Jamie Lappin laid a brown paper square on his mother's kitchen table. His first wages: two pounds nineteen shillings and ninepence. Josie Lappin waited until he was out of the kitchen before she opened the packet. Then she burst into the living room, ordering her next youngest after Jamie out of his chair. 'Sean! Out of it. Let Jamie sit down, he's been out earning. Get away up to Shielses and bring a Fray Bentos for his supper. Here's the money. Hurry up now.'

Young Sean, thirteen, jumped out of the chair and took the money, a bit unsure. Fray Bentos steak and kidney pies in their flat round tins were a rare treat. He might get a bit of the thick, flaky crust. Jamie, glancing at Big Jamie sitting in his armchair, stopped his brother before he got to the door.

'Wait a bit, Sean. Mammy, can you give me a shilling for chips?'

Josie, surprised, said 'You'll have nine and ninepence in the morning. Why do you want chips? You can't eat a Fray Bentos and a shilling of chips as well.'

Jamie said 'Give Sean another shilling, Mammy. I want to do something.'

Josie did not understand, but she gave Sean another shilling. 'Eight and ninepence tomorrow then, Jamie. Sean, get chips as well. Run there and back. Out!'

Jamie Lappin approached his father, who was sitting in the old armchair with its back to the window for light, reading as usual.

'Daddy, Mammy's going to do a fish and potatoes. I saw it in the kitchen.' He stopped, searching for words, fearful of offending the big man looking up at him, his eyes amused.

'Daddy, there's plenty for everybody. But if you shared my Fray Bentos and chips we'd all have a great feed.' He waited, uncertain.

Big Jamie smiled his big slow smile. 'Josie, I'll eat with Jamie. I think I saw a tin of butter beans in your kitchen. Spread it out, my lovely. We're celebrating Jamie's trade.'

Josie, flushed, left the living room and showed pleasure in her boy's thoughtfulness by banging her pots and oven door a bit more than was really necessary. Jamie, later, with a belly full to bursting, felt proud that he had done something special.

6 July 1966
BELFAST

Sergeant Peter Ewart turned left off the Falls Road, strolled slowly past St Paul's church, keeping the church railings on his right, turning right again toward his station. The upper twenty-three feet of grey brick wall surrounding the station yard, topped with three strands of barbed wire, was unmarked and unbroken except for a vehicle gate, painted dark green. Below the six foot line the wall was a mass of multicoloured graffiti so interwoven that only close inspection could untangle it. Strangely, the gate bore no graffiti, except a small black and white sign that said KEEP CLEAR VEHICLES EXITING AT HIGH SPEED KEEP CLEAR. Official graffiti to deter the unofficial. The wall, so high it seemed to lean outwards, blanked out the morning sun, and cast a heavy shadow.

To Ewart's front, seen and heard through the shadow of the wall, the Springfield Road hummed with people and traffic. Ewart stopped, examining the shadow, seeking the unusual, the furtive movement, the unexpected presence of a man or woman who should be somewhere else. The usual July tension filled the air, making people jumpy as they heard the Lambeg drums and marching feet of the Orangemen preparing for the big march on the Twelfth drift across the city. But there was nothing in the shadow. Bored, Ewart strolled on. As he reached the Springfield Road his eyes scanned left then right. Something out of place caught his mind and eye.

Two constables leaving Ewart's station caught sight of the patrolling sergeant and stepped out smartly for the little street opposite. They were late out, nearly ten minutes. There was no hope that Sergeant Ewart had not noticed, but they were grateful to be away from his immediate grasp. Both had the pouched and bloodshot eyes of a late, rough night. Beer fumes still clung round them and their boots were less than shiny bright. A close encounter with the station sergeant was a thing to be avoided. Eyes front, they crossed the road, ignoring the traffic, knowing the sight of a bottle green uniform was enough to make any driver, even the taxis, slow, stop or swing around it. Ewart smiled to himself. Not bad lads, a bit thick, but not bad. They just needed a kick up the arse now and again. He'd see them later.

Sitting at his desk, Sergeant Ewart scanned the Yellow List, fresh in that morning. Named after the RUC's habit of printing it on yellow paper the list detailed those selected for promotion to inspector this year. There were only two names for the city area: Jackson and Adams. Other names could and maybe should have been there, but weren't. Ewart was pleased. This looked good for the future: McBride, Smith, Edmonson, Toner and old Jock

Dennis had been passed over. All were good, reliable policemen, but ageing. Jackson and Adams were only two years his senior, both thirty.

I passed my promotion exams the year after they did. I can expect to see my name next year. Ewart's ears pricked up. Outside, an ambulance roared past the barracks, on its way to the Royal Victoria Hospital, cracking the air with its new two-tone siren. He glanced at the clock: four minutes past ten. 'Bloody cowboys,' he muttered. Reaching for his intercom, he called the outside desk.

'Sergeant Ewart here. Ring the Royal. Find out where that ambulance came from. Check if it's a real emergency. I'm fed up with those crews banging on the blue light every time they're late for their tea break. If it's Terry Higgins driving it book him for speeding anyway. His excuses have run out.'

Ewart prided himself on his local knowledge, with more than a little justification. He knew everybody in the district: where they lived, worked, drank, gambled, had a bit on the side, went to church. He knew the fathers, the mothers and the kids; knew the baddies and the decent. He knew where to find each and every one of them at any moment of the day or night, knew who knew whom in the tight little community, the enmities and the friendships, and by instinct and knowledge of the streets he knew who to lift and question if somebody got more of a hammering than he deserved or if a real crime was committed. That intimate knowledge would carry him through. As the Falls people had it, he could 'look at your face and know its people and its people's people'. He always got his cups of tea when he patrolled in the daytime and the odd large Jameson's when he clouted a pub door with his nightstick any time after closing.

The years working out of Hastings Street until his promotion to Springfield had been good to Peter Ewart. He had grown to just under six feet and had filled out to nearly fifteen stone, with wide, powerful shoulders and thick strong body. His face, smooth and unmarked under heavy brows, had taken on a grave, solid look, a little fleshier than he really liked. But he thought it fitting in a policeman; people rarely argued with him these days.

His mind wandering over the implications of the Yellow List Ewart thought about his future. Inspector Jeavons, head of Springfield Road barracks, retired next year. Five good men had been passed over for promotion, at their last chance. The old men were being phased out. *With luck I can throw away my boots, buy myself a white shirt and black brogues next year. I can get rid of this bloody gun on my belt and carry a blackthorn stick instead. I can get a tailored uniform of bottle green barathea instead of this rough old wool. Inspector Ewart I will be, and God save anyone who stands in my way.* Ewart's eyes and jaw tightened, thinking of the future. *There's much wrong with this Province, but there's much to be treasured too. I'll see to my bit of it.*

The intercom on his desk buzzed. 'Constable Conlon, Sergeant. The ambulance driver was Terry Higgins. But the wardmaster at the Royal says he had to speed. He had a boy hurt bad in the back, an industrial accident.'

'What's the boy's name?'

'Lappin, Sergeant. Jamie Lappin, from Conway Street.'

Ewart's stomach turned over. *Big Jamie's boy! Industrial accident my arse. It's July. Some overheated bigot has dropped a hammer on the boy.* 'Get Big Jamie from his work. Bring him to the Royal. Keep him away from the doctors until I've sorted things out. I'm going to the hospital now.'

In the main foyer of the Royal's Casualty Department Sergeant Peter Ewart bent his head to look into the face of a middle aged and diminutive consultant. Studying her expression as she talked, his face was deliberately serious, to reflect his own professional standing and to hide his layman's awe of the learned professions. In her well starched white coat, worn open over a simple blouse and straight, plain skirt the consultant physician, called in by a nervous houseman with his first serious head injury on his hands, was Ewart's senior in every way. The stocky, slow-moving policeman was impressed by the brisk little woman and content to accept her judgement. He wanted it simple and clear, for he had to tell Big Jamie himself when he arrived.

The doctor gave it to him in terms he understood, and for that he was grateful. Young Lappin she thought to be badly hurt but not fatally. He had a skull fracture and was badly concussed but did not show indications of internal cranial bleeding. His upper back and right shoulder were heavily bruised and he had minor scrapes on his hands, knees and to the left side of his face, probably caused as he fell. He was young and not well developed but he was fit enough and his vital signs were strong. It was too early to say with confidence but she thought the boy would recover without permanent damage. She had heard an outline of the cause of the boy's injuries from the ambulance crew. A heavy steel bar had fallen on him as he walked under it, catching him more on the shoulder than the head. In her opinion he had been very, very lucky.

A few minutes later Big Jamie Lappin arrived, sawdust in his hair. Ewart made it to him before he could start asking questions, bowling straight in 'I know you, Big Jamie, and you know me. I'll not lie to you. Your boy's hurt bad, but the doctor says he'll be all right.'

Big Jamie thought quick and deep, but spoke slowly and carefully. 'What's happened? RUC sergeants about the place say it's bad.'

Before he answered Sergeant Ewart considered young Jamie's condition and the calm, slow control of a man he knew to be both clever and capable of taking the law into his own powerful hands.

'Step easy, Big Jamie. We're all ten years older and ten years wiser. There was an accident. There'll be an investigation at the factory. Mackie's don't like accidents, you know that. I'll take an interest, because of the time of year. You know what can happen in July, Big Jamie. Decent people get the head staggers and do stupid things. If anything out of order has happened I'll see to the guilty myself. My word on it, Big Jamie. I'll put them behind bars. I've contacts up there at Mackie's. Leave this to me.'

Big Jamie half turned, putting his hands in his trouser pockets, his head turned back to look the policeman in the eye.

'See that you do. You and I both know that bad accidents up there are few and far between. I think somebody tried to kill my son. Bars for them, as you say. Or I'll see to them myself.'

Chapter Five

14 August 1969

BELFAST

Conway Street was in flames, the row of two-up, two-down houses facing the mill collapsing inwards as their roofs fell and their walls cracked and split in the heat. Shattered slates and smoking, blackened roof joists lay all over the road, mixed in with shards of glass and broken brick. Smoke rolled upwards in thick clouds, almost invisible except where the glare of the flames picked out dense swirls made by hot air and cool wind colliding about a hundred feet above the street. The stars were nowhere but sparks flew everywhere, driven through the crowds of people trying vainly to save something, anything, from the fires, driven through the smoke and through the neighbouring streets, sparkling and dying in the turbulent air. Shouting men trying to build a barricade broke off their work to pick up bits of flaming wood and hot brick, using them as missiles to drive back the howling mob pushing its way down from the Shankill.

Inspector Peter Ewart lay against a wall, protected by two constables as another dressed the wound in his head. Young policemen milled about, leaderless, some trying to keep between the fighting crowds. A few, abandoning training in favour of their instincts, had joined the crowd from the Shankill and were directing the mob's efforts to smash through to the Falls.

Big Jamie Lappin hustled his family through the crowd to the relative quiet of the main road, where hijacked trucks and vans waited to ferry burnt-out people to the huge Ballymurphy estate, where the school hall of St Bernadette's had been turned into a refugee centre by the local priest. There he could leave

34

them in safety while he returned to do what he could here. Bombay Street, up by Clonard monastery, and several streets around the top of the Crumlin Road were also burning: mobs waving Ulster and Union flags were attacking the Markets and there was heavy fighting near the bottom of the Grosvenor Road. All over the city Catholic ghettos were being burned by their neighbours from the Protestant ghettos. Heavily armed police in Shorland armoured cars patrolled the quiet middle-class areas of the Malone and upper Stranmillis Roads, assuring their occupants that everything was under control.

Young Jamie Lappin and Gerry Madden were throwing bricks and bits of heat-cracked paving stones for all they were worth, not bothering to pick out individual targets: there were too many attackers, too close, packed tight in the narrow confines of the street and being packed tighter as pressure from those behind drove them forward into the fire zone, squeezing them against the mill wall, as far as possible from the flames.

On top of the half-built barricade a middle-aged man in an old duffle coat and a scarf over his face surveyed the scene with surprising calm, concentrating his mind to pick out the things that mattered; the things that could affect the outcome of this local battle and decide whether or not this crowd from the Shankill could reach the Falls. For the last eight years Tom McSherry had been the senior IRA officer in Belfast. In theory he commanded the IRA's Belfast Brigade and was responsible for defending the Catholic areas against exactly the kind of thing that was happening now. But his brigade was a joke. Less than forty over-age and poorly armed volunteers followed his lead.

For thirteen years McSherry had waited for this, enduring the sneers in the pubs and the bitter smiles of the doubters in the meetings of the Brotherhood: the 'Fifties campaign had been a disaster. But there would be no more sneers. The people had nobody else to turn to for protection. And protection they needed now. If they could, this petrol-bombing mob would join up with others pushing down North Howard Street, parallel to

35

Conway Street. And if they made it the whole Falls would burn. They could make it if they got close enough to the barricade to spread out again. The battle, McSherry determined, would turn on whether or not the mob could be kept in the fire zone, pressed against the wall of the mill and with only a few able to do any real fighting.

Beneath his outer calm a deep rage burned in Tom McSherry, filling his chest, cutting off his breath and building up to hammer behind his eyes. He knew the symptoms well and tried to fight them off, for it was always the same: frustration and anger grew in him until he vented it in the savage violence of a bottle-swinging brawl; or trembling and nauseous he blindly staggered through the iron clamp of agony that bound itself for days around his head. Migraine, the doctors had called it years ago, and sent him to a psychiatrist. Self-induced stress, the psychiatrist said. Learn to take it easy, be calm. McSherry sneered inwardly at the memory. It's machine guns I need, not pap.

He felt the first thin tendrils of hot wire creep from behind his eyes. In a little while they would join and twist together at the base of his skull in a solid knot of agony. He willed himself to look into the attacking crowd, watched the hate-filled faces, open-mouthed, scream and bawl the vilest of obscenities. He shook his head, trying to clear it. No good. He did not hate these people who were doing their best to kill him, but he feared their numbers and understood their fear of his ambition to unite the country. They were, he thought, just trying to keep hold of the little they had.

Aware of the power of his anger and the effect it could have on his thinking McSherry allowed his hands to travel over the top of the barricade, seeking. His left hand found the distraction he was looking for, a long screw protruding from the hinge of a ripped-off cupboard door. His hand closed around it, concentrated his anger on it, freed his mind to think: a different kind of pain would have to do in place of drugs. He looked up the left side of the street. About twenty houses were burning, set alight by petrol bombers. The screw dug into his palm, hard, forcing him to divide his mind between ignoring the pain and assessing the military situation. *Good*, he thought, *pain sought and welcomed, carefully controlled, has a clean cold purity that not even migraine can match*. He rocked his hand on the screw, feeling it force itself between the bones in his palm. The hot wires unwound, drew back behind his eyes. *That's the way*, he thought, a bitter smile curling one corner of his mouth down. *That's the way to chill the head*. He flicked his eyes over the yelling crowd as the muscles of his neck relaxed, sending little thrills of pleasure down his back.

These people are not the enemy, McSherry reminded himself. Their masters are the enemy. Think cold. About an hour would see the fires die down enough for the crowd to widen their attack. That would not be long enough. As the screw began to press against the skin covering the back of his left hand he decided to gamble, to trade space and houses for time in the hope that the mob would stick to their intention of burning every Catholic they could out of house and home, hoping they wouldn't realise what he was doing. Five men in their early forties and two older men stood on the pavement behind him, waiting. He turned to them, signalling them closer. Glancing again at the attacking mob, he noted that it had gained ten yards. As an inch and a bit of screw thread drove through the back of his hand he made his decision, gave his orders.

McSherry turned back, peering through a gap in the makeshift barricade. He paid close attention to the people doing the fighting, watching his own men begin to take control of the wild mêlée. As his eyes roved he made mental notes of those that fought the hardest, on both sides. Gerry Madden caught his attention, then Jamie Lappin. Lappin he closed out of his mind: the kid fought hard, but without sense. He turned his attention back to Madden, who was fighting with detached intelligence.

Madden was in constant movement, never with his feet in the same place for more than a few seconds, usually managing to keep someone between him and the attacking mob, using a living body as a shield while he fought with a calm, intense ferocity. Gone was the wild brick-throwing. Now he was throwing bits of window glass and smashed slate, picking a living target and spinning the small, jagged-edged sheets with an economical twist of the wrist. Some he hit in an exposed spot, the face, hands or head. Some he missed, and the missile hit others in the close-packed mob. Sometimes he hit the ground. The hits and misses seemed to have little effect on him. He didn't jump for joy or get depressed. He just chose another target, one of those who seemed to be leading the mob, and threw the glass.

Gerry was enjoying himself. For the first time in his life he felt free. Grunting with the effort he spun a piece of slate at the head of a man wearing the bright sash of the Orange Order over his chest. Gerry knew the man and stood still just long enough to watch the sliver of slate hit him across the mouth and nose. The man fell bleeding under the feet of those around him, bringing two of them down with him. Gerry laughed aloud. *Eat that you Orange bastard.* Recovering, he reached for another chunk of slate. Hot and sweating freely, he flung it into the crowd, trying for a man waving a banner. Missed. He threw again and again. Out of the corner of his eye he saw Jamie Lappin, throwing bits of brick. 'That's it Jamie!' he shouted. 'Smash their skulls in. This is great.'

The danger did not bother Gerry Madden. He dodged and weaved behind other people as he aimed and threw. All the insults, all the abuse he and his mate had suffered boiled out of him. One time two men had hauled him out of his seat at the cinema when he hadn't stood for the playing of 'The Queen' at the end of the film. They had held him upright between them until the anthem was over, then shoved him to the floor and kicked him until he had to crawl away under the seats. He wished the slate and glass he was throwing now were hand grenades. Gerry grinned as another of his missiles took a man across the face.

Tom McSherry pulled his duffle coat tighter round him and

checked that the scarf still covered his lower face. There was much still to be done. These vicious street battles could continue for many hours or even days, if the government didn't put the army on the streets. Reports from Derry said the RUC were reeling on their feet and had given up trying to beat down the Bogside. The Ministry of Home Affairs was transferring police in hundreds to Belfast, but they were nearly finished here too. Discipline had broken down and some police had joined the mobs. McSherry was very worried. For the first time in his life he hoped to see a British soldier on a street in Ireland. His own few, scattered across the city, couldn't be relied on for much longer and their ammunition was running low. They might just be enough for now, but recruits would be desperately needed. This was going to be a long war. Young Madden and a couple of others showed promise. In the meantime British bayonets were needed to bridge the gap.

Inspector Peter Ewart, back on his feet, tried hard to gain control of the situation, but felt it slipping away from him. His own station sergeant was playing a leading role in directing the mob intent on burning the Catholics out. Most of his constables were injured or at the end of their tether, dark rings of fear and exhaustion forming half-moons of defeat below their eyes. Some of them had come to him as reinforcements pulled out of the savage rioting going on in Londonderry, had been exhausted on arrival and were on the verge of collapse now. There wasn't much more he could ask them to do.

Ewart longed to rush out, shouting, to impose his authority on this madhouse, but could not. He knew it would be futile. For over a year the peace of the province had been disturbed by rowdy marchers and demonstrators, demanding one man one vote. The government had overreacted. It put thousands of police on the streets, but allowed marching demonstrators proceeding peacefully from Derry to Belfast to be brutally attacked by Protestant militants. The débâcle at Burntollet Bridge had been filmed and shown live around the world. The government, panicking, played the Orange card for all its powerful worth and stepped aside while Orange leaders and fundamentalist demagogues raged their seventeenth-century slogans, whipping up all the old terrors, driving decent, ordinary Protestants half mad with the fear of a united Ireland, an Ireland in which they believed they would be second-class citizens forbidden to practise their religion in peace, would lose their jobs and homes and be forced to flee the province their ancestors had bought with blood and held for centuries. Ewart feared the province really was meeting its end. The Catholics would be burned out in their thousands, driven over the border to the south until the Republic could take no more. Then, he thought, the Republic would put its own soldiers over the border and the storm of civil war would burst on the heads of all the Irish, north and south. The alternative was probably even worse: the Irish Army would sit tight. Ulster's British Army garrisons would march out of their barracks to impose order and the IRA would rise again, a phoenix from the ashes of the houses burning around him.

'Jesus Christ,' thought Ewart, looking at the shambles, 'how can I do anything?' The answer came as he felt his legs wobble under him with exhaustion and the shock of the wound he had received earlier. *Show an example*, his mind told him, *you're a senior officer of the RUC. Stand up and be counted. Put a stop to this. Enforce the law. At least be seen to try.*

Afraid, more afraid than he had ever been, Inspector Peter Ewart pulled himself together, checked that his tie was straight over his bloodstained white shirt and strode unsteadily into the space between the fighting crowds, his blackthorn stick clamped tight under his left arm, intending to stand there as a barrier. His voice, a strong bass, wavering slightly, called his constables to him. If all else failed he could and would shoot the first man who attempted to rush past him to the Catholic barricade. In this his mind was clear, his duty clear: *never mind the rights and wrongs, never mind the politicians; I must try to enforce the law.*

McSherry, on the barricade, saw Ewart step out. For years he and the inspector had been enemies, knowing each other well. For years Ewart had tried to prove McSherry a member of an illegal organisation, the IRA. For years McSherry had bobbed and weaved, leaving Ewart nothing to get hold of. Now, in these most difficult of times, McSherry saw Ewart at his best and was impressed. He watched the inspector put his life on the line, pulling the revolver from the holster of the constable accompanying him, determined to prove the police to be on no side.

You're sadly misled, Peter Ewart, thought McSherry, *but you're a brave man, God save you.*

A nineteen-year-old in the Catholic crowd misconstrued Ewart's intentions: he saw only an RUC inspector with a gun in his hand at the head of the attacking Protestants. As Ewart turned to face the Protestant mob a piece of glass struck him on the side of the neck, cutting him from the jawbone to the ear, missing his carotid artery by a fraction of an inch. He fell, feeling the hot rush of blood from his throat drench his shirt as the mob surged over him.

On the barricade Tom McSherry saw Ewart fall. The mob of Protestants was spreading wider as the flames on their right cooled and died for want of fuel. He filled his lungs and roared over the fighting. 'IRA back! IRA back! IRA back!' He stood fast as the defenders, led by his own few, tumbled over the rickety barricade. He looked back over his shoulder and got a hand signal from the roof of the Bernard Hughes & Co bread van buried in a welter of tables, chairs, old settees and mattresses that formed the second barricade. The rear barricade was ready.

McSherry called forward one of his men. 'Get petrol from the van. Soak this lot I'm standing on.'

The man, his face streaked with sweat and smoke, yelled back, 'The houses behind us are already soaked, Commandant. Big Jamie Lappin did it. He's coming now to do the barricade.'

McSherry, surprised, looked for the big man Lappin. Big Jamie was not long in coming. He carried a ten-gallon drum of petrol and diesel oil siphoned from any vehicle he'd happened to come across on the Falls; it was now nearly empty from his spraying of the houses. He seemed beside himself with rage as he threw the remainder of the drum's contents over the barricade.

'Get the hell off this, McSherry, you useless bastard. I know your plan. You'll let those animals burn our houses to keep them trapped against the mill wall. Damn you, McSherry, are you blind? The peelers are leading them. They might burn nothing more and just charge on. Get the houses going now, it's our only chance, God forgive me. Let's hope the British put soldiers out before we run out of houses to burn. Have you guns?'

McSherry hesitated, glancing at the new barricade, the attackers and Big Jamie in turn, knowing what had to be done, but unwilling to be seen to be the one to do it. 'Two old Thompson guns. Very little ammunition. I'm sorry. It's all I have.'

'Fuck you, McSherry,' yelled Big Jamie, 'you're wasting time. I'll do it my bloody self. They'll be over this in a minute.'

Big Jamie turned and ran, picking up a burning roof beam as he went, throwing it into the first of the houses on his right, on the corner of Conway and David Street. Then he threw other flaming ties into the next houses, 72, Mrs Conlan's; 70, old Da O'Shaughnessy's; 68, his own house; 66, Mrs Brannigan's; 64, Danny Fisher's, then another and another, and another, then two more, last of all the widow McCaillim's. He caught sight of Marion McCaillim's distraught face as he did so. She was standing alone, her sons nowhere near, the little redhead Siobhan clinging to her, the seven-year-old watching with frightened eyes that saw everything and understood nothing, frightened for her dollies, strapped safely into their miniature TanSad pram, inside her house that Mister Lappin was burning. Big Jamie fell, collapsing in on himself as he reached the second barricade. Hands pulled his sobbing figure over. Behind him flames, light blue and yellow, licked at curtains, spreading quick and certain over hundred-year-old plaster and twisted window frames. He struggled from the helping hands, forcing his way through to Marion McCaillim, expecting her to spit at him, claw his face as he felt he deserved. She stood, Siobhan now on her hip, watching him come.

'I'm sorry Marion. It had to be done. I'm sorry.'

Marion said nothing at first, but held little Siobhan out to him, offering the child as a token of her sincerity. He took Siobhan, wondering. 'Don't you say sorry to me, Jamie Lappin. I have eyes. The Prods would have burned me out anyway. I'd have sent my own man to do the same if he was alive and had the guts for it. I'm proud of you, man.'

Big Jamie watched Marion's face. She was still a pretty woman, had turned away many a man from her door. But behind the prettiness there was strength and courage. 'Marion. Thanks. Come with me now. Bring the kids. I'll take yours with mine up to Ballymurphy out of harm's way. Where are your boys?'

Marion's face twisted. 'They're the sons of their father. They were away like lilties the minute the fighting started. I don't care where they are. They're old enough to fend for themselves. They can go to their father's people in Dublin and stay there. I'll go to my Daddy's with Siobhan, until I find a new place. Give her back to me.' She hefted Siobhan astride her hip. 'God bless you and keep you, Jamie.' Upright, brave, she turned and walked away, heedless of the pandemonium around her.

Tom McSherry, ashamed of his own weakness, had seen enough. Most of the defenders were over the first barricade. The attackers were less than twenty yards away, but the houses behind him were burning well. Slowly and with care he spread the fingers of his right hand, thrusting them under his left palm, easing it off the screw driven through it. He clenched his hand, watching the blood squeeze darkly out of the hole in its back. He smiled grimly. His migraine was gone, but his heart was empty. Big Jamie Lappin had shamed him in front of his own, had seen and grasped the moment he had waited and prayed for, thirteen years in the coming, but had failed to take when it came. From here on in there would be no hesitation, no compassion, no mercy, no second thoughts. From here on in there would be war. There would be war today and war tomorrow, war unending until he saw his country clean and whole, free of outside interference, free of inside interests crying 'WOLF' to her ignorant masses. He would lead his brigade. He would hesitate no more, but wade through blood knee deep to avoid the sight of a man burning his own home.

Three hours later Tom McSherry felt his coat tails pulled and turned to see the puller. Dawn was breaking behind him. The mob had been held at the second barricade and the battle was almost over; only a few still tried to fight their way into the Falls. *A Pyrrhic victory if ever there was one* was the thought in his mind. But his attention was drawn to the end of the street. Advancing up it was a three-deep line of British infantrymen, helmeted, bayonets fixed, their steel throwing silver stars of morning sun through the trailing streamers of smoke still hanging in the air.

Beside him a big and dirty face stared hard at him. 'Well now, Tom McSherry, here come the cavalry. How long before you're fighting them?' Big Jamie did not wait for an answer but turned and walked away, calling young Jamie to him.

McSherry called a man to him, told him to fetch Gerry Madden and Sean McAllister, another lad who had caught his eye, to a meeting in the Hibernians' hall at ten o'clock sharp. Young Madden had the makings of a fighting man, he thought, with brains and understanding. He only needed education and a guide to see him through. McAllister was a savage with no brains at all but he had the heart of a bull and the single mindedness of a snake with a belly to fill. McAllister had seen Gerry Madden in action and had mimicked his every move, less one – he had failed to use the bodies of his friends as a shield. But he might learn, with experience. Already the two lads were coming together, with Madden in the lead. Madden was a great prospect; McAllister less so. But the two together, McAllister's axe to guard young Madden's foil, could be useful to the Cause.

His scarf pulled tight about his face McSherry left the barricades. Watching Big Jamie Lappin's retreating back, one arm around the shoulders of his son, McSherry thought it a pity that the lad was not a patch on the father. Gerry Madden and Sean McAllister would have to do.

The Hibernians' hall was cold, bare and stank of wet scorched mattresses despite the windows shut tight against the tributary of smoke eddying down Clonard Street to join the main river flowing along the Falls Road, held close to the ground by fine, misty rain. There was no furniture in the hall, other than a few folding chairs leaning against the walls. Bare floorboards, swept clean, curved at their edges, showing the wear of uncarpeted years, nailheads bright and clear. Gerry Madden felt insecure, unsure of why he was there. The man who had lifted him had been uncommunicative; he had just carried out his orders, brought Gerry and Sean McAllister here. His job done, he stood silently by, waiting. The great bell of Clonard monastery broke the chill quiet. Gerry counted the tolls. Ten o'clock.

'You two, follow me.' The shout boomed around the hall, making Gerry jump. Sean McAllister didn't even blink. Together they moved, following the skinny figure through a short corridor into a small, ill-lit box marked Committee Room.

There was a table, two men and very little else. Both men were hooded and had guns in front of them, between their arms, which were spread open on the table. One of the men spoke, his voice muffled by the hood, but unmistakably west Belfast.

'You have been seen to fight well. You know the present situation. Will you fight for Ireland? Say no and you're out the door. Say yes and you're volunteers, subject to the military discipline of the Irish Republican Army. You know what that means – nothing matters but the Cause, for life. Nobody ever leaves the IRA unless he's headed for Milltown in a box. You shoot your brother if you're told to. What's it to be? Yes or no?'

Gerry Madden felt his insides contract, felt the urge to relieve himself then and there. He knew the rules of the IRA: everybody did. The reference to Milltown cemetery frightened him. Who were these people? If he said the wrong thing he could be killed. Since last night Gerry had wanted very much to join the IRA, but he also wanted to be sure of who he was talking to. If these were not the IRA but some bunch of head cases who were trying to take the IRA's place he wanted out, and quick. Then he saw the hands of one of his interrogators twitch and tremble. A weakness. He moved his eyes to the hands of the other, felt them widen as he saw the tiny swallows tattooed between the thumbs and index fingers. A bandage was wrapped around the man's left hand. He knew those swallows. *Tom McSherry.*

This was real. He was being offered a chance to join the Brotherhood. No one was ever asked twice. Just then Sean McAllister began to edge away from him, as if getting ready to bolt. Stupid, thought Gerry, the door will be covered on the outside. He made his decision. Frightened as he was, something cold inside his head told him what to do. He stepped forward, grabbed the revolver nearest him from between the hands of McSherry's trembling henchman and swinging, pointed it at the head of Sean McAllister, pulling back the cocking handle as he had seen people do it in the films.

'I swear by Almighty God that I will fight for Ireland. Sean, you're not going anywhere. You know I'm volunteering, so you know too much. You're volunteering too, or I'll blow your fucking head off.'

Nobody moved. Gerry, determined, growing in confidence, shoved the gun harder against the other lad's head and shouted, 'Sean McAllister, are you with us or against us?'

The hooded man with the twitching hands threw his chair back and was half erect when McSherry shouted, 'Stop, Jack. Stop still!'

McAllister, near paralysed, felt the gun barrel hard and cold just in front of his ear, pushing upwards. He panicked, nearly falling to the floor in fear. 'I'm with you Gerry. For fuck's sake don't shoot me. I'll do anything. Don't shoot me, Gerry. In the name of Christ, I'm your man. I'll volunteer.'

Gerry, his fingers trembling, put the revolver back on the table, next to McSherry's own, wondering why McSherry hadn't grabbed for it. 'We're volunteers, Commandant. There's no need for hoods. I know who you are.'

The tension eased perceptibly. Tom McSherry pulled off the hood and threw it to the floor as he stood up, controlling his breathing with a visible effort.

'Volunteer Madden,' he shouted, leaning heavily on the table that separated him from Gerry Madden, 'don't you ever do the like of that again. You could have been shot. And we don't recruit by putting a gun to anybody's head.' McSherry's voice dropped back to normal. 'I'll give you the oath in a minute. Go in there.' He pointed to a door on his left and waited until Gerry had gone through it.

The other hooded man sat back down in his chair. Sean McAllister stood shaking, his face grey and sheened in sweat. McSherry had to do something. 'Are you all right, Sean? Nobody is going to shoot you. You're not a volunteer yet. You can go home if you like. But keep your mouth shut about what you've seen. Or I'll shoot you myself. All right?'

McAllister surprised him. His voice still full of shock the words tumbled out of him in a tight stutter. 'I'll volunteer, Mr McSherry. I've always wanted to fight for the Cause. I know my history. I know what it's all about. I'll do my best. It's just that Gerry really scared me. I thought he was really going to do it, you know. It scared me. I couldn't help it. Can I still volunteer, Mr McSherry?'

McSherry shook his head, disbelieving. 'All right, Sean. You can volunteer. Don't worry about what happened. Wait here while I talk to Volunteer Madden. Joe will bring you a cup of tea. Here's somebody you know. He'll take your oath.' McSherry gestured to the sitting man. Sean watched him pull his hood off: it was his Uncle Jack, his mother's brother.

Inside the small room off the committee room Gerry Madden took his oath of allegiance to the Cause. He was exultant. He was now a soldier for Ireland! He allowed his joy to shine in his eyes.

Tom McSherry hefted the revolver Gerry had grabber earlier. 'Would you really have shot Sean?'

'Yes, Commandant. I would.'

'Good. Never point a gun at somebody if you don't intend to use it. Now, a lesson for you.' McSherry broke the gun open, flicking the chambers out. The gun was not loaded. 'The other gun wasn't loaded either. We're not stupid people here. You or Volunteer McAllister might have turned on us. In which case' – McSherry pulled a small automatic from his belt – 'this one is loaded. Come on out and make your peace with Volunteer McAllister. You're going to be very busy in the next wee while, Volunteer Madden. Volunteer McAllister you will need.'

September 1970
BELFAST

Well over a year after the loss of his home young Jamie Lappin was still out of work, afraid to go back to Mackie's, despite the company's repeated offers and willingness to continue with his apprenticeship: his memories of drilling swarf blown into his eyes, the great steel bar falling on him, made him wary of the same happening again. Gerry Madden had gone down south, to Dundalk, to get work with the Irish Post Office, he'd said. Gerry dropped him a note now and then, telling big boys' lies about sticking his hand up country girls' skirts and throwing pints of Guinness down him faster than the barman could pull them. He hinted at dark secrets and trips to the hills, but never said 'come and see'. Big Jamie, Jamie's father, had lost weight and seemed to draw in on himself, rarely speaking; he had not been seen with a book in his hand since the riots. On the one occasion Jamie tried to ask his father for advice the big man just said, 'Get out of this place. Go somewhere else and make a life for yourself. Get out of Belfast before it pulls the life out of you.' Then he relapsed into silence. A week later he had come reeling home drunk, and had been sick for days. It did not stop him getting drunk again, as often as he could.

Jamie, at a loss and drifting, stayed at his family's pre-fabricated wooden house, one of those the City Council had provided as emergency homes for people burnt out in the riots. Sometimes when the weather was good he slept out, walking up Divis, taking a well worn path up the side of the mountain until he could look back across the city, as far as the Harland & Wolff shipyards. It was quiet up there and he could think.

Belfast was becoming an increasingly dangerous place to be, especially his home area. He thought about the rights and wrongs of what was happening, tried to reach conclusions, but could not, because he felt he did not know enough or did not really care. Sitting in his favourite copse high on the mountain Jamie felt less and less affinity with the city, began to hate its poverty, bigotries, hatreds and violence, the rain, the lack of work, the oppressive weight of defeat and despair he saw on people's faces, the hopelessness that seemed to hang in the air. Men not yet forty looked tired and beaten, their wives worn down by too little money and too many children.

As the months passed Jamie felt a growing restlessness, an urge to go and do something, or just run away. People had approached him, hinting that he might 'like to attend a meeting' or 'listen to a man talk about what the British are really doing in Ireland'. He had fobbed them off, instinctively feeling unready to commit himself to anything. But they were becoming more insist-ent: people were having to take sides, they said, were having to show where they stood in the struggle against the British and the Stormont parliament.

For a while Jamie worried about it all. Unless he chose soon he could be in danger from all sides. A splinter group, calling itself the Provisional Irish Republican Army, had broken away from the old, Official IRA. The Provisionals were accusing Cathal Goulding, leader of the Officials, of having sold the Cause's guns to the Free Wales Army and of having abandoned the armed struggle in favour of extreme left-wing socialism. They accused him of having left the Catholics of the North defenceless against anything Stormont might whip up against them. Matters were coming to a head, with the Provisionals and Officials assassinating each other on the streets.

In his heart Jamie Lappin, unconsciously absorbing much of his father's thinking, had no strong feeling either way, no hatred of the Prods, no urge to free Ireland from anybody. He just wanted a chance to get out from under it all, get away from the hard-faced men on all sides, get away and make something for himself. He went to offices full of Australians, South Africans, New Zealanders, all of whom offered assisted passages to their countries. But he had no trade and couldn't even find the ten pounds an assisted passage cost. The pictures they had shown him were of another world of happy people in the sun. He wanted to be part of that. He wanted out of Belfast.

One day, in Cupar Street, Jamie stopped to talk to a soldier in a different uniform from the others he had seen: a dangerous thing to do, but an idea was growing in him. The soldier was young, about twenty, his own age, tall and tanned. His name was Harry Summers and he was in the Parachute Regiment. The Paras were the elite of the British Army, he claimed. That's why he had the special jacket, a Dennison smock he called it, in large blotches of camouflage colouring. The dark red beret he said was exclusive to the army's airborne forces. Jamie was intrigued. 'What's it like in the Paras?'

Summers grinned, showing strong white teeth. Recruiting

was part of every soldier's job, they said, and it looked good on your reports if you got somebody in. 'It's OK. Money in your pocket. Plenty of sport. Grub's a bit rough sometimes, but there's always a lot of it. I've been in three years and I've been to Canada and Kenya on exercise. And I've been to Cyprus. Great place, Cyprus, loads of brandy sours and long blonde Swedes on holiday, all going topless on the beach. Comforts for the boys, know what I mean?' He grinned again, glancing up and down the street, keeping an eye on his mates. 'Officers are bastards, but you can keep out of their way, and your mates are great. You watch out for each other, see?'

Jamie considered this, all the time watching the bright alertness of the soldier. He seemed somehow more alive than the boys of Belfast. Even the other soldiers Jamie had passed the time of day with seemed sluggish in comparison. Jamie wanted to know more.

'Is it hard, getting into the Paras? I'm strong and I like hurling and Gaelic football.' Jamie paused, thinking. What were the drawbacks? His thoughts were interrupted by Summers, who had never heard of Gaelic football but had seen hurling on TV and thought it a game for lunatics.

'Of course it's hard, hauling a 60-pound Bergen rucksack up and down the mountains in Wales, then digging in, then going patrolling in the rain. I was on an ambush once where we had to lie still until the snow buried us to hide ourselves. It's tough in the Paras, but we weed out the wankers in P Company. That's our training company. Only the toughest get through. Then you do your jumps, get your red beret and join the Maroon Machine. The best infantry battalions in the world we are, a whole brigade of us. Nobody fucks about with Paras, not even Jocks. Paras are the evillest there is.' He made a short jerking movement with his rifle. 'See this? Self-Loading Rifle. 7.62 millimetre. It can throw a bullet two miles straight through a brick wall. Compared to our machine guns, it's a toy: 600 rounds a minute they can throw. And we've got mortars and anti-tank rockets.'

Summers suddenly stopped his flow of talk and sprinted

across the street, hard targeting; angling his run every few strides, changing his speed in mid-stride, now darting, now slowing, then darting again, an impossible target to hit. He stopped in the doorway of a shop.

Jamie looked about, puzzled. Soldiers always moved like that, to avoid IRA snipers. But there were no snipers about. There was none of that odd feeling in the air that warned people something was happening. Didn't the soldiers feel it when it came? Obviously not. He walked over to Summers and asked what had happened.

'Nothing happened. My mates moved, so I did, to cover them. I told you, we look after each other. You want to be a Para?'

Jamie was interested. Maybe this could be his chance. Harry Summers seemed to be so self assured and very much in control of himself. 'I could do. Maybe.'

'Then get yourself down the recruiting office. Tell them I sent you. Now fuck off, you're attracting attention to me. See you if you survive P Company. You can buy me a beer.'

And Harry Summers was gone, sprinting slantwise across the road, never more than three strides in the same direction. Jamie watched. 'Get out' his father had said. Now he knew how.

For four days he thought hard about leaving his family, cutting himself off from them. He would have to. The Provisionals and the Officials would never forgive him if he joined the British Army, would kill him if they got the chance, would harass and maybe even harm his people if they knew for sure where Jamie Lappin had disappeared to.

After a night on the mountain Jamie went home and told his mother he was going to England, was joining the British Army. He talked to her about his feelings, how he was worried about leaving them all at home, and confessed to being scared of being on his own, cut off.

Josie Lappin did not fail him. Her heart went out to him, wanting to keep him with her safe for ever, but her mother's instinct knew he needed to go. She looked at Big Jamie sleeping off a hangover. 'I don't blame you, son. It's time you left us to make your life. Don't forget us. Don't forget we love you. Your Daddy's not well, but he'll be brave again. Try your hardest and remember your Daddy as he was. Bring honour to his name. Don't come back until all this fighting is over. God bless you, Jamie.' A kiss, a tearful hug and he was away.

The slightly portly sergeant in the Army Careers Information Office in Royal Avenue was sharp, smart and all business. Every bit of his uniform that could be polished shone like gold or black glass. Jamie, a bit intimidated, answered up as best he could. Name? James Lappin. Address? 17 The Huts, Whiterock. Phone number? None. Age? Twenty. Any criminal record? No.

Then came the tests, simple enough. English and arithmetic. Then the forms. Everything about him: school, family, exams, relatives in communist countries?

'You're a likely lad, Lappin. We could make a soldier of you. I think we could even make a gunner of you. Field artillery myself. Twenty years, 1st Regiment, Royal Horse Artillery. A great life for a lad. And prospects of promotion. See these? Sergeant's stripes. I'm a member of the sergeants' mess with a pension coming my way, and a great life behind me. Been everywhere, me, all over the world. The Royal Regiment of Artillery for you, OK?'

'I want to join the Parachute Regiment, please.'

'What? A Para? Listen son, I've had a look at your tests. They're not the best but they're very good. You can join any regiment you like. Or you could get yourself a trade. Engineers or the Ordnance. You could even apply to those maniacs in the Ordnance bomb disposal if you wanted. They need clever lads. Paras are just thick infantrymen.'

The recruiting sergeant thought of his job – to recruit for the army, not just his own regiment – but decided to press on, to get this lad for the Guns if he could. He could not quite put his finger on it, but the skinny lad had something about him. The boy seemed young for his age and unsure of himself but there was something unusual showing in his eyes. He stared at the boy and thought about it. Determination. That's what it was. He tried again, one of those disparaging bits of doggerel the regiments threw at each other springing into his mind.

'Son, Paras have the speed of racehorses, the strength of carthorses and the brains of rocking horses. Once you get to the selection centre at Sutton Coldfield you'll see. There's lots you can do. But you want to be with the fighting soldiers, not support troops, I can see that. Go for the Guns, lad. You won't regret it.' The sergeant leaned his arms on his desk and hunched his shoulders, throwing everything he had into convincing the thin, rough-accented kid.

Jamie did not understand a lot of the sergeant's talk. He'd never heard of Sutton Coldfield, didn't even know what Ordnance meant. He was silent, afraid of saying the wrong thing.

The old Horse Gunner sighed. He supposed Paras needed the odd intelligent lad. This one was no intellectual giant, but he showed promise. He could be a good Gunner, and rise to sergeant or more. Every regiment loved its own and poured bile on all the others. Most of it was bullshit. But Paras were different: they really were the animals they claimed to be.

'OK, son. I'll put you down for the Paras. But if you don't like them or you don't pass for them, transfer to the Guns. You'll be all right there. We even have our own Paras, the 7th Regiment, Royal Horse Artillery. 105 millimetre pack howitzers, to support the Parachute Brigade.'

Jamie Lappin, confused by the numbers and the jargon, had no real idea of the variety of careers the army offered. He just wanted out of Belfast, and to be accepted for what he could do. He just wanted to be somebody, and the Paras were the best. Harry Summers, tall, strong and tanned, had said so.

'Thanks. I'll do my best when I get there. Bye bye.'

As he watched young Lappin carefully close the door on his way out the recruiting sergeant suddenly felt very tired. Thank God he had only two years to push. Then he would buy a piece of mistletoe, pin it to his shirt tail and invite his colonel to kiss his arse. Soldiering was great until you turned thirty. After that it was all downhill. He felt a hypocrite, recruiting these kids. But he had a pension to come and a family to feed. Heaving himself out from behind his desk he glanced at the plain round clock on the wall. Twelve twenty. Lappin, and all the others, could learn the hard way, the same as he had. Time for a couple of pints.

Six weeks later an exhausted recruit was crawling along the towpath of the canal behind the Parachute Regiment's training centre in Aldershot. His uniform was covered in mud, his smock and trousers worn through at the elbows and knees, showing not much skin and a lot of flesh not far from the bone. On his back was a Bergen rucksack and in his right hand an SLR. Only the rifle was free of mud and dirt. Walking slowly beside him as he crawled were a captain and a tough-looking sergeant, talking about him as if he wasn't there. The sergeant's tone was hard and rough, his Glaswegian accent thick and heavy.

'No guts. Can't keep up. His platoon are back in barracks by now. We should bin him.'

The captain looked at the sergeant, playing the straight man. 'Surely not, Sergeant. He's trying. He's just tired. Maybe he should wear boxing gloves in bed. Or could he be one of those, you know, not as other men?'

Sergeant Jeff nodded, speaking loud and clear. 'You're right, sir. A wanker, maybe a queer. Never make a Para as long as he has a hole in his arse. I'll prove it.' He prodded the crawling recruit with a booted foot. 'YOU! STAND UP!'

Jamie Lappin hauled himself to his feet, unable to stop the tears, unable to speak. The last six weeks had drained him, killed him, left him with nothing more to offer, and with sixteen weeks of basic training still to go. He stood as best he could, swaying.

Sergeant Jeff stuck his face into Lappin's and took him by the throat. Watching Lappin's eyes, he roared, 'You're a wanker, you! You've let yourself down. You've let your platoon down.

Anything to say before we bin you and send you off to be a clerk somewhere?'

Jamie fell over. The captain and Sergeant Jeff picked him up. Again he stood swaying, mouth open, staring hard back at the sergeant. 'I'm not a wanker. I'm not a queer. My rifle's clean, Sergeant. I can shoot it.'

'Like fuck you can. You've still a mile to go. You can't get there. You're binned. Give me that rifle.'

'No, Sergeant. I can get there. This is my rifle.'

Jamie Lappin stumbled off, in the wrong direction. Jeff dunted a shoulder against his, turning him. Jamie made about twenty yards before he fell and started crawling again. His superiors walked behind him, talking quietly. Jeff said 'His pulse is strong and even, only about ninety a minute. I checked it at the artery in his throat. He's exhausted, totally bollocksed, but he won't give in. Did you see the look in his eyes? If he had the strength he'd strangle me. Look at the state he's in. I like this kid. I want him, sir.'

The captain, dressed as any other Para captain would be, was in fact the centre's medical officer, a doctor. He watched Jamie as he replied. 'No. He will not pass P Company. He's had enough. His heart's bigger than his body. He's underfed, has been for years. He just doesn't have the strength. Not enough muscle bulk, far too light. Brave lad, though. Shame, really. Bin him for his own good.'

'I want this kid, sir. I was like him once. He's good material, sir. Only a natural athlete could have such a low heart rate for the effort he's putting in. He just needs building up. Invent an injury for him. Achilles tendonitis, stress fractures in the shins, anything that'll give him six months' light duties. I'll feed and train him. If he isn't doing the business any time during that I'll send him elsewhere. Give this lad a chance, sir. Just look at the fucker, crawling. He deserves a chance.'

The doctor watched a little while. 'All right. He's got stress fractures of the tibia, both legs. Reassessment on P Company in six months. Get him into the medical reception station. I'll clean up his knees and elbows, rest him and feed him up for ten days. After that he's yours. I want to see him once a fortnight, OK?'

Jeff walked forward and leaned over the crawling figure, bawling in simulated rage. 'You lucky fucker. The doctor won't let me bin you. You're going to hospital. You've fooled him, but not me. I'll have you, Lappin. I'll have you on a kebab stick. You're idle, Lappin, idle. Crawl faster. Unless you make the finish line you're out on your Paddy arse, no matter what the doctor says. Move your bloody self!'

Chapter Six

15 August 1972

FRIMLEY

In a great Georgian mansion set in thirty acres of Surrey country-side, Elliott's rich, deep tones carried easily along the long, wood-panelled study, echoing slightly near the door.

'Come and sit down, Charlotte. Please make yourself comfortable.' Elliott pointed to a delicate-looking Louis Quinze piece to the left of his desk. 'There is coffee on the table.'

He spun his considerable bulk in his own more practical swivel chair to face his other visitor, a tall, very elderly, almost ascetic-looking man who, despite his age and need of the stout ashplant he used as a walking stick, had the unmistakable stamp of a man long used to the possession and exercise of power.

'A moment with your granddaughter, General. There are some things I ought to say.'

Elliott, the fifth of the line to carry the name as headmaster of Elliott's school swung his chair once more and directed his view at the young woman sitting, very composed, in the delicate period piece. Charlotte Aitken was tall and slim, still a little gangly and occasionally awkward, like a young thoroughbred not yet sure of its legs. But there was an uncultivated beauty in her; thick dark hair cut sharply at shoulder length for ease of maintenance framed a face not classical in its proportions but full of life and health. Her eyes, a blue that varied with her mood and the light, shone with intelligence.

Elliott shifted in his chair, easing an imaginary physical discomfort. Something about the girl had always disturbed him, something he could never put his finger on, something in her eyes, a compelling, terrible certainty. He cleared his throat.

'Charlotte, as you know it is time for you to leave us. I have considered the options open to you and the spread of your abilities. It is my duty to advise you with regard to your career. I have not yet discussed this matter with your grandfather but we will, I hope, reach agreement.' He smiled, expecting her to make some polite reply. She said nothing, but stared back at him, a hint of amusement in her eyes. The Headmaster, again discomfited, paused to consult his papers.

'You have two A-level passes, one A and one B, and five O-levels, with a bias towards the sciences. You have represented the school at swimming and sailing and you have led two school expeditions into the Cairngorm mountains, earning the only Winter Mountain Leadership Certificate ever held by a girl from this school. I am told by those who should know that you are also an offshore sailor of some potential.'

The headmaster lifted his head to smile, hoping to ease the tension he knew she must be feeling 'You are not brilliant academically but quite capable of taking a good degree, and your sporting activities make you a good all-rounder. I believe that you should go up to one of the better provincial universities, take your degree in a general science, enjoy yourself as much as possible and then consider your future.'

Elliott glanced at Charlotte's grandfather. 'General?'

'Thank you, headmaster.' The old general's voice was strong, showing no sign of his advanced age, with only the slight roughness of the lifelong devotee of single malt whiskies to guide the hearer. 'Your view is of course most valuable, and in dealing with an ordinary girl would no doubt be correct. But Charlotte is not ordinary; she is working to a plan. She will have a month's break and then attend the Regular Commissions Board at Westbury in preparation for a career with the military. There is no room for university. The WRAC College and the Staff College at Camberley will be quite sufficient to train her in how to think. My granddaughter's career objective has already been decided. Charlotte intends to be, headmaster, the first woman ever to reach general officer rank.'

Surprised, for this was the first he had heard of a plan for Charlotte's future, Elliott closed his eyes and thought hard. Now he realised why Charlotte had worked so hard at such a range of activities and why her fees had been paid by her grandfather, why the general had supervised her education and sat here today in place of her mother and stepfather. The girl had been taken over and virtually programmed by the old general, for reasons of his own.

Elliott was bitterly disappointed. Never before had he come across so cold-blooded a hijacking of the future of a young woman. Men often wanted their sons to follow in their footsteps or into their businesses, sometimes forcing them to do so. But to plan a military career for a girl not yet twenty, knowingly plan to rob her of a settled home and children? It seemed outrageous. Compassion for Charlotte Aitken made him hope that she would mature quickly, see through this nonsense and break free to lead her own life. At last he said 'I see. Charlotte, would you please leave us. I'm sure you want to get on with your packing. Good luck and God bless you.'

When Charlotte had left, Elliott clasped his hands together and thought. His Quaker faith had not stopped him studying military history, including that of the First World War. A passage from a history book long out of print sprang into his mind: *Hopkinson, Alexander, major-general. Military Cross for the action at Mons. Once the youngest major-general in the Army, thought of as the man most likely to be our youngest ever Field Marshal, but was held responsible for the disaster at Huguenot Wood after he lost 7,500 men killed and wounded out of a division less than 10,000 strong in under a day and refused to press on with the attack. Relieved of command by Kitchener for failing to achieve his objective and retired to his family estate in Suffolk, aged 29.*

The headmaster unclasped his hands and stood up to pour coffee for the general and himself, thinking that other generals in the same war had lost more men in less excusable circumstances and had got away with it, gone on to pour more men into the same charnel houses. Huguenot Wood had been a morass of mud dominated by machine guns in concrete pillboxes, a crucial piece of ground. Its capture would have broken the German line at a point close to the main railway terminal supporting their entire front. General Hopkinson must have had powerful and ruthless enemies, jealous of his meteoric rise to divisional command. Ordering him to attack Huguenot Wood with only one division had been an act of madness. Killing his career for refusing to continue the slaughter was an act of supreme callousness. It must have been a terrible blow. His reason for planning Charlotte's future seemed obvious: sixty years of bitterness had corroded the general's moral judgement, leading him to live through his granddaughter. It was understandable, but still despicable. The headmaster chose his words carefully.

'I must confess to surprise and some disappointment, General. I had hoped to see a second generation of Aitken girls before I retire.'

The implication was not lost on the general. 'Perhaps you will Headmaster. But I doubt it. Charlotte can be very single-minded.'

17 April 1973
VOGELSANG: WEST GERMANY

On the sixth day of Exercise Final Fling the rain still fell, sometimes heavily, sometimes nothing more than a fine mist, always cold, incessant, sister to the dispiriting wind that could empty the lungs of the East in blasts that bent the Ardennes pines, but then on other days would die off, giving hope that better weather was on its way at last; a wind that teased tired bodies, tired minds with promises never kept, infuriating in its uncertainty.

Huddled over his old A41 radio, Officer Cadet Mark Coolidge shifted his shoulders to ease the pain caused by the chafing of the radio's canvas web straps, thanking God for the chance to get the bloody thing off his back. His platoon had just covered nearly twelve nightbound miles through the forest, avoiding all tracks and firebreaks to negate the chance of enemy ambush. With his personal equipment and weapons weighing just over 60 pounds, the A41's 40-plus pounds were an irksome but essential addition to Coolidge's load, forming his platoon commander's only means of communication with the world inside and outside this dripping, heavily forested offshoot of the Ardennes.

Coolidge glanced around in the dark, noting the figures of the rest of 3 Platoon's headquarters personnel slumped against trees or flat out on the ground, maintaining a guard or fast asleep, dead on their feet after six 24-hour days of constant movement and fighting in the cold and wet, with the minimum of sleep and all rations eaten cold to prevent the distinctive smell of hexamine cookers giving away their location to the enemy. Then Coolidge caught the tiny red gleam of a torch shielded under a poncho: his platoon commander studying her map for her next foray against the enemy. Coolidge groaned, rubbed eyes full of the blood and grit of sleeplessness and flicked on his radio, calling the Directing Staff, DS, for a radio check. The first thing Charlie would do when she drew her head and shoulders out from under the poncho would be to ask were comms good. He wanted to be ready.

'Zero this is Three, radio check, over.'

There was silence for a few seconds then Officer Cadet Mike Tedder's anxious tones came through Coolidge's headphones. 'Three this is Zero. OK. Receiving you five five. Where the hell are you? The DS are going crazy trying to find Boadicea. You must tell me where you are. Over.'

'Zero this is Three. OK. Out.' Coolidge grinned in the dark. He switched off the radio to prevent the Directing Staff officers from bothering him further, knowing there would be hell to pay. His sympathies went out to Mike Tedder, a good man nursing a broken leg, one of the 'sick lame and lazy' unable to deploy to the field through injury. Tedder had been detailed off to act as base camp radio operator for the DS based in Vogelsang, the Belgian army complex of firing ranges reputed to have once been the home of the Hitler Youth Waffen SS Division. Coolidge jumped, startled. Officer Cadet Charlotte Aitken, revered platoon commander of 3 Platoon, Alamein Company, the Royal Military Academy at Sandhurst, was at his elbow.

Charlie Aitken was one of only three female officer cadets still surviving the sudden and arbitrary decision of *someone very very senior* to silence the feminists clamouring for equality of training and opportunity, for women in the trenches, once and for all. Nine nineteen-year-old potential officers had been lifted out of their training course at the Women's Royal Army Corps training centre in Camberley, moved a couple of miles up the A30 and thrown straight into the male potential officers' Standard Military Course. Here they would face seven months of close contact with young men they would eventually know far better than the men's wives ever would, with no concessions to their sex other than a hard-fought battle for separate bathrooms. The Commandant of the WRAC College, taken by surprise, had chosen which of her young women she could send quickly but wisely.

At one time the attempt to preserve the male-oriented status quo had looked like succeeding, with six of the nine young women falling by the wayside through injury, inability or plain physical and emotional exhaustion in the first two months. But the girl known to the Sandhurst DS as Boadicea for her ferocity was still around, along with the elf-like Wilhelmina 'Willie' Guthrie and the 6' 1" Alerose 'Big Al' Friendship, both women in the Aitken mould, women who out-savaged the most savage of the male cadets with their female pragmatism and willingness to consider courses of action the men would have balked at. The reason they had survived was simple: the men, at first sceptical and dismissive had come to admire their sheer determination in

63

the face of physical impossibility, their refusal to ask for help but willingness to accept it if offered, their obvious ability in other areas and their exceptional personalities. Living with them 24 hours a day and sharing their pain and exhaustion, the men had come to think of them as much the same as the less physically able men, but with better heads.

In a gauche attempt to show their feelings, the men had elected 'our women' as honorary men and given them male names, not as a certain kind of gay gives men women's names, but as a token of solidarity. The tiny, perceptive Willie Guthrie, destined to become a legend in her own lifetime for resigning her commission to lead an all-woman expedition down the Nile from source to the sea – but not before winning the Queen's Gallantry Medal for coolness and leadership under fire – had urged the other women to see things from the men's point of view.

'They're not being sexist. They're trying to show us some respect but haven't got far enough yet to see that men and women really are different. They think the best they can do is make us equal by making us men. They're really trying hard. That's what matters. We should accept that.'

The women did, and the men ignored their female bodies and listened to their female minds. It wasn't ideal, but it was workable. Even the godlike academy sergeant-major MacAlpine, late of the Scots Guards – who had been heard to say that women had no business being soldiers because they had no concept of honour or respect for the enemy – came to accept them, if gruffly, while pretending not to in his public utterances. Terrorists in uniform they were, he said, smothering his admiration for 'my girrrls' as they fought their way with bleeding feet and tear-stained faces over killer route marches and the appalling Sandhurst assault course with brutally strong and extremely fit young men, carrying equipment and weapon loads that should have killed a pack mule, occasionally with their equipment carried for them for short distances by the biggest, strongest of the men, occasionally literally carried between two men, occasionally, unceremoniously, thrown bodily over a six-foot red brick wall set in the middle of a bog of shin-deep mud.

But after the log race, a physically devastating six-mile run in which teams of eight carried a telegraph pole by whatever means they chose, MacAlpine had seen enough. A man known to have the ear of Her Majesty the Queen, he had faced down the DS, demanding that 'my girrrls' be recognised as exceptional young women, and that they should not be the subject of blind, unthinking abuse.

'They are special,' he burred, 'but they are not men. They cannot carry these loads at the speed they must to keep up with the men. They can do anything the men can, but I will not have them overburdened.'

The DS, assuming with some justification that the academy sergeant-major's voice spoke the words of Major-General Smythe, General Officer Commanding The Royal Military Academy (the GOC RMA) accepted with alacrity the direction of the prevailing wind, with one eye on the Queen and the other on the GOC RMA, with a cursory glance at the Army Board. Thereafter the academy sergeant-major's 'girrrls' carried the same as the men, with the exception of the heavy weapons, the General Purpose Machine Gun, the frightful Carl Gustav anti-tank gun and the brutal old A41 radios. With time, the DS had seen the wisdom of the academy sergeant-major's thirty-two years of soldiering.

First the DS took the women seriously, then began to wonder, then admire, then protect, then treat as equal, then watch with suspicion as the women adopted more and more unorthodox tactics to compensate for their physical limitations and maximise their intellectual and emotional insights into the wholly male world of war-fighting, watched the women thinking like men but still *feeling* like women, always and forever probing for weaknesses in the cold male logic of how fights, however great in scope, should be fought. 'Big Al' Friendship, debating on a set subject 'The Need for Morality in Warfare', had given the DS nightmares. Standing

65

at the lectern of the academy's Churchill Hall she had given it to them in a single, solid punch.

'There are the Geneva Conventions, to which we are signatories. There are in addition unwritten rules that you do not do immoral things, like tie enemy civilians to your tanks to prevent the enemy firing on you. There is talk of honour and glory, decency, humanity and Christian principles. I say it is all bullshit.' She paused for effect.

'I say the Conventions and other Rules of Warfare were dreamed up by civilised people thinking civilised thoughts, thinking that wars can be fought in a moral, civilised fashion. I say that we should recognise that wars are not civilised or moral: nor are they glorious or honourable. I say that wars are dirty, brutal, painful in the extreme: utterly amoral. If we cannot avoid a war we must end it, end its amorality, to restore morality in our lives. There are only two definite ways of ending a war: you accept defeat or you win. If it is assumed that you cannot surrender, then you have no alternative: you must win, in order to end the war.

'It will be argued by those who oppose my view that I am saying that supposedly immoral, certainly amoral actions, like tying enemy civilians to your tanks, are acceptable. I will save them time: that is exactly what I am saying, because war-fighting is amoral. If such actions shorten or end the war they are not immoral, or amoral: they are moral in the highest sense, because if you act otherwise and lose, the enemy wins — and he may plunge the world into a new Dark Age of amorality, as Hitler would have. If you win, morality is triumphant, not just restored. I say again, war is amoral, not immoral. The best way to end amorality is to end war. The best way to end war is to be victorious, to do whatever you have to do, as Truman did when he atom bombed Nagasaki and Hiroshima. I say again, all the rest is bullshit.'

'Big Al' Friendship, sitting down to a shocked silence, had been punished for her use of colloquial language, nothing more.

A very senior officer had been called in to give an opposing argument to the same audience, to 'give a balanced view', the reaction of horrified DS to a vote in which Alerose Friendship had been defeated by the narrowest of margins.

Charlotte Aitken, reflecting on the issue, was not convinced by either argument. She determined that issues of morality were irrelevant: should she ever fight a war she would do anything in her power to win it; the presence of an enemy prepared to fight her was an opportunity, his efficient destruction visible evidence of her right to high command. Exercise Final Fling was giving her just such an opportunity and she was seizing it with both hands.

'Are comms OK, Mark?'

'Yes, Charlie. The DS are getting really serious about finding you. They are not happy. What's happening?'

'Sod the DS. I don't know what's happening. I want you to tell me. Get on listening watch and copy down anything 1 and 2 Platoons say. I think they're coming after us and I want to know when and where. Where's Colour-Sar'nt Willcocks?'

'Over there, by the tree with two trunks.'

As Charlotte moved off silently into the murk, Coolidge shivered with cold and wet but grinned happily, flicked on his radio and reached inside his combat smock to pull out 1 and 2 Platoons' Slidex and Mapco settings. Getting those had been Charlie's first great tactical success, achieved within an hour of deploying out of Vogelsang. The three platoons of Alamein Company had been given overlapping patrol areas and separately told to consider anyone they came across as the enemy, effectively pitting them against each other, every platoon for itself against the others, for a period of ten days.

Charlie had been given command of 3 Platoon as her test exercise. She had reacted faster than anyone had anticipated, split up her platoon into sections and ambushed 1 and 2 Platoons' headquarters before they could melt into the forest. Her section commanders had, on her orders, captured 1 and 2 Platoons' radio operators and surreptitiously copied their codes before claiming successful attacks on the enemy to an unprepared Directing Staff.

That little stroke of audacity and aggression had impressed the DS and paid dividends over and over again. The DS had tried to redress the balance by leaking her codes to her enemies, to find she had abandoned them in favour of a colour and number code devised by Roger Jacks, another officer cadet in 3 Platoon. Her enemies could hear her, but had no idea what she was saying. 3 Platoon knew where everyone else was most of the time but nobody, including the DS, knew where 3 Platoon was. Or so Charlie thought.

Charlotte's first Orders Group to her platoon had made her intention clear: she intended to fight as if this were for real, relying on her own resources, her own Intelligence-gathering. She was going to fight 24-hour operations without let-up until the DS admitted that her enemies could not function as fighting forces. With the total commitment of every member of her platoon – something she assumed went without saying – she was going to fight the other two platoons into the ground. Standing in the pouring rain with a rifle in one hand and the other clenched in a fist held close under her chin she had been magnificent, spellbinding, her face fixed in absolute determination, the power of her will catching every man by the throat, by the balls, forcing them to see and listen, *feel* her drive to win.

Charlie's men, after nearly seven months sharing their lives with her, had not been surprised, did not feel threatened, did not even see her as a very pretty young woman: Charlie, they assumed without thinking, was the right man for the job; they would fight 1 and 2 Platoons into the ground. Anybody who couldn't hack Charlie's pace was a wanker and didn't deserve to be in 3 Platoon anyway. Charlie had grinned and taken their silence, then driven them on to success after success. Tonight they were cold, wet, tired to the point of exhaustion but content, with morale sky high: 3 Platoon were winners.

'Morning, Staff. It's just about fifteen minutes to first light.

I'm going to rest the men for a couple of hours, until I find out what 2 Platoon are doing, then I'm going to move against one of their patrols. OK?'

Colour-Sergeant Willcocks of the Coldstream Guards grunted himself upright, passing a hand over his chin to feel the night bristles and promising himself a shave at the first opportunity. 'Very well, Miss Aitken. But not a couple of hours. Four hours at least, no argument. They need it. You need it. Overtired commanders make mistakes that cost lives. You can afford four hours.' The colour-sergeant pulled his beret down over his eyes. 'Away you go. Get some sleep.'

Charlotte Aitken stood still a moment, looking defiant. She was striding stiffly off when she heard Willcocks call her back.

One of a small band of Foot Guards senior non-commissioned officers hand-picked as officer cadets' first contact with soldiers, Willcocks had undergone a six-week selection course in the freezing forestry blocks of Sennybridge in the worst a Welsh mountain winter could offer, just to prove he really wanted to help train the British Army's officers of the future. Since then he had spent most of his waking hours with officer cadets, 3 Platoon being his fifth batch of raw would-be officers, from the day of their first arrival at Sandhurst, teaching them just about all they would ever need to know about handling soldiers at platoon and company level. Sometimes he almost bullied them, sometimes cajoled them, sometimes had them near to tears, sometimes built them up when they were on the verge of quitting. Always he was with them, and had never let them down. Now he felt conscious of nearly having failed to offer his best to Charlotte Aitken; for a moment he had forgotten why he had come to Sandhurst.

'Miss Aitken. A word if you will, ma'am.'

Charlotte swung about in mid-stride, forcing the anger out of her face. When Willcocks asked for a 'word' she could be certain she was in for a major-league bollocking or something worth listening to. In either case it paid to react with speed.

69

'Yes, Staff. I'm here.'

'Good. Listen in. Things are going well for you. Don't blow it. Aggression and willingness to fight day and night are great. Especially if you can motivate your men by giving them successes. But pride comes before a fall, ma'am. Think about it.'

Charlotte, tired beyond anything she had ever felt, was impatient and irritable. 'What do you mean, blow it? I'm defeating my enemies. That's what I'm supposed to do. What more can I do? I don't understand and I think you're talking in riddles. I'm sorry, Staff, but I haven't the time for this.'

Willcocks nodded to himself, his instincts were right once again. Charlotte Aitken, self-appointed supersoldier, needed a touch of reality and a bit of advice. 'You have all the time I think you need, Miss Aitken. Talk to me like that again and I'll not hesitate to relieve you of command.'

Charlotte saw the danger signs flashing. *Relieved of command for lack of judgement. That would be a disaster. Willcocks wouldn't threaten such a thing unless he's really concerned.*

'I'm sorry, Staff. But what more can I do?'

'You can give these young gentlemen the leadership they deserve. You've shattered them and they're still giving you the best they have because they believe in you. Do you deserve it? No, you don't, because you're allowing yourself to think of them as if they were machines. They're not. They need hot food and rest in these conditions. Most of all they need a commander who is thinking clearly and logically, not somebody who's out on her feet. Do you understand me?'

Charlotte's mind was back in gear, the gnawing fear that she had made a great error in trying to finish off her enemies too quickly coming back to haunt her. She felt weak, mentally and physically. She was cold and wet and filthy after a week in the field with no more than token attention to her personal hygiene. She felt close to defeat, and despair, and close to tears. She felt, as the men put it, as if she couldn't say shit without somebody's arm up her ass and her voice coming out of somebody else's mouth.

But she was still willing to fight, though unsure how, with her nightmares haunting her.

'Yes. I understand. We still have four days to go on this exercise. I'm worried that even if I finally defeat 1 and 2 Platoons today the DS will not accept that, and dream up something to keep the exercise going. My platoon won't be in condition to fight on. I'll be beaten by myself. I understand that very well, but I can't see what more I can do. Christ Staff, I'm at my wits' end.' Charlotte paused, forcing back her tears, biting on her next words. 'I need help.'

Willcocks shrugged his shoulders, pretending to scratch an itch against his tree, to cover his admiration of the young woman in front of him. He studied every line of her. Charlotte Aitken's head was down, not a good sign. He knew her well enough to believe that any second now her head would snap back up. He had to see it happen. If it did not she was broken, prepared for defeat. If it did she would fight, with or without his help, until she saw an opportunity to snatch victory out of the jaws of defeat or was overwhelmed. He watched as a tremor went through her, saw her head come up, saw the hurt in her eyes turn back to defiance. Willcocks felt his breath, unconsciously held, blow out with relief. In his heart of soldiering hearts he knew that this was the moment he had waited for, believed that this young woman could become the great commander every soldier dreamed of serving under. This was what he had come to Sandhurst for: to find and help shape such a commander. He would start serving her now.

'Very good, Miss Aitken. I know you need help. Every commander worth his rations needs help. I'm going to help you as your enemies are being helped. I'm going to give you the advice a good platoon sergeant would. My advice is go to ground for twelve hours, then resume operations. You can afford that. I can assure you that you will not be attacked in that time.'

But Charlotte's mind was now fully aroused. Her early training snapped her into logical thought, throwing her exhaustion aside for the time it would take her to absorb and use the new information at her disposal. 'How can you know that?'

'Miss Aitken, be realistic. Use that very good mind of yours. You've pulled off one of the most original approaches to this exercise ever devised by an officer cadet. But don't think you thought of it first. The DS are very professional officers. They wouldn't be allowed anywhere near Sandhurst if they weren't. There is no way they would allow you to roam around at will, without even basic safety cover. They are assessing your performance, hour by hour. Do you imagine they don't know where you are? You are guilty of the sin of seeing what you want to see.'

Willcocks reached under his combat smock and pulled out a PRC 349 radio. 'These are new. Range about a couple of kilometres. I talk to the DS helicopter every four hours. Get it now?'

Charlotte slumped to her knees, rifle across her thighs. 'They know everything? Then why didn't they tell 1 and 2 Platoons where to find us? Why have they let me think I was winning? I don't understand, Staff. Are they playing with me?'

'No. The DS have come to expect the unusual from you. They wanted to give you every chance, but they're geared up to meet whatever you throw at them. They expected you to lie low 24 hours ago. You didn't. They got worried. Their problems are that you've been too successful and that 1 and 2 Platoons' commanders are very near the end of their tether. OK so far?'

'Yes. I understand.'

'Good. Think about this. The DS have 1 and 2 Platoons' commanders to think of. They're not going to let you destroy the self-belief of two very good young men. Nor are they going to allow you to drive yourself or your platoon into the ground. They have to redress the balance. The DS will co-ordinate an attack on you by 1 and 2 Platoons, to restore their morale.'

'Yes, I thought they might do that, the bastards. It's what I've been watching out for. What if I'm ready for them?'

'The DS have a secondary plan. They're prepared in case you

see the attack coming. If you manage to sidestep it the DS will be pissed off. They can't complain about you doing your job, so they'll forgive you, but only if you have the sense to have your men in a fit condition to fight. If you do you'll have your victory: and possibly win the Sword of Honour.'

'Hmm. Yes, I see. What then, Staff?'

'You'll have to back off and allow the other platoons to trap you and give you a hammering. They will see themselves as having nailed you in the end. You will know that you beat them hands down. Everybody's happy. The DS think you're something special, they're on your side, ma'am. But if you blow it they'll rip you apart. Understand?'

Charlotte gathered her thoughts, excitement building in her. 'Yes. I've won. They'll give me twelve hours to rest, then set 1 and 2 Platoons on me some time soon after that. I'll avoid that attack and counter-ambush 1 and 2 Platoons if I can. Then I'll have to let them catch me and kill me. But when and where will the enemy set their ambush? I need to know, Staff.'

'I won't tell you. That would be going too far. I need your word that you'll let them catch you.'

'Got it, Staff. You have my word. I'll let them get me — tomorrow. I'm going to crawl into my sleeping bag now, after I've told my platoon what's happening. OK?'

Willcocks grinned in the growing light. 'OK, Charlie Aitken. I'll enjoy seeing you march out to take the Sword, even if you aren't up to much on drill.'

'Thank you, Staff. Don't forget I'm female. I'll need someone to march out with me to take the sword from me. I'm not allowed to carry a Sam Browne belt and scabbard to put it in.'

Willcocks smothered a grin. 'You're a born diplomat, Miss Aitken, or a born general. I'll march out with you and carry your sword. Now bugger off, ma'am.'

Fifteen minutes later Willcocks spoke to his company commander, after listening in to Charlotte's briefing of her platoon. 'She sees the light. She says she's going to lie low for twelve hours. Plan A won't work. She's been expecting something like it. That's why she hasn't gone to ground before now. I had to tell her the plan in outline, to convince her that she has time to rest her platoon. She will probably manage to avoid the attack when it comes. She will counterattack if she sees an opportunity to do so. I have her word that she will then allow 1 and 2 Platoons to trap her, probably tomorrow, after she has a barbecue with all the hexamine her men have saved this week. They'll all be in their sleeping bags with bellies full of hot grub when 1 and 2 Platoons catch her. She'll have her men roll out of their maggots and fire a few blanks in token defence. That's about it. Over.'

Willcocks listened and thought hard, composing his answer to the question ringing in his ears. Then he spoke, crisp and concise.

'She's an outstanding commander. She's bright and she's able. She's a great motivator. She's learned that everyone, including herself, has limits. Miss Aitken is the best cadet I've known, if only because she is selective about who she takes advice from. I'm asking for the Sword for her. Over.'

He listened to the reply, then answered 'I know she can't carry a sword. With respect sir, that's no excuse. The Academy Sar'nt-Major is the authority on drill. He'll sort it out. I want the Sword for Miss Aitken, sir. She's bloody well earned it. Out.'

Major-General (Retd.) Alexander Hopkinson, sitting in uniform on the tiered ranks either side of the King's Walk watched with great pride as his granddaughter marched forward, a colour-sergeant of the Coldstream Guards one pace to her left, one pace to her rear. Academy Sergeant-Major MacAlpine stood four square in the centre of his parade ground, bellowing orders. Around him 400 officer cadets presented arms, rifles or swords according to their Sandhurst standing, the General Officer Commanding raising his own arm in salute. The academy adjutant, on Alexander, readied the big grey horse to walk up Old College steps.

On the saluting base Her Royal Highness the Princess Alice,

Duchess of Gloucester, Colonel Commandant of the Women's Royal Army Corps also watched Charlotte Aitken march forward, proud that one of her own was to receive the academy's highest award.

Exactly three minutes later Charlotte Aitken saluted Her Royal Highness, executed a somewhat less than perfect left turn and offered the Sword of Honour, her sword, to Colour-Sergeant Trevor Martin Willcocks, Coldstream Guards. Willcocks accepted the sword and scabbarded it immediately, to march off the only colour-sergeant ever to carry a sword on a British Army parade.

Up in the tiers Major-General Hopkinson sat, almost slumped back, content and confident that he had done his duty and could face his Maker with a clear conscience. Charlotte Aitken, second-lieutenant, would be his salvation.

June 1973
BELFAST

Siobhan McCaillim twisted the knife in her brother, watching him squirm. 'Mammy says you're useless. She says you're cowards and hoods. Why don't you stay down in Dublin with Tommy? You talk like one of them. You should get away before she comes home and sees you.'

Liam, aged nineteen, had no defence against his eleven-year-old sister. She just sat there on a stool, beside the fire, staring. Her eyes never seemed to blink. They just watched him, boring into him as if they could see inside his brain. Even her hands never moved. She was like a little witch, with her hair flaming in the light, and her dress a black thing well below her knees. Liam tried.

'Shut up, Siobhan. What do you know? Tommy's with the Officials. I'm doing my bit, raising money. We're not cowards or thieves. You know nothing. Mammy knows nothing. You're only a wee girl.'

75

But Siobhan was merciless, smiling now, feeling for his weakness with an instinctive knowledge of the fragility of a male ego lying to itself, never pausing, watching his face for signs, striking harder as she felt him weaken.

'I know enough to know you're talking shite. Tommy talks shite too. The Officials are a load of old shite. They're talking about shooting Brits. They're not shooting any. All you do is pass round the hat in pubs. All Tommy does is drink and sing rebel songs. Why don't you come back here all the time and join the Provies? They're shooting Brits. You're afraid, that's what you are. Mammy's ashamed of you. She won't talk about you unless she's angry. Even in the Cumann na mBan they'd spit on you. Mammy's high up in them now. I'm joining as soon as I can. One of these days Mammy's going to get you and Tommy fixed. You'll get kneecapped for hitting her.' Siobhan laughed. 'You'll be in trouble passing round the hat to get your drink money with no knees.'

Liam jumped up, surprised, suddenly afraid. 'High up is she? Jesus. Jesus Christ. I never hit her, Tommy did. He was just drunk. He didn't mean it. She wouldn't give us the price of a pint. Ah, it was years ago.'

He bent to sit down again. Siobhan, in a move she had seen her mother use, suddenly stood up, speaking as she rose, catching him off balance. 'It was last year. I haven't forgotten. I'm going to get you fixed if Mammy doesn't. I have friends. Mammy knows Gerry Madden. Sean McAllister buys me sweets. I'll tell Sean you knocked Mammy about. I'll tell him you drink the money you collect. Sean would kneecap you. Gerry's worse. If Sean tells him Gerry would nut you for sure. Gerry hates people like you, and he likes Mammy.' She watched the fear creep through him, as if he couldn't believe he was hearing his eleven-year-old sister threatening to have him killed.

'Away with you, wee one, you're all talk.'

Siobhan smiled sweetly. 'I'll get you a cup of tea. I'll get Sean before you drink it. You'll see if I'm all talk.' She moved into the kitchen behind the little sitting room. The kettle wasn't even on the gas before the front door banged shut. Siobhan made herself some tea and took it back to her stool in front of the fire. *Mammy was right. You can frighten them. All you have to do is know something about them and make them believe you. It's easy.* She jumped up, smiling as her mother came in, shaking the rain out of her hair.

'Was that Liam I saw running down the street? What did he want?'

'Yes, Mammy. He wanted money. I frightened him. I told him I was going to get Sean McAllister to kneecap him and Tommy for hitting you. He was away like a liltie. He'll tell Tommy. They won't come back. It was a good laugh watching his face.'

Marion McCaillim took the tea out of Siobhan's hand and sipped it, thinking. She spoke carefully, softly. 'Why did you do that, Siobhan?'

'They're dirtbirds the both of them. They take our money. They're afraid of the Brits. I hate them. I wouldn't kneecap them. I'd put hoods on them and nut them if I could. I will when I'm bigger.'

'You'd shoot your brothers in the head? They're your brothers, Siobhan. They're big men and we're women.'

'I don't care. They're shite, you said so to them when they hit you. I'm not afraid of them. I can frighten them. I want to hurt them, Mammy. It'll be good practice for shooting the Brits.'

'All right, Siobhan. Make some more tea.' Marion McCaillim was both horrified and excited. *Such a wee one! Talking about killing her brothers, shooting Brits, frightening Liam. She meant it. She would do it, or get it done.* Listening to Siobhan in the kitchen, she resolved to take more notice of her. A throwaway line Marion's father had made the day Siobhan was born came back to her. *Maeve, the flame-haired warrior Queen of Eire.* Maybe so. Marion smiled as a thought flickered playfully around her mind. In her mind's eye she saw Siobhan in a toga-like shift, a great fan of flame-red hair flying in the wind, swinging a sword from a chariot, standing on the bar between the horses the way the old warriors had in Maeve's battles against Ulster.

As she was staring at the fire Marion's fantasy coalesced into a question. Why not? She had hoped her husband, then her sons, would fight for the Cause, but had been bitterly disappointed. So she was doing what she could herself, running intelligence-gathering operations to identify undercover Brits. She was doing it better in the Cumann na mBan than her male predecessor had managed from the staff of the Provisionals' Belfast Brigade. Why not? Why not a woman? Why not Siobhan? Maybe Marion's despair of Ireland's men ever winning the country's freedom could be lifted. Siobhan had no fear, no background of being ground down by men. She delighted in scaring them. She believed in the Cause because that's how she had been brought up.

Marion decided to bring Siobhan into the Cumann na mBan as soon as she was old enough, but not allow her to rise in it. She would teach her more history, develop her means of controlling men, teach her about them and their weaknesses. If she wanted to, Siobhan Maeve McCaillim could take on the men. Marion would watch out for her, lead her in, give her a start at the right man. She would not push her, but help her if she wanted to do it. *It must come from herself. It will show if it's there.* A vast dream opened up in Marion's mind. *What a glorious thing! A woman to lead the Cause!*

As Siobhan came back, cups in hand, Marion looked at her with new eyes. The priests and the teachers were always crying about the effect of the bombing and shooting on the children, about the pictures they drew of hooded bodies, bomb blasts, armoured cars, soldiers carrying rifles bigger than themselves. They worried about the nervous coughs, symptomatic asthma, unnamed fears the children suffered. Siobhan had no illnesses, was not nervous. She thrived on the war, was always talking about it, loved watching the TV news. Siobhan was different. Marion smiled on her daughter, thinking of the future. If nothing else, Siobhan would be her revenge on the men who had betrayed the Cause, the men who had dragged her down, beaten her, laughed at and ignored her. Siobhan, if she wanted to, could rule over them all.

December 1973
GUILDFORD, SURREY

Charlotte returned the salute of her platoon sergeant and walked stiffly back to the officers' mess, hoping to be in time for lunch. Behind her Sergeant Jill Hines contained her fury long enough to dismiss her platoon and get into the foyer of her own mess. Then she screamed, as long and loud a scream as she could manage. Women warrant officers and sergeants rushed out of the bar and dining room. Even the WRAC centre's regimental sergeant-major, a woman used to the unusual and surprised by nothing, moved slightly faster than her usual stately pace. They found Sergeant Hines stamping her feet and struggling to rip her beret apart, building up to another scream.

'What the hell's all this then, Sar'nt Hines? Stop that and stand still. Answer me, Sergeant.'

Seeing the quick gesture of the RSM's right hand, the rest of the mess members faded from sight, keen to find out what had set the normally even-tempered Hines off.

'I told you to stand still, Sar'nt Hines. Look at me.'

Sergeant Hines heard the RSM through the fog of her rage and reacted as a soldier should: she snapped rigidly to attention and said in a clear, precise voice. 'Yes, ma'am. I'm sorry, ma'am. It won't happen again, ma'am.'

The RSM nodded. Quite relaxed and completely in control, she spoke in normal, conversational tones. 'You're damned right it won't. How dare you leap about like a madwoman, screaming in my mess, upsetting people.' She smiled gently. 'We'll have half the centre's senior NCOs complaining of indigestion! That'll never do. Right then. You're under control. Scream again.'

'Ma'am?' A small, embarrassed voice.

'I said scream again, a good one. Get it out of your system. Wait a minute.' The RSM leaned back into the ante-room. 'Sar'nt Smith, Sar'nt Galsworthy! Out here now!'

Placing the bewildered sergeants in a triangle facing each other the RSM said, 'Scream on my command. Good screams now. As hard as you can. Show some solidarity. Ready? SCREAM!'

The three sergeants screamed, a bit insecurely at first, then, under the RSM's frown, louder and louder. Fists hard on their thighs they competed with one another, screaming in each other's faces until their necks were brick red and their shoulders quivering with the effort, their feet involuntarily joining in, drumming on the floor in concert with their screaming.

Then they stopped, suddenly, as if on command, falling with their arms around each other in a terrible fit of the giggles. Tears streamed down their faces as they settled down, looked at one another, looked at the RSM and collapsed again, hooting at the silliness of it all. The RSM merely remarked 'Sar'nt Hines, you owe us a drink.' She walked into the bar and ordered four large gin and tonics.

A little later a red-faced Sergeant Hines approached the RSM, unsure of what to say. The RSM said it for her. 'Never mind, Sar'nt Hines. I know; Miss Aitken, wasn't it? Complaining that your platoon's accommodation is not up to standard? Bearing and turnout of your recruits poor? How dare they appear in front of her in that state? How dare you allow them to? All that sort of thing when you and they have been bulling up the place and themselves half the night. I know. Don't worry. You handled it well. Next time be ready. Don't let her get to you. Stare her in the face and let her know you see through her. She's just nervous and finding her feet. She'll come round when she sees that Sandhurst isn't the real army. You'll have to look after her and see her right. That's your job. No more of this silly screaming, eh?'

'Thanks, ma'am. I've never been so embarrassed. But it was great of you to do that. I really enjoyed it, it was better than anything. Thanks, ma'am.'

'All right Sar'nt Hines. Don't worry about it. That's why I'm a regimental sar'nt-major. But do anything like that again and I'll scoff you for lunch. Got it? Away you go. Look after your platoon and Miss Aitken. Do your job.'

'Yes, ma'am.'

In her mess Charlotte Aitken heard the screaming and flushed, noting the grins of more senior officers, and with the cry 'Who's been winding up the Seniors then?' ringing in her ears. The Commandant of the WRAC centre, a beautifully groomed full colonel looked up from her soup and remarked to no one in particular 'Second-lieutenants should be seen and not heard. The RSM will be wanting a word in some young lady's ear. Oh well!'

Charlotte flamed. *Oh God. The colonel knows it was me! My first day with my first platoon and I've made a cock of it. I knew I was being too hard on Sar'nt Hines. I was nervous. I didn't mean it. The RSM will give me extra duties and everyone will know who's caused this scene. Oh God, how embarrassing.*

In the RSM's office Charlotte was defiant, prepared to stand on her dignity as an officer. The RSM looked bored. But out of the office a much chastened Sword of Honour winner emerged, rather more aware of her twenty-year-old-importance in the scheme of things than she had been ten minutes before, with five extra duties as Officer of the Day to remind her. The RSM went back to her work.

Two weeks later Sar'nt Hines thought she had Charlotte's measure and was nudging her in the right direction, easing her into command of her platoon of raw recruits, helping her cope with young women the like of whom Charlotte had never dreamed existed. Most of them had no real education beyond the age of fifteen, and some were not terribly certain of basic hygiene. Some were calm and self-assured, others bundles of scratchy nerve ends; some quick and helpful, others surly and permanently discontented; some looked like china dolls, others like crop-haired thugs, but most were normal, decent working girls who wanted to do something more than punch a supermarket checkout till. All were soldiers, all her personal responsibility; together or individually they could give her great personal satisfaction, a sense of doing something worthwhile, but any one of them could wreck her career. Before the month was out Charlotte had made a decision: she would not, if she could avoid it, ever directly command more than a handful of soldiers, male or female. She would follow the Intelligence road, make her career where she could use her abilities and not be hostage to people who were as foreign to her as men from the moon. She remembered Colour-Sergeant Willcocks, remembered the intelligent, fit, beautifully turned out Sandhurst cadets with a painful yearning. These people she had the honour to command were very different, beyond her experience, and she had no wish to broaden her knowledge of them. Her grandfather had been right. These were the mob. They were there and she would use them where possible, avoid them the rest of the time. She would not let them use her, bog her down in the morass of their petty worries, debts and scandals.

Near Christmas one of Charlotte's fellow subalterns suggested a visit to a party at the Queen Alexandra's Royal Army Nursing Corps mess in Aldershot. It would be fun and there would be men there, attracted by the nurses. Charlotte agreed. Anything to get out of Guildford.

At the party was one Andrew Leggath, a man with a problem. Very tall, very slim, very handsome in a pale blond English way, very rich in inheritable wealth, very good with horses, dogs, minions of the human kind, very cultured, very thoughtful, very well bred, very everything: a veritable example of the English class system's perfect product, designed, educated and formed, custom built to perpetuate itself for ever, but like the system that had produced him, deeply flawed.

Andrew Leggath believed without the slightest shadow of doubt that the world and everything in it existed for his personal gratification: nothing in his experience had ever indicated otherwise. At thirty-two he was just about to step into his father's shoes as chairman of the family merchant bank, a sinecure that gave him access to financial society while others did the work. Just down from Yorkshire where he had been 'supervising' his younger brother's handling of their grouse moor, Leggath saw Charlotte Aitken in her party dress and smiled the smile of the idle sophisticate.

Charlotte he saw as slightly overdressed for this particular party, in a Droopy & Brown evening dress of understated elegance. It encouraged him: not many girls could run to Droopy's in Oxford or Bath whenever a party was in the offing. The girl had money, old money, but not experience enough to dress for the occasion. It would be amusing to play with her, at least until she bored him.

Charlotte seemed more at ease than she felt, looked very beautiful. Watching her closely, Leggath, with the instincts of a shark, saw through her studied poise to the nervous uncertainty beneath, noticed her irritation at the schoolboy humour and antics of a bunch of very junior Parachute Regiment officers, then moved. Charlotte saw Leggath's quiet approach as salvation from the Paras. He exuded the public school's greatest social gift: he could talk to anyone on their own level, was never ill at ease, and never seemed to try too hard, if he seemed to try at all. To Charlotte, he had seen her in difficulty and moved to help, to return her to her own with great civility and without threat, stated or implicit.

As the party became more noisy and boisterous Charlotte found herself maintaining Leggath within reach, using him as a shield against the more overt approaches of the Paras, trying not to allow him to see her doing so. This was her first real party out

83

on her own, away from her family and away from the protection of the men at Sandhurst. The wine and an odd sense of freedom were having an effect too. She felt like being irresponsible, like joining in, but did not know how to without seeming gauche and unsophisticated. She felt small droplets of perspiration between her breasts and down her back, felt restricted by the underwear bought specially from Gossard to help her feel good. She wanted to drink much more wine than she should, pull out the pins holding her hair up and bounce round the tiny dancefloor in the ante-room. But she couldn't. She felt a fraud, looking cool and collected while she was so ill at ease. She felt frightened by the overt sexuality of the men and had no idea how to handle it in an easy, smiling way as the other women did. She could, if she wanted to, freeze any approach in its tracks. But she didn't want to.

She had been thinking about sex for some time and had caught herself up in a web of confusion: she wanted a man, to see what one was like, to find out if all she'd heard and read was true. She wanted to break out, be rid of her virginity, yet wanted to keep it out of fear, and for someone special. She wanted a friend, someone who would understand what *she* wanted. Someone to allow her freedom, but protect her. She wanted to be cared for. In a momentary flash of honesty she saw that she wanted to be rid of the fear that she wouldn't be able to do it, that there could be something wrong with her, that a man would laugh at her: but she wanted a man. Andrew Leggath was good-looking and one of her own kind. Maybe he . . .

'Charlotte, this party is getting to be a bore, don't you think? But it's impossible to leave so early without seeming ungrateful. I've found a small room down the hall. Most people there seem to be in couples. Shall we take a look? I'll bring some champagne.'

'Champagne? Lovely. Where did you get it?'

'From here, dear heart.' Leggath reached behind him to produce a silver bucket with a freshly opened bottle of Krug nestling in the ice. 'I wouldn't dream of travelling without it.'

Charlotte took the invitation at face value and responded with a brittle brightness she did not feel. 'Lead on, MacLeggath, Champagne Charlotte is my name. If it's too quiet in there I can always run back here.'

The small room was different indeed. The walls were covered in Indian Army memorabilia, with the odd item from the Zulu wars and the Crimea. The rug on the floor would have bent the eye of any conservationist out of shape; it had been made in Bengal in about 1898, of four huge and beautifully matched tiger skins, a head at each corner, animals shot at the height of their powers, varying not more than an inch or two in length. Or so Leggath told Charlotte as he steered her gently across the rug, a hand not quite touching her elbow, guiding her more by inference than touch. In deep leather armchairs a number of couples, older than the rest of the revellers, had carefully established themselves, seemingly close enough to be sociable but just too far apart, enjoying a little privacy in a crowd, the women in the chairs, the men sitting easily on the broad, curving arms.

Charlotte felt at ease, more comfortable here, more in control. Leggath behaved impeccably; he set out to amuse and entertain her, keep her feeling good about herself with a jumbled-up mixture of anecdotes, tales of humorous situations, terrible scrapes, self-deprecating little confidences and the odd slightly arch observation on life in general, with occasional glances that lingered a little, never too long, that told her he saw her as a beautiful, interesting young woman. The champagne flowed, a second bottle appearing as if by magic. Charlotte felt wonderful. Leggath seemed the right sort, the kind her grandfather had told her she could find if she looked with care, someone of like mind who could be a companion on her way to the top. But that was a long way away, and she was having fun.

As the evening progressed a young-looking major moved to an upright piano and began playing, really rather well, a mixture of romantic ballads and light classics, offering to play on if anyone wanted to dance. Most did. Leggath led Charlotte by the hand,

85

having taken it in a casual, unaffected way; it was the first time he had actually touched her. On the floor he danced beautifully: light and strong, moving Charlotte around with ease and skill. She enjoyed the dancing, letting herself go a little, enjoying the bubbles in her head, the warmth and strength of his hand across her back.

This, for Charlotte, was romance as she had expected it: a suitable young man, confident in himself, treating her well, wooing her gently, listening to what she had to say, never too intense in his choice of subject for conversation, making her laugh and letting her know without saying so that he found her beautiful, fun and interesting. She decided she liked Leggath and would respond positively if he offered her dinner at a later date.

The realisation that she had allowed herself to be drawn closer to him came as a little electric thrill. The music had slowed. The pianist, sensing the mood of his dancers, played Nat Cole's haunting version of 'Perfidia', and 'On the Street Where You Live'. Now he was playing a lovely adaptation of J.J. Cale's 'After Midnight', a favourite of Charlotte's. She laid her head on Andrew Leggath's shoulder and crooned peacefully, softly humming. Leggath moved to hold her closer, not in an overtly sexual way, just enough to make her feel as if he were cocooning her, protecting her from the world. He kissed her lightly, just above the ear, almost unnoticeably. Charlotte lifted her head to check his eyes. He was smiling with them. He winked, turning his head in an odd, slightly wicked gesture, still unthreatening, still charming. Charlotte unconsciously eased herself into him, not wanting this lovely feeling to end.

It did, very quickly, when she became aware of his physical arousal.

Sudden panic swept through her, tensing her. She wanted to move away from him. But he held on, apparently unaware of her panic. Her mind raced. He made no effort to press himself on her, but neither did he move away; he was feigning ignorance of his own body and its effect on her. When the music ended he stepped back, bowed from the neck and said 'Champagne?'

Charlotte, her throat dry, nodded.

Leggath was back to his charming self, if a little closer than before, a little more personal. Charlotte felt her mind recoil but her body respond to him, a strange paradox she had not encountered before. It was as if her body was telling her mind what to do, her physical instincts overruling her common sense. She felt she knew what she was doing, yet her inner voice said No you don't. Her body said Yes while her mind said Run! So she sat, paralysed by uncertainty, attracted and repelled, insecure and utterly confused. She wanted Leggath and asked herself, 'Why not?'

Charlotte broke out of herself to look at him. He was talking. '. . . hope you won't. I'd like the chance to talk rather more privately. You must have noticed how I've been looking at you. You know I think you're the most gorgeous girl I've ever seen. I want to take you out, to somewhere we can be alone, somewhere we can talk. I really want to get to know you, and it's difficult here.'

Leggath watched Charlotte's face close down a fraction, saw he was moving too quickly. He rushed on before she could speak. 'I know I'm saying far too much far too soon. I shouldn't be saying anything at all if I were behaving decently. I'm afraid of not seeing you again. I haven't ever behaved like this with someone I've just met. It's all a bit much for me to take in. You're probably used to men reacting to you like this: you're gorgeous . . . I think – Oh Lord, how stupid of me – you *must* have a boyfriend. I'm being a fool. I'm sorry. Maybe it was a bad idea.' He saw her face change a little, softening, not quite so unsure. *Definitely better, Andrew. Like a fish on the hook. She's coming round.*

Charlotte reached for her wine. Sipping it gave her time to think as she tried to cut through her confused emotions and the champagne bubbles. *Oh! He is really interested in me. What can I do? What should I say? I'm blushing. He looks very handsome.*

87

I want to go home. I want ... I'm so confused ... Maybe he'll do something ... I'm not ready ... I am ready ... I'm ready now ... His hands were so strong as we danced ... He'll think I'm a tart ... He'll despise me ... I don't know how to do it ... Jesus, he doesn't know I'm a virgin ... She swallowed hard, trying to keep the tremble out of her voice, her sudden burst of sexual longing threatening to choke her.

'It is a bad idea. We've only just met. I don't have a boy-friend at present, I don't have the time. But you may call me at Guildford if you wish. I must go now. It's late and I have a parade in the morning. Perhaps I'll hear from you. I'm sorry. Goodbye.'

She grabbed her handbag, stood up abruptly and got away as fast as she decently could.

Leggath took his failure philosophically. If not now, then later. It would extend the fun. *Frightened her off like a doe in the rut. How very amusing. Plenty of time.* He strode after her and caught her just outside the door.

'Charlotte, I'm sorry. I shouldn't have said so much. I just didn't want you to think I wasn't interested. Too much cham-pagne. Forgive me. I'm truly sorry. I'll call you tomorrow if I may?'

Unable to face him, she kept her eyes down and nodded. 'Yes. Tomorrow. Goodnight.'

Alone in her room, face down on her bed Charlotte Aitken at last put a face to the looming male figure that had come more and more frequently to haunt the dark emptiness of her nights, standing over her, demanding her submission, caressing her with hands that felt like silken steel and handling her passion with care. In her mind's eye she saw Leggath's serious-smiling eyes, felt his warmth and strength. At last she had a face to look at and real hands to feel run over her. Weeping softly, in desperate need of someone to love her, she sucked the thumb of her left hand as the fingers of the other brought relief and deep, dreamless sleep.

Reality came brutally, three candlelit dinner dates later. After an evening of romance, on New Year's Eve, Andrew Leggath took an excited, fearful, highly aroused and trembling Charlotte Aitken to her own bed, a little while after she had felt him press more and more urgently against her as they stood breast to breast, belly to belly, kissing with growing passion. He ensured that she saw the sad, pointed look in his eyes that told her 'This is not fair on me'; and he had stepped back from her, still holding her. In a rush of abandon and guilt at his unspoken accusation of prick teasing she had blushed furiously and blurted out, 'I can't fight this any longer. Let's go to bed.' Even then he had played the gentleman, stepping away to pour a glass of wine for her, saying softly 'You're trembling, like an earthquake somewhere high up on the Richter scale. Are you sure?'

No. 'Yes. I want to.'

He handled her quickly and efficiently, not needing to arouse her further. Her own need and starry-eyed view of him allowed him to sidestep all but the most basic preliminary kisses and caresses. He moved down over her body, kissing her breasts, her belly, plunging between her legs, using his tongue where she normally used her fingers to bring her to a quick, intense, solely physical orgasm. He rose over her, tied his fingers in her hair and entered her. A short, stabbing pain, then Charlotte lost herself, needing more, wanting to give, give, give. She opened her eyes as she felt his pelvis hard against her, felt him inside her, tried to grip him the better to feel and draw him to her, lifting her knees either side of her breasts, arching her back to receive him further, opening herself to him . . . He was standing over her, had left her, was walking across the room toward the washbasin in the corner, was standing over it, jetting hot water into it. *Surely not . . . No . . . He's washing . . . He's . . . what?*

Confused, uncertain, her body crying out for the deeper physical and emotional release she so desperately needed Charlotte watched, wide-eyed, as Leggath covered himself, picked up his clothes, cast her a glance of hatred, his face a mask, whispering fiercely 'Bitch' at her, a stream of filth, ending in 'Stupid, useless bitch. Your knees up round your ears. I thought you were a decent girl. I'm going to be sick.' Then a shout, bouncing off the walls. 'Why aren't you ashamed? You should be ashamed. You're like a bitch in heat. A bitch playing the lady. You're nothing but a whore, grunting and sweating like a pig. I can't make love to you. Fuck you, Charlotte. Fuck *you*.'

The bang of the door. Charlotte, twenty years old but feeling twelve, rigid with fright, humiliation, deeply shamed, screaming inside, shock, frustration, horror and hatred of her body flying in and out of her, kaleidoscoping in her head, punching her in the guts. She leapt out of bed, tears blinding her, and scrabbled through to her bathroom. Tearing at the shower head, she sprayed herself with hot water. Great handfuls of creamy thick soap she squeezed from a tube; scented with almonds, she had used it for her back before dinner. Now she threw it over her, scrubbing scrubbing scrubbing, retching and choking on her tears. Then she saw it: a thin grey-white snake of semen oozing out of her, down the inside of her thigh, mixing with the blood of her lost virginity. Her gorge rose again, leaving her sobbing, retching and shaking, curled on the floor of her bath, utterly disgusted, grateful for the flow of hot water over her.

In the hot, cleansing stream Charlotte's mind began to function once more. Leggath had not been inside her more than a few seconds. She knew enough to realise that he, not she, had failed. She would have understood. He hadn't given her a chance. He had used her, spent himself inside her, rushed to wash himself and run away. He had called her filthy names. What was wrong with him? It did not really matter, but she felt dirty all the same.

On New Year's Day General Hopkinson arrived to pick Charlotte up, to take her to Essex for a family get-together, his traditional New Year's dinner. He thought she looked pale. 'Why didn't you come to Tollesbury yesterday as you always do? Out gallivanting at a party I suppose.'

'No, grandfather. I was a bit confused. I borrowed a car and went for a long drive, to consider my future. *Never, never, never again.* I'm all right now.'

'A young man?'

'Of course not. I was alone.' *You are the only man in the world I can trust – and now I'm lying to you. What does that make me?*

5 January 1974
TOLLESBURY

Colonel Jacobson, nearing eighty, her grandfather's oldest and most trusted crony was doing his best, seated in the main hall of Tollesbury Manor while Charlotte Aitken paced around him, hands clenched behind her back. It was not easy for him, for two reasons: Charlotte unnerved him, so like her grandfather was she; and he was aware of her contempt for her mother, his wife, and her barely concealed view of him as little more than a family retainer. He kept his statements short, even terse.

'The burial will be tomorrow, Charlotte. I have arranged it in accordance with the general's wishes. It will be at three o'clock, a simple affair, just ourselves and the vicar, in the churchyard of the estate chapel. Sar'nt Platt will drive you.'

Charlotte was pale and icy-faced. 'Very well. I have nothing to do. You have seen to everything. Why?'

'Charlotte, the general had very clear views on protocol of all kinds. You are mistress here now. It is not your place to be intimately involved in what are essentially administrative matters. That is what the estate management are for. In this case, because of its nature, the general wished me to oversee things for you. You are responsible: I am just acting for you.'

'How can you assume these things? My mother may be mistress. Grandfather's will has not yet been read.'

'Don't be obtuse. You know very well that Tollesbury is yours. It was always intended so. Provision has been made for my wife, both by the general and myself. Tollesbury is yours.'

'How do you know?'

'I know because I have a copy of the general's will and I am under instruction from him to tell you of its contents before it is read. Only you and I will be present when the general's solicitors read it. Your mother will be indisposed. The other beneficiaries will be informed by letter, except Sar'nt Platt. You are to inform him that he may retire now. But should he wish to he may continue in your service until age disables him. He will retain his full salary for life, as will Mrs Platt. They will retain their cottage for life. As for the estate, it is yours, held in trust, with one proviso: you must achieve general officer rank before your forty-second birthday. Should you fail to do so the estate will maintain you to the sum of £50,000 per annum, index linked. The remainder will go to the Huguenot Wood Fund for the widows of British soldiers killed in action. That's all, apart from a letter, which I am now to hand to you personally. The letter, Charlotte.'

'Thank you.' Charlotte reached out automatically, taking the letter in its thick vellum cover. 'Thank you for everything. Grandfather has acted for the best, as always. I would like some privacy please.'

'Of course. I will be in the drawing room if you need anything.'

'That is very kind, but I wish to have the house to myself tonight. Sar'nt Platt will be here to look after me. Thank you.'

Jacobson huffed a little, but left immediately. Charlotte had taken over and he had no place here, except as guest. The general had warned him it might happen this way.

Charlotte called without turning her head. 'Sar'nt Platt. You heard. It will be so. Are you content? Have you anything to say?'

Platt marched out from his usual lurk, in Number One Dress uniform, boots shining, lifting his arthritic knees in a still-sharp *halt*. Standing in front of Charlotte he saluted formally, barking, 'No complaints, ma'am.'

'I would consider it an honour to have you serve me as you served the general. However, should you feel unable to I would understand.'

'Ma'am. Followed the general since he was a subaltern and I was a drummer boy. Die if I retired. Like to see another general at Tollesbury. Nothing more to say, ma'am.'

Charlotte wanted to thank the old soldier from her heart for his lifelong friendship with her grandfather. The two, general and sergeant, had been very close. Sar'nt Platt must be feeling the general's loss badly. He would know how she felt, as she knew how he felt. Platt would consider it unnecessary, even unsoldierly, for her to say anything about it. She chose another way.

'Very good. Give Mrs Platt my best wishes. I hope she feels able to carry on with her duties. I'm going out now. A hip flask and some coffee, please. Thank you.'

Out on the saltings Charlotte sat in the shelter of the old pillbox, out of the wind. She carefully poured her coffee and added a little whisky from the general's hip flask. Ever since the general, whisky in hand, had literally keeled over in front of herself and his guests she had seemed to feel nothing, had watched and moved and acted like a machine, with no emotional responses. Dr Wallten had certified the general dead of a cerebral haemorrhage, a massive stroke. The doctor, aware of her closeness to the old man, had warned her of the sudden shock of bereavement, told her that she would need people around her, people she could talk to. There was no one, except Sar'nt Platt, and she could communicate with him without words. As Platt had observed, there was nothing more to say: they must bear up together. Right now she was frozen up, as if there were a space inside her, an emptiness that chilled her emotions, her feelings, preventing her from reacting at all. Even the shock of her experience with Leggath had not touched her since: she had no feelings but guilt and shame. Charlotte tore open the general's letter, expecting several pages of advice and some guidance. There was one page only. It read:

My Dear Charlotte,

I have given you every advantage, every asset I could provide or draw out of you. I am content that it will be enough. Have no fear. You are ready. Do your duty and all will be well.

Huguenot Wood destroyed me as it destroyed so many of my beloved soldiers, but left me living, to tell myself I had done my duty, obeyed the orders of my superiors as they were given to me. But I had obeyed orders I knew to be wrong and lost a battle I knew could not be won with the division I had to hand. I failed my soldiers because I did not have the moral courage to refuse to order them into the morass. I failed them because I did not have the strength of character to ignore the conventions of command and fight for them in the dining rooms of the General Staff, forty miles behind the lines, lest I put my own career at risk. I failed them because I did not have the physical courage to show the Staff how strongly I felt by ordering my soldiers to stay in their trenches and personally leading my officers out into the storm in their place. Instead I sat safe in my dugout and sent my soldiers out to die, telling myself I was only obeying orders. I have never forgiven myself, or expected others to. I have never forgiven myself for failing to stop the slaughter sooner. Kitchener did not sack me. I had what is now called a nervous breakdown and was quietly retired on medical grounds. I was not a good general. I did not deserve the loyalty and faith my soldiers put in me. I have tried to atone for my weakness: in you I have tried to give their successors a general fit to lead them. Do not fail them as I did. Let me face God with a clear conscience. Pray for me.

Charlotte leaned back against the pillbox, all the pent up emotion in her bursting through, clearing her mind, dropping all the pieces into place. *For sixty years he lived with himself, despising and hating himself, in some sort of mental agony, never showing it for a moment. How very lonely he must have felt. He had done a terrible thing, but his sense of honour, his courage had come through to show him his error and he had stopped the slaughter. He had seen the truth, the folly of blind obedience. He had stood up and stopped it, in the face of the rage of his superiors, for the benefit of his soldiers. Then he had resigned, his final, honourable act, to live a long life of shame and self-hatred. He had, in his way, given his life for his soldiers, but could not see it.*

But that was not all. Charlotte allowed the alternatives to come as he had taught her. In the lee of a pillbox not very different from those of Huguenot Wood she felt anger rise in her as the truth came with brutal clarity. *You stupid, stupid man. They needed you. You were the best general the British Army had. You were the soldiers' only hope, the only man who had the courage to stop the useless slaughter. You should have stayed. You should have fought Haig and Kitchener. You should have told Lloyd George. Only you could have beaten them. Only you had the courage and the standing in the eyes of the little people to fight the fools and win. You should not have resigned. You should have fought for greater commands, fought for a corps and then an army and then led all the armies as their Field Marshal. You could have used Huguenot Wood as a stick to bludgeon your enemies down. You could have led the British Army out of the morass. You could have retreated into the higher ground behind you, let the enemy take that useless swamp and let them fight their way out of it to get at you. The German General Staff would never have accepted such terrors for their men. You could have stopped the war. You would have been a hero. Instead you failed your country. You failed the British Army. You failed your men. You failed yourself. You were beaten by yourself. Damn your honour. Damn your self-pity. Damn your ego. You should have fought harder. Huguenot Wood did not destroy you. You destroyed yourself because it was easier to run away under cover of your honour than to stand and fight. You were a coward in*

the face of the enemy, enemies in the same uniform you wore.
You can go to hell.

There were no tears as she sat sobbing silently, her rage at, her love of her grandfather burning out the chill emptiness inside her. Much later, the tears came. The general, had he been able to hear her thoughts, would have been content. He knew her well and had chosen his words with care. Nothing would stop her now, not honour, dignity, fear or opposition. No loss would be too great, no prize be of value high enough to divert her.

Chapter Seven

12 June 1976

THE BRECON BEACONS

In a long unbroken snake the baby Paras fought their way up the stony path leading to the peak of Pen-y-Fan, the highest mountain in the Brecon Beacons in Wales, turning their heads to vomit on the move and sweating out the beer swilled the night before in the bars of Brecon, learning all the way: *never believe the Directing Staff. Never believe it's going to be easy tomorrow, never believe any fucker. Don't even believe the colonel. Look after yourself and your mates and bollocks to anybody else. Trust your mates while they're still moving. Forget them if they fall. Keep going forward. Paras don't ever give in. That's the way it is.*

The recruits tabbing fast up the mountain wore camouflage caps with long wide peaks known as cunt caps: Paras regarded anybody who hadn't earned the right to wear a maroon beret as a cunt. The recruits themselves had a variety of disparaging nicknames, but were mostly called Toms, after the archetypal British soldier, Tommy Atkins. Sergeant Jamie Lappin, standing next to the white concrete trig point on Pen-y-Fan's summit watched the snake climb closer, each Tom carrying 60 pounds of food and equipment in his rucksack; with the water on his belt, and rifle in his hand it made 70-odd pounds in total. Lappin spoke to the young second-lieutenant, fresh out of Sandhurst, who was squatting down beside the trig point, sweating heavily.

'They're getting it hard today, sir, but it'll help weed out the wankers. Yesterday they were helping each other, today they won't have the energy to spare. Tonight they're going on a night march round Ystradfellte reservoir and over the bog on

97

the other side Fan Fawr, the mountain behind you, over Fan Fawr itself then back over this in the morning, round the base of Cribin and down the Roman road to Torpantau.' He paused, seeing the young officer's difficulty in following the course he was describing on his map.

'Put the map away sir, I'll point out the course.' For a few moments he went back over his briefing, pointing out landmarks where necessary. 'Then from Torpantau they'll be picked up in trucks and taken back to Brecon. Then a day off. Then on to Senny Bridge for live firing exercises. Now then sir, what do you think?'

The question was a courteous search for approval of Lappin's plan, since the second-lieutenant was nominally in charge of this part of a six-week exercise. The young officer, John Hartly, was ill at ease. He too had believed he had a rest day today and had spent the previous evening trying to get into the knickers of a big-arsed barmaid in the Sarah Siddons pub in Brecon, a lady whose wide-eyed stupidity was balanced by her knowledge of the ways of soldiers. He had not been successful and had woken at 7.30 to a thumping hangover and a brief sight of the tail end of his command disappearing out of barracks.

'A few questions, Sar'nt Lappin. They're puking all over the place. I can understand that. I had a multicoloured yawn on the way up myself. But why do you want them to stop helping each other? I thought they were supposed to work in teams. And the course is very tough without any breaks. Are you sure they can cope?'

'We're teaching them, sir. And we're selecting the best.' Lappin's face was impassive and he chose his words carefully. 'Lesson One – don't blindly rely on what people tell you, because plans are subject to change. I lied when I told them they would have a rest day today and gave them the night off to get a few swills in Brecon. This morning we needed to be throwing them at the mountain by eight o'clock at the latest, so we rifted them out of bed at five. It took us two hours to get them ready to march because their kit was all over the place and their Bergens not packed. Some of them were still drunk. We expected that and allowed for it. But they won't make the same mistake again. From now on they'll pack ready to move before they head out on the town, just in case.'

Hartly nodded, the hangover threatening to pull his head off. Thank God he hadn't emptied his Bergen.

Sergeant Lappin appeared not to notice his discomfiture and continued 'Lesson Two – look after Number One and don't expect anybody to look after you, because they won't. They'll be too busy trying to make it themselves. At this stage we're still sorting out the weaklings. This tab will do that. Those that are left will know who can make it on his own and who can't. Then we'll let them sort themselves out into teams. The rejects will be obvious; the Toms will do the job for us – they'll form teams they trust. Any kid with no team is an automatic reject.'

Hartly nodded again. Lappin was very experienced in recruit training, but he had to be sure, 'And the supervision? We don't want any to die on us.'

Lappin grinned, his face pared down into that thin, ill-looking mask that only long distance athletes at the peak of fitness ever acquire. Second-Lieutenant Hartly, watching Lappin consider his question, thought the Irishman looked every inch a professional soldier, but not like a Para. Relatively short at about 5' 9" the sergeant's wide shoulders and muscular build gave him more the air of a Marine. Lappin took off his red beret and ran a hand through short dark hair, fixing Hartly with humorous blue eyes.

'Quite correct sir, dead ones cause too much paperwork. See the Red Hats running alongside, without rifles? Those are the Directing Staff from the training wing in Aldershot. They have first-aid kits and PRC 349 manpack radios in their Bergens. If one of the Toms wobbles too much the DS will radio me. I'll use my 320 to call up a chopper and Casevac the kid they're worried about to the medical reception station in Brecon. But it shouldn't happen. My Directing Staff know which ones to watch by now and will slow the leaders down if too many are suffering too much. We'll be with them all the way. Every so often we'll find an excuse to stop and look the kids over. They won't know what we're doing and it'll give them a rest. We'll push them very hard sir, but not too hard.'

Hartly nodded, 'OK, I'll rejoin them as they pass us.' He strapped his web belt around him, picked up his Bergen and hefted it, cocking an eye at Lappin. 'All right?'

Lappin grinned again, a wide guileless smile. *Arsehole, who do you think you are?* The way the water bottle had swung on the young officer's belt as he strapped it on had alerted Lappin to its emptiness. Chances were the boy was trying it on with an underweight Bergen as well. He couldn't possibly have overtaken the Toms if he had started late and carried the same. He had broken the Paras' golden rule: nobody — not even the colonel and he over forty — went tabbing with heavily laden Toms unless they carried the same or more than the men. Lappin reached out and grabbed the top strap of the rucksack, weighing it one armed. It seemed a little light, not much more than 50 pounds. He threw a glance around him and selected a couple of rocks, about ten or twelve pounds each.

'Not quite, sir. And you aren't carrying a rifle. Drop these in your Bergen. That'll put you right. I suggest you fall in at the head of the snake and watch the DS for guidance on your speed. And I suggest you fill your water bottle at the first opportunity or you'll flake out from dehydration before midday. Wait one, please sir.' Lappin searched around and found a rock weighing about fifteen pounds. 'Take this as well sir. You lost your name when you weren't at the front in Brecon. I'll tell the Toms you're carrying penalty weight as penance for being late. So long as you stay at the front they'll forgive you. Fall back and they'll never follow you again. I'll be at the back to shepherd the stragglers. You lead, I'll drive. Please be so good as to watch and obey the signals my DS will give you. You've got about ten minutes to get ready.'

COLCHESTER

Major Richard Warren sauntered into the small office opening off the brigadier's, left the door open behind him and parked himself on the arm of the one armchair in the room. Chin on hand he smiled at the WRAC captain behind the grey steel desk. She didn't even look up at him, so he waited, idly turning the riding whip in his free hand between his fingers. Captain Charlotte Aitken was worth looking at, he thought, noting the slim legs under the desk, remembering the healthy sheen on her face and the frank blue eyes that had intrigued him when they had been introduced a couple of nights ago in the mess. Not perturbed in the slightest at her ignoring him he pursed his lips and began to whistle softly, 'Colonel Bogey'. That usually worked. He had no doubt of his ability to charm her. At thirty-four, unmarried and with a string of conquests behind him he knew himself to be very good looking, a cavalryman of independent means and as the newly appointed chief of staff of this infantry brigade a very important fish in a small pool. But no response was forthcoming. He began to get irritated, this was going on too long.

'Do you normally ignore your Brigade Major, Charlotte?' he said in a quiet voice, with just the beginning of an edge to it.

That brought her head up. 'Brigade Major, sir? I thought you were the chief of staff. Or have things changed again?' Charlotte's tone and expression were flat and neutral. Warren flushed; the title of Brigade Major had been abolished years ago, but some, himself included, still clung to it because it sounded military and dashing.

This was not the response he had expected. 'Are you trying to insult me, Charlotte?' He was standing now, looking down at her.

'Of course not, sir. I don't know you.'

'Then why are you adopting an insubordinate attitude?'

Charlotte Aitken shifted her position in her chair. Her hands clenched into fists and every line of her rigid figure echoed the fury in her suddenly very dark eyes.

'Sir, if I appear insubordinate it is because you have just ignored every military courtesy usually applied by one officer visiting another. You walked into my office without knocking, failed to salute as you should have, sat down without asking if I was busy and failed to state your business. I happen to be working on a briefing paper needed by the brigadier this afternoon. If you have something for me that takes priority please say so. If not I will come to your office when I have finished the brigadier's paper.'

Warren blanched. Nobody had ever spoken to him like this. His handsome face blank as he tried to think of something to turn her anger, he cursed himself for his stupidity. Aitken was right. He had treated her as if she were some dizzy typist and not a top-drawer officer, and top-drawer she had to be to hold down her job. As so3 g2, a staff officer grade three in a g2 (Intelligence) post Captain Aitken was the brigadier's first port of call if he wanted to discuss anything to do with Intelligence. Warren tried another tack.

'I apologise. I wasn't thinking.' His smile was broad and full, his hands spread wide in penitence. 'Why don't we have a drink or two after dinner and put this behind us?'

'I don't think so, sir. I have things to do. Don't you?'

Seeing that his famed charm wasn't working, Warren bristled. 'You are treating a senior officer with contempt, Captain Aitken. I require an explanation.'

Charlotte sighed, secure in the knowledge that the brigadier had four days ago signed a confidential report that graded her performance as excellent in the highest bracket, the best that could be achieved by a captain.

'You flatter yourself, sir. I am not treating you with contempt.

I am treating you with indifference. Until you start behaving like a senior officer and stop treating me as anything other than a fellow professional I see no reason to treat you in any other way. You provoked this confrontation sir, not me. I will be happy to forget it and accord you the respect due to your rank as soon as you grant me the same courtesy. Is there anything else, sir?'

Defeated, Warren silently considered his position. He needed the holder of the G2 job to actively co-operate with him in planning brigade exercises, for it was on his performance in the field that the brigadier would judge him. The warning the SO3 G3, his operations captain, had given him about Charlotte Aitken's fierce professionalism and notorious determination to exclude consideration of her sex from every aspect of her military life had fallen on deaf ears. Warren had made a serious mistake and knew it. Besides, Captain Charlotte Aitken was clearly on the way up and had the ear of the brigadier. Warren decided to back off.

'My apologies once again, Captain Aitken. We seem to have got off on the wrong foot. I would be most grateful if you would dig out the current Organisation for Battle of the Group of Soviet Forces Germany. I need to bring myself up to date.'

Charlotte relaxed and smiled, her fists unclenching into hands devoid of rings, the nails cut short and square. 'The superintendent clerk has it ready for you, sir. I suspected that since your last job was commanding an armoured squadron in Cyprus you might ask for it. I will have it sent to you.'

Again Warren cursed. He had made a complete bloody fool of himself. Charlotte Aitken was on the ball.

'Thank you, Captain Aitken. And thank you for your foresight. Don't bother calling the super clerk. You have work to do. I'll collect it on my way back up the corridor.'

He turned and strode to the door, pausing as she called to him: 'Sir!' Facing her once more he saw that she was standing, holding out her right hand. He shook it as Charlotte Aitken smiled again, her eyes a brighter shade than before, lighting up her face. 'God,' he thought, 'I must seem like an arrogant idiot.'

'Please call me Charlotte, sir. Captain Aitken is a bit formal.'

11 August 1976
WARMINSTER

Chief Inspector Peter Ewart stood solidly behind the lectern in the main lecture hall of the School of Infantry in Warminster, Wiltshire. Dressed in a charcoal grey pinstripe suit, white shirt and black knitted tie he felt completely in control of himself, if not entirely at ease. The remnants of a hangover, the inevitable result of a late night spent drinking best Fermanagh poteen with the commandant of the school throbbed faintly behind his eyes. An hour ago it had been debilitating, but a surreptitious quarter bottle of Jameson's before lunch had come to his aid.

Behind Ewart, curtains rolled smoothly back to reveal a cinema screen and two back-projection screens. The main screen, not in use today, carried a projection of the school's emblem, a naked sword. In front of and to each side of Ewart sat the Intelligence officers of every regiment likely to be sent to Northern Ireland over the next eighteen months, plus other interested individuals drawn from all over the United Kingdom Land Forces area. The sea of soldiers ranged upwards in banked tiers reaching to just below the roof, each dressed in regimental working dress, giving the lie to the popular notion that the British Army had a uniform.

In the centre of the lowest row of seats sat the Commandant, a full colonel late of the Life Guards, legs thrown forward and crossed at the ankles, his own style of dress unique to himself.

He had faintly bloodshot eyes, a cavalryman's shirt, Guards belt, parachute boots and tropical lightweight combat trousers. The rolled-up right sleeve of his shirt bore a small set of wings, very different from those worn by members of the Parachute

Regiment: they were smaller and curved up, not down. From a distance they looked like a small blue and white boat.

Casting his eyes higher up Ewart caught sight of the two corporals of the Royal Military Police who had carefully monitored the identity of everyone entering the room. They checked their watches and moved to close the doors. Both men wore combat dress and carried Browning 9 millimetre pistols in webbing holsters. Before closing the doors they removed their pistol belts, put them into a small safe set into the wall and drew two Sterling submachine guns out of the safe. One military policeman stepped outside into the foyer. The other locked the doors behind him. They would stay in place throughout Ewart's presentation. Anyone left outside would stay outside. The guard inside the door made a brief hand signal to a captain, the colonel's adjutant, who stood at the foot of the steps leading down to the presentation floor. Turning quickly, the adjutant moved to the seat next to the colonel.

The colonel, a very tall and apparently easygoing individual bent his head to listen to a word or two from his aide and slowly, with studied care, rose from his seat. The hubbub of voices and scraping feet lost volume as the occupants of the higher tiers saw him stand up. As he reached Peter Ewart, the colonel turned about and said in a conversational tone 'Ladies and gentlemen, please do be quiet.' Instantly the huge room was filled with silence.

Colonel Harry George, despite his languid manner, was not a man to ignore; he held the Military Cross and the Queen's Gallantry Medal. All present knew that he had commanded not only the Life Guards but also the 22nd Special Air Service Regiment, source of the small winged badge on his right sleeve. The man's personal charm and toned-down Sloane Square drawl failed to hide the total professional behind the facade. His opening remarks were not the usual bland introduction of a guest speaker; his choice of words indicated a set of orders, not advice.

'You are privileged today to hear an up-to-date briefing on

the Intelligence situation in Northern Ireland. You are to listen carefully. You are not to make notes, but are to ask any question you think relevant. For the first time a senior RUC officer has agreed not only to answer any question put to him, but to give sufficient background information to enable you to fully understand his answers. You are to take full advantage of the opportunity. Chief Inspector Peter Ewart is second-in-command of the Belfast office of the RUC Special Branch. That in itself is of major importance. But I would have you know that I, in previous commands, have not only been grateful for the advice of Chief Inspector Ewart, I have relied on it. One thing more – this briefing is classified SECRET.' The colonel half turned, spoke privately to Peter Ewart for a moment, and strode back to his seat.

Ewart started on a joke, praying that one of these bright young people would act as his straight man. 'Ladies and gentlemen. I expected to see before me men and women in the uniform of the British Army. But I don't see two people dressed alike. Am I in the wrong place?'

For a long moment he thought his broad accent too much for them, but a young gunner with a sense of occasion rose to his feet and called out, 'No sir, you are in the right place. I and my brother officers of the Royal Regiment of Artillery are dressed as British officers should be. That chap down there in the middle, the awfully senior chap who just spoke to us, dresses oddly, but we're afraid to tell him so in case he creeps up on us and kills us. As for the rest of this motley crew, they come from a ragbag of lesser regiments. Those in skirts are either lady officers or from regions north of the Fortnum and Mason line. Please be so kind as to ignore them, sir.'

The great room dissolved into roars of simulated rage and invective. The colonel smiled indulgently and marked Captain Willie Smethurst RA as an officer who seized opportunities and thought on his feet. He jumped up and orchestrated the chant of 'Drop short, Drop short' that infantrymen habitually taunted gunners with, accusing the gunners of killing more of their own troops than the enemy's.

Ewart allowed the roaring to go on until the colonel sat down, then threw his hands up and waited for silence. When he got it he quietly remarked in a slow and ponderous voice, careful to let them get used to the accent 'Well now, a gunner is it? I recall a story told me by my aged and sainted mother. She and a sister of hers who had a soldier son watched a parade one day when all the regiments were gathered, and her sister remarked, "See all those soldiers? Not a man knows how to march except my Billy. They're all out of step except him." And I have to say to you, ladies and gentlemen, Billy was a gunner!'

It was an old joke and a good one; it all depended on how it was delivered. Ewart had done well. Feet thundered on the tiers and calls of 'Damned gunners. Well said, sir,' echoed round the hall. Once more Peter Ewart held his arms up.

Confident that he had them he stepped out from behind the lectern, trailing the wire from his signal button behind him. The button would alert the visual aids staff to move on to project the next picture in the carefully arranged sequence he had briefed them on.

'Here we go, then. We'll start with an overall brief, then get down to the nitty-gritty. Don't wait until the end of my presentation if you have a question. Ask questions as they occur to you. Listen in . . .'

Pictures flashed up of the tactical areas of responsibility of the various military formations in Northern Ireland; these were talked about. Then came a detailed commentary on concentrations of Provisional IRA strength and activity around the province, followed by a brief on current PIRA objectives.

Captain Charlotte Aitken, listening intently, was occasionally disturbed by unintelligible mutters from the man on her right. She had met him that morning and was alternately surprised and pleased to see him here. Sergeant Jamie Lappin of the Parachute Regiment had caught her eye as he stood on the short grass below the viewing galleries of the infantry firepower demonstration she had attended that morning at Battlesbury Bowl, about three miles away. The short, powerful figure directing and commenting on the activities of the sniper detachment firing at targets up to 1,200 metres away had grabbed her attention. His performance was impressive, his commentary over the PA system informative and interesting. A word with the major running the demonstration had been sufficient to secure a chance to talk to him – she wanted to know how the use of specialist snipers could enhance her own brigade's capability in dealing with enemy reconnaissance troops. When the focus of the demonstration had moved away from the snipers Sergeant Jamie Lappin came up to meet her.

'Sar'nt Lappin, ma'am. You have a query about snipers?' The strong Belfast accent did not surprise her but the depth and timbre of his voice, undistorted by the PA system, and the steady gaze of his eyes, a blue that matched her own, caused her to pause before speaking.

'Yes. I'm Captain Aitken, SO3 G2 at 19 Brigade. But I don't think we'll be able to talk.' She waved a hand at anti-tank crews swinging the long barrels of 120 millimetre Wombat recoilless guns into position. Lappin grinned. Wombats were probably the noisiest weapon the army had.

'You're right ma'am. There's a refreshment tent behind the main stand. It should be quieter there.' He moved off without another word, leaving her to gather her belongings together.

Charlotte Aitken caught up with him, swinging her small day sack over her shoulder as he rounded the back of the stand. He glanced at her but kept walking, making no move to take the little rucksack from her. His abrupt departure had been a surprise. Feeling perverse she asked, 'Aren't you going to offer to carry my pack, Sar'nt Lappin? It's not heavy.'

Lappin stopped abruptly and grave faced, caught her eye. 'I've never seen a Bergen so small, ma'am. I thought it was your handbag.' Disconcerted for the second time in as many minutes she stared hard at him, wondering if he was trying to patronise her. Then she saw the beginnings of a smile creep around the corners of his mouth and into his eyes. She couldn't help but smile back. 'OK Sergeant, I'd have hit you with it if you had offered.'

Lappin threw back his head and laughed in a full, unselfconscious bellow. It was difficult not to laugh with him, but she made the effort, conscious of the hundreds of officers nearby. Lappin got a grip on himself and remarked, 'I believe you would, ma'am – lady officers who don't carry their own equipment don't ask questions about snipers. Lady officers who do might carry a brick in their handbags.'

Charlotte Aitken was still uncertain, a little shaken by her instinctive reaction to him. Determined to assert herself, she was about to tell him that carrying heavy packs over mountains was nothing new to her. But he didn't give her the chance.

'Lead on, ma'am. Best laugh I've had in yonks. I'll get the coffee.'

Later, coffee and sniper talk finished, they walked down the hill towards the car waiting to take her to Warminster for lunch, then on to Chief Inspector Ewart's briefing. Lappin had his own Land Rover. Charlotte assumed he would be going straight back to his battalion in Aldershot. Lappin thought that she was on her way back to Colchester, to 19 Infantry Brigade.

At the parting of their ways there was a moment of awkwardness. Charlotte, looking sideways at Lappin, thought he was the sexiest man she'd ever met. She had studied him carefully while they talked. He was an inch or so shorter than her, very broad across the shoulders and obviously solidly muscled. Short, thick dark hair spiked at the crown of his head and dark blue eyes fringed with almost feminine lashes looked out at the world with confidence and humour, as if he believed himself capable of anything. His face was smooth, lightly tanned, with a big straight nose, his lower lip almost sensuously full. Very handsome. His voice, burred by his accent, was soft, deep and seemed to vibrate deep inside her. His small strong hands moved constantly as he talked, their gestures sometimes stopping in mid-move as his mind jumped ahead of his tongue. She had shut her eyes as if concentrating on what he was saying to give herself time to pull together an overall picture of him, but couldn't. She had the impression of strength, energy and humour, good looks and powerful sex appeal, but there was more, there was a certainty about him, a solid core of self-belief that was immensely attractive. The man was extraordinary, an elemental force, like a squall that catches the best of sailors by surprise. Then she had it – he was *real*. No pretence or artifice. What you saw was what you got.

Now, standing with him at the bottom of the hill she suddenly became aware that he was watching her intently, as if weighing something in his mind. A shock of recognition flowed through her; she had seen that look before, the look of a man debating whether he dared proposition her. Then the look faded from his face, replaced by a brief smile. Relief and disappointment fought for possession of her. *Thank God he hadn't said anything.* She didn't know what her reply would have been. The realisation that he was interested in her gave her pleasure, but the knowledge that he must have noticed how he had affected her caused the beginnings of a blush to creep across her throat. But it was going to be all right: they both knew that officer-other rank relations were severely frowned on.

Lappin broke the moment. 'Thank you for your interest, ma'am. It's been a pleasure talking to you. It's a pity time was short.'

Charlotte thought the possible double meanings deliberate, but he was wearing his grave face again, giving her the chance to ignore anything but the most obvious interpretation of his words. She lifted her chin slightly and said in a formal tone that failed to hide the meaning of her reply 'Thank you for taking the time to talk to me. It *is* a pity time has been short.'

Bang, there it was, out: a flash of intimacy passed between them. It would have to do. *Flirting is fun, but that's as far as it can go.* They both knew that. Lappin smiled, keeping his mouth straight, letting the smile show only in the crinkles at the corners of his eyes. He drew himself up and saluted smartly, saying, 'Good day, ma'am.' Charlotte returned his salute and walked to her car, knowing he was watching her. She made a deliberate effort to prevent an almost unconscious swing of her hips, thinking 'Dammit, why does he have to be a soldier?'

When they met again in the foyer of the lecture theatre they did not speak, but tacitly chose seats together, approaching from opposite ends of the row, as if their sitting together was pure chance. Nothing could come of it, both were sure, but the attraction was strong. She wondered what the hell he was doing here and what he was muttering about. She rapped his left knee with the back of her hand. 'Shh!' He jumped and flicked her an apologetic look.

Chief Inspector Ewart was talking about the Provisional IRA command structure in Belfast. '. . . the rising stars. These people have been around for a few years and managed to avoid capture or being killed.' A photograph flashed up on the left-hand projection screen. 'Ruari O'Hagan – He is currently acting as Belfast quartermaster, with control of all arms and explosives dumps. He is also a master bomb-maker and probably made most of the bombs used in the incendiary attacks on the city centres of Belfast and Londonderry about six months ago. He's probably destined to take over from old Sean O'Hara down in south Armagh. And now for a real baddie. Gerry Madden.'

All heads swung to the right-hand screen, expecting a picture. The screen remained blank. Beside her Charlotte Aitken sensed rather than felt Sergeant Lappin go rigid in his chair. She glanced at him and saw his hands clenched over his knees and the muscles of his jaw standing out in corded lines. Inspector Ewart continued his monologue.

'No picture of Madden is available because we've never been able to put our hands on him to arrest and interrogate him. He is potentially the most dangerous of the up and comers. A slippery boy is Madden, and a very bad one.

Others we've interrogated and turned have told us a lot about him. He's of middle height, fair hair, pale complexion, speaks fluent Irish and is much brighter than the average. He is known to be a student of the history of revolution and apparently gave a talk in Dublin a few months ago on the dynamics of guerrilla operations to senior members of the Provisionals' planning staff, a talk which influenced their decision to adopt their current twin track approach – gun in one hand and ballot box in the other. He is the nearest they've got to an original thinker, a cold-headed, ruthless and totally committed terrorist. But don't imagine he just sits around and philosophises. Madden is known to have planted numerous bombs and to have been directly responsible for the deaths of at least eight soldiers in sniping attacks. He will almost certainly be co-opted on to the Army Council planning staff in Dublin on his return from his current assignment, training with the Palestinians in Libya. We must get him soon. Now, Seamus Healy . . .'

Outside the lecture theatre Charlotte Aitken stood talking to Jamie Lappin, her face neutral, as if she were discussing nothing more than the weather, but her voice intense and a little strained. 'What is going on? Why are you here?'

'I'm from Belfast. I know Peter Ewart, he used to be in my district. I had the afternoon free and asked our Intelligence officer if I could come along. He took the opportunity to skip out of coming down here and asked me to represent him. I didn't know you would be here, ma'am. I'm sorry.'

Charlotte decided not to let him go. Her discovery that a man, any man, after all these years of self-imposed celibacy could interest her enough to risk her career intoxicated her. A flashing glimpse of Andrew Leggath crossed her mind. But Lappin was not, could never be, like Andrew Leggath. Lappin, she instinctively knew, was the genuine article.

'I'm not sorry. Let's drop the pretence, shall we? There's nobody close enough to hear us. There's something that needs to be said and I'll say it because you can't or won't. I want to know more about you. I think you want to know more about me. I know the rules and so do you. Right so far?'

Charlotte felt her throat tighten. This was a crazy thing she was doing. Men came to her: she used them for her social needs, always army men and always highly eligible, to escort her when needed as a visible sign of her heterosexuality, dropping them at the first hint of physical intimacy. And this man probably had had more women than he could count. Never before had she acted like this, but she wanted to see more of Sergeant Lappin. Lappin did not answer, but he nodded.

She felt her face flame with pleasure and embarrassment. This was stupid. She felt like a silly schoolgirl with a crush on the boy at the bus stop. She tried to think of something to say, but Lappin beat her to it.

'Captains don't get close to sergeants. You might be doing this to amuse yourself at my expense. But I'd like to see you again. Why not name a place and time? If we're there we'll see what happens next. If we're not we forget we ever met. OK?'

Charlotte felt the tension ease out of her. 'All right. I spend most of my free weekends in London and I sometimes lunch on Saturdays in the Italian restaurant in Battersea High Street, about one o'clock. I might be there this weekend.'

Lappin smiled the big, open smile he'd inherited from his father. 'Right then. Let's go and think about whether we want to know each other's first names. My career is as important to me as yours is to you.' It was Charlotte's turn to nod wordlessly. Lappin stepped back and was about to salute when she spoke again, pricked by curiosity. 'What's special about the man Inspector Ewart had no picture of? You seemed shocked when you heard his name.'

Lappin's face froze. 'We were brought up together and he was my best friend. I thought he was working for the Post Office in the Republic of Ireland and I thought he stopped writing to me because I joined the army. It was a shock to hear he's been bombing and sniping all along. Did you see the scar across the inspector's throat? Gerry Madden put it there, years ago, and Ewart knows it.' He shook himself. 'Time to go, ma'am. Good afternoon.'

His salute was sharp and correct. Her return was equally correct. 'Good afternoon, Sergeant Lappin.' Neither looked back as they walked away.

9.30 a.m. 15 August 1976
BELFAST

Peter Ewart felt sick; sicker than he had for a long time. Staring at the mirror he felt a fresh wave of nausea and self-disgust wash over him. His hair was tufted and unkempt, his eyes red and deeply pouched, his facial skin a fishbelly white laced across the cheekbones with the fine red and blue lines of burst capillaries. Drunk last night, he thought, too drunk this time, was sick on the bathroom floor. Place is stinking. Must shower. He grabbed a toothbrush and swabbed it round his mouth, forgetting to put toothpaste on it until he noticed the absence of taste, squeezed too much out of the tube and put the brush back in his mouth.

The strong mint smell hit him first in the back of the throat, then the belly. Heaving, he leaned over the basin. He splashed his face and walked carefully back to his living room, thinking, too much drink and not enough food yesterday. He checked his notebook, the one he used as a combined diary, address and phone book and for noting down anything that jumped into his head that he wanted to remember. Good. Nothing till this afternoon. Bed. Sleep. Shower then a bit of lunch and a couple of snorts and I'll be ready. Saturday afternoons often bring something in. Passing through the hallway of his bungalow Ewart failed to see the small red indicator lamp glowing on a flat grey panel set into the wall. The light indicated which of the seven infra-red detector beams set at chest level around the bungalow had been broken during the night. It was the one across his garage door.

A few years, maybe only a year or two ago he would have seen it, would have checked it as a matter of course. But the drink was beginning to tell on him and he knew it, was trying to limit it to manageable proportions, to keep his work unaffected. Mostly he was successful, but sometimes the pressures, frustrations and physical fear of hunting terrorists for a living were just too much. He never planned it, never said, 'Tonight I'm going to get drunk'; he just let it happen as and when he needed to.

Sometimes music took the edge off, sometimes not, as he lay in a bath and allowed himself to drift off to Bach or Beethoven. Sometimes Mrs Adamson, his cleaner, did a bit for him, not for cash or even for friendship, but because she knew him and what he did and when he needed an hour or so of a woman's time. But the drink was his ever-present friend, had been for years and years, growing more dependable as the going got tougher, but like a friend, liable to snap at him when he abused it. He knew how to handle it, could manage, just as his father had, running the farm by day, dead drunk by nine at night, up and working by six in the morning, for more years than a dog had fleas. Ewart, falling into bed, knew he would be all right.

12.15 p.m. 15 August 1976
LONDON

Jamie Lappin walked slowly down Battersea High Street, wondering still if he was doing the right thing. Most of last night, in his battalion sergeants' mess in Aldershot he had beaten around the subject of meeting up with a WRAC officer with a crony of his, Tony Aldiss, sergeant-major of B Company, until the whole story of his meeting Charlotte Aitken had come out. Tony's advice had been simple. 'No future in it, Jamie lad. Happens sometimes.

Forget about it. Better still, fuck her and then forget about it.'

'Yes, I know. But there's more than just a jump in this. I feel odd about it. She's different. Tough. Straight up and down with no bullshit. Beautiful as well. Looks fit. Sort of woman that doesn't whinge. More likely to chin you if you got out of order. Or just walk out on you. I don't know, Tony.'

'Get a bloody grip on yourself, Jamie. A tart's a tart. I've been married twice and divorced them both for the same thing. They all pretend to be different until they think the hooks are in and then it starts. Always the same. Gimme gimme gimme. Where are you going? Where have you been? Trying to make you feel guilty for getting wrecked in the mess with your mates on dinner nights. Whining about never getting out. Telling you you're wonderful, being nice nice nice then screwing the first bastard they find with a wide line in bullshit and a hard-on when you're away doing your job. Fucking tarts and liars, all of them. For fuck's sake Jamie, why am I telling you this? You know what it's all about – Shut up. Don't interrupt me when I'm talking to you – Get a few wets down you and go and see that WRAC Lance-Jack in the CommCen. She's had the hots for you for months. Go and give her one and forget this bloody officer. She's either looking for a bit of rough or pissing you about.'

'OK, but–'

'No sodding buts. Have a pint.' Aldiss waggled an arm at the mess barman. 'Two pints. And two large Scotches.'

'OK. OK. You don't want to hear any more. But Jacko Timms married a WRAC officer, didn't he?'

'Jamie, I'm pissed off with this. You've got a good career ahead of you. Twenty-six-year-old sergeant with an "Outstanding" grade on your last confidential. You'll get colour sar'nt on the next vacancy. Company sar'nt-major two or three years after that. And then what? RSM before you're thirty-two. Ten years still to serve with nowhere to go but up. They'll have to commission you. You'll make major as a quartermaster at least. Everybody knows it except you. What the fuck's wrong with you? Jacko

Timms had to quit when he married the WRAC. Wasn't going anywhere anyway. And what's he doing now? A fucking house husband. Can't take a job below her majesty's status. Wouldn't do, old boy, and made to feel like a prat when he has to tag along with her to mess functions. Those fuckers over there in the officers' mess don't talk to ex-rankers unless it's to give them a job they can't soil their command status hands on. Fuck that. You're right, I don't want to hear any more of this shit. Met a tart with a pretty face and a captain's pips and you're talking about marriage. Bollocks. Go and get your leg over like I told you. You'll be better in the morning. Now fuck off. I'm going for a game of snooker.'

Lance-Corporal Jennie Wilson was willing; more than willing. But for the first time in his life Jamie just couldn't do the business. Every time Jennie's fingers and tongue seemed to be getting somewhere a pair of earnest blue eyes, edged with anxiety, returned to haunt and unman him. Jennie was very good about it. 'You've had a dram or two, Jamie darling. But not that much. You're in love man, and not with me. Tell me about it.'

Jamie told her, not mentioning names; Jennie's soft Western Isles voice and complete womanliness were hard to resist.

'Ach, man. I know the lass. General Aitken, it must be. There's not many of us don't know about her. Captain still, I think. But a general she will be. Hard on the men, and all the lezzies drool about her. A lovely lass, but something odd about her. Get out of my bed, Jamie. Come back when she's finished with you. I'll be good to you.' Jamie Lappin left Jennie's bed thinking a lot more of her than when he'd got into it.

But now he was committed. Standing outside the little Italian restaurant he could see the raised bar and kitchen section at the back, and the tables, a dark wood surrounded by splashes of colour marking the positions of the diners, but all of this in one section of his mind. The rest was occupied by two very blue eyes in a face surrounded by thick dark hair, gazing back at him in a mixture of apprehension, relief and happiness. He expected to feel his doubts dissolve, but they remained to prick him. The difference was that he did not care.

12.30 p.m. 15 August 1976
BELFAST

Three extra hours' sleep, a shower and a pint and a half of full-cream milk made a new man of Peter Ewart. He still looked rough, but no more than might be expected of a man who hunted terrorists for a living. He felt better and poured a very large Jameson's as he dialled his office number. The detective-sergeant on duty relayed a series of messages of no real importance. But one message, apparently innocuous, caught his attention: Gerry Madden was said to have flown into Shannon International four days ago. No positive ID at the time, but a call on the Confidential Telephone received this morning confirmed it. Madden was back in Ireland.

Ewart shaved carefully and rinsed his eyes with Optrex, thinking about Madden. Destined for the Provisional IRA planning staff, almost certainly. With a Libyan education. Bastard. They'll try him out, and soon. They would select a carefully chosen and reconnoitred target and tell him it was a fleeting target of opportunity, to see if he performed under pressure. Probably they'd go for an army mobile patrol somewhere near the border, with a culvert bomb planted years ago just in case a Brit unit got careless about travelling at odd hours over different routes. They'd let Madden blow the Brits away just to test him and give him confidence in his planning. The questions were – where and when?

Walking through his hall on the way to his front door Chief Inspector Ewart at last caught the red glow of the warning lamp on his alert panel. The garage. False alerts on the front door were not uncommon – milkman, paper boy, posters of junk mail. But the garage was different. Ewart swung into self-preservation: this was the third time in two months his garage beam had been broken. It smacked of Provisional IRA reconnaissance. A phrase out of a James Bond novel jumped into his head: *'Once is happenstance, twice is coincidence, three times is enemy action.'* There was a fair to middling chance the enemy had wired up his car to a couple of kilos of high explosive.

Ewart walked into his living room, took a couple of deep breaths to calm himself and whacked more Jameson's into a toothglass. Drinking deep, he called his office number again, passing a code that indicated he thought himself to be under bomb attack. The desk sergeant asked him to remain inside the house and advised him of the dispatch of an RAOC EOD team and an RMP close protection detail. Ewart relaxed: a forewarned RMP team could handle anything a Provisional IRA active service unit could throw at someone in their charge.

While he was waiting, Ewart thought hard, made a decision and moved into his study. Behind his desk was some personal reassurance: a single barrelled Remington self-loading shotgun, its magazine pre-loaded with five rounds of no. 4 shot, its barrel shortened to a little over ten inches. Ewart had 'acquired' the gun from a Provisional IRA arms dump a friendly infantry battalion had found as a result of information Ewart had passed to them. At close range the gun would put a hole as big as a dinner plate in a man; much better than the .38 calibre Smith and Wesson the Special Branch had issued to him. There would probably be no need for either weapon, but the Provisional IRA might know about his alarm system; if they did they might have deliberately triggered it knowing he would call for assistance and remain in the house.

Out in the street a man in Post Office overalls straightened up from the open door of a green metal box standing close against a wall. Wires trailed from two of the hundreds of telephone connections housed in the box, leading to a pair of headphones on the man's head. He spoke into the open window of a small Bedford van. In the back of the van two men checked and cocked their weapons. 'OK, boys. He's still in there. He's just called in some sort of code. The bomb squad and Military Police are on their way. Let's go.'

The men jumped out of the van and ran down the street. Turning into Ewart's driveway, they stopped to signal to the man at the telephone junction box. As they reached Ewart's door they heard his telephone ring, triggered from the box. One of the men pulled a seven-pound sledgehammer out of his belt and swung it up. On the fourth ring the telephone stopped. As planned, the men were now certain exactly where Ewart was – standing in the hallway with a telephone receiver in his hand. The leader of the two Provisional IRA volunteers nodded. Down came the sledgehammer, full on the door lock, smashing it with a splintering crack. Simultaneously the leader kicked the door open and stepped into Ewart's hallway, firing as he moved. Jolting to a stop, he saw nothing but a bare hall. The second man dropped the sledgehammer and pulled out his pistol. 'Where the fuck is he?'

The answer came in a deafening roar as shards of splintered door smacked into both men's faces. Ewart stepped out of his lounge, firing straight at the doorway. The leading terrorist took the full blast of the sawn-off shotgun in the throat; it severed his head and spattered his support man with blood and bits of shredded flesh. Shocked and confused, the man fired wildly down the hall as he turned to run, hitting Ewart in the chest more by luck than marksmanship. But the small bullet was not enough: Ewart just stood there, still firing into the doorway. He caught the fleeing man in the side, then the back and legs as he fell forward. Ewart's last round hit the top of the door as he dropped the shotgun and began to pull his pistol out of his belt. But suddenly he felt the effects of his wound. Blood filled his throat, choking him, dimming his vision.

The RMP staff-sergeant listened carefully and made notes as

the young Ammunition Technical Officer, the operator leading the bomb disposal team, briefed him.

'The area is clear of IEDs. There's one man dead, decapitated, in the doorway. Another one dead, just outside. He's a mess from the knees up. There's a third casualty, your man, seriously wounded in the hall. My Number Two has radioed for an ambulance and is looking after him.

'There's a .357 magnum revolver, a Colt Cobra, one round fired. It's lying in the doorway. There's a .32 Beretta automatic, one round fired, in the porchway. There is an impact area at the far end of the hall, one round, the Colt. Your man was lucky, he took the Beretta round. The Colt would have killed him outright. Your man had a .38 Smith and Wesson, police issue, unfired: my Number Two has it in possession. There's also a sawn-off shotgun, a self-loading Remington, lying near your man, all five rounds fired. He did rather well. Best guess is they tried to jump him but he was ready and caught them in the doorway with the shotgun. Vicious bit of kit, that. At that range it ripped them to bits. Tough shit on them, I say. But your man's possession of a weapon like that might raise eyebrows. Your business. I need my Number Two back. We have another call,' he smiled tiredly. 'Probably a hoax to pull us away from here. That's it; I have to go.'

The military police staff sergeant took over, preparing the way for the inevitable RUC crime squad, detailing one of his own men to relieve the bomb disposal operator's Number Two. Moving into Ewart's bungalow he called the Special Branch duty room and reconstructed events as best he could, walking around with the phone as he talked, knowing that PIRA rarely botched jobs like this and searching for the reason why. He found it as he stepped over Ewart, realised what he was doing: *they tried to catch him in the hall by bursting in as he answered the phone. But he'd moved the phone into the lounge. Careless. They should have known he'd have a cable long enough to carry the phone around the house.*

'I have a question. Did he have a shotgun licence? You don't think so? I'll ask you again. Did he have a shotgun licence? Of course I understand. You're under pressure, a senior officer after all. You're not sure? Be sure . . . he did or he didn't . . . two dead terrorists . . . shotgun wounds . . . good lad, you understand . . . Coroner's court . . . perfectly entitled . . . minimum force in a life threatening situation . . . of course I understand . . . he had to use a licensed shotgun in support of his issue weapon . . . I need to see a shotgun, any shotgun, here, within the hour . . . good lad . . . that's the way it is . . .'

1.20 p.m. 15 August 1976
LONDON

'Hello, Miss. Mind if I share your table?' Jamie Lappin's voice echoed his nervousness and reflected the turmoil in him.

Charlotte Aitken smiled the smile she'd practised so hard for so long in her bathroom mirror, determined to say what she wanted and had to say, knowing that nothing but complete honesty would ever do for this man. However shocked he might be, she knew he would respect it. 'No, not at all. I'm Charlotte.'

'Jamie. Thanks.'

They sat and stared, blue on blue. 'I'm glad you came.'

'I'm glad you did.'

'There could be problems.'

'I don't care.'

'Neither do I.'

He ordered ravioli in a sauce heavily laced with garlic, she Calamari fresco with a light salad — and a clove of fresh garlic, chopped fine. Despite her tension she had seen it coming: she had named an Italian restaurant and garlic and love don't mix. Unless both eat it of course.

'I suppose we're friends now?' he said, looking into his clenched hands.

Be brave. State the truth. 'I want you.'

His head came up with a jerk. 'I want you too. But not now. Maybe in an hour. Maybe in a week, or a month.' Jamie Lappin found it hard to believe he'd said that. He tried again. 'That's not true, I want you right here and now. I want to have you over this table, or under it if you prefer. But I'd like you to know who's having you.'

Charlotte Aitken flushed. *I was right. There's not an ounce of bullshit in him.* 'You must think I'm very forward, Jamie. I've never been like this before. But I'm very happy right now. I want you to want me. I'm embarrassed talking like this. I don't know what to say. I just want to know all about you. I'm nervous. You might just use me and laugh about it. I just —'

'Sorry, I'm interrupting you. You're afraid, I'm afraid. You want to be a general. Don't ask me how I know that, I just know. I want to be RSM of the best battalion in the finest regiment in the world. You want to be top of your tree and I want to be top of mine. I don't want to know you, because you're a threat to me. I think you think the same. So we fuck each other's brains out and go our separate ways. Or we . . . I'm not sure. I don't know what to think.' Jamie Lappin gathered his thoughts, caught, held her eye and took the plunge every man must take at least once in his lifetime. 'I think I'm falling in love with you.'

Charlotte Aitken took a deep, deep breath, feeling her heart jump inside her for the second time that day, a dizzy, lovely feeling. There had been no sideways glance, no flicker in his eyes, no fidget in his hands, flat on the table, a gesture in itself. *He means it. Thank God for that.* 'I've already fallen in love with you. The moment I saw you through the window my heart jumped. I'm not sure why, but it did and I know I love you. I think it's because you're real. I can trust you. I'm trusting you not to use me. If you want me now, I'm ready. But like you said, I'd like to know who's having me. I'm frightened of you. You could hurt me.'

Then came the big, slow smile. 'Now, later, next week maybe. Next month possibly. Who cares? Women to screw are two a penny. And you can't be short of admirers. Let's not make love until we decide the time is right. I'd like to hold your hand.'

Lappin paused, taking a breath, holding it, dropping it. 'You could hurt me more than you can imagine.'

Charlotte reached over the table, took one of his hands in both of hers, drew it toward her and kissed it softly. 'You really are an amazing man, Jamie Lappin. You're right. I'm not short of admirers. But I've only ever had one boyfriend I could have cared about, a long time ago.' She gripped his hand tightly, her blush fading to a pale intensity. 'I don't know much about making love.'

Again came the smile, and Jamie said, 'You'll know. As you love me you'll know, my Charlotte. We have all the time in the world.' Devilment crept into his eyes. 'On the other hand, what's wrong with good old-fashioned lust? I can't just look at you. You look so . . . so–' Interrupting him she fished, a minor coquetry, expecting a compliment. She got it, but not the compliment she expected. 'What? I look so what?'

'Well, you look so . . .' he paused again and then said in a low, deep voice, holding her eyes with his, 'You look edible.'

Charlotte's flush became a blush, and then a raging bush fire burning her cheeks. She dropped her head to hide behind her hair and kicked him under the table.

Strolling along the Embankment two soldiers found a unique way to show a unique love. Holding hands is normal for lovers; total physical separation normal for soldiers. Unsure for a while they walked along, hands behind their backs in military style until they reached their omen: a quiet, powerful, sleeping warship: HMS Belfast, a heavy cruiser enjoying her honourable retirement, her great guns in their armoured turrets pointing port at the prow, starboard at the helm. Then the lovers found their way: little fingers linked they walked along, in balance, one plus one equalling one.

3.00 p.m. 15 August 1976
BELFAST

The man in his shirt sleeves switched off the radio with a snap. The flat, unemotional voice of the newscaster had stabbed at him like a spear. Standing with his back to the other two men in the room, he allowed the tension, already bowstring tight, to build into an almost physical presence. 'Your plan failed, Gerry. Ewart is still alive, we have a lieutenant and a volunteer dead. Explain.'

Gerry Madden pushed back the thick lock of dirty fair hair that hung over his forehead, a gesture of nervousness. His voice trembled with anger. 'My plan did not fail. Volunteer Connery here –' he jerked a hand at a short middle-aged man in Post Office overalls – 'no matter what he says now could not possibly have seen what happened. He was too far away. Ewart just wasn't where he was supposed to be. Something was missed on reconnaissance. Connery admits everything worked perfectly until the boys hit the door. So I started thinking and checked back.' Madden lifted a cheap cardboard file off the table next to him and flicked it open.

'I first saw this twenty minutes ago, after Connery came back. Question: does Ewart have an extension phone? The Post Office records that Connery copied say he hasn't. But the original fitting instructions, here, – ' he handed a flimsy piece of paper, a carbon copy of Ewart's Post Office order form to the shirt-sleeved man – 'read this. It specifies an extra long cord, 24 feet, to be exact. With that he could have been nearly anywhere in a two-bedroomed bungalow. And there's this.' He produced two slips of paper stapled together. 'Reconnaissance reports. Nobody told me that Ewart had been recce'd twice in the last few months. The bloody man was waiting for us. Somebody on your brigade staff needs to be seen to. This is out and out incompetence. There's no way you're going to pin this on me.'

'Don't talk to me like that. I'm Commandant here, not you. I'm sending you back to Dublin. You were here to be tested and you failed. And you have the brass neck to try to shift the blame on to my staff. My report will sort you out Madden, once and for all. I've told the Army Council before that sending people off to swan about in the desert is a waste of time. You'll be lucky if you ever set foot in Belfast again.'

For reply Madden turned on Connery. 'Get out. This is not for your ears.' Surprised by the note of command in Madden's voice Connery backed out quickly.

'Wrong, Tom. It's you who'll be sorted, not me.' Madden pulled a thick brown envelope out of his coat pocket. 'This contains my orders from the Army Council. I was told to carry out one operation and then investigate why nearly every operation planned here over the last eighteen months has been aborted or botched. If I found you or your staff to blame I have the authority to relieve you of command. I'm doing so now. It's been a long war and will be longer still. You're tired Tom, burned out. Try to defy me and you'll face an investigating committee.'

Tom McSherry, shocked, turned suddenly agonised eyes on the young man he'd selected and sworn in himself. He had suspected that the Army Council was watching him, but hadn't expected anything like this. He pulled himself together and shouted, 'Don't give me that! I'll have you fucking shot before I hand over this brigade to you. I built it up from nothing. The Brits are sauntering about in Derry and down on the border, but they're still hard targeting here for fear of us. Fuck you, Madden. You're a dead man.'

He charged across the room and pulled open the door, shouting 'Connery, get–' He froze: he was staring into the barrel of an Armalite assault rifle held by Sean McAllister. Connery lay crumpled in the corridor, a thin streak of blood across his forehead.

'You'll remember Sean, Tom. I've had him transferred from Newry to be my bodyguard. Move and he'll kill you.'

Strung out too far for too long, Tom McSherry caved in. 'Don't do this to me, Gerry. I'll put the brigade back in shape. It's just that the migraines . . .' He flapped an arm, stuck for words, searching Gerry Madden's face. He found no compassion.

'I'm sorry Tom. You have to go. Things are different now and the old ways aren't good enough. The brigade's riddled with touts. That piece of shit in the corridor is one of them. The first thing Sean did here was put a tap on the lines into Palace barracks. I have a tape of Connery telling the Branch that I was back from Libya, and there's more. Connery and two others will be court-martialled and shot before the day is out, but not before Sean interrogates them. We'll find the rest of the informers, if there are any.' He paused, as if in thought. 'You've served the Cause well, Tom. I take back what I said about relieving you of command. You can save your face. I'll tell the Army Council that when I showed you the result of my investigation you were shocked that ill-health was preventing you from sorting things out yourself. I'll tell them I took over at your own request. As brigade commander I can allow you to retire on health grounds. You'll still be a soldier and an honoured man, Tom. That's the best I can do, for old times' sake.'

McSherry seemed to shrink before Madden's eyes, ageing twenty years. 'All right Gerry. Touts is it? I wondered . . .' Strength seeped back into his voice. 'The brigade's yours. I've been betrayed by my own. Find them and rip them to fucking shreds if you have to. Then kill them all.' A thought seemed to strike him, stiffening him, giving a little height. 'As their former Commandant I claim the right to preside at their courts-martial; and to execute them.' He pulled his head up. 'You can't deny me, Gerry.'

Madden considered for a moment. This seemed a heaven-sent opportunity to remove any ill feeling McSherry could hold against him and put the older man in his debt. He offered his hand in reply.

'Thanks, Tom. I was hoping you'd offer. I'm grateful. You know them well and will be able to pass judgment on them. Our people trust you and will know the sentences have been fair. But you can't execute them. Sean will see to that. The likes of Tom McSherry don't dirty their hands on informers. I won't give you orders, Tom, but I'd like to see you back here at eight o'clock tonight.' McSherry took the offered hand and shook it.

'I'll be here, Commandant.'

Straight-backed he brushed Sean McAllister out of his way and strode off for home. Halfway there he bit the tears back. He had known this must happen some day. In a way he was glad it had been Madden. He had been retired with honour and could still wield influence in the Cause. This way even the Brits would have to show him some respect.

Gerry Madden closed his eyes and shuddered. Opening the brown envelope he allowed its contents, several sheets of routine instructions, to fall to the floor. Three muffled voices that could have belonged to anybody born in west Belfast were safe on tapes in his pocket, two telling of recently botched Belfast Brigade operations. A couple of hours with the files had identified the not too bright volunteers who had carried out those operations. He would claim it was their voices warning the Special Branch that the attacks were coming off. The third voice, which was supposed to belong to Connery, told of Madden's arrival back in Ireland. None of the three to be accused had ever called the Special Branch: all the voices were variations of Madden's own. But by the time Connery and the other two got before McSherry's court they would have spent eight hours in Sean McAllister's hands. Two hours would have been enough. They would admit anything, blame each other and name any name he chose to feed them in return for the promise of a quick bullet and no more pain.

Madden handed the tapes to McAllister. 'You won't regret throwing in with me, Sean. These people are useless anyway. Don't let me down.'

McAllister nodded and left. Madden threw himself into an overstuffed armchair and pounded its arms in triumph. The first step had been taken; McSherry out and he in command, with Sean as his enforcer. All it had taken was balls and planning. The three volunteers who would be shot could easily be replaced.

A thin dark Palestinian face, forming out of the air, seemed to grin at Madden, congratulating him on lessons well learned. Madden laughed aloud. Yes, he had learned. One day he would sit on the Army Council as chief of staff. He would turn the Provisional IRA into a real instrument of terror. The Brits would drown in their own blood, and he would wield the knife.

Chapter Eight

14 and 15 February 1978

GERMANY

Nearly eighteen months to the day after their first meeting Jamie Lappin, Colour-Sergeant, watched Major Charlotte Aitken walk naked across the big room, arms behind her, her every movement a delight to his eye. Slim, graceful and lightly tanned she pretended to become aware of his scrutiny.

'Never seen a naked lady before, Colour-Sar'nt?'

'Yes ma'am, but I've never seen a major with an all-over tan before.'

Together they stood before the big picture window in a former ski hut high above St Andreasburg, the Harz mountains soaring up into the night sky around them. Dark sky, white snow, stars twinkling blue-red in the clear mountain air and the earth, all rock and snow, falling hard away into the frozen forest. Beautiful. The hut was theirs for ten days, rented in celebration of her promotion from a German nobleman who'd guessed wrong and built it before the ski lift routes were chosen. Way off piste it was quiet, secluded on the edge of the forest and romantic beyond the wildest dreams of fantasy.

Their life together had not always been so good. At first it had been difficult, bloody difficult; hard and uncertain enough to have killed most love affairs. Time after time snatched evenings, whole weekends had been cancelled or spoiled as one or other of them were called by their duties. It had been frustrating, enraging, sometimes disappointing to the point of tears. Over all hung the spectre of discovery, public embarrassment and military disgrace. The need for secrecy had made life doubly difficult, doubly tense, intruded on those moments that other couples used to find themselves as a couple. Sometimes they felt like adulterers, hiding, deceiving their friends. He loved her in his heart but felt himself inadequate, unable to hold her. She had no doubt that he was everything she wanted and needed, but worried about her ability to reassure him. As the first months passed Jamie had become increasingly insecure, Charlotte more desperate.

The crisis came as Jamie cancelled at short notice a weekend eagerly awaited and planned for, a date meant to replace one he had also had to cancel. It was unavoidable, he said. He was a recruit instructor, he said. He had to be available to his recruits at all times, ready to support his staff of corporals if things were going badly or someone was injured or ill. He had cancelled more dates than she had. Desperately embarrassed he had suggested she might find it all too much to bear, that she would be better off without him complicating her life. Charlotte had been disappointed, but was ready for his suggestion: Harriet Coles had stepped in to save them.

A few weeks before Jamie hit bottom Charlotte had become intensely aware of the root of his insecurity: the differences in their backgrounds. On one of their few evenings together in her London flat Jamie had idly picked up a silver-framed photograph, whistled and asked if she liked visiting stately homes. Thinking about something else she had smiled and said 'Don't be silly, Jamie. If I want to see lions I'll go to Africa. That's Tollesbury. I inherited it from my grandfather. The estate comes all the way down from Charles II. You'll be Lord of the Manor one day, if you do the decent thing by me.'

His pain at her tactlessness had cut her to the core. 'I thought you lived here,' he said. 'I thought this flat was something special. Now there's this Tollesbury place. That's a mansion. Who are you, Charlotte?'

She had tried to tell him, but it had taken time for him to absorb it all: her background, education, ambition, Tollesbury, the sheer weight of personal wealth that surrounded her. She had worked hard to recover her error, reassure and convince him that none of it really mattered, that she loved him and had no wish to change him, that her background was full of sophisticated frauds, men with no meaning to their lives. That it was what and not who he was that mattered to her, she needed him to be as he was, real. He had seemed to understand, sometimes, but then he would look uncertain, as if he could not really believe that she really, truly loved him. The photograph of Tollesbury had unnerved him, reminded him of the gulf between them. He had refused her invitation to visit it. Charlotte had become very afraid.

Harriet Coles, Charlotte's best friend, a Roedean girl whose parents seemed to own two-thirds of Yorkshire, was serving as a lieutenant with the Royal Army Medical Corps. Harriet had seen changes in Charlotte, noticed her unaccustomed uncertainty, taken the brunt of sudden outbursts of irritability. Over dinner one evening she chided Charlotte, remarked 'It must be love', and was shocked to find a suddenly distraught Charlotte in tears on her shoulder. Confession followed confession.

Charlotte told Harriet all about Jamie, and how she feared losing him. Harriet told Charlotte that she too had a boyfriend, a Welshman called Charlie Waters, whom she loved very much. A soldier in the Medics, he wanted to work his way to a commission, then marry her. Charlie was tall and skinny, not very physical, a gentle, sensitive man who really cared about other people. At one time he had felt insecure, ignorant and inadequate. When he had found out just how wealthy Harriet's family were, he was almost unable to believe her family holdings were bigger than his home valley and felt he wasn't good enough, would embarrass Harriet in front of her people. He had refused to meet them. Harriet's platoon sergeant had seen it all before. Her solution was simple, inelegant – and extremely effective.

Harriet and Charlotte shared their feelings about their impossible men. Harriet predicted that Jamie would do as Charlie had:

he would suggest that it all might be too much for her rather than admit it was getting to be too much for him. She suggested that when it came Charlotte should do to Jamie as she had done to Charlie: hit him as a woman from his own world would. She should stop trying to reassure him, and attack. She should kick him where it hurt, throw the onus on him to prove his love for her.

So when Jamie's call came Charlotte was ready: she gave a very good impression of a woman in a towering rage of rejection and jealousy. She accused Jamie of playing with her, deceiving her, accused him of having another girlfriend tucked away in Aldershot. She swore at him and told him not to call her again until he had dropped whatever little tart he was fooling around with.

Jamie was stunned. He quite literally took to the hills, disappeared into Wales for a week, and reappeared with a reconstructed diary to prove his whereabouts on every day since they had first met. He sent flowers. He even cancelled a coveted ten days of adventure training in Norway just to spend an evening with her watching an old film about offshore sailing in the 1920s. Charlotte was difficult, distant, refused to apologise for her behaviour and warned him that she wouldn't share him. He swore that there was no other woman. Charlotte gave him the impression that she knew better but chose to believe him. Jamie was mightily relieved; and reassured that she really did love him. Then she made clear to him exactly how she saw him: she took him home to Tollesbury, to meet her family, and introduced him as her fiancé. Mrs Platt fussed over him, and took care that he slept in a room of his own. Sar'nt Platt drank beer with him and gave him a hard time about modern soldiers with their waterproof clothing and feather-filled sleeping bags. Charlotte chose her moment carefully. Jamie, dressing in his own room, overheard the conversation as Mrs Platt set out breakfast on the terrace.

'What do you think of my fiancé, Mrs Platt?'

'He's lovely, ma'am. He's a nice young man. I think he's from a good family. He's a bit skinny. He doesn't look very well. Platt was like that when he came home from the Great War. Mr Jamie needs looking after, ma'am. I'll feed him up for you.'

'Sar'nt Platt?'

'Not sure, ma'am. Not an officer. But he's a proper soldier, ma'am. Think he's all right. Think he will look after you. I like him. That's all, ma'am.'

Their duties still clashed, but this caused no problems. They accepted it as the way of the military world and a part of their relationship. It had been nearly three months after their first meeting that they slept together, on a weekend in a tiny hotel on the edge of the Radnor Forest, not long after Jamie had stayed at Tollesbury. Their lovemaking, after a day of walking through the forest trails, the tension building hour by hour, had been quick and fierce, then slow and gentle, engendering a physical emptiness and emotional fulfilment that left them sleeping, dreamless, to wake more in love than either could have dreamed of. But not until they had been together six months or more had they really begun to ease into peacefulness, feel comfortable and quiet, not needing constant reassurance from each other. Now there were no doubts. Life was better, difficult only some of the time.

'It's months since you came back from Portugal,' said Jamie. 'How do you keep that colour?'

Charlotte eased herself away from him, away from the staggering beauty of a full moon doing its damnedest to light and bathe the midnight Harz in winter. 'Women's wiles and a beauty parlour with a sunbed. Anyway, that's none of your business. Enjoy it while you can.'

She slipped an arm behind his head and kissed him deeply, moving against him, moulding herself to him. She whispered in his ear, 'Mountains and dark pine woods. A belly full of beef. A log fire, a bearskin on the floor and a woman who's wildly in love with you. What more could a Para want?' She pressed against him, allowing her knees to loosen and her hips to lean into him.

Jamie smiled, keeping his eyes on the mountains, an arm around her. 'Look at that out there. I wish I had the words to describe it. I'd tell it a poem.' He tore his eyes from the window. 'I'd tell it it's nowhere near as beautiful as you are. Now let go of me and give me a drink.'

Charlotte stuck out her lower lip in an accentuated pout. 'Animal. I love you too. Here.' She swung her hidden hand from behind her back. In it was a thick glass tumbler swirling with two inches of amber liquid. Jamie smiled again, took it and sipped it. No water, no ice, just pure Bushmills Black Label, the glorious Black Bush. Feeling the familiar smooth bite on the edges of his tongue he said, 'Ach, you're a wonderful woman. Where'd you get this?'

'I brought it with me, to tempt you. And I'm keeping it hidden. Every time you make love to me I'll give you some.'

For a moment she thought she'd gone too far, had triggered some unknown bomb lying deep in him. He stiffened for a second, then relaxed. It was not unusual, for experience had taught her of his prideful sensitivity: he had come from nowhere by the strength of his will and his need for recognition. Then she felt the laughter begin to form, rumbling, deep in his chest. It was going to be all right.

'You're a hell of a woman, Major.' He dropped the glass, half full, and stepped back from her just enough to catch the bearskin by its ears, swinging it up off the floor, over his back and around them both. 'Who needs the floor?'

Charlotte made no answer, but crossed her arms behind his head and lifted her legs to lock them around his back, searching for him, feeling his tongue caress her own as he opened and filled her.

'Mmmm. Would you be so kind as to walk forward, Colour, and lean my shoulders against the wall?'

'To hear is to obey, ma'am. Hold tight.'

As her shoulders hit the pinewood wall and she felt the first of his thrusts drive her up and back Charlotte nuzzled her face deep into his neck. Sometimes this was the best way. A stand-up fuck with the only foreplay a mocking reference to the gulf that separated them. This way she said to him, and he to her, I love you, and to hell with the army.

Bright sunshine filtered down through the pines, picking out the bright red hoops on Charlotte's one-piece ski suit. She was laughing, bent over at the knees, holding her arms tightly against her sides. A few seconds previously a solid fist of fear had struck her in the chest as Jamie had tumbled headlong down the slope, bouncing off the trees, his skis off his feet and whirling round him on their retaining straps. But it was all right. He was on his feet again. Standing up shaking himself and roaring abuse at the novice skier who had cut across him he looked like a crop-haired snowman, loose snow coming off him in showers. Hearing her laughing he turned and bellowed up at her, the Irish in him thick in his voice, 'And what the hell are you laughing at, witch? I'll give you laugh. Just you stay there. I'll put these bloody skis to good use across your arse.'

Charlotte put a hand across her mouth and tried to control herself. But it was no good. And he was now only a few yards down the hill, bulling his way up through the powder snow, skis trailing behind him. Slipping to one side she whipped past him on to the piste, turning gracefully downhill, laughter streaming behind her. Oh God, she thought, he'll be furious. But I can't help it. Better stay out of his way for a bit. Over her shoulder she saw him struggling to get his skis on. She calculated. She had a head start and was technically a better skier, but he was incredibly strong and skied like a wild man, oblivious to the dangers. Head down, arse up and go for it was his philosophy. Typical of him.

Jamie Lappin, angry but not as angry as Charlotte thought,

charged down the hill, following the fall line, elbows tight in and feet together, knees braced. Seeing the streams of novices across his path he kept going, picking spaces, throwing himself through gaps in the lines. When he turned at the bottom of the hill he did so in a display of sheer physical power that instantly had a small knot of brightly clad Germans around the Glühwein stall throw up their arms and applaud, stamping their feet and shouting, 'Bravo, Herr Schneemeister, bravo, bravo!'

Jamie, surprised, stayed where he was. They had obviously followed his suicidal charge down the fall line and had mistaken his red and black ski suit for the uniform of the Bergwacht, the mountain rescue patrol. He grinned, anger evaporating as Charlotte swung around him. Executing a perfect stem Christie, she stopped close enough to touch him, then leaned over and kissed him. 'My hero. One of these days you'll break your legs.' Noting the edge to her voice he opted for conciliation; Charlotte was notorious as a bad loser. 'Fine. I'll buy you a Glüh. OK?'

'Don't you dare patronise me. You can cook dinner for that. One more word out of you and you can sleep on the floor.' Seeing the darkness in her eyes he backed off. She was also notorious for her quick temper. 'And you threatened me. How dare you shout at me in public! Yes I would like some wine.'

Crestfallen, he moved off to the Glühwein stand. Charlotte smiled to herself; there are more ways to win than coming in first. When he came back she would forgive him.

Later, lying back on the big bearskin in their ski hut she said, 'That was a fantastic run you did today. Stupid, but fantastic. But you mustn't do it again. You really will break your legs.'

'OK. I was cross at you laughing at me. But did you see the Germans? They thought I was from the Bergwacht.' He threw a log on the fire and lay back, quiet. 'I wasn't always so strong. I even failed P Company the first time.'

Charlotte, alerted by the quiet indifference in his tone, said nothing at first. It was rare for him to talk about himself, particularly about the times before they had met. She would have to be careful and make the most of her opportunity. She loved him very much and wanted to know all there was to know, yet respected his privacy. But when he talked like this, she listened.

'My father was a great man. Enormous he was. Not short like me. Near six and a half feet tall and big built. And he was intelligent. He knew all about social history and could talk the leg off three professors when he wanted to. Big Jamie they called him. Even the peelers stayed out of his way. Not that he was violent. He was quiet. He just did what he thought was right. He used to tell lovely stories to us kids.'

'What happened to him?'

'Nothing. He's probably still running about. But the riots changed him. He started drinking and wouldn't talk any more. It was him who told me to leave home. So I joined the Paras.'

Carefully she rolled over and laid her head across his thighs, feeling the warmth of him through the rough texture of the scruffy old towelling bathrobe he insisted on wearing.

'What happened then?'

'I was a wimp. I only lasted six weeks. They were going to throw me out but the platoon sergeant spoke for me. He took me off the course and made me eat five meals a day, and run until I collapsed. Then he put me on the multigym and made me pump the weights until I cried. Bloody old bastard. Every time I tried to cry off during Bergen runs with him he'd stop and throw a sandbag into my Bergen to make it even heavier, so I stopped whingeing and just tried to keep up. In the end I was carrying more than he was, so he claimed that because I was fifteen years younger than him I had an advantage and made me hit the weights for an hour before we went running. It took him five months to get me ready. I passed out top of the next course.

'He's retired now. Runs a pub near Ashton-under-Lyne. Rough pub full of Hell's Angels. He has no problems with the Angels, they're all terrified of him. I go up and see him sometimes. He's OK. His Mrs told me he's very proud of me.' Jamie sat up suddenly and reached for his whiskey tumbler, a roughness in his voice. 'Sorry girl, war stories. My glass is empty.'

Charlotte rolled away from him and reached for the bottle, conscious of his embarrassment. Pouring carefully she said, 'I have a war story too.' Then she told him about her grandfather, long dead, but still the biggest influence on her life.

9.00 p.m. 15 February 1978
BELFAST

Feet thundered on bare wooden stair treads, their owners' nostrils twitching against the sour smell of boiled cabbage and their eyes squinting in the dim light of the single bulb hung shadeless high on the landing ceiling. A door at the top of the stairs, sheathed in metal, barred the progress of the assault, but not for long. Wasting no time on useless attempts to batter the door down the leading policeman motioned to the soldier immediately behind him. Two thundering blasts shook the hallway, bringing flat lumps of plaster down from the ceiling and off the damp-streaked walls. Two .177 ball bearings fired from a 12-gauge shotgun hammered into the armoured door's hinges and ripped them away from their reinforced mountings. Men poured through the gap, shouldering the door out of their way. Inside, three men struggled to get out from under blankets thrown over mattresses on the floor. Two others armed with handguns tumbled out of a back room, still disoriented from sleep, trying to replace comprehension with reflex action.

'Armed police! Stand still, stand still. Drop your weapons now!'

One of the befuddled gunmen tried to run back into the back room, shouting incoherently. He fell across the doorway as the thin rip of a low-velocity Heckler & Koch machine pistol stitched a line of red-black spots across his back and shoulders. Two soldiers leapt across the room, lifted the other gunman bodily off the floor and threw him backwards into the hands of two of their companions following close behind them. He screamed as his arms were goosewinged and his hands pressed back and upward until they lay close behind his head, his old Makarov automatic falling to the floor.

The men on the mattresses lay still, watching a third pair of soldiers armed with the lethal little German machine pistols advance to stand over them, knowing that to move a hand could kill them. Inside the back room another man sat up in bed, waiting. Facing him the two leading soldiers had taken up positions in two of the corners, nearest the door. They stayed, all three a frozen tableau, while the outer room was emptied, the men in their underpants thrown roughly down the stairs into hands which caught and held them, guiding them at a run out into the armoured vehicle which stood, rear doors open, backed up against the doorway of the pub in Leeson Street.

Chief Inspector Peter Ewart stepped over the body of the dead man sprawled across the back room doorway, filling the space formerly occupied by the door, his thick figure massive in a long, double-breasted black overcoat. The man in the bed, up on his elbows, twisted his face into a grimace of grinning hate.

'Ewart. I might have known. Armed police my arse, you evil, black-souled bastard. It'll never stand up in court. Those pigs in the corners are SAS. I suppose you're going to murder me too?'

Ewart said nothing, but flicked a finger over his shoulder. The policeman who had led the assault appeared, a pistol in his hand. Ewart drew a .38 revolver from his pocket. As he did so the soldiers in the corners backed out of the room, pausing to drag the dead gunman out of the doorway and haul him down the stairs. Ewart stayed silent until the high-pitched whine of the Saracen armoured car's engine faded into the night. Then he spoke, his voice flat and hard.

'There's you and me and this police officer. We're armed police. I see no soldiers. I see no dead body. Get up, McAllister, you're under arrest' – Ewart stopped and picked up the dead man's Makarov – 'for possession of an unauthorised firearm and ammunition. That's ten years at least. But I could just walk out of here. Answer me a question. Where's Gerry Madden?'

'Who's Gerry Madden? I've never heard of him. Try harder, Ewart.'

'Oh I will, Sean, I will. The Intelligence boys tell me they have something special in store for you. Get out of that bed.'

Two hours later Sean McAllister stood spreadeagled against a wall, wearing nothing but an oversized army coverall, his feet and arms wide apart, bearing his full weight on his toes and fingertips. He had a double-thickness black hood over his head, blocking out the light. Earlier he had been drenched in freezing water and then led into this room, almost suffocating in its moist heat, the coverall and hood chilling and clinging to him from the dousing with the fire hose, turned on full blast, that had thrown him off his feet and tumbled him, whooping for air in the freezing blast, all over the cobbled yard of Palace barracks.

Now McAllister was hot; the hood seemed to smother him. He had lost all sense of touch, his hands and feet numb from carrying his weight. No sense of smell, for there was nothing to smell. No sense of taste, nothing to eat. Nothing to see but the inside of the black hood. A noise like hissing static filled his ears, punctuated by an odd thudding sound, like a diesel engine revving hard, driving up his heartbeat to try to match it in the absence of any other sensory input, filling him with the fear of a heart attack. He couldn't breathe, sweated, was sick inside the hood, felt panic rise and rise in him, felt hot urine sweep down his legs and his bowels open. He fell. Strong hands lifted him and threw him back against the wall.

'Sensory deprivation. Experimental technique, of course. But we know it causes total disorientation, saps the will, generates a complete loss of control over the bodily functions, creates a feeling of shame and fear. Fascinating. After a while their minds can't cope and start inventing input, nightmares and hallucinations just to keep themselves going. They can't tell if they're awake or asleep and can't separate reality from what they think they see. I've often heard them babble on about giant rats and tigers hiding in the corners. The doc says it's a bit like having a severe attack of the DTs. He believes that if we kept it up long enough we could induce irretrievable mental breakdown, a kind of permanent anxiety state. As for him in there; another three or four hours and he'll tell you anything you want to know, just to have someone to talk to. If he doesn't, just hint that you'll send him back to the wall. Then he'll talk. Good technique, isn't it?'

Gazing steadily at Sean McAllister through the soundproofed window, Peter Ewart tried hard to ignore the smooth, eager face and fruity chuckle emanating from below the bright green beret. Dear God, he thought, is this what we're reduced to, torturing men into mental illness? He turned his eyes to the sack-like shape of the Intelligence Corps officer beside him. 'I think this is sick. I think you're sick. I'm invoking police primacy here. Get him off that wall and into a cell. And get him cleaned up. I'll see him in the morning.'

Out in the cold air of night Peter Ewart felt his gorge rise. He had promised Sean McAllister something special. But not this. The cold bite of the February air in his chest reminded him of the loss of most of one lung. Almost involuntarily his right hand reached, up to trace the line of the scar across his throat. Twice Gerry Madden had tried to kill him, and hurt him badly. His hunt for Madden was becoming an obsession, a fight for survival, for next time Madden might succeed. Not wanting to go home to his sterile little bungalow Ewart reached inside his overcoat and pulled out an oversized hip flask. Half an hour later, lying fully dressed on a day cot in a transit room he took a final pull on the flask, emptying it. He leaned back and closed his eyes; he would put McAllister back on the wall if he had to.

Six hours later he was up, showered, shaved and smelling faintly of Old Spice. Sitting in a comfortable leather swivel chair he awaited the arrival of Sean McAllister. The interrogation room was familiar in size, shape and content: one leather swivel chair, an unvarnished pine plank table in front of it, one stool made out of a dining chair with its back cut off at seat level, set on the other side of the table.

Ewart straightened himself as the door opened, expecting Sean McAllister to be brought in. Instead the fat Intelligence officer stuck his head round the door, a know-it-all grin on his face. 'Wrong room, RUC. McAllister's not coming here. He'll be brought to you shortly. Come with me.'

Ewart jumped out of his chair, his face dark with anger. The fat man's lack of respect was infuriating. 'Who the hell do you think you're talking to? I'm Chief Inspector Ewart to you,' he shouted. 'Come in here right now and explain to me what's going on.'

The door opened a little further and the fat face peered round it again. ' 'Fraid not, old chap. I'm not answerable to you. If you want to see McAllister he's two doors down on your left, in the special interrogation room.' The face brightened. ' 'Bye now, RUC.'

Outside the room two doors down stood a thin, stooping figure. 'I'm Dr Wheeler. I would like to speak to you,' he said.

The voice was like the man, thin and reedy, lacking in substance. The doctor seemed nervous; he twisted his hands together and swayed from side to side. Ewart, still furious, barked, 'Talk then. What's going on here?'

The doctor paled. 'The subject is not fit for interrogation. The subject has not stood up well to the experiment.'

'Subject? Experiment? Are you talking about McAllister?' The doctor nodded. 'Then fucking well say so. What's wrong with him?'

'He is incoherent and does not respond in a normal way to normal stimuli. It's not my fault.'

Ewart forced calm on himself. The skinny medic looked as if he were about to burst into tears. 'Very well, doctor. Please tell me what you're concerned about. I was told that a couple of hours on the wall wouldn't do any real damage. Will McAllister be ready in an hour or so?'

'No. He had more than a couple of hours on the wall. You upset Major Osborne last night by ordering him about, so he took it out on the subject. McAllister only came down here an hour or so ago. He may never be ready for interrogation.'

Ewart swore. 'Where is he?'

'In here.'

The doctor threw open the door behind him. Peter Ewart took a long stride into the special room. Everything was as normal, except the colours and lighting, altered to suit subjects of sensory deprivation. The floor, ceiling and three walls of the interrogation room had been painted a non-reflective matt black, the remaining wall shiny white. Four spotlights fixed to a rack on the ceiling threw searing blue-white light directly on to the white wall. Sean McAllister sat on the stool facing the white wall. Ewart moved round to confront him, realising that to McAllister he must seem a menacing, faceless black bulk. McAllister looked terrible, a twitching shuddering wreck. Slumped over the table he kept rubbing his fingertips over its cigarette-scarred surface, feeling for each grain in the wood. His eyes shut tight against the light, he was muttering to himself. Ewart rapped sharply on the table to get his attention. McAllister screamed and threw his arms up around his ears. Startled, Ewart drew back, then tried talking to him, but every time he spoke, no matter how softly, McAllister screamed again and poured out a stream of incoherent speech, as if begging him to stop shouting. Ewart strode out of the room and collared the doctor hovering in the corridor. 'What have you done to him? He's useless.'

'Nothing, I've done nothing. He's just had too much. He can't stand light or noise, that's all.'

Ewart reached for the light switches on the wall, but the doctor stopped him. 'Don't. Please don't. If it goes dark suddenly he might pass out from fear. Here, use this.' He held out a small key. 'It fits the lock on that panel over there.

There's a rheostat in the panel. You can turn down the light slowly.'

'You do that. I'm going back in.'

The doctor jumped forward. 'Sir! Please do everything slowly. He's got no reality to hold on to and he's afraid of everything. He'll feel a desperate need for protection. If you get through to him he might even think you're his mother. Please be careful.'

Facing McAllister, Ewart pulled a thin linen handkerchief out of his pocket and drew it over McAllister's hands. The hands stopped moving over the table and snatched the smooth cloth, holding it tight at first and then caressing it. As the light dimmed McAllister seemed to relax a little, his shoulders less hunched.

Feeling sick for having any part in this, Ewart reached over the table and grasped McAllister's hands, holding them tight, willing the twitching man to pull himself together. After twenty minutes he leaned over and whispered softly, 'What's your name?' McAllister shouted, *'Sean McAllister! I'm Sean McAllister! Who are you who are you who are you?'*

'I'm a volunteer, Sean,' whispered Ewart, 'I've a message for Gerry Madden. Where's Gerry, Sean?'

'Gerry Gerry Gerry Gerry. Away for Gerry want Gerry bring bring bring. Bring bring. Bring Gerry. Kill wall.'

Ewart shut his eyes and moved to place an arm round McAllister's shoulders, to reassure and steady him. 'I'll bring Gerry, Sean. I'll bring him. He'll kill them, the ones who put you on the wall. Gerry will kill them all and take us home. Tell me where he is before they come back Sean. They'll be back soon Sean, tell me where I can find Gerry so I can bring him.'

McAllister broke into high cackling laughter, then screamed again, *'Killwall Gerry. Makestopnoise. KillGerry. KillKillKill. Makestop. KillWaaaaaallll.'*

He stood up and fell over backwards, still screaming, seeming not to feel the impact of his head on the floor.

Ewart leapt round the table, lay down and stretched himself,

145

pulling McAllister to him, cradling him in his arms. 'It's all right, Sean. It's all right. Gerry's coming. I'll go and get him now. Where is he, Sean?'

'Bone. GerryboneboneGerrybringGerry. Aaahhhh! Stop-stop–'

McAllister slumped suddenly, clinging to Ewart with both arms, sobbing, his breath coming in great whoops between the sobs. Ewart signalled, waving an arm at the square of black glass set into the wall. Two men ran in and pulled McAllister away from him, screaming and struggling.

Ewart stood up and marched out of the interrogation room, rigidly under control. Inside the comms room across the courtyard he clamped both hands around the shoulders of the young soldier sitting with his back to him, in front of the communications desk. 'Get the brigadier for me, son. Put it through the speakers.'

'Brigadier, this is Peter Ewart. I have reliable evidence that Gerry Madden is in the Bone. I need a cordon and search immediately.'

Brigadier Harry George, Commander 39 Infantry Brigade reacted fast, his Sloane Square drawl showing no sign of urgency. 'The Belfast Resident Battalion will be deployed in ten minutes. Two Companies of 7/10 UDR will be in support in fifteen. Meet me at Flax Street mill. Goodbye.'

In the ops room of the battalion headquarters deep in the derelict linen mill Ewart and George stared morosely into cups of cold coffee. The Bone, an area of back-to-back terraced houses central to the Ardoyne ghetto, just a few hundred yards up the Crumlin Road from the old mill, had been surrounded and thoroughly searched. Every man over twenty in the ghetto had been subjected to search and a P–check of his identity. Madden had not been found and the whole area was now in the throes of a savage riot.

'Fuck it, Peter. Madden could have had any number of aliases set up just in case this ever happened. Is there nobody in this city who can reliably identify him?'

'Nobody that could would, Brigadier. I was hoping to capture somebody on the staff of their First Battalion and put the screws on him to finger Madden. But we got nobody. The whole bloody lot of them must have gone on the run as soon as they realised we had Sean McAllister.'

'What about McAllister? Couldn't he have helped?'

Ewart sighed. 'He's a gibbering wreck. Can't even stand up. He had too long on the wall.'

'What wall? What are you talking about?'

'Sensory deprivation, Brigadier. I imagined you knew about it. It's an experimental technique to prepare suspects for interrogation. McAllister had a couple of hours of it before I ordered him taken to the cells for a rest. But the officer running the show kept him on the wall throughout the night. The doctor reckons he'd only been taken down an hour or so before I interrogated him. McAllister's a murdering bastard, but his mind's gone. It'll be months before he's even half right.'

The brigadier's face tightened. 'I've heard of SD. Its use is against the law, here and anywhere else.' He paused. 'It's a dirty little war, Peter. I am not concerned about McAllister's health, mental or otherwise. But I am concerned that someone failed to obey your order and robbed us of a potentially useful informant. What is the name of that officer?'

'A Major Osborne I believe, sir.'

The brigadier stood up, stalked over to the Comms desk and picked up a telephone fitted with a voice lock. 'This is the Commander. Get me the chief G 2, now.'

Within seconds the voice of the Intelligence Corps lieutenant-colonel responsible for uniformed Intelligence Corps personnel in the 39 brigade area boomed out of speakers fixed above the Comms desk. 'Wilson. What can I do for you, sir?'

The brigadier answered quietly. 'Colonel, have you at any time authorised the use of sensory deprivation techniques in my brigade area?'

'No sir.'

'Are you aware that I might require their use?'

'No, sir. SD is proscribed by international law. Were you or anyone else to require its use I would not and could not obey you. If you are considering the use of SD I must strongly advise you against it.'

'Good. We are of like mind. Do you have a Major Osborne on your staff?'

'No, sir. Major Osborne is an adviser to the Northern Ireland Office at Stormont. He is attached to my staff for administrative purposes only.'

'You are to place Major Osborne in close arrest pending court martial on a charge of disobeying a direct order. Other charges may follow. SD techniques have been in use here, under Osborne's direction. You are to investigate who authorised his use of SD techniques in my brigade area and are to order their suspension immediately, regardless of the seniority of the authority concerned. No further experimentation is to take place in the 39 brigade area without my written authority. You are to interview Osborne and prepare an oral brief on every occasion these techniques have been used, quoting the conditions and authority under which they have been employed. On completion of your investigation you are to order that Osborne be relieved of his post with immediate effect. Osborne is to be out of Ulster within twelve hours. You are to deliver your oral brief in person to me at 0700 hours tomorrow. Are there any questions?'

'No sir, your orders are clear. Is there anything else?'

The brigadier thought for a moment. 'Yes. There must be a doctor involved, probably not from the Royal Army Medical Corps. Call my brigade medical officer. Inform him that I require him to be in attendance at your briefing tomorrow and will be obliged for his informed opinion. Call the head of Army Legal Services at HQ Northern Ireland and request his attendance at your briefing. I want to know how we stand should we be accused of illegal methods of interrogation. That is all.'

Peter Ewart, listening, allowed the breath to whistle through his teeth, thinking 'That's power with a capital P'. One three-minute phone call and God only knew how many careers teetered on the brink of the abyss.

'Those people and a lot of others are going to be up all night, Brigadier. You know this must have had ministerial approval?'

'Yes, Peter. But one day soon it's going to hit the headlines. I'm damned if my brigade is going to carry the can for some shortsighted politician. Shooting mad dogs is one thing. Torturing them is quite another. Let's go for a drink.'

1 October 1980
DUBLIN

Seven men sat at the long table. Padraig Hanna, President of the Army Council of the Provisional IRA, and as far as the IRA was concerned, legal President of a 32 County Republic of Ireland, listened with growing irritation to his chief of staff.

'I really don't see what the problem is, Padraig. We've weathered this sort of thing before. I've issued my orders.' Short, thick bodied, with the wide-fingered hands of a butcher and the purple mottled face of a frustrated, rage-filled man long overdue a massive stroke, Turlough O'Donnell fought for his political life.

'Surely to God the boys in the North can handle a few informers,' he went on. 'After they've seen to that all they have to do is keep on stiffing as many Brits as possible and blowing every factory they see into dust. We'll bomb the North back into the Stone Age and leave nothing for the Brits to rule. It's what we've always done.'

Padraig Hanna shifted in his seat, irritation clear on his big, weatherbeaten face, his Kerry brogue edged with the iron that had seen him through fifteen years of British and Irish jails. 'That's enough, Turlough, you've had your say. The Army Council will listen to the representative of the northern brigades. Keep silent

149

now.' He turned to the man on his left. 'Mickeen, would you be good enough to call the man in?'

Mike Jordan, a veteran of the 1950s campaign and the son of a man who had fought with Patrick Pearse in 1916, got up and moved stiffly, bending to lock the knee of his artificial leg, the legacy of three machine gun bullets which had smashed his right thigh beyond repair. 'I will Pat. I've had enough of this nonsense.'

He stopped limping halfway down the length of the great room and pointed backwards. 'Turlough O'Donnell, fine was the blood you shed for Ireland, but I add my counsel to that of the President. I will not hear a word more of your "stiff the Brits" outpourings. You've had six years as chief of staff. The war in the North is a shambles and we're losing it. You will give the man his say. He might have a good idea or two. The Army Council will decide.'

He moved on and pulled the great oak double doors of the council chamber apart. 'Commandant Madden. Come in.'

Gerry Madden did not rise immediately, but waited until he heard Jordan's uneven footsteps fade, giving him a chance to get back to his seat. It was a minor courtesy, but Jordan would notice it. Once through the big double doors Madden stopped to get his bearings.

A vast expanse of dark green carpet stretched in front of him. To his right, near the doors, sat a female secretary, there to record the debates and decisions of the Army Council. To his left four huge windows ran from floor level to the twenty-foot-high ceiling. At one time, some said, it had been a private ballroom, fit to hold a thousand dancers. Madden believed it. All around the pale green walls hung portraits, dark with age, in ornate gilt frames. From the centre line of the ceiling hung three chandeliers, a matched pair either side of the room's main glory; two and a half tons of Waterford crystal, stunning in its wedding cake symmetry. At the far end of the old ballroom a mahogany table, built to seat 200, stretched across the width of the room. Dwarfed behind it sat the seven members of the Army Council of the Provisional Irish Republican Army, Padraig Hanna, President, in the centre. Before starting the long walk down to them Madden flexed his fingers and composed himself, determined not to be intimidated by the room or the people in it. Today was to be his day. He would announce himself from here.

Adopting the traditional 'at attention' position Madden called 'Commandant Gerard Madden, Commandant of the Belfas—' He stopped, confused, his voice booming back at him, sounding like a shout in a cave. Damn it, he thought, the bloody acoustics! He gripped his hands into tighter fists, feeling the fingernails bite into his palms, mentally kicking himself. He should have paid more attention: why else would the secretary be near the door? Because she could hear every word spoken at the table from there. He continued in a normal speaking voice, his face and neck suffused with embarrassment 'Commandant of the Belfast Brigade, reporting as ordered'.

Padraig Hanna suppressed a chuckle. 'Come and sit down, Gerry. And please forgive us our little joke. We never warn anybody about the sound effects in here. It's one of the few things we have to laugh about these days. Come and sit down, there.' He pointed to a chair set squarely facing him, but still twenty feet from the table.

Gerry Madden still stood silent, at attention. The secretary stood up and whispered to him 'Go on down there Commandant, they're waiting.'

Madden strode firmly down the centre of the room, picked up the chair set out for him and carrying it with him took up a place directly opposite Padraig Hanna, close enough to put his elbows on the table. As he sat down he smiled, a broad disarming smile that never came near his eyes. 'I'm sorry, gentlemen. I'm a bit deaf. High-velocity weapons. Armalites and Woodmasters. But you would know all about that, of course.'

Turlough O'Donnell was on his feet instantly, rage purpling

his face. 'You cheeky bastard! We were stiffing Brits before the best half of you ran down your Da's leg!'

Madden smiled again. Not a man on the other side of the table, including the chief of staff, had heard a shot fired in anger in more than a quarter of a century, and they were sensitive about it. O'Donnell's outburst was a mistake: it confirmed to Madden that it was the Army Council, not he, who was on the defensive.

Padraig Hanna, eyes hooded below thick, bushy eyebrows, was also angered, but the hints coming out of the North seemed verified: Gerry Madden was not a man to be taken lightly. Hanna sought to regain the initiative, keeping his voice low and soft.

'Sit down, Turlough. All right Gerry, the fun's over. Your report if you please.'

'Gentlemen, a moment of preparation if I may.' Before anyone could comment he rose, a 'thank you' on his lips, and turned his head to address the distant secretary. 'Call my people, please.'

Two men hurried into the room, overawed by it and their presence before the high command. Quickly they set up a screen and a vufoil machine, placed a box of transparencies beside the machine and withdrew as silently as they had come. Without further preamble Madden launched into his presentation, using flow charts, pie diagrams and block indicators to punctuate and illustrate his talk. The Army Council, surprised by the unaccustomed method of reporting, sat silent throughout one and a half hours of Madden's ruthlessly objective presentation.

He closed with a summary. 'So, gentlemen, to sum up. Over the past year we have lost 39 volunteers and 8 officers killed in action. We have lost a further 117 volunteers and 14 officers captured and incarcerated by the Crown forces. We have lost 348 volunteers and one officer through desertion, mainly to the UK mainland. Over the same period we have lost 4,800 pounds of high explosive of varying types, 680 rifles and handguns, nearly a quarter of a million rounds of ammunition, 12 hand-held rocket launchers with 86 armour-piercing rounds and one .50 Browning machine gun, complete with its tripod. We have also lost two major arms shipments intercepted on the high seas.' Madden paused to let his words sink in. 'On the other hand we have killed four British Army regular soldiers, thirteen RUC police and police reservists, six UDR soldiers, two of them retired, one prison warder, the wife and daughter of another prison warder, 248 other civilians – 86 of them minors – and fifteen informers. Our bombing campaign is responsible for most of the civilian casualties. There are questions to be answered. I am ready.'

Mike Jordan spoke first. 'You have more to say. Don't play games with us, Madden. Get on with it.'

'Sir. We have lost a large number of our own people for a variety of reasons. Our people are measuring Brit success against our own. They are looking at the failure of the campaign in the cities. They see us forced to concentrate in the border areas where we are vulnerable to all kinds of Brit Intelligence gathering. Their gut feeling is that every time they set out on operations the probability is that they will die or spend the next twenty years in a British jail. So they desert. The morale of those remaining is at an all-time low.'

Padraig Hanna stood up, motioning both Turlough O'Donnell and Mike Jordan to remain in their seats. The other members of the Army Council stirred, except one. Malachy Young sat cold and calculating, waiting. An accountant by profession he alone had seen the writing on the wall, its path traced by the finger of the man from the North.

Hanna asked, 'What are you telling us, Gerry? Diagrams and numbers, talk of desertion. Talk of Brit Intelligence. What's the bottom line?'

Before Madden could speak Malachy Young broke in. 'Commandant Madden has shown us much, but not all. I have followed with interest his presentation and await his final diagram. If I am not much mistaken it will be a critical path analysis of our progress towards military victory in the North. Please proceed, Commandant.'

Padraig Hanna, at a loss, sat down.

'Thank you, sir.' Madden's voice was cold and calm. 'I do have one last vufoil. The red line represents Brit military success in terms of killed and captured, men and equipment. The blue line represents Brit regulars killed or wounded. The black line shows the level we have always believed we need to achieve to drive them out.' Madden flicked on his last card. From a point set at 1970 the lines diverged, the black line forming the basis of success to be achieved: it sat in a horizontal line set at 200 British regulars killed or wounded each year. The blue line never came near it, but declined further and further away from it. The red line rose further and further up from it. At the year 1982 the red line went off the graph and the blue to zero.

'That's it, gentlemen.' Madden's Belfast accent grated harder than it had before. 'By the autumn of 1982 we will be defeated.' He sat back and waited.

Most of the men in front of him came up shouting, damning him for his lack of belief in the Cause. Silent, relaxed, he waited, certain that the question he needed and had prepared for must come. It took a little while, but then Malachy Young stood up and stepped back from his chair. Deliberately he pushed the chair back to the table. The action, simple enough, had the effect of a gunshot: Young had opted out of the debate, relinquished his seat on the Army Council. He could only reoccupy it by invitation, but still held his vote until he left the room.

'What the hell are you doing, Malachy? We need you here today. What's going on?' Padraig Hanna's voice came as near to shrillness as the bigness of it allowed.

'The man has something more to say, Padraig. I think it's something the Army Council won't want to hear. But I want to hear it.' Young fixed pale, almost colourless eyes on Gerry Madden. 'Tell me, Commandant, your view of what we must do to avoid defeat and then how we may achieve victory?'

Madden felt the muscles at the base of his neck relax. He had an ally, a man who had foreseen the wind of change and awaited its messenger. He stood up and moved away from the table, just far enough to hold the eye of any man he focused on.

'We will be defeated. That is a fact, a statistical inevitability, should we carry on as we do at present. To avoid defeat there must be radical change. To achieve victory there must be an internal revolution. The structure of our army served us well in the twenties and before. It caused us disaster in the fifties, yet we are still using it on the threshold of the eighties.

'We must drop the idea of thousands of volunteers banging away at the British. We must adapt to the urban environment. We must have small active service units, totally independent of each other, assisted by Intelligence gathering and support organisations. The ASUs must swim in a sea of information provided by others. I've tried it in Belfast and it works. We must retrench before we can move forward. To avoid defeat we must restructure the Provisional IRA. To win the war we must be able to fight the war in Ireland, to fight the war in England. If necessary we must be prepared to fight the war wherever British troops are to be found. We must abandon the huge and very expensive effort we have made to win the popular vote, at least for the time being.

'First the Armalite, then the ballot box, when the people have seen what we can do. On the military front we must fight with smaller, better forces. We must abandon the military battle that pits us one for one against a well-equipped, well-trained and well-informed professional army. We must adopt a true guerrilla approach, striking and running, preserving ourselves. We must fight, fight hard, our active service units hidden in the mass of the people. Then we might achieve victory. At worst we can never be defeated.' Madden stopped abruptly and sat down, waiting.

The Army Council sat silent, overwhelmed by the cold logic and appalling ruthlessness of the young man from the North. He had made no excuses, no apologies for the failures, had brushed aside as irrelevant the dreadful civilian casualties caused by O'Donnell's bombing campaign. Without mercy and with deliberate cruelty he had savaged the direction of the war and by implication those charged with its direction.

Padraig Hanna wavered, tempted to order Madden's arrest and the removal of his command. Turlough O'Donnell glared ferociously at Madden, determined to have him shot at the earliest opportunity for his lack of respect for the lawful government of Ireland, the Army Council itself. Malachy Young stood silently behind his chair.

Mike Jordan broke the deadlock, his voice soft, almost inaudible. 'You are proposing fundamental changes as well as being the bearer of bad news, Commandant. You have attacked every member of this Council personally, since we are collectively responsible for the guidance of the Cause. Are you calling on us to pass a vote of no confidence in ourselves? Or are you telling us that the fighting units in the North are going to split the Cause yet again?'

Madden took his time in answering. Although he was in great danger, he felt committed by his earlier words as well as encouraged by Hanna's indecision and Young's tacit support. He decided to go for broke. 'Each of you must examine his own conscience. It is a fact that the fighting strength of the Cause is in the North and that the war could be carried on, admittedly with difficulty, without assistance from Dublin. But I have consulted my colleagues in Armagh and Derry. We are of one mind: the Cause must not be split. There is, however, a need for change.'

'Are you proposing that we all, including the President, resign in favour of yourself and anybody you choose to appoint?' Jordan's voice had taken on a silky quality, edged with warning.

Madden, for the first time, looked shaken. 'No sir, I am not.' He thought for a moment. 'The President's position is unassailable until he decides to retire. But I feel that he has been badly advised.'

Jordan smiled a wry, careful smile. Madden's answers were a masterpiece of political backstabbing. If Padraig Hanna chose to retire, Madden would be a challenger for his presidency. If

Hanna stayed on he would have to accede to Madden's demand for changes at the top. Or Madden, despite his stated support for the unity of the Cause, would lead the men of the North in a breakaway.

'What then, do you propose for yourself?'

'I propose nothing, sir. I have said what needs to be done. We can do it. It is for the Army Council to decide if I am to be permitted to play a leading role in the restructuring of the Cause.'

Near the end of his tether in the tension crackling like the edges of a thunderstorm in the great room, Madden decided to end it, one way or the other. 'Are you prepared to offer your own resignation?'

The question exploded like a bomb on the table. Madden's audacity was unbelievable! How could he stand there and time after time insult and face down the Army Council?

Padraig Hanna expected an outburst of rage, wounded pride and threats against Madden. So did Turlough O'Donnell. None came. A chair scraped the parquet floor behind the table. Mike Jordan joined Malachy Young in standing behind his chair. 'I think you are a very brave or a very stupid young man, Gerry Madden. You may yet suffer for your arrogance. I also think you are right in what you say, though I deplore your choice of words. But I am convinced. I am prepared to resign rather than preside over defeat.'

Madden looked at him, careful not to smile, allowing his gratefulness for Jordan's support to show through a small inclination of his head. Beneath the cold exterior Madden's heart was banging away as if he had run ten miles: sweat gathered under his armpits and slid coldly down his sides. He felt bubbles of it pepper his upper lip and resisted a strong urge to wipe it away. *No weakness must show, lead or die.*

Padraig Hanna's great leonine head swung to his right as he heard another chair scrape the floor. Art Connery, leader of the Cork and south-west branches, stood behind his chair.

As successor of Michael Collins himself Connery's name carried great weight. Hanna considered: three standing, three sitting. His was the casting vote. On his left he felt the beseeching eyes of O'Donnell. Kill this presumptuous bastard and fight on in the old way, the eyes said. Hanna procrastinated, hoping that one of the standing men would break with tradition and sit down again, or that another man would stand up and relieve him of the need to cast his vote. He bowed his head, trying to think through the extreme tension that filled the room. A deep sobbing reached him; the secretary, a good and loyal girl, was unable to cope with the stress and emotional charge of the past two hours.

Hanna chose his side. 'As President of the Provisional Army Council and Head of State of the legal government of Ireland I feel it would be cowardly of me to retire at this time. Much needs to be done. I must accept the realities of the situation we find ourselves in and am most grateful to Commandant Madden for his advice. I will accept that advice. Those that cannot may resign with their characters unblemished.'

Two more men stood up, trying to ignore both the agonised roar of Turlough O'Donnell and the audible sigh of relief that Gerry Madden, despite himself, just could not suppress.

O'Donnell took defeat badly. Throwing his chair back against the wall he stamped down the room, throwing threats and curses over his shoulder: he would lead his own people out of the Cause; he would see to it that Madden did not live a day longer than he could prevent; the Council were cowards.

Padraig Hanna motioned his colleagues to sit down, then he called for a vote. Less than a minute later Gerry Madden took his seat on the Army Council of the Provisional Irish Republican Army, confirmed in his appointment as their new chief of staff. His first Order in Council was that a separate Northern Command, officered by people loyal to him and him alone, be established forthwith. His second was that PIRA's political wing should abandon their current campaign in favour of his new grassroots approach. His third was that Turlough O'Donnell be advised that should he attempt to carry out any of his threats he would be declared an enemy of the Cause and pay the extreme penalty.

One hour later Madden called Jack Agnew, his second-in-command in Belfast. 'Jack? OK? This is Gerry. I'm chief of staff ... Thanks ... Take over as commandant of the Belfast Brigade ... You deserve it ... Be prepared to act as second-in-command to Dennis Hughes in Armagh. I have just appointed Dennis as quartermaster-general for Northern Command as planned. His brigade operations officer will take over from him.

'Yes, we're on our way, Jack. One thing for you. The lists we made before I left for Dublin ... Yes those, the colour-coded lists ... Put them into effect: the blue ones are people we need for the ASUs; pull them off the street and send them down to Drogheda; I'll meet them there and tell them what's happening ... OK, that's fine, the Curlew Hotel ... The yellow lists are the Cumann na mBan, the women we can trust. The green are people we need to dump, they're a liability, just tell them they're being held in reserve ... the pink are Brit informers, suspected informers or just idle. Nut all the informers we're sure of, plus some of the suspects at random. Kneecap the rest ... I don't give a fuck what you think, do as I say ... Don't forget that Brit ex-squaddie living in Sorella Street ... I know he's married to your wife's sister. For fuck's sake Jack I don't want to hear this! So what if he retired ten years ago? Kill him. Make sure he dies hard. Let them all know for sure that any of our people joining the Brit army can never come home ... this is a fucking war we're fighting here ... Don't let me down, Jack, I'd hate to think you were unreliable. Remember your oath and obey me. Goodbye.'

Siobhan McCaillim talked quietly with her mother. All over the Republican areas of the city men were dying or screaming from gunshot wounds to the head or legs. The British Army, bewildered at the sudden outbreak of violence, was out in force, blundering about without any real Intelligence guidance, hoping to take advantage of whatever internal split was racking the Provisionals, trying to find out what was happening, who was killing and kneecapping whom, and why. Peter Ewart knew why: overnight he was losing a network of informants painstakingly built up over years of effort. As the soldiers rushed about his city like blindfolded bullocks he sat peacefully, sipping Jameson's straight from the bottle, weeping to himself and knowing that Gerry Madden had come of age, that his personal war was only just beginning.

Two years with the Cumann na mBan had sharpened Siobhan McCaillim, two years in which she had longed for a more active role, volunteering to join first the Markets, then the Falls, then the Andersonstown active service units. But her mother had always denied her, had sent her to train as a nurse in the Musgrave Park hospital. Siobhan had had to find other ways of amusing herself, mainly by attracting the attentions of any man in sight, playing the innocent, vulnerable little girl, deliberately and cruelly winding men into a state of confusion and frustration. Mostly she kept her knees together – unless the game was fun enough to make sex interesting – if it gave her the chance to get in deeper, do more damage, gave her a greater sense of power and control. She did not hate men: she did exactly the same to any woman vulnerable to her. She punished them all for allowing her to get inside their heads.

Siobhan had once watched, fascinated, a French-made wildlife documentary in which a fisherman had bloodied the sea, caught a shark, opened it up without killing it then thrown it back overboard to watch it tear at its own entrails as they streamed around it. When other sharks came the fisherman drove them all into a feeding frenzy while he sat back and laughed as they fought and ripped lumps out of each other. The film crew had held the fisherman up as the ultimate barbarian. Siobhan had understood him completely: he was having fun, just didn't realise it was even more fun if you could use people instead of sharks. It was just his game, like hers, nothing serious.

'It's said Gerry Madden is taking over from old Turlough, Mammy. Things are changing. What do you think?'

'Aye, daughter, they are. I've been watching Gerry Madden. He's the one. It'll be a wee while yet. You're young and Gerry Madden is full of himself. We'll watch and wait our chance. Don't worry, he'll get tired. They all do. I'll tell you when Madden is ready.'

'All right. But it's not nice to plot against the chief of staff.'

'No, acushla, it's not nice. It's a war for Ireland and we have to count our own men among the enemy. The bastards with their priests have kept us big with their kids and small with their Hail Marys long enough. They've talked big and fought small. It's time for us women to take a hand. You're the one. You know that. You're the new Maeve. Fuck them. Feed them. Use them when you're ready. Madden is the target, Siobhan. You might only get one chance. You have to be ready. Get him and you've got the country.'

'Aye. Gerry Madden it is, Mammy. You tell me when.'

Out in her mother's kitchen Siobhan smiled to herself at all this Maeve, Warrior Queen, Chosen One thing of her mother's. All shite. I'm not Maeve, I'm Siobhan McCaillim and by Christ they'll all know about me. Power over stupid men was one thing, her mother's revenge a part of it. She could enjoy that. But what mattered was having power enough to strike real fear into people. Power over everything and everybody. Compared to that, money and all it could buy were nothing. Siobhan was sure Gerry Madden had power now and she wanted it from him. She imagined the feeling: the power to sit back and turn whole cities into antheaps of people running for their lives, hiding under beds, power enough to break the hearts of your enemies and terrifying your friends, all with a few words. Deep in her abdomen the little softness grew, flowering inside her, her aching need for the power to horrify, terrify, wield power over life and death opening her. She squeezed her thighs together. Gerry Madden could wait. She cast her mind around, searching. Yes. Seamus Long. If anybody was out kneecapping he would be among them. She knew where to find him.

'I'm going out, Mammy. I won't be long.'

The man in the dirty entry behind Sorella Street was crawling about, keening softly from the pain, the blood from his wrecked knees smearing the dirt as he crawled. A heavy boot reached out and hooked itself over him, turning him on to his back. His eyes were shut.

'Open your eyes, Brit. Say your last contrition.' But the eyes squeezed tighter, refusing to look. The boot dug into one of his legs, bending the knee. The ex-soldier screamed. 'Don't, don't. Oh Jesus! Jesus! Please God. Please don't.'

'Open your eyes I said.' He did, wracked with fear and pain.

'Ask her like I told you, Brit.' The boot was poised over his knee again.

'Bitch. Fucking bitch. All right, all right. Sweet Jesus have mercy on me. Do it. Do it you fucking bitch. Get it over.'

'That's not nice. Don't talk dirty in front of a wee girl. She's only eighteen. Ask nice.' The foot crunched down, a searing, red-hot agony. 'Oh. Mother of Christ pray for me. Do it please. Please do it. My legs. Please shoot me, Miss. Please. No more ... Oh my God I am heartily sorry for all my sins ...'

The man in the heavy boots handed the gun to his companion. She moved slowly, almost caressingly, straddling the man on the ground, sitting on him, sliding the gun barrel over the weeping, praying man's face, forcing it between his teeth. Shuddering, she pulled the trigger, her whole body shaking with the lust of it. She moved to get up but could not, could hardly breathe. The man with the boots grinned and lifted her, spinning her, lifting her skirt. She clung to him, letting it happen, paying as agreed.

She dropped her skirt and watched him lean against the old brick wall that was streaked with dirt and age. The gun was still in her hand. He looked at her, holding his hand out for the gun. Siobhan held the gun up, smiled sweetly, stepped in close and shot him in the chest, then again in the back of his head, as he fell. No witnesses. No tales. By morning her mother would have the gun back with the ASU quartermaster, rescued from the scene by her daughter, a frightened girl who had heard it all but seen nothing in the dark, hadn't been able to identify the third man she had heard running from the entry, the one who had shot Seamus Long.

Chapter Nine

0815 a.m. 13 June 1982
GMT (Zulu time)

LONDON

Major Charlotte Aitken smiled tightly as she returned the salute of the MoD policeman guarding the entrance to Fleet Headquarters in Northwood. Deep below the building, in the complex built to house the Admiralty in times of war, she joined others in the green and brown of the army and the light blue of the RAF sprinkled among the dark blue of the navy. Joint HQ they called it, the command centre of Operation CORPORATE, known to the general public as the Falklands war. J2, the Intelligence branch, lived in a series of air conditioned concrete hutches where fluorescent lighting burned night and day. Almost always J2 knew everything first. Satellite communications links allowed those authorised or senior enough to talk to commanders on the spot, jumping across nearly 9,000 miles with only a half-second delay. The Prime Minister herself could, if she wanted to, ask a platoon commander crouching on a wet hillside what he was doing and why.

This morning, as she read quickly through the night's signal reports in preparation for taking over duty from the night shift Charlotte Aitken felt the weight that had prevented her sleeping move from low in her stomach to the centre of her chest. The attack that had been planned for the night had gone ahead, despite advice from JHQ to Downing Street. Charlotte felt the dread creep through her. It was Jamie's battalion that had been earmarked to make the assault.

But during the night Downing Street had spoken: the signal message was clear and unequivocal: *The assault on the Crab*

Ridges is to proceed as planned. A victory, the more startling the better, is politically necessary to maintain diplomatic pressure on Argentina and to reassure British public opinion. Two frigates are to offer Naval Gunfire by night if the Paras need it. A full Commando of Royal Marines is to be made ready to continue the assault in daylight, backed up by Harrier ground attack aircraft and a third frigate if the Paras fail.

In other words, the Cabinet wanted a British victory against superior forces to intimidate the Argentine government. If the Paras failed by night the Royal Marines, fresh against a tired and depleted enemy and with overwhelming fire support, would overcome any Argentinian counterattack and succeed by day.

The Paras, the signal message continued, *if defeated, may retreat as the Royal Marines advance.*

Flicking ever more rapidly through the signals Charlotte cursed the Cabinet for their ignorance. She, like any other professional soldier, knew that Paras did not retreat; it was foreign to every instinct they possessed. Paras, she thought, are not like ordinary soldiers. Once committed to the attack their colonel could lose control of them if he ordered them to retreat. She imagined her Jamie, brave as the best and stronger than most still fighting on some freezing hill, refusing to give in, no matter what the odds. He'd said it to her so many times, smiling with his eyes, the steel in them shining bright with pride in his Regiment. 'Paras never give in.' She felt an urge to drop the papers from her hands and scream her rage and fear for all to hear. Page after page streamed through her trembling hands, transmissions from Task Force HQ, Op CORPORATE, telling the story of the assault, report by report, all in Zulu Time. Charlotte checked again: Falkland Islands local time was five hours behind GMT, Zulu Time. The first signal was timed at 130200Z; two a.m. on the 13th Zulu. Seven a.m. GMT, my time, 8 a.m. Alpha time, British Summer Time.

130200Z Jun 82. 1 Para X SL. Aslt on 1 Para objective begun.

Charlotte shut her eyes tight, thinking fast through the jargon: It is the First Battalion. They're over their start line. Jamie's fighting. What time? 2100 hours local time, full dark in southern winter. That's something. Keep safe keep safe keep safe Jamie.

130300Z Jun 82. 1 Para taking cas from dug in machine guns and en arty but have gained crests of both Crab Ridges. 7 RHA firing CB in DS. 1 Para adv along crests. Our Paras are being hit by machine guns and artillery. 7th Regiment Royal Horse Artillery are firing Counter Battery at the enemy artillery in Direct Support of the Paras. Good Good Good. I hope they kill all of the bastards trying to kill my Jamie. We're winning, our Paras are advancing. Yes!

130315Z Jun 82. 1 Para aslt slowing. Adv continues. 1 Para inflicting heavy cas on en inf. Uh Uh! They're slowing down, but still advancing and giving the Argie infantry fighting them a beating. Mixed thoughts. The fighting must be very heavy. Jamie Jamie, keep safe keep safe my darling.

130410Z Jun 82. 1 Para aslt on Crab Ridges breaking down. 42 Cdo RM prep for adv. Oh My God! It's not going well. Yes, stop them stop them. Jamie's done enough. Let 42 Commando's Marines go in, please. Where the hell are the Navy? Why aren't the frigates firing to help our Gunners?

130440Z Jun 82. 'A' Coy 1 Para held on West Crab Ridge. 'B' Coy adv slow on East Crab Ridge. 1 Para cas heavy. 42 Cdo prep to mov at first lt. You bastards. You callous bastards. Charlotte counted quickly, fingers trembling. My Paras are taking heavy casualties. My Paras are being killed. Get the Marines in now. Now. First light is four hours away. The Argies will counterattack. Fuck you, get the Marines in to help my Paras. Get the frigates firing. My Paras have done their bit. Jamie Jamie Jaaamie!

130500Z Jun 82. 1 Para aslt stopped. 'A' Coy 1 Para digging in. Bde Comd about to order 1 Para to hold gd gained. Yes you bastard. Let them stop attacking and dig in before the Argies counterattack. Get the Marines in now. Keep safe, Jamie, keep safe. Where are those bloody frigates?

130520Z Jun 82. En inf counterattacking on West Crab Ridge. 1 Para req NGF on West Crab Ridge. 7 RHA to switch to close sp. 1 Para prep to continue aslt. What? What the hell are you doing? Why Naval Gunfire now? Where have those bloody frigates been all this time? Get out of there. This is crazy ... crazy ... I SEE I SEE I SEE.

Charlotte's head flicked up, eyes shining as her mind caught a lateral thought, caught in a flash of insight the Para Commanding Officer's intention. Why hadn't Task Force HQ realised it? The Paras were going to win, without the Marines' help. The Paras' Commanding Officer had fought as far forward as possible, using his Gunner support to fight off the Argentinian artillery, not to pound the enemy trenches. The Argentinians would think that was all the artillery he had. When they saw the Paras digging in they would counterattack, get out of their trenches and attack the 'defeated' Paras. The Argie infantry would be out in the open, caught without protection, then BOOM they would get two frigates and 7 RHA concentrating fire on them. Then the Paras lying doggo would get in amongst them again. *I Love You I Love You, you clever clever bastard, whoever you are. Keep safe, Jamie my darling, keep safe.*

Charlotte glanced at the clock on the wall, set for Zulu, Greenwich Mean Time: 08.30. That was 03.30, Falkland Islands Time. The last dispatch had been at twenty minutes past midnight, Falklands time. There had been no dispatches for over three hours. Why? It could only be because the Paras had destroyed everything in front of them. Or ... Charlotte felt a clutch of fear grip her heart, weaken her knees. *We should have heard by now.* What's *happening?* The run of battle, according to the signals, was clear. *But there's nothing about the Naval Gunfire the Paras asked for. Oh Jesus. The Navy have let them down. The Gunners couldn't do it on their own. It's over, over. My Paras have been defeated. Christ, Jamie, where are you?*

EAST CRAB RIDGE
130520ZJUN82

'What can you see, sir? The boys're gettin' a stonkin' up there, what the fuck's happenin'?'

Private Coleridge turned his face, frightened, tired and streaked with chocolate brown camouflage cream, and looked over his shoulder. Five feet away Jamie Lappin leaned out of the boghole he shared with Coleridge, half-frozen bog water seeping like congealing black blood around the outline his body had pressed into the sodden peat. Both men, engrossed in B Company's battle raging above them, ignored the water and the cold; death, if it came, would hurtle roaring out of the sky. They had learned that the old soldiers' tale claiming the shells you could hear wouldn't kill you was bullshit, and anyway it didn't apply to mortar bombs coming straight down at you.

It was not quite pitch dark, a sliver of moon showing as a faint grey glow above and through the rainclouds. Rain pelted down in soft, semi-solid lumps as big as billiard balls, the cursed, ever-present wind shattering and scattering it into a deceptive near-frozen spray that curled and crept its way into every fold of cloth and wrinkle of skin, the odd unbroken lump beating the men and the short, sheep-cropped tussock grass flat into the peat. Most of what the two men could see were the flashes of exploding heavy artillery shells and mortar bombs, reflected and diffused by the rain, and grey clouds streaming from smoke grenades thrown by their comrades to blind and confuse their enemies. Long strings of red tracer bullets, belt fed in 200-round ribbons into the machine guns supporting the Paras' attack, curled into the Argentinian positions, ricocheting at all angles into the dark all along the ridge their company was attacking. Compared to the artillery display the tracer streams seemed puny, but between every two tracer bullets there were four other copper-coated bringers of peace hidden in the stream.

Off to the west, on the other side of the valley, the same was happening on the twin ridge being attacked by A Company. Quick, small flashes — shrapnel grenades — flared here and there, flickering like fireflies in the dark. The noise was horrendous, pounding into the two men in the hole, a mixture of heavy explosions, machine gun fire, the banshee wails of the ricochets and a weird, incessant chanting carried on the wind. 'AIIRRBOORRNNE AAHH! AAIIIRRRBOOORRRNNNE ΛΛΛIIHH! AAAIIIIRRRRBOOOORRRRNNNNE AAAAHHHH! A deep, savage, drawn-out fighting song that chilled the heart and turned the guts of men to water, over and over and over again, never ending. The ground underneath the soldiers seemed to live and breathe, trembling and twitching as shock waves from the artillery came through it in even, pulsating tremors. Jamie Lappin lowered his night glasses and glanced at his radioman, a nineteen-year-old from Carlisle. The lad was nervous, a compound of fear and exhaustion; he needed reassurance, Para style.

'What the fuck's wrong with you, Coleridge? We're winning, no problem. That chanting is just our lads putting the shits up the Argies while they dig themselves in. Mind your own fucking business and stop asking stupid fucking questions. You just do your job and help me here. Get on your radio and send Corporal Anderson forward, or we'll have the OC on the net shouting for ammo. If you don't get Anderson moving in two minutes I'll rip your fucking ears off. When you've done that get your stove out and make yourself a brew. I'm going up there to take our snipers out; listen out for me and do what I tell you, sharpish. OK?'

Private Coleridge relaxed and reached for the handset of his radio, clipped to the yoke of his webbing, embarrassed that he'd got frightened and not done the business. If the sar'nt-major said everything was OK, then it was. *We're winnin'. Fuckin' Argies are all fuckin' wankers. Fuckin' boys'll kill them all.* 'OK, sir, sorry sir, no problem.'

He passed Lappin's message sending Callsign 2 Golf, Corporal Anderson's ammunition resupply party, forward to the platoon sergeants of B Company. Sure that Anderson was moving, he started digging into the side pockets of his Bergen for his brew kit. Within minutes he had dug a shelf into the earth of the boghole, just above the water level, to hide the glow of his little petrol stove, the precious No. 7 burner given to him by a wounded marine he had helped after the last battle. Hunched over against the sleet and wind Coleridge thanked the marine from the bottom of his squaddie heart; the hexamine blocks issued with the 24-hour ration packs burned hot and smelly but were bastards to set light to with the paper matchbook included in the pack. In these conditions it would have been impossible. The powerful little stove was a godsend.

'2 Foxtrot, this is Seagull 2. Where is 2 Golf? Over.' Jamie Lappin's voice, calm and clear in his headphones, cut into Private Coleridge's mental diatribe against the rain running down his back, the weight of his Bergen, the fucking Argies and anything and everything remotely connected with the Falkland Islands.

Coleridge reacted to the voice immediately. 'Seagull 2, 2 Foxtrot. Well on their way. Should be with you in minutes one zero, over.'

'Seagull 2. Ten minutes. OK. Move up to Bravo HQ and talk in the choppers taking the casualties out, over.'

Coleridge grinned. Seagull, the radio nickname adopted by the colonel's adjutant and regimental sergeant-major had filtered down to B Company's sergeant-major, with a number to identify which company he belonged to. Good nickname. All the bastards that had it could shit on you from a great height. Mind you, he thought, Lappin wasn't too bad, a tough fucker who would ream your arsehole for you if you didn't do the business, but a Para to the core. Do the business and he looked after you like your granny. 'Foxtrot 2. Moving now, out.'

Coleridge poured tea into the black plastic mug, the top of his waterbottle, added a sachet of sugar and drank the first of it, still scalding, as he packed his kit away. He had just started moving, mug in one hand, rifle in the other, when the full weight of a concentrated Naval and Field Artillery barrage fell on the western ridge, seventy-two high-explosive shells a minute blasting back and forth over a piece of ground no bigger than three football fields in a welter of flame and screaming shrapnel.

Not many minutes later it was all over. On the western ridge a few Argentinians wandered aimlessly through a midnight made light by starshells fired by the frigates, like jerky figures in a very old black and white movie, weaponless, confused, unsure of anything. They were in the state of helpless shock common to all defeated soldiers, incapable of resisting the Paras of A Company advancing through them, bayoneting any man still carrying a rifle, flinging phosphorous grenades into any uncollapsed trench that might contain an armed man.

On the eastern ridge the enemy conscripts were dumping their weapons and stumbling back, demoralised and horrified by the terrible force of the concentrated barrage they had witnessed falling on their comrades in the west, made worse by the co-ordinated streams of heavy machine gun fire the two Para companies had thrown in to help destroy their best infantry. Those of the conscripts still carrying weapons walked and ran into murderously accurate sniper fire coming from their rear. They crumpled loose limbed as high-velocity bullets struck them at ranges no sniper could miss from.

Jamie Lappin was absorbed in the battle. He lay flat, chest slightly raised, elbows made firm against the soft peat, and breathed slow and steady as he swung the barrel of his rifle in even, steady arcs, left to right and back again, covering the arc

171

of fire he had allotted to himself. At any moment, he thought, he and his would be overrun, shot or bayoneted by the retreating enemy, unaware in his concentration of the terrible destruction of the enemy to the west. Certain of impending death he froze his mind, cutting down with chill precision the enemy conscripts as they appeared, until there were too many running into his field of vision. To left and right his snipers did the same, taking as many with them as they could.

But then there was the crying. The enemy conscripts were weeping as they ran, calling on their mothers and their God to save them from the guns and from the Paras, *los sombreros rojos*, the red-hatted chanting devils who were said to dip their headgear in blood to give it better colour.

Lappin stood up, knowing it was over, calling his men to him. As the starshells faded the three snipers walked through the battlefield, back towards their company HQ. Long before they got there they realised that the lines of human rag dolls they were walking through were separated by a wide band of bullet-shredded grass from those grouped around the enemy trenches. That gap was important: those around them they had killed themselves, those around the trenches were somebody else's. Lappin saw both his subordinates on their hands and knees, vomiting on to the turf, the smoke and stink and adrenalin and the enormity of the meaning of every well-placed round they had fired falling on them like a hammer blow. Then they got up and joined him, legs rigid, walking with him through the serried ranks of their dead.

Lappin counted. Counted and rechecked. Fifty-seven. Three snipers. Nearly twenty each. Fifty-seven mothers' sons whose wives and children and girlfriends and sisters and brothers and grannies would see the telegram telling of death and refuse to believe it and then accept it and scream and weep and call upon each other for support in this their hour of grief. Lappin did not fall to his knees, nor did he ease his forward stride, but the gorge rose high in him, his stomach trying to empty itself across the mottled camouflage cloth covering his chest. He leaned to one side and emptied himself as he walked. Cradling his rifle across one arm, he slid the zip of his combat smock down, put a hand inside and felt the smooth flat surface of the photograph, warmed by his body heat, that might sustain him now.

Close to his chest, in the warmth and darkness, Charlotte Aitken smiled the smile that told him of her love for him. It was enough. Lappin wiped his face with a handful of grass. Other battles had yet to be fought. As he dropped the grass a stray bullet, ricocheting off a rock to the west, struck him just forward of his right ear. He fell nerveless on the grass.

LONDON

A piece of paper torn from a scratch pad was stapled to the latest signal. 'Call JI. Juliet Lima. MID. Harriet.'

Charlotte's fingers scrabbled against the pad of signals, terror flooding through her. Harriet Coles, Charlotte's best friend, was now a captain in JI, the Branch that looked after personnel. Harriet could be trusted; her own soldier, Charlie Waters, was now a warrant officer in the Medical Corps, doing his best to patch up the wounded in a barn not far from the Crab Ridges. Jamie Lappin – Juliet Lima – must have been hit, killed or wounded, for Harriet to know about where he was. There was something about him being mentioned in dispatches. The bastard had done something brave and stupid and had been killed. Charlotte, knees shaking, called Harriet on the internal telephone.

Nearly screaming with excitement Harriet cried 'Jamie's OK. He's OK. He came to Charlie's aid station to get treatment for a slight head wound. A spent bullet hit him and concussed him, but he's all right. Charlie put his name down as "lightly wounded" so we would know he was all right. Isn't it amazing? The Paras took a frightful hammering but they did it. They really did it. Against all those Argentinians. They conned the Argies into counterattacking, then let the Navy and the Gunners blow half of them away. Jamie sneaked round behind the rest with snipers, went right through their trenches and killed masses of them. The Argies broke and ran. Jamie's been mentioned in dispatches and might get a medal. Isn't it wonderful?'

Harriet's Roedean tones finally broke Charlotte's last vestige of reserve. In the shelter of the wooden wings of her telephone cell Charlotte let herself fall into the small steel and canvas chair set against the wall, tears streaming unchecked down her face and dropping from her cheeks to the floor. Nearly choking with relief she curled up, elbows clamped tight around her knees, head down, sobbing, 'Thank God. Thank God. I thought he'd been killed.'

As Harriet babbled on Charlotte gained some control of herself; pride and anger swept through her, straightening her in the tiny seat. 'Those bloody, bloody Paras. They probably don't even realise what they've done. Of course it's wonderful. But they're too brave, Hari. They don't care about anything. Jamie's as bad as the rest of them, worse. He'll do something stupid and be killed. I know he will. I'm frightened. I need him. I couldn't manage without him. What am I going to do if he's killed?'

14 June 1982
COUNTY ANTRIM

Peter Ewart was driving along the Antrim coast road. He pulled into a layby to listen to the news. The Argyll and Sutherland Highlanders had made a small arms find near Newry. An off-duty UDR soldier had been shot dead by hooded men as he lay in his bath; no one had as yet claimed responsibility. A battalion of the Parachute Regiment had launched a night assault on a heavily defended Argentinian position blocking their advance on Port

Stanley. Casualty figures were not yet known but the assault had been successful and Royal Marines had been brought up to pass through the exhausted Paras and continue the advance. Nothing interesting.

Ewart reached out to switch off the radio but noticed a distinct tremor in the fingers of his outstretched hand. He left the radio as it switched to light music and pulled his hip flask out of his coat pocket. Holding it with both hands he carefully unscrewed the brass cap and drank deep, thinking of the day ahead. Ten more minutes and a couple more pulls on the flask cleared his mind and stilled his hands. He switched off his radio and pulled back on to the road leading to Waterfoot, a small village nestling in the shallow curve of Antrim's Red Bay. He had an appointment he intended to keep.

6 p.m. WATERFOOT, COUNTY ANTRIM

Peter Ewart nodded sagely as Sean McAllister tipped the last of their first bottle into his own glass. McAllister's body swayed, his arms weaving from side to side as he poured, holding the mouth of the bottle hard against the lip of the thick glass tumbler. Ewart watched as McAllister bid him 'Slainte' and threw the whiskey down him.

'Done like a true drunk, Sean. Never spilled a drop. Open the other bottle, now, like a gentleman.'

McAllister cracked the new bottle and poured for them both, leaning against the wall of the little caravan to steady himself. 'Aye, drink up Peter.' McAllister paused, thinking, then bawled, glass raised high, 'Death to the enemy! Confusion to the legions of the damned!'

Ewart responded, 'And to hell with the Scarlet Whore of Rome!'

Immediately McAllister became contrite, 'I'm sorry, Peter, I was forgetting that you're a black Protestant.'

Looking into McAllister's drunken eyes, like oysters floating in tomato sauce, Ewart said gently, 'And I'm sorry too, Sean. I forgot that you'd found the Lord. I thought you were just playing, like me.' He sought something, anything, that might distract his friend. 'I thought you were talking about the Loyalists.'

'Fuck the Loyalists. Fuck the Brits. Fuck the IRA and bedamned to the devil. Well then man, another wee one?' Sean shouted as he splashed whiskey into their glasses.

'Thanks, Sean. I will.'

Ewart sat thinking, as McAllister fell into a reverie of his own. *It doesn't take much to knock Sean over these days, thank Christ. It's only a matter of time, and not much of it, before his liver gives out. Terminal cirrhosis, the quack says, a classic case of chronic alcoholism.*

A blessing, thought Ewart, who had sat through the early days and long dark nights of Sean's release from Purdysburn mental hospital, wiping his face and sometimes his backside when the horrors were on him, the horrors of the wall. Over the years Sean's dreams had become more peaceful, but the once muscular frame had softened, bellied, ravaged by the drink that gave him a few hours of oblivion. It was better this way. Better Sean's mindless wandering, day to day, until the day he didn't wake, than the absolute terror of a sober minute, for in a minute Sean was back on the wall.

Ewart shifted in his seat, easing himself. The thin foam cushions in the little caravan brought poor comfort. But Sean seemed happy enough. The widow woman up at the farm saw to most of his needs and the owner of the village's one bar saw to the rest. Not that Sean was allowed to drink there, but the woman at the farm picked up Sean's ration from the pub as she bought and cooked his groceries for him. The 'oul girl' thought Sean a victim of the Troubles, a 'dacent man wricked b'the antics a hooleegans', a poet destroyed by the violence of his surroundings.

True enough, on his better days Sean scribbled down bits of rhymed nonsense, was often to be found crosslegged on the strand, whatever the weather, staring sightlessly out over the bay, as if contemplating, soothed by the sound of the waves, made safe by the wind, his face washed by the rain.

Every month or two Ewart came up to settle Sean's bills and drink a couple of bottles with him in the little caravan Ewart had bought on site just before Sean came out of hospital. Somewhere near the sea, the psychiatrist had advised, somewhere small where people are simple and out of the Troubles, where they will look after him. Waterfoot had been perfect: the caravan, the elderly widow whose married middle-aged sons ran her farm from their own homes, leaving her looking for something to do. Sean had only to step across the narrow country road to the beach, or sit alone through long, quiet nights safe with his bottle: everything he needed. He was snoring now, sitting on the floor, drunk, at peace. Ewart got up and stepped carefully over him, trying to minimise the rocking of the caravan as he shifted his weight.

Out on the beach it was cool. The wind came off the sea, as it always did here at the end of the day, storms excepted. Ewart studied the dial of his watch, fast disappearing in the gathering gloom of evening. Ten o'clock. Late. Christ it's lovely here. Been sitting here for hours, dreaming. He picked up the bottle beside him: empty. Irritated, he drew his hip flask out of his pocket: empty. He considered. No, not enough, not yet. His car, only feet away, had another couple of bottles in the boot.

Near midnight, leaning against a tussock of waist-high dune grass, Ewart looked up at the moon sailing high above him and turned his eyes down to the sea. A boat, ketch-rigged, sailed silently across the silver road the moonlight paved on the gently heaving sea, a thing of beauty. *And I am sailing, on a broken, empty road paved with bones on a sea of blood.* He closed his eyes, slowly. *Aye. I'm getting maudlin. It's enough.* He got up, weaving on his feet. Half buried in the sand was his bottle of Jameson's, two-thirds full. Ewart searched but couldn't find it. Then he remembered the last bottle in the boot of his car. Before he left Waterfoot he pulled it out of the car and left it on Sean's table; he might need it in the morning.

Out in the arena sailors, soldiers and airmen stood still, in lines, surrounded by the spoils of war. Captured Panhard four-wheeled armoured cars, their ugly short-barrelled cannons dipped in defeat, stood at the corners of the great oblong of Earls Court. Scattered here and there were 155 millimetre heavy howitzers, captured near Port Stanley, their stubby barrels and chassis heat seared, shrapnel scarred. A Harrier jump jet carrying a 'smart bomb' and a pilot with his heart in his mouth had flown at near-Mach speed straight up the side of Mount Kent to receive a signal from a lonely, frightened, half-frozen RAF Forward Air Controller sitting in the centre of a ring of Paratroopers, well behind enemy lines. The laser-guided bomb, seemingly arriving from nowhere, flicked over the mountain before the little plane crossed the skyline, had devastated the gun line threatening the British approach route to Stanley, breaking the morale of the Argentinian gunners for the rest of the war. Jamie remembered it well, for he had led the patrol escorting the RAF officer himself.

Now the remnants of those guns shook to the pounding of thousands of British feet ranged in wooden tiers around Earls Court arena, stamping in time to the strains of 'Land of Hope and Glory' thundering around them. A few minutes earlier, startled Japanese tourists and visiting French, Germans, Belgians, Dutch and Americans had involuntarily risen to their feet as the huge crowd around them, led by the massed bands in the arena, leapt up to sing 'Jerusalem' in celebration of the Falklands victory. This, the last night of the Earls Court military tattoo of 1982, had a special flavour. Pure atavistic pleasure flowed through every British citizen present. Stamping hard, sweating in the press of their tightly packed thousands, roaring pride in their nation, the British viewed the captured guns and corded their throats in song. In their minds were their losses: soldiers killed, ships sunk. But most of all they thought of their victory: the defeat of the enemy, the tiny population of Britons on the Falkland Islands freed from brutal tyranny – 'Rule Britannia, Britannia rule the waves. Britons never never never shall be slaves.'

Jamie Lappin stood impassive, trying not to let go, desperately trying not to let the tears show his pride. *It was worth it. Yes, it was bloody well worth it.* Beside him Charlotte Aitken grasped his hand and reached round to pull his face to her own, her eyes shining. It was her man, *her* man that had caused those guns to be here. He couldn't hear what she said, but he could see. 'I love you, Jamie Lappin. By God, I love you.'

Standing in the foyer of the great hall Jamie found himself mobbed. He had gained a little weight since his return from the islands and had lost that pared-down look of the athlete. Immaculately turned out in Number Two Dress uniform he wore his red beret and the Falkland Islands campaign medal on his chest, the discreet little rosette on the medal's ribbon indicating his presence throughout the battles for the islands. The Military Medal to the right of it proclaimed him a living, breathing hero. He looked very handsome, pulling the people to him. Men wanted to shake his hand and girls wanted to kiss him. A few of the younger girls' mothers pressed folded pieces of paper into his hand, telephone numbers hastily scribbled out of their husbands' sight. Standing back in civilian clothes Charlotte was proud. *They all want him, they all want him, my Para, but he's mine, every lovely bit of him is mine.*

As the great crowd began to disperse Jamie took Charlotte in his arms and kissed her deeply. 'It was the thought of you at home that kept me going, Charlie. Sometimes I was scared out of my head. You kept me going.'

Charlotte was very proud. She really did love this quiet,

self-contained man. In the months since he had come home they had spent every weekend together, seeing shows, attending concerts in the Festival Hall (at which he fell asleep), eating, drinking, walking, talking, making love, sometimes just being alone, growing ever more absorbed in each other, ever more careless of being seen together. At first Jamie had been more silent than usual. Sometimes he woke in the night, drenched in sweat, and would not let her ease him. In time it had got a little better; when he woke with the shakes he allowed her to fold herself around him and soothe him back to sleep. But he would never speak of the war, never tell her what it was that had woken him. At times he muttered in his sleep, but not so she could understand. Maybe now he would rest easier. She moved through the thinning crowd to take his arm. 'Home, James. I've something special in store for you.'

'Special? What?' He seemed excited by the emotional outburst of the crowd and the attention showered on him. 'What's special?'

Charlotte stepped close to him, her hands creeping over his shoulders. In truth she had no idea: it had just come to her to say it, to pull his attention back to her, away from everyone else. Charlotte caressed her lips with her tongue, thinking. 'Wait and see, Sergeant-Major. Wait and see.'

'I'm all yours, Charlie ma'am. Let's go home.'

Near the doors a tall, slim lieutenant-colonel of the Cavalry turned away. He had seen enough.

2 a.m. 17 September 1982
NEWRY, COUNTY DOWN

At precisely two minutes past 2 a.m. the phone rang for the first time ever in a deserted, barely furnished studio flat in Clapham, London. A small, tap-sensitive electronic device attached to an American-built PMX 108T answering machine illegally linked to a standard British Telecom line took the call, checked it, acknowledged it and let the caller know the call was being transferred. Fifteen seconds later another phone rang in Newry, County Down. Gerry Madden picked up the receiver and listened for a moment to a Tyrone voice.

'The operation is aborted. Pure bad luck. A policeman is standing in out of the rain in the foyer of the target.'

Madden felt a flush of exasperation. Would these people never see the bigger picture, never take a chance?

'Kill him. He's a bonus. Then plant the bomb as planned.'

The Tyrone voice took on a note of alarm. 'We can't kill a policeman! The whole fucking country would be up in arms! They'd be sure to find us in the end.' The voice stiffened. 'The mission is aborted.'

Madden felt his fury build, thumping behind his eyes. This mission was important, the start of a carefully planned and provided-for campaign. The logistics of pre placing the weapons and explosives and guaranteeing safe houses, had taken over a year and cost more than half a million.

'Kill the policeman. Plant the bomb. Then go to the place planned. I'll see to it that you're on your way to Holland before the Brits can seal the ports. You'll –'

'You don't understa –'

Madden seemed to implode. Controlling his anger he channelled it into his voice: where other men might have shouted he whispered, almost inaudibly, very slowly, holding the phone with both hands, shoulders hunched over it, pouring a stream of cold clear viciousness down the line.

'No, you don't understand. Listen to me now. Calm down and listen very carefully to me. You come from a good family, don't you? . . . Yes, that's true, they are decent people . . . No, they can't be kept out of this, we're fighting a war . . . There are no innocents . . . I am not going to argue with you . . . I have this to say to you: disobey me and I promise to you that your father will be dead within the hour. I'll have him shot with a hood on his head and a placard round his neck telling the world that he was a Brit informer. Your brother, I recall, is treasurer of one of the Tyrone Republican clubs. I'll have his kneecaps blown out of his legs, because he will be found guilty by a court martial of stealing the Cause's funds, regardless of his innocence. I'll pass the word to the Cumann na mBan that your youngest sister is suspected of seeing a Brit squaddie. She'll be tarred and feathered as a Brit whore. Your mother will be spat on in the streets as the wife of a tout and the mother of a thief, a whore and you, a coward in the face of the enemy. Do you understand me now? . . . Good . . . That's enough unpleasantness . . . Anyone can have a touch of cold feet . . . I understand, it's just the nerves playing you up. Don't worry. You'll be long gone by the time the Brits get moving. Be brave now, kill that policeman and plant the bomb.'

Four hours later, as a massive explosion ripped through the Conservative Party's Central Office of Information, killing the doctor and scene-of-crime detective who were examining the corpse of a young police constable found huddled in the office doorway, the leader of the Provisional IRA ASU that had planted the bomb hit the bottom of a gravel pit in Essex, shot through the head, a bag of cement tied to his chest. Transferred at an hour's notice from the Moseley ASU in Birmingham the man who dumped the body carefully cleaned his pistol and drove to London to assume command of the Kilburn ASU. Once there he made a quick call to Newry.

Madden sat back, satisfied for the moment. The death of the old, unreliable ASU commander at the hands of the new might be useful in the long run: the new man would not question orders in case he wound up in a gravel pit himself. The target had been destroyed; a policeman had been killed; an unreliable commander had been found out and replaced. All in all not a bad night's work.

Madden closed his eyes and let his mind wander back to the desert. Sometimes, when his plans succeeded, the face of Abu Horaj would come. He felt the tension at the back of his neck as he tried to relax and waited, allowing the memories to flow back . . .

Gerry Madden crouched under a rock projecting out of a low cliff deep in the desert, trying to squeeze his body into the scant shade it offered. Around him other young men, mostly hot-eyed Palestinian volunteers from the vast refugee camp ten miles to the south of Tripoli, were hunkered down in the sun, holding *kheffiyeh* over their heads to make their own shade.

After the soft grey drizzle of Belfast the dry searing heat of the Libyan summer, heat that dried your shirt faster than your sweat could wet it, seemed incredible. Thirst clawed at Madden's throat and made the salt-raw skin of his armpits and around his crotch feel like fine sandpaper, so that it was difficult and sore to move. He squinted at his watch – it must be nearly time for him to go, time to earn his water for the day. A headache brought on by dehydration banged away behind his eyes, matching its rhythm to the hammering beat of the machine gun strafing the wire. Maniacs, he thought, fucking maniacs will kill us all. His turn must be soon. Time and time again he'd told these bloody Arabs that conditions in Northern Ireland bore no resemblance to the Golan Heights or the Israeli fence along the Lebanese border. Always his protests had been ignored. They just didn't seem to ca –.

'Ma'ad'Den. You go!' The timekeeper's high-pitched shout cut into his thoughts and galvanised him into action. His irritation and discomfort were instantly forgotten, driven out by the more consuming need to survive the next two and a half minutes. *The stopwatch is running. To hesitate when called means death.* He flopped forward, legs and arms moving before his belly hit the ground, crawling hard and fast on his knees and elbows toward the lane of criss-crossed strands of razor wire spread like a net over a low forest of six-inch stakes driven into a patch of cleared ground fifty yards long. Grunting with the effort and praying for speed he kept low and flat to avoid snagging his loose cotton trousers on the wire as he drove himself under the first few strands. Three seconds after the Palestinian's shout a burst of fire from an AK 47 assault rifle tore up the ground he had been crouching on, fired by a fifteen-year-old Palestinian girl standing next to the timekeeper. Elbows already raw and knees pumping hard to grip the rough, sandy ground, Madden had only one urge: to keep moving faster than the single hand of the timekeeper's stopwatch. *To slow or tire when under the wire means death.* No excuses were accepted. You moved or you died.

A barrage of machine gun fire blasted the sand and rock under the wire, timed second by second to match the standard Israeli response to a real or imagined penetration of their border defences by a Palestinian commando. First the Israelis fired a full 200-round belt of ammunition loaded into pre-set machine guns ranged to rake their twelve-foot-high fence, paused for three seconds to fit a new belt of ammunition and then razed the ground under the low wire entanglement stretching 50 yards back from the inside of the fence at a rate of one foot a second. Then they started where they'd finished, going back over the same ground again. You had to be quick or you were dead. The Palestinians copied the Israeli pattern exactly, making no allowances, not for any reason. Better the slow and weak died here, they said, than under the Israeli wire, where they might cause the deaths of their comrades, or worse, the failure of a mission.

Drenched in sweat and lying open mouthed well beyond the end of the firing lane Gerry Madden cursed these Arabs again, grateful for the momentary coolness of the sweat fast evaporating off him. Five minutes later, his shirt dried by the sun, he sipped water out of a goatskin bag chilled by deep burial under the sand in the freeze of the desert night. He watched without compassion as a boy of nineteen was pulled dead from under the wire, the sixth in the last month. Too slow. Too bad. Plenty more where he came from. Not realising how much of their philosophy he had unconsciously absorbed, Madden marvelled again at the absolute ruthlessness of the Palestinians.

Death meant failure, failure meant death. But a tiny success meant everything, with human lives weighing nothing in the balance. Four months he'd been here, learning. He'd mastered every small arms weapon manufactured east of the Elbe river, knew how to make and trigger bombs out of the most innocuous of materials, knew how to use the latest technology to make his bombs better, less detectable, more effective. But most of all, he'd learned how to survive. And he'd learned a lesson more: unless you lead you're a pawn and pawns are expendable. It was simple, really simple. You led and survived or followed and died. Too many times he'd carried and planted roughly made bombs built and set by other men, knowing that each job might be his last. His survival had been a matter of luck, nothing more. Later, as a sniper, he'd been safer, but the Brits kept getting better and better at cutting off his escape routes. Now as a seasoned PIRA soldier he had the benefit of this training. When he got home he would use it to get on the staff and send other people out to fight.

But now the face of his old instructor would not come. Madden tried to pull it into his mind, but it would not come. In its place he felt a burning in his guts; he opened a small silvered packet and swallowed a couple of aspirin-sized white pills. His doctor called them Zantac, a defence against ulcers. Madden called them his shield against the weak, his defence against the furies that drove him over the weaknesses of others. Maybe he needed something more to help him relax. He picked up the phone. 'Send in a girl, the new one with the red hair if she's there.'

Ten minutes later Siobhan McCaillim, twenty, a pretty full-breasted young woman in her last year of nursing training at Musgrave Park hospital, was kneeling between Madden's legs as he lay sprawled in an armchair. He had made no effort other than to undo a button and slide a zip. As Siobhan's lips and tongue moved over his flaccid penis Madden closed his mind. It was only a matter of time, if the girl was any good. She was, better than any other had ever been. Siobhan, rolling him around her mouth, had

185

no doubts. Some of the middle-aged doctors she had played with had similar difficulties; she had taught herself how to overcome such things. Madden was just another big name with a dick that bent in the middle. She worked smoothly, easily, to tease him to erection.

As Madden felt himself engorge with blood, come erect at last to fill her mouth, he began to see the face of his personal djinn: the Palestinian face, Abu Horaj. Dark it was and full of hate, the eyes burning cold either side of a nose that challenged an eagle's beak. As the girl between his knees brought him close Madden saw the cold eyes smile, the coldness vanish, the mouth show its teeth in a smile of respect and comradeship. 'Ma'Ad'Den, you know. *To hesitate when called is death.* You have done well.' It was enough.

As he burst into the girl's mouth Madden grabbed her hair in both hands, forcing himself deeper into her throat, heard and felt her gag and choke. Careless of her he held her there until he was spent, forcing her to swallow the sperm flowing out of him. Looking down at her he saw the thin rime at the corners of her mouth as he allowed her to lean back, a tentative smile beginning to crease her pretty face, her duty to the chief of staff himself done as he wished.

Madden pulled a handkerchief from his pocket and handed it to the kneeling girl. He leaned forward, resting his elbows on his thighs. 'Here, take this. You're Siobhan McCaillim, aren't you? I know your people, Siobhan. I knew your mother years ago. You're very like her, aside from that lovely hair. What job have you?'

Wiping her mouth Siobhan controlled her urge to spit in Madden's face. Starting with her brother she had played the game again and again, fighting for supremacy, the ability to inflict pain, physical and mental. Right now Gerry Madden was in complete control, she a bit of meat off the street. Her time would come. One day she would manipulate him as he had manipulated her, but with stakes infinitely higher. The game was just beginning.

She kept her head lowered as if in embarrassment and whispered 'I'm a nurse at Musgrave Park, sir. I watch out for Brits visiting the military wing to see if there's any pattern. It's not much, but I've been able to report the cars they use. Maybe one of the ASUs will ambush a Brit car soon.'

Madden reached out and placed a hand either side of the girl's face, lifting it gently, strongly, forcing her to look at him. His eyes were intense, his voice low and soft. 'Don't belittle your work, Siobhan. It's very valuable. Without information we can do nothing. What are you doing here in Newry?'

Siobhan blushed, looking even younger than her years. She would have to be careful of what she said now, or her whole plan would go out the window. Madden, still holding her face, could feel the heat of her blush on his palms.

'My friend Maire told me you'd be here, sir. I wanted to meet you. You're a great man, sir.'

Madden's face did not change, but something flickered in his eyes, something scary. Siobhan misinterpreted the flicker, her face flaming again. *Say something quick, distract him.* 'I've not done that before, not all the way like that. I'm sorry I choked.'

Madden stroked her hair with his fingers, watching the play of light on it, more distracted by it than by her words, watching it flame, dull, flame, turn red-gold, liquid fire.

'Don't worry, Siobhan. I'm happy enough. I have work to do now. Do you mind if I call for you again?' Madden smiled, 'Practice makes perfect, they say. Or maybe something different?'

Siobhan eased herself to her feet, shy and awkward, as if pleased that he was pleased. 'Whenever you like, sir. Anything you like. Thank you.' *Bastard. I'll do what I have to do. I'll smile and say Thank You Sir. Until I'm ready.*

When Siobhan was gone Madden reached for the telephone. 'Send in Billy Walsh.' Billy Walsh nearly filled the door as he came through it. Successor to Sean McAllister as Madden's bodyguard and personal enforcer he was a huge man, a farmer's son from south Armagh. 'You going out, Gerry?'

'No. That girl, Siobhan McCaillim, she's not the usual. Keep her around, I like her. Go and see her mother. Her name's Marion McCaillim. She still lives on the Falls somewhere. Tell her Siobhan's with me and I'll look after her. Nobody else but me gets use of her, understand?'

Walsh nodded. 'Nobody but you, Gerry.'

Madden got to his feet and began pacing about, speaking in short, jerky sentences, thinking and talking about several things at once. His time as chief of staff had been successful so far, but not easy. He rarely seemed to sleep and was often erratic in his behaviour.

'Siobhan told me she came here to see me. She said her friend Maire told her I would be here. That's bad. I don't like too many knowing about my movements. That Special Branch bastard Ewart never gives up trying to get wind of me. The man's a maniac, obsessed. Find out who this Maire is and find out who's been talking to her. Frighten Maire. Hurt the one who's talking too much. Remind them both that people with loose tongues need heads to carry them in. Be as severe as you have to be. I won't be endangered by loose mouths. I'm going to bed. I'll see Ewart in hell yet. Send for Doctor Rafferty. These pills are no fucking good. And send Siobhan up to me when the doctor's finished. Find out where Ewart goes when he drives up the Antrim coast road.'

Siobhan smiled to herself when Billy Walsh told her Madden was asking for her. For years her mother had suffered under the fists of a drunken husband, until the bastard had fallen under a lorry, drunk as usual. The years of disappointment, of listening to public house heroes who were nowhere to be seen when the bullets started to fly, had taken their toll on Marion McCaillim. Thirty years of disappointment, seeing her sons grow up into miniatures of their father, her passionate belief in the rightness of the Republican Cause ground down under their stupidity.

But in Siobhan Marion had seen the spark, had coached and trained her, taught her that the Cause was not safe in the hands of men, told her of Maeve, the Warrior Queen of prehistory, who had fought for and recovered the land of Eire when the men had sold it to marauding Danes, who had led the three provinces of Leinster, Munster and her own Connacht to war against the most powerful of them all, Ulster, in an attempt to unite the country. But Maeve's armies had melted away after initial successes, melted off home with their booty before the Ulstermen could gather, leaving her to face the wrath of Ulster on her own. Maeve had failed, through no fault of her own except that she had put her faith in her men. When Siobhan had reached fifteen, Marion McCaillim had been adamant, setting her daughter on her way.

'They sold Ireland for drink then, they did it again in 1798, in the famine year of 1847, in 1921, in '56, and they're doing it again. They're brave men Siobhan, some of them, but they have the curse of the Celt in them, the darkness in their souls that will not let them rest. They're children, Siobhan. Big strong cruel children. They need a woman to lead them, to look to the future for them. It's always been that way. But they are dangerous. Never trust them. Use them as they would use you. Fill their bellies and empty their balls, then use them. Use them to raise yourself above them. Use them for the good of the Cause. Teach yourself their ways, be obedient, be quiet. When you are ready, bend them to your will. Save the Cause from them, for they will surely destroy it if you don't.'

Siobhan thought back over it all. It was all crap. Power was what mattered, not that sort of shite. Gerry Madden was her route to it. Slowly, as if embarrassed by the stares of the other women in the farmhouse kitchen, Siobhan Maeve McCaillim walked to the door, up the stairs and into her chosen battlefield.

9 a.m 19 September 1982
LONDON

... Main Battle Tanks: 448 × T72 are being moved from

Tbilisi to 3 Shock Army, it is thought to replace some of the T62 fleet experiencing signs of metal fatigue in turret mechanisms . . . Charlotte Aitken stopped reading the weekly Intelligence summary circulated around the MoD to answer the general's intercom call. She would have to find a way to put him off: normally she arrived at her office before seven on Monday mornings in order to read and interpret the latest Intelligence summary before General Patrick read it and raised questions she would have to answer. This morning she had arrived shortly before 8.30, delayed by Jamie's lust attack in her bathroom. It had been fun, but it had thrown her routine out of kilter.

'Charlotte, this is the general. Come to my office now please.'

'I'm sorry, General, but I'm not ready to comment on the IntSum. There are aspects of it I want to look into before I brief you.'

'I'm not calling about the IntSum. Please be good enough to come along now.' Major-General Patrick Forth's voice indicated some irritation.

'Very good, General. I'll come right away.'

Walking along one of the MoD's endless brown linoleum corridors Charlotte turned over in her mind anything the general might have heard over the weekend that could have made him tetchy. Nothing special came to mind. Once through the two closely set doors guarding the general's privacy Charlotte knew she was in trouble. First the ascetic, almost emaciated head of the Intelligence Corps did not ask her to sit down. Second, he had a tray on a side table near his desk, holding a silver coffee pot, the usual milk and sugar, and only one cup and saucer. Warned by these signs Charlotte did not adopt her normal easy but respectful stance and instead came to attention in front of his desk, wondering what the hell was the problem.

Looking up at her the general was clearly upset. The thick single eyebrow that sat like a bar across his lower forehead was bent in the middle by the bitter scowl on his face. His voice, surprisingly deep for his spare frame, barked at her, 'Major Aitken, have you got married?'

Charlotte was confused. 'No, General, I have not got married. If I had it would be recorded. I don't understand the purpose of this interview, sir.'

'Purpose? My purpose is to determine whether you have gone barking mad. When I walked in here this morning the Military Secretary himself called me direct. Do you know Lieutenant-Colonel Richard Warren, a cavalryman?'

By now thoroughly off balance Charlotte answered, 'Yes I do sir, if he's the same Richard Warren who was chief of staff of 19 Infantry Brigade when I was SO3 G2 there.'

The general laid his hands flat on his desk, casting around for some explanation, some mitigating circumstance he could find acceptable, something he could pass on to the Military Secretary. 'He is not likely to be in error then, should he be asked to identify you. He's an old boyfriend of yours, dumped for someone else, is that it? There's bad blood between you, that sort of thing? Has Warren any reason to want to damage you?'

'I wouldn't have thought so, General. He was never a boyfriend of mine, he had more girlfriends than he needed. We got on reasonably well, after I'd let him know I wasn't interested in him. I haven't seen him for a long time. May I ask what this is leading to?'

'You may well ask. You will meet Lieutenant-Colonel Warren again soon, if I think it necessary. I believe it would be an embarrassing meeting for you, so I will try to avoid it. It would appear that Warren took your lack of interest in him rather more personally than you believed. He has waited his chance and planted a spear straight between your shoulder blades. You are in deep trouble.'

The general sighed, lifted his hands and drew them down over his face, not wanting to proceed with this charade. He continued, 'I must formally ask. Are you involved in any personal way with a warrant officer of the Parachute Regiment? It is reported to the Military Secretary that you were seen in what could best be called compromising circumstances in the main entrance hall of Earls Court three nights ago. It is reported that you embraced a uniformed warrant officer of the Parachute Regiment immediately after the last performance of this year's military tattoo. Is this true?'

Charlotte felt faint. There was a darkening of the room and her legs felt unsteady. *Oh my God, we've been seen. How could I have been so stupid?*

She fought for control of herself, feeling the blood drain out of her face. There was no point in lying, it would only make things worse. Warren had put the knife in to the hilt.

'Yes, sir. It is true. Before you ask further questions I should tell you that the sergeant-major and I have had a stable relationship for some years now. There is no question of any security risk occurring through either of us being blackmailed.'

The general lost his temper for a moment, shouting, 'I'm not talking about blackmail or security risks. Do you think I didn't know about this relationship of yours? I'm the head of Military Intelligence, for Christ's sake. I've turned a blind eye so long as you exercised discretion. I'm talking now about plain bloody stupidity. You know the social rules of the army. If you choose to break them you damn well make sure you're not going to be found out. Or you pay the penalty. For Christ's sake, Charlotte, what do you think you're doing? You couldn't have chosen a place more public or anywhere more likely to have someone who knows who and what you are close by.'

The general calmed down, 'I can only assume that you were temporarily out of your head, and I am very glad you did not try to lie to me. I have instructions from MS to ask for your immediate resignation if you had lied. The facts are here.'

The general drew two folders from a drawer in his desk and laid them on the desk's polished surface. One was headed MAJOR C. AITKEN WRAC, MoD, the other WO2 (CSM) LAPPIN J. MM, Depot Para. 'People have been busy over the weekend, Charlotte. General Rogers was informed at lunchtime yesterday. I need hardly say that he is furious. He has, however, left you a loophole. Read these.'

The general drew two sheets of paper from Charlotte's folder.

The first was a notice telling her that her Positive Vetting was under review and that 'for the period of the review' her PV was withdrawn. In addition she was to have no access to material classified higher than Restricted. The paper was signed by Lieutenant-General DBH Rogers, Military Secretary. For a mainstream Women's Royal Army Corps officer who had nailed her colours to the Intelligence mast it was a professional death knell – unless she behaved as expected. Maybe, just maybe, if she corrected her error in the 'period covered by the review' she could salvage her career. The other paper was a posting order, with yesterday's date and also signed by General Rogers, ordering her to report forthwith to the WRAC Depot at Guildford to take up 'a supernumerary post pending administrative action'.

General Forth waited as Charlotte glanced through the papers. Then he said, 'You know what this means, don't you? In case you are in any doubt, MS is giving you a chance. You are to end your liaison with Sergeant-Major Lappin immediately and have no further contact with him. You are to go to Guildford, into a clerk's job, out of the way. If you decline to give up your Para you will remain at Guildford until hell freezes over or you do something, anything, that could be construed as conduct unbecoming to an officer, at which point you will be cashiered. I spoke to MS not ten minutes ago, Charlotte. Make no mistake; he means it. There is little I can do for the moment. You may go.'

As she found her way to the door the general called her back, something like pity or compassion showing in his eyes.

'Charlotte, I have read the sergeant-major's file. People are not awarded Military Medals for nothing. Sergeant-Major Lappin is a brave man, a hell of a soldier and certain to be commissioned in time. I can see how you were attracted to him; any woman would regard him as a good catch. But you are not any woman;

193

you are — were — a military officer with a bright future of your own, holding a senior Intelligence job. I find all this incredible. I have to assume that you got carried away by the crowd.

'As for Lappin, he may well end his career in his present rank, or lower. It depends on how he reacts to what has happened. Hopefully he will do the right thing, as I hope you will. You can both recover from this, if you are sensible. In the meantime he, like you, has been posted. He will be interviewed by his Commanding Officer as soon as he gets back to Aldershot. This afternoon he will be on an RAF aircraft out of Brize Norton, destined for Zimbabwe to join the British Army Training Team out there. I tell you this so you know he is not being harshly treated. All he has to do is keep his head down for a while and all will be forgiven. I suggest that you do not try to speak to him. A short letter telling him of your decision to end the relationship will be sufficient for him and acceptable to MS. That's all.'

When Charlotte had gone the general called for Richard Warren. Warren marched in, smiling. He saluted, removed his hat and turned toward a chair, expecting an offer of coffee, a brief chat and the general's thanks for exposing a security risk. Warren was already into the chair when the general exploded out of his.

'Stand up, damn you! Where the hell do you think you are? Get your head-dress on and get to attention!'

Warren jumped, jammed his hat on, stood rigid at attention and faced the raging general. In answer to a buzzer the general's ADC rushed in. He took the situation in at a glance, feared his general was about to strike the colonel, and moved to stand between the shaking Warren and General Forth.

'General! Be calm, sir. This is not right, sir.'

'Get out of my way. Write this down. Interview between myself and Lt. Col. Richard Warren, this date. Warren congratulated on bringing to the attention of the Military Secretary a matter of importance to MoD security. Get out.'

The ADC went, quickly. The general rounded on Warren.

Standing straight in front of him he shouted, 'You heard. That's what will be on record. But I want you to know that I was fully aware of this situation. I have known about it for a very long time. You could have, should have, approached me in confidence. I would then have dealt with this matter with discretion and common sense. But no, this was not business. This was personal. You wanted your pound of flesh, you miserable wretch. You went over my head, trying to do the most damage possible to the career of an outstanding officer, in revenge for some small slight she gave you years ago. I have lost the best SO2 I've ever had, for your self-esteem and an old grudge. I'll give you grudges, Warren. You have made a bad enemy in me. Watch and see. Get out.'

Chapter Ten

12 February 1983

GUILDFORD

Charlotte sat in her odd-shaped room in the WRAC centre's officers' mess, gazing with hatred at the walls, none of which seemed parallel; they sloped this way and that, unrelieved by pictures or decoration of any kind. She had refused to bring any personal belongings with her, preferring to live out of a suitcase and get away to London as often as possible. Outside her suite of two rooms a couple of officers stood gossiping, their outlines visible through the bubble-glass insert down the side of the door. Charlotte wished they would go away, or indulge this peculiar Guildford habit of conversing in corridors somewhere else. As if aware of the hate rays coming through the door the women moved off, leaving Charlotte relieved but without human contact, however tenuous.

She hated this place and everything and everyone in it. In her jaundiced eyes nothing had changed since her days as a second-lieutenant. She saw the same wicked bitches who seemed to be here forever. Even if they had different names and different noses, their faces were the same: hard, self-centred, out for the preservation of their little privileges above all else. They were dead wood, most of them the female equivalent of what the fighting soldiers called base rats, people who ventured out into the field army only when forced to, scurrying back to the security of base-depot routine and mindless bullshit as quick as they possibly could. *I could kill them all*. They congregated in cliques, jealous of any newcomer who might rock their cosy little boat. They banded together to exclude all threats, all attempts at change, delighting in the opportunities the WRAC's policy of sending naughty girls to Guildford gave them to lord it over women often their superiors in rank, nearly always their superiors in ability. The lesbians were the worst of all, a small but solid core of viciousness that spilled out over anyone not of them but forced to live with them, refusing to join them and threatening their stranglehold over the centre.

Bitches. Cows. I HATE them.

The reason for Charlotte's current rage lay on her knees, a forecast of duties for the month. The average Orderly Officer duty was supposed to come up once a month, with a weekend duty once every two months. Her name appeared on this list five times, three of them weekends, despite the fact that as a major she should not appear at all, but act as duty Field Officer, on call for a week at a time once every three months. She should not have gone out of her way to irritate the centre's staff, but was in no position to argue about their treatment of her. The day of her arrival her new Commanding Officer had made that crystal clear, telling her she was very much under the microscope and could expect 'tests of her fortitude', a euphemism for what others were later to tell her straight to her face or through false commiseration: 'You've blown it, Little Miss High Flyer. WRAC not good enough for you? Intelligence Corps better for you? Well you're back here now and we're watching you. You look down your nose at us and we'll fuck you about until you come crawling for the WRAC to take you back – or we'll see you out on your arse.'

Charlotte had been given a nothing job, with nothing to do except shuffle bumf for an embarrassed chief clerk; for hours and even days nothing crossed the desk she shared with a second-lieutenant who had sense enough to stay out of the office. But she had to sit there, from 8.30 in the morning until 4.45 in the afternoon, precisely. Any absence from her desk meant raised eyebrows and queries regarding her whereabouts from the raddled battleaxe appointed to oversee her.

Five months of this and not a word from Jamie was too much to bear.

'I'd like to speak to the director. This is Major Charlotte Aitken.' To Charlotte's surprise General Patrick Forth came on the line almost immediately.

'Forth. Speak.'

'General, this is Charlotte Aitken. Get me out of Guildford, please.'

'And your Para?'

'I have no Para.'

'I know. I also know you are having a thoroughly miserable time in Guildford. I know too that Sar'nt-Major Lappin is doing an excellent job with BATT Zimbabwe. He writes to no one and there isn't an international telephone within 200 miles of him. I'd say he's written you off. He's back in the Para good books. His career is safe. And you?'

'I have not tried to contact him. General, I cannot lie to you. If Jamie Lappin wants me he can come and get me, any time he chooses. If he does, I'll go. But it has been five months and he hasn't tried. I've lost him. I want to come back to work.'

'Thank you for your honesty. I expected nothing less. In some ways I envy Lappin. All I can say is that he seems to be all right. Enough of that. You are on leave as of now. Report to me personally on Monday morning, in the rank of lieutenant-colonel. We've been holding a job open for you, you bloody idiot. Welcome back.'

At home in Essex Charlotte banked up the fire, put on her grandfather's old Barbour jacket, went out on to Tollesbury saltings and cried until she could find no more tears.

'Ewart's playing very safe, Gerry, and very clever. We know exactly where he goes, what he does and who he sees. He probably knows that. But he never goes on the same day. Sometimes he goes twice in a month, then nothing for two months. Sometimes he stays for an hour or two, sometimes all day. Once or twice he went at night, paid the old woman and never saw Sean at all. There's no pattern we can get hold of to plan an operation against him. We've tried following him but it's a waste of time. He always cottons on to us and uses a radio to get the RUC or the army to intercept us at a surprise road block. We can't set up an ambush because we never know when he's going or what route he'll take. We can't risk following him with guns in the car. The chances are we'd lose the weapons, and the men would get ten years a skull for carrying. It's not possible, Gerry. I'm sorry.'

'Bollocks, Billy. There must be a way. Go away and think again. Talk to Belfast Brigade. Maybe somebody on the staff will have an idea.'

Gerry Madden, pale, thin and ill-looking, stared up out of the armchair. 'Ewart has to go. Only last month that bastard set up Willie McGlone down at the border. The fucking SAS murdered Willie on his way to Mass, ran him over with a tractor and escaped. Ewart has to go, Billy. See to it.'

BIlly Walsh looked uncomfortable. He knew McGlone had been run over, but by a kid with no licence to drive, helping out on the family farm. But Madden would not have it. The SAS haunted him, as they had his predecessors as chief of staff ever since the war had started. Everything he could blame on them he would, not knowing he was a victim of SAS psyops, psychological warfare aimed at breaking his will to fight, creating a mystique about SAS operations that might lead him to believe the SAS saw everything, knew everything and would not hesitate to set him up and murder him if they got half a chance.

When *An Phoblacht*, the Republican newspaper, had carried a vitriolic article written by Madden 'proving' the SAS had murdered the unarmed McGlone the Brits had neither admitted nor denied it. But a drawling Englishman calling himself 'one of Flecker's pilgrims' had rung up McGlone's brother and told him that Gerry Madden was next for the chop: there was nowhere he could hide; it was just a question of time. It had taken Madden a while to work that one out, but he got the message when an ASU commander in East Belfast, a student of literature, told him the SAS used a quotation from a play called *Hassan*, by James Elroy Flecker, as a tribute to their dead, who were scattered all over the world. Madden had looked it up.

> We are the pilgrims, master; we shall go
> Always a little further: it may be
> Beyond that last blue mountain barr'd with snow
> Across that angry or that glimmering sea.

Madden had collapsed in a mixture of rage and paranoid fear that left him incapable of effective action for days. He recovered, but was convinced that the SAS would go to any lengths to find and kill him. It was one reason why he was determined to remove the threat posed by Peter Ewart: Madden needed to concentrate on one personal enemy at a time.

'I know a way to get Ewart.'

Madden jumped out of his chair. Billy Walsh smiled a smile verging on a sneer. The bitch was at it again. Maybe this time Gerry would put her in her place, once and for all. Siobhan McCaillim, quite calm, sipped at a tumbler of whiskey.

Madden leaned over her, almost shouting, bent over to hold the arms of her chair. 'How? What would you do?' But Siobhan was not about to be intimidated or give up her advantage. Using the age-old power of women she calmly remarked 'Don't shout at me, Gerry. I want to stand up.'

Madden straightened and looked at Billy Walsh. Nobody else, if they wanted to live, would dare speak to Madden like that. Walsh shrugged his shoulders. He did not want to get involved in something between the chief of staff and his mistress. Things had not been going well for the Cause for the last year or so, despite Madden's successes. As things went from bad to worse Madden's mental and physical condition had deteriorated, but he had rallied over the last few months as he seemed to draw strength and comfort from the twenty-year-old woman who accompanied him everywhere.

At first Billy had been well disposed toward her because she seemed to ease the burdens his worshipped boss had to carry, but then he had begun to worry. The more time Madden spent with Siobhan the greater her influence over him became. And the more her confidence grew. Some of the more senior Provisional IRA commanders had also been concerned, until they realised Siobhan McCaillim didn't just pump Madden up: she increasingly concentrated his mind and drove him on to be more creative, more imaginative in his plans.

Watching Madden plan an operation the head of the Armagh ASU had noticed that he glanced at Siobhan from time to time, as if checking that she was listening and approving. Twice more the same man had gone out of his way to watch the interplay of the two. One night, after a conference of ASU commanders, one of the men had made a remark about Siobhan's legs. The Armagh man rounded on him. 'You're a stupid bastard. You don't know what you're looking at. That girl is watching and listening to everything. A lot of what the chief is doing is coming out of her, not him. One of these fine days you'll make a remark like that and find yourself with three eyes. That girl is out to make her name and doesn't give a fuck who knows it. You watch your mouth, just in case.' The assembled terrorists laughing and making mock of the Armagh man had nearly brought the house down. But since then they were careful of what Siobhan got to hear.

Siobhan stood up quickly, her small, neat feet almost hidden by the wide trousers she seemed to wear all the time now. 'Why don't you sit down Gerry, you're tired. Billy, get a drink for Gerry.'

Billy Walsh was in the act of pouring a can of Harp lager when he realised he had obeyed her without thinking. He bit his lip. One day, when Gerry realised what was happening and threw her out on her arse, Billy would see to her personally, with pleasure.

Drink in hand, Gerry Madden sat huddled in his chair, waiting. Siobhan took her time, beginning only when she sensed Madden was about to tell her to get on with it.

'Billy has done a good job on Ewart, Gerry. We have everything we need. The answer is simple. We put a radio-controlled bomb under McAllister's caravan and detonate it when Ewart is there.'

'For Christ's sake Siobhan, you're talking nonsense. It's out of the question. It's not technically possible. It couldn't be concealed for long enough. Even if it were Sean would be killed along with Ewart.'

Siobhan glanced at the impassive Walsh to see if he had registered her compliment. Nothing. She dismissed him from her mind and concentrated on her irritated lover. Her voice, normally soft and feminine, took on a harder edge, as if exasperated. 'So what if McAllister is killed? He's no loss. He did good service once but he's done nothing for years. He's a burned-out drunk of no use to anybody. He'll be dead of the drink soon anyway.'

Billy Walsh shifted his feet, thinking *thank you, Lord*. Madden would never take this. Madden would go mad. He might even kill the cow himself.

It seemed as if Walsh was right. Madden was out of the chair, his beer slopping over the floor among the shards of his smashed beer glass, his face wild, a .38 Smith & Wesson Saturday night special in his right fist, inches from Siobhan's head. 'Don't talk like that! I've known Sean McAllister since we were kids. He was a good man and the Brits destroyed his mind. Even now that bastard Ewart is trying to work on him. I won't have this. I will not have it. Say one more word and I'll fucking kill you here and now. Do you hear me?'

Siobhan stood very still, head lowered, feeling the anger flowing out of Madden, testing it. It was hot, the anger of the moment, not the chilled rage that lay deep in him and caused him to act. It could be all right, but she would have to be very careful. Her voice back to normal she said softly 'I hear you, Gerry.'

As Madden subsided she caught him half in, half out of his chair. 'But I think you're making a mistake. Ewart will catch you, or finally get somebody to talk. He'll tell the SAS and they'll set you up and kill you. I don't want that to happen, Gerry. You're too important to the Cause.' She paused, just for a half-breath '. . . and I love you.'

Madden, his hands on the arms of the chair, was caught unbalanced, physically and psychologically. He opted to sit down first, then think. But she didn't stop to give him the chance to dismiss her. Billy Walsh couldn't believe it. *You clever, vicious little witch.*

'Ewart is dangerous. You know that. He has to go or you will in the end. He has to die, no matter what it costs. I know what you think of Sean, but Sean's dying. He can serve the Cause one last time, even if he doesn't know it. He's our only chance to get Ewart. We have to take that chance. It would all be over in a second. Sean wouldn't even know it had happened. What's more important, Gerry? The life of a dying man or your freedom? If Sean had the choice and could understand he wouldn't hesitate, he'd detonate the bomb himself. We can't afford to lose you, Gerry. Please think about it.' Siobhan sank to her knees and grasped his hands. 'Please Gerry, think about it.'

Madden seemed confused, emotions flickering over his face. Billy Walsh was stunned, confused himself. *Either you mean it or you should be looking for an Oscar, Siobhan.* Still, he couldn't help but admire her. He waited for Madden to put his mind to work, confident that the chief would do the right thing.

Madden stared at Siobhan, his eyes no longer wild. Something had changed in him, like the throwing of a switch. He spoke, flat and emotionless. 'A technical matter. Tell me how you think it's possible.'

'I don't know a lot about bombs. But I think a command wire would be discovered. It might have to be in place for months. It can't be any kind of trigger or timing device because Ewart is so unpredictable; something else might set it off and then Sean would be lost for nothing. It has to be radio controlled and it has to be able to be switched on and off to avoid the Brit scanners. We have to have someone to switch it on for us and to call in the volunteer who will fire it. The old woman up there has sons. Take one of them and tell him exactly what to do. He has to watch out for Ewart. When Ewart comes he calls the volunteer and switches on the bomb. Or something happens to his mother.'

Madden nodded. The plan seemed logical. 'Why not a timer switch? It's more reliable than the electronics. All the farmer would have to do is start it.'

'He would have to go to the caravan. Ewart might get suspicious. Or Ewart might leave or go out just after the switch was activated. We have to be sure he's in the caravan when the bomb is fired. There must be a power line from the house to the caravan. We can run a line to the bomb's power supply from that. The farmer can switch it on from inside the house. Before you ask: a command wire along the power line is no good. We have to give the volunteer a chance to get away and we don't want the farmer to see him. The first place the Brits will look is the house so it's better if the volunteer has never been there. The bomb will just sit there, switched off until we need it. The Brit scanners can only find bombs that are active.'

Madden smiled. 'You're not just a pretty face, Siobhan. I always knew it. Billy?'

Billy Walsh had listened carefully. 'It's a terrible end for Sean, Gerry,' he said. 'But I think Siobhan has thought of everything. It would work. We would get Ewart at last. I can't see how it could fail if nothing goes wrong during the setting up or something unexpected delays the volunteer. Even then we could switch the bomb off again until next time. It's a good plan.'

Madden looked undecided, thinking. Siobhan kept up the pressure, knowing that this was the best chance she would ever have to impress the ASU commanders enough to be taken seriously in future.

'There are other things, Gerry. Not even Ewart would think we would use a live man, one of our own and a hero of the Cause as bait. That's a weakness we can exploit. And there's propaganda. Killing Ewart would be a great blow. You can write an article for *An Phoblacht* reminding our people of what the Brits did to Sean. You can tell them how Ewart has badgered a sick man for years. You can tell them Sean realised he was dying and volunteered to sacrifice his last days. You can tell them he deliberately set and fired the bomb himself, to make sure. Sean would be a hero again Gerry, a martyr for the Cause. It would be a just reward for all he has suffered.'

Madden made a characteristic decision-making gesture, snapping the middle fingers and thumbs of both hands. 'Do it. Make the bomb big enough to totally destroy the caravan. I don't want Sean to suffer.'

Siobhan sighed and kissed his right hand, still holding the snub-nosed gun. *You've let him suffer for years, you bloody hypocrite. But you'll use him just like you use me, and throw him away. You won't throw me away. One of these days I'll use you. Then I'll throw you away.*

18 June 1983
LONDON

Charlotte Aitken sat, hands folded in her lap in front of the

205

little Olivetti portable in her flat, pulling together in her mind the words she wanted to use. She looked tired and her face had aged, thinning down into tighter lines. The first silver hairs had begun to glint in her thick dark hair. That morning she had looked in her mirror and grimaced, thinking it impossible that she could have changed so much in less than a year. Now thirty and very beautiful, some men would have thought her more attractive than ever if it weren't for the lack of interest that showed in her eyes. At her elbow was a plant stand, minus the potted palm that belonged there. She had turned out the lights and her sitting room was aglow with the light of five candles. It was important to set the scene: it had taken her a long time to gather the courage to write this letter. Even the decision to type it rather than write it had been painful. She reached for the bottle on the plant stand and carefully poured a small Glenfiddich.

It was way beyond midnight when the letter was finished, and a third of the bottle was gone. Unused to drinking, Charlotte read the letter through, the lines blurring one into the next. Carefully, more carefully than necessary, she sealed it into an envelope and burst into tears, feeling guilty; even the paper she had chosen to write on was a plain, stark white.

25 June 1983
BULAWAYO

Jamie Lappin, alone as usual in his tent, resting through the hottest part of the Zimbabwean day, held a plain white envelope, not noticing how the paper quivered with his trembling. He knew it was from Charlotte and longed to rip it open, read it greedily. But a part of him was afraid of what it might contain. He carefully sliced open the top of the envelope, using the tip of a bayonet.

Dear Jamie,

I think you know what happened. We were seen and reported. You were sent away and I was stripped of my security vetting and sent to Guildford for the worst months of my life. I heard nothing from you. I thought hard about what I had to do. I was and am very much in love with you, but love does not make careers. I had to choose and I chose my career. It seemed more secure and I need it. I could not see myself as anything other than what I am and I could not see you as anything other than what you are. I am told you have been forgiven and are doing well. I have been promoted lieutenant-colonel, seven years before I am due promotion. You should be promoted soon, well ahead of your time. Jamie, we are not ordinary people, we must face up to our abilities. Please work hard and be commissioned. Come home and marry me.

Charlotte

He read the letter again, and then again, searching for nuances, every possible hidden meaning. Slowly it came to him. Charlotte did love him and was suffering without him, but her course had been fixed by her grandfather and she couldn't break out. She wanted them to be together, but only in the context of the army. For him to leave and do something else would not be good enough, for to Charlotte he was everything a soldier should be, except that he was not an officer. If he were commissioned and came back to her life for her would be perfect. But if he were not commissioned he should not come back at all: he should stay away and let her follow her chosen path. She seemed to have missed the most important thing of all: his love for her. Over the past months he had had much time to think about their years together and had come to look on himself as a kind of spare part, called on by Charlotte when needed but put back in his box when she wanted to get on with more important things. It was an unfair assessment of the role Charlotte played in his life and self-pitying, he knew, but that's how he thought. This letter seemed to confirm it.

For what seemed a long time Jamie tried to think about how he felt now, but could feel nothing. No pain, not even disappointment. He just knew it was all over. Something deep inside him was telling him he was being called to heel, that his partnership with Charlotte was over, that if he went her way he would forever be dependent, always have to defer to her needs, would betray everything he had become, everything he had worked so hard for, everything he believed in. For years he had kept no God. The regiment was enough: feeding him, clothing him, making sure he kept himself healthy, offering the companionship of like-minded men, setting goals, holding out the promise of advancement through his own efforts. If he kept on going as he was he must become RSM, he must be commissioned, in probably not more than two or three years. Then it would be inevitable that he would drift back to Charlotte as a supporting actor in the drama of her pursuit of generalship. He must not let that happen, if he were to remain whole and his own. He would never be commissioned, never even make RSM. With this letter Charlotte had killed his career, stolen from him the motivation always to search for more. His pursuit of excellence was over, his driving ambition destroyed by Charlotte's obsession. It was over between them and between him and the army. Lappin stood up and walked calmly out of his tent. The discipline of long-range shooting always eased his mind and brought clarity to his thoughts.

The sergeant at the armoury was tempted to point out that it was against regulations to draw weapons and live ammunition without written authority, but remembered that Lappin had written the regulations. Besides, there was something odd about the sar'nt-major. Outwardly he seemed perfectly normal, smart, sharply creased, boots shining, the red beret an exact half-inch above his eyebrows, its silver winged badge centred above his left eye. But he was different.

Inside the cool and dark of the armoury Lappin threw a box

of ammunition into a small canvas bag and reached for the long rifle leaning in its rack. He paused for a moment, as if reassured by the rifle's weight and perfect design, and ran his hands over its blued steel and darkened wood, a hint of oil caressing his fingers.

In theory a standard L42A1 sniper rifle, the weapon was a rebarrelled, rebuilt Number Four .303 inch Lee Enfield short-magazine infantry rifle. Its stock and foregrip had been replaced by weathered and linseeded hickory wood tailored to his needs, with small indentations placed to guide his fingers and jawbone into the perfect firing position. The rifle's new, thick-walled 7.62 millimetre barrel and working parts had been given critical inspection and carefully re-engineered to meet a standard far beyond the reach of any factory.

Lappin glanced at the wooden box holding the rifle's x 4 optical sight, picked it up, removed the sight and carefully fitted it to the rifle. There were no adjustments to be made, no need to choose a position on the rifle slide to fit it, for it fitted in only one place, to within one tenth of one thousandth of an inch, on both horizontal and lateral axes. Like the rifle the sight was a one-off, adapted from a deerhunting sight built by the Carl Zeiss factory at Jena, East Germany.

Rifle and sight had been reworked by a gifted craftsman, a Royal Electrical and Mechanical Engineers weapons artificer wholly employed by the Small Arms School Corps in Warminster. Together the gun and sight were a near ultimate expression of the gunsmith's art. Low down on the stock the gunsmith's initials, *RB*, were placed under *J Lappin MM*, burnt into the wood with hot wire.

During initial test firing of the complete weapon Lappin had achieved five rounds inside a three-inch circle at 600 metres, five rounds inside a fifteen-inch circle at 1,200 metres, four rounds out of five into a twenty-inch square at 1,500, all over undulating ground, with the wind swinging, the trees along the range altering the airflow, causing unpredictable eddies the rifleman needed to feel and sense rather than see. He had been ecstatic. In effect he could guarantee a first-round head shot at 600 metres, a body shot at more than double that. The watching NCOs from the Small Arms School Corps had nodded gravely. The weapons artificer had merely grunted 'Near enough'.

Later, over a beer in the mess, the SASC sar'nt-major had been blunt. He was due to retire in a couple of years and there would be a vacancy. He had held the post of Rangemaster (Snipers) for eleven years and had no natural successor. Some of his colleagues could step into the gap, but were better at other things. What the Corps needed was a dedicated, natural rifleman to take over the post. Lappin's case had been discussed. An application for transfer from the Paras to the SASC would meet with no opposition.

Lappin had been surprised, to say the least. The SASC were probably the best small arms weapons instructors in the world, certainly the most professional. There were few members of the smallest fighting corps in the British Army, but their influence was enormous. Anybody could apply to join, but only the very few who had achieved A gradings in the SASC weapons instructor courses had the ghost of a chance and even then they still had to have something else, something exceptional to offer. To be invited to apply was unusual in the extreme. Flattered, Lappin had declined with thanks. He thought he had a lot left to achieve with the Paras. The rifle was reward enough for his Falklands contribution to rehabilitating an often derided infantry skill. Snipers were back in fashion and the SASC sniping courses filled for months ahead.

But things were different now. Looking at the rifle Lappin saw another kind of beauty, saw his future open up before him. His search for excellence might not be over after all. He could remain in his present rank safe from Charlotte Aitken and devote his career to his second great love. He would teach and he would practise, finding and training great battlefield riflemen, honing his skills to stay ahead of the best of them, become the sniper's sniper, the finest rifleman of them all. His new challenge would replace the old; officers were two a penny, even Para officers. But there was only one Rangemaster (Snipers). Lappin felt the old charge of excitement tingle through him. The SASC would be his new home. *What better time to start than now?*

9 July 1983
WATERFOOT, COUNTY ANTRIM

It had not been a bad day. Not special, but not bad, even though it had begun before four in the morning. The phone call telling him that J.J. Macall had been captured had pulled Peter Ewart cursing and grunting out of his bed and into his street clothes. Macall was a known player, a veteran of the H blocks and currently a very slippery member of the Markets ASU. They would get nothing much out of such an old hand but the questions he wouldn't answer might lead them on to something or someone else. But six hours on and off with Macall had been disappointing: Macall had refused to say anything at all, even to identify himself. Still, the contents of his pockets might be useful.

There had been the usual comb, wallet with a few pounds, a pocket knife, cigarette packet and throwaway lighter. There had also been four used Ulsterbus tickets, one to Armagh and three to Castlewellan. Macall had been stupid not to have thrown them away, but maybe even the Provos required receipts these days if a man was to claim his expenses. The dates on the tickets told them Macall had visited Armagh on the day that Joelly Bright had been released from custody at Armagh jail after serving eight years for the incendiary bombing of a Belfast bookshop. Bright had been sighted in Castlewellan ten days after her release. Obviously Macall had gone to Armagh to collect her and deliver her to the boys of County Down. The other tickets indicated he was keeping in touch with her, once a week, preparing her for reintroduction into active service. It was useful intelligence. Bright would be watched out for. The rest of the day had been the usual slog through written reports, producing nothing.

Drifting slowly along the coast road Ewart suddenly changed direction, swinging inland, heading over the hills toward the landward end of the Red Bay. In the boot of his car were a couple of bottles, in his jacket pocket an envelope for the old lady. Examination of his mirrors showed nothing and Ewart looked forward to a quiet night with his dying friend: Sean McAllister had only months now, maybe only weeks. Ewart hoped that this would not be his last visit to the little caravan. His visits there kept him going, kept him believing he had not sunk so far into the covert war that he had ceased to believe in the value of people.

Up in the farmhouse a middle-aged man unaccustomed to dealing with violent men agonised over what he had done. In the farmhouse kitchen he could hear his mother crack eggs on the edge of her ancient cast-iron frying pan. Although he was not hungry, it was his mother's habit to feed her boys whenever they appeared, whatever the time of day or night. The farmer knew that his actions would kill the stumbling drunk down in the caravan, and with him the man who paid his bills.

Who the man from Belfast was the farmer did not know and did not really want to know. His mother was in danger. The four men who had taken him off his own farm, hooded and beaten him, clicked gun hammers against his head and told him what he had to do had left in him no doubt that his mother and maybe he too would die unless he did as he was told. Earlier today he had seen the visitor's car but had done nothing until he had seen the man himself and was sure that he was the one that had been coming here for years. The farmer moved like an automaton, unwilling, a thinking robot, to do the will of those who pulled his wires.

In Whitehouse, a northern suburb of the city, a thin and unwholesome woman answered the farmer's call. She called another number, sending a quiet schoolteacher on his way. The schoolteacher, a man carrying the burdens of a BA Hons (Econ.), an MSc in business studies and a PhD in political science on his philosophical shoulders left the comforts of his wife and home to put the theories of his youth into action. It took him less than an hour to get into position; on his way he collected the fat white DISKXPRESS floppy disk box superglued closed and fitted with a short black button on its top. All he had to do was gain the high ground above the little caravan, ensure the presence of a middle-height, thick-bodied man of middle age he did not know and press the black button. The box would send out signals on a television channel, act like a remote control. Easy enough, but an act of great faith for an educated man.

Peter Ewart, tired, had no thought beyond the man who shared his bottle. Sean seemed a little better now. Gone were the bloodshot eyes and bloated body. He had lost a great deal of weight and moved with the years of a younger man, but in his brightness there was emptiness. His self and his body were lost. There remained only a hulk, dependent on the whiskey for its life. Ewart strained to reach the long-lost man, defeated before he tried. In his mind's eye Peter Ewart saw his loss. It was not months or even weeks. In days Sean McAllister would be gone, a shadow in his past. Ewart felt – the lights flickered – 'Have you a problem with your lights Sean? I'll tell the old woman.'

Sean answered. No, there was no trouble with his lights. A TV man from Belfast had come to check them a week or two ago. Sean laughed, a TV man for the lights! Time for another jar or two.

Ewart stood up as far as he could under the low roof of the caravan, using the moonlight to scan the field between him and the farmhouse, noting the power cable running on poles from house to van. There was nothing more to see, but the lights of the van were just a fraction dimmer than before, as if a refrigerator had switched itself on.

'Have you a fridge, Sean?'

'No, Peter. They took it away because I kept things too long. The oul girl thought I would poison myself.'

Ewart felt the first little prickle of fear. Nothing had changed in the caravan: no extra lights had been put on, no TV, no refrigerator, nothing. *No TV.* But the lights had dimmed. Why? There must be an extra drain on the power somewhere. If not here then in the house. Why had someone checked Sean's lights? *And why had there been no bill for the work?* Ewart's suspicions and sense of self-preservation were now fully aroused. He looked at the lights again: standard caravan lights, 12 volt . . . *12 volt.* The power cable from the house was 240 volt, running into a transformer in one of Sean's cupboards, which cut its voltage from 240 to 12. *No TV . . . a TV man from Belfast . . . Christ! a video . . . that needs 240 volts . . . a video with a built-in timer . . . and remote control . . .*

Ewart jerked open the cupboard door, pulling a pile of jerseys out on to the floor. The transformer was there as before, with its old wiring intact. But a new, two-strand wire was joined to the power cable, neatly tacked to the cupboard wall, running down, bypassing the transformer. Ewart pulled open the lower cupboard, his mind sharp and clear, his mouth dry. A burst of nervous sweat wet his armpits. *Holy Jesus.* The thin wire ran down to the floor, but did not bend away to an appliance, it carried on straight through a small hole in the floor surrounded by a corona of drilling dust. A fist of real fear grabbed Ewart's heart, darkening his vision for a moment. Certainty hit him. As his head cleared he leapt to his feet, banging his head on the low ceiling. Sean laughed, a glass of whiskey in each hand. Ewart dared not shout. Sean might panic. Someone outside might hear and be prompted to act, send a signal to trigger a timer set to zero delay, blow them both to hell. Ewart reached for the door with his right hand and pulled it open. Wrapping his left arm round Sean's almost weightless frame, he lifted him off his feet and threw them both out the door. As they hit the ground Sean began to react, struggling and complaining. Ewart let him go and whispered savagely, 'Come with me, Sean. Stay close to me and crawl across the road and down the bank. Come on.'

Ewart scuttled on hands and knees out on to the road, the tarmac rough on his hands, then across the road and over the bank, sliding down through the sand and beach grass. 'Stop here —'

He looked for Sean, but he was nowhere to be seen. Ewart cursed himself and heaved himself back up the bank, his feet sliding in the sand. Sean was upright, standing in the doorway, a bottle in his hand. Oh God, thought Ewart, his poor mind hasn't grasped what's happening. Ewart moved to stand up and motion to Sean, call him over the road. He put his full weight on a tussock of beach grass clinging to the slope. The tussock broke away, unbalanced him and threw him backwards down the slope.

Three hundred metres from the caravan, up the hill and off to one side of the farmhouse the schoolteacher was panicking, his palms sweaty on the plastic box. The caravan door on the side away from him had opened, he could see the light spilling out, a man's shadow outlined in it. It was worrying that he couldn't be sure. Even more worrying was the patrol. On the road he could see a Makralon-covered Land Rover moving slowly towards the caravan, lights out: a UDR or Brit patrol coming to check out the village. Or had something gone wrong? Maybe the Land Rover had a scanner in it, was searching for the source of the electronic emissions it had picked up. He was tempted to wait, to try to get the vehicle level with the caravan, do a bit of damage there too. At least that would add to the confusion and aid his escape. But what if the scanner neutralised the trigger mechanism of the bomb? He stopped thinking, panic growing in him, his mind full of what-ifs. The shadow thrown by the man in the caravan doorway was big and bulky. He must be the one.

As Ewart struggled back up the slope Sean looked at his own foreshortened shadow and grinned inanely. What was Peter playing at? He had put one foot on the ground, stepping down out of the caravan when the teacher pressed the small black button. As Peter Ewart got one hand on to the top of the bank the bomb detonated its twelve kilos of Semtex, a gross overkill, blowing the caravan and Sean McAllister into nonexistence. The huge power of the explosive was concentrated upwards and outwards, its great flash brilliantly lighting up the countryside for a millisecond before the blast wave swept out over the road and up the hill, smashing in the windows of the farmhouse, upending the Land Rover on the road, sweeping on to knock down telegraph poles and lift roof slates in the village. Then came the bang, a huge thunderclap of sound that blattered all around, hemmed in by the hills, throwing itself for miles out over the sea.

Minutes later Peter Ewart was hauled roughly to his feet by a shocked, frightened and very angry soldier of the Queen's Lancashire Regiment, his nasal Liverpudlian speech speeded up by the adrenalin running through him. 'Whothefuck're you? What'reyou doing? Standupwillyou! Stand up!' Ewart shrugged the soldier off. 'Get your hands off me. I'm an RUC officer. That bomb was meant for me. Get an officer.'

The young soldier reacted instantly to the voice of authority. 'Mr Ball sir! Over here sir!'

Another soldier detached himself from two more who had appeared, running down the slope. 'OK, Private Janes. I'm here. What's going on? Who's this?'

Ewart felt an edge of anger. 'Talk to me, not him. I'm Chief Inspector Ewart, Belfast Special Branch. The bomb was meant for me. Where did you come from?'

'Second-Lieutenant Ball sir, QLR. We were on routine patrol, coming down the road when the bomb blew. Knocked our vehicle over. Only cuts and bruises. Are you all right, sir?'

Ewart shook his head. His nose was bleeding from the tiny fraction of the blast he had caught; he had been sheltered by the slope. 'Get on your radio. There are only two ways anybody can escape without going past you and both of them start at the T junction at the end of the village. Ask for road blocks on both those roads about five miles out. Ask the Belfast resident battalion to send the NightSun over this area in case the bombers are trying

216

to get out overland. We'll catch these bastards. Raid that house up there with your own men and arrest anybody in it except for an old woman. Then report back to me. There was somebody in the caravan. We'll have to search the area for his body.'

The young officer was not accustomed to taking orders from a policeman, but the burly, blood-smeared man was senior enough and seemed to be talking sense, until he talked about a body. There would be no body. There *could* be no body.

'Very good, sir. I'll do all that. May I see your ID?'

In less than twenty minutes the area was sealed off for miles around; the farmer was in custody, being held in the village pub; two platoons of the Queen's Lancashire Regiment were on their way, led by their company commander; Special Branch and uniformed RUC were coming from Belfast and the NightSun, a helicopter fitted with a huge searchlight, moved in ever increasing circles overhead. Ewart was slumped on the road. *I'll see you in hell for this, Madden. If I have to kill you with my own hands I'll see you in hell for this.*

As dawn broke one of the QLR platoons sweeping the ground found the transmitter, dropped by the fleeing teacher. The teacher had been caught two hours before, pinned blinded into the middle of a barley field like a fly on a board by the solid white bar of the million-candlepower beam thrown by NightSun. The farmer had confessed to everything, sobbing uncontrollably. Ewart gazed at him with contempt. 'Charge him with the murder of Sean McAllister and the attempted murder of myself.'

The farmer looked up. 'I'm sorry. I'm sorry. But I had to. They beat me and put a hood over my head. They threatened to kill my mother. I had to do it!'

Ewart shook his head. 'No. You had to do no such thing. You had to tell the police. You would have been put under protective surveillance. Nothing would have happened to you or your mother. The Provisionals are not stupid people. They know they can't risk much in this area, not when the security forces have been alerted. They tried it on and played you for a sucker. And you did exactly as you were told. You knew what was going to happen and you aided and abetted it. You're going to jail. And you're going to stay there.'

Though he tried very hard Ewart could not get near the teacher. His colleagues shook their heads and said, 'Sorry, sir. The superintendent says no. You're too close to this case. You will be kept informed.'

10 July 1983
STRABANE, COUNTY TYRONE

Gerry Madden had been up all night. That in itself was not unusual, for as time had gone by he had become more and more nocturnal in his habits, rarely turning in before 4 a.m.

Around the table sat eight men, and one woman who was little more than a girl in appearance. Madden took his seat, a straight-backed kitchen chair, and said flatly, 'The operation was a failure. Everything went as planned, but a bloody Brit patrol turned up at the worst possible time and panicked our man. Sean McAllister is dead, God rest his soul, but that evil pig Ewart is still alive and unhurt. The schoolteacher is in custody. That is not a problem because he knows nothing and nobody and was chosen as being expendable. But Ewart is still alive. Has anyone anything to say?'

The commander of the Armagh ASU spoke to the point. 'The plan was good. It worked. Sean's loss is sad, but your contingency plan to make him a hero and a martyr can still go ahead. We can deny knowledge of the schoolteacher and claim that the Brits have taken an innocent man as a scapegoat. We can claim that the SAS found out about the bomb and sent in the patrol to detonate it with their scanner. It's unfortunate that Ewart survived. He must have slipped out to take a leak or something. He's been lucky this time, as he has been before.

But we only have to be lucky once. He knows that. I think we'll see less of him as he concentrates on his own survival. He might even quit and go somewhere safer. No blame can be attached to anyone. We should be grateful for the contribution of Woman Volunteer McCaillim in this operation. I propose that she is promoted to the rank of lieutenant for her clear-sightedness and tireless efforts to ensure the operation's success.'

Not everyone around the table wholeheartedly agreed with Armagh, but they saw the direction of the wind. The vote was unanimous. Lieutenant McCaillim thanked the assembly for their vote of confidence. The chief of staff announced that she would be appointed to the central planning staff with immediate effect. Then he abruptly left and went to bed.

When all but one of the men had gone, Siobhan McCaillim said, 'I owe you a favour. That could have gone badly for me. What can I do for you?'

The man from Armagh pretended uncertainty. 'I'm not sure. I'm not looking for much. I'm best where I am and I don't have the brains for politicking. I want to keep what I've got. I'm thinking that when Gerry retires from active service or gets picked up and jailed there'd better be somebody to take over. It has to be somebody from the North. Those old men in the Republic are good enough for getting money and guns, but they're out of touch. I've been watching you. I'll have to watch you closer. I'm thinking that you'll need some support. What's in it for me?'

Siobhan McCaillim folded her hands in her lap, suppressing the excitement flowing through her. This man was the most powerful in the North, next to Gerry Madden. She had underestimated him. He knew his strengths. He also knew his limitations and was preparing for the day when a brighter man would lay claim to Armagh. He was offering an alliance. More importantly, he was taking her seriously.

'I think you're a wee bit early. Gerry will be fighting on for years yet. He will not be picked up and jailed, he's far too clever for that. The Brits don't even have a photograph of him. Don't let his appearance fool you. All this ulcer problem and insomnia is nothing to worry about. It's just that the Brits are getting to grips with the ASU structure he brought in. Eventually he'll think of ways for us to protect ourselves. Then he'll be all right and back to his old self. Our failure to get Ewart was a blow and he's taking it hard. We need a success to get the Army Council off his back. You should work at that.'

'And in the long term?'

'Gerry has a long way to go. I think that one day he'll be looking for a more political post. He's got his troubles at the moment but he has a lot of support on the Army Council and Padraig Hanna has to retire some day.'

Siobhan stopped and turned away, standing with her back to the man to prevent him from reading the excitement in her eyes. 'I think somebody has to be ready to take over as chief of staff, but whoever it is will need powerful friends in the North. And whoever that somebody is will have to be prepared to guarantee that good and proven fighting men are not replaced by bright lads of no experience. If I were asked for my views I'd say that we must look to the future, but that we must remember that experience can't be bought or learned from a book. A man like yourself now, not looking for promotion, could hold his place until he chose his own successor. He could then move on to the staff, to provide the voice of bitter experience to a chief of staff who lacked it.'

'Aye, I would go along with that. Armagh is dear to me. I'd like to hand her over to a man of my own choosing. And to be the elder statesman, like? To have no responsibility but to offer good advice if asked. That's perfect. I'd hate to be bummed out with nothing to do. We'll get along, Siobhan.'

I have him. 'No, we'll not get along. You'll support me from now on. You'll work among the others to see me on my way. And I'll see you retired an honoured veteran, with a voice on my council.'

'You're a girl and a half, Siobhan. I'm in. And by the way, you have no friend in Billy Walsh.'

'That's your problem. Remove him when the time is right. I'm glad that we have an understanding. You must be tired. It's a long way to Armagh.'

'I'm going to get a couple of hours on one of the truckle beds and get away before morning. I'll be fine.'

'Good. Plan for doing something soon in Armagh. Bring it up at the next meeting. I'll help you plan it and get Gerry involved. It will strengthen our position and help get Gerry out of this state he's in.'

'Aye, OK.' He allowed his eyes to wander.

'Don't even think it.' Siobhan had the upper hand and intended to keep it. Men like this thought that sex and domination were the same thing. 'There's a waitress in the hotel dining room that looks after Billy Walsh. Use her. Goodnight.'

Chapter Eleven

14 July 1987

WARMINSTER

The great lecture room at the School of Infantry at Warminster was abuzz with voices. Officers of many corps and regiments, in their varying dress, sat awaiting their lecturer. The chief guest was Lieutenant-General Sir Harry George MC QGM, Commander United Kingdom Land Forces. Other dignitaries sat around him, sweeping upwards and outwards, mere battalion commanders and their like relegated to the higher tiers of the auditorium. Even so, by the general's written direction one complete side of the great hall had been set aside for officers ranking second-lieutenant to major. Competition for places in every part of the hall had been fierce for all twelve of the planned series of special lectures. This lecture was to be the third. Subjects ranged from 'The Capabilities of the Warsaw Pact' delivered with unusual panache by the eminent Russia watcher Dr Chris Donnelly, to 'How You Will Be Perceived by History' by John Keegan, historian, military commentator and author of *The Face of Battle*, a seminal work on every thinking officer's bookshelf.

Today's lecture would be 'What Price Accuracy? The Value of the Rifleman'. It would be delivered by the army's premier rifleman, the Small Arms School Corps' Chief Instructor in Musketry, an ancient title that obscured its holder's true vocation. He was better known as the army's one and only Rangemaster (Snipers).

As the clock hit 11.30 precisely, Jamie Lappin marched out from behind the heavy curtain, halted, executed a perfect left turn, faced the general and saluted. The general stood up to return the salute. As a courtesy, every other officer in the auditorium rose to his feet.

'Warrant Officer Class Two, Rangemaster (Snipers) Lappin J. reporting as ordered, General. May I have your leave to carry on sir!'

'Please be so good as to carry on Sar'nt-Major. The floor is yours.'

'Thank you, sir.' Lappin paused for a second, still twenty paces from the lectern and called out 'Corporal!'

A corporal of the Parachute Regiment marched out and relieved Sergeant-Major Lappin of the pace stick he carried under his left arm, replacing it with a blued steel and hickory wood rifle. The rifle secure, Lappin marched forward to the lectern.

'So far so good, ladies and gentlemen. That's the military courtesies over and done with.' He placed the rifle across the leading edge of the lectern, where it could not help but be constantly in their view.

'Let's get down to business. I see myself confronted with the best minds the army has to offer. I am not an intellectual. Should you engage me in argument I may well be defeated. That is as it should be. You are paid to think. I and my like are paid to do. But remember this, if you would: I have a rifle, you don't.' He paused as a ripple of laughter flowed down from the tiers, welcoming it with a smile before continuing.

'It is not my purpose today to say that a man with a rifle is the solution to all military problems: that would be patently untrue. What I intend to do is to convince you that there is value in having men who have the training, developed skill, natural ability and equipment to destroy and disrupt our enemies at the times and in the places those enemies feel most secure, that individual riflemen, properly selected, trained and equipped can swing the course of a battle, that individual riflemen can have an impact on the fighting capability and morale of an enemy out of all proportion to their numbers . . .'

'. . . Warsaw Pact's huge armoured forces are led into position by the Soviets' Commandants' Corps. They are a valid target for riflemen. Hit the right four men at the right four road junctions and a full Warsaw Pact armoured division may find itself heading in the wrong direction, its hundreds of tanks moving confidently across its sister divisions' paths, getting in their way, slowing them down, confusing them and at the same time exposing itself to a devastating flank attack . . .'

'. . . Soviet corps and divisional generals would not take kindly to being brought abruptly into the front line like any common soldier. Such men know their own value too well. If our riflemen could not kill them outright those same riflemen could conceal themselves for days, moving with and continually harassing the targeted HQs. The generals' plans would be seriously disrupted by continual forced moves of their HQs, not because they feared the riflemen, but because an enemy who has the capability to shoot down a general in his own HQ knows exactly where that HQ is: we might decide to withdraw our irritating riflemen and replace them with an even more irritating airstrike. No senior commander could tolerate that possibility . . .'

'. . . close my presentation with a small observation.' Lappin raised a hand. Three men dressed in the ragged camouflage of snipers trained for a European war marched out from behind the curtain. Lappin moved to join them.

'How easy would you rest, ladies and gentlemen, if you knew with perfect certainty that I, any one of these men or possibly all four of us, lay lurking in the undergrowth a mile from your own HQ, with the sole intention of killing you?'

The four snipers marched out, to the best applause of all: total silence. The audience was stunned.

Behind the curtain Jamie Lappin took a deep breath, expelling it hard and fast to relieve his tension, expecting to hear the shuffle of moving feet. For many minutes, it seemed, there was silence. Maybe he had gone too far, failed to impress his distinguished audience. *Well, fuck it. I tried. I tried my best.* He reached out to touch the shoulder of the nearest rifleman, to say 'Sorry, I let you down.' Before his fingers could reach the man a chanting roar and a heavy drumming of feet thundered through the curtain. Surprised, he jerked back. His riflemen were grinning, swinging round to thump him on the back, trying to shake his hand. The roaring became clearer. Lappin risked a quick look round the edge of the curtain. The area of the auditorium set aside for the young officers was on its feet, chanting 'RIFLES, RIFLES. BRING ON THE RIFLES,' while their more senior and dignified superiors grinned indulgently and satisfied themselves with hammering on the arms of their chairs.

Lappin pulled himself together. For a moment he had forgotten that officers politely clap hands to applaud civilians – but among their own they stamp their feet and pound on anything handy to show approval of something they think well done. He'd only seen it happen once before, years ago in this same hall, an accolade to a policeman they'd taken to themselves, the day he'd first met Charlotte. It seemed impossible, but today it was happening for him. A great rush of emotion swept through him, unmanning him and threatening him with tears. His riflemen politely saw nothing, waiting for orders. Lappin rolled his neck, straightened his shoulders and forced himself to calm down. There seemed only one thing to do.

'Right then, lads. We've won the day. Let's finish it with style. There's at least a dozen generals and more colonels than I could count out there, so wipe those smiles off your faces and listen in. Some of the old boys on the other side of that curtain have been in more shooting wars than they would care to admit. They know what a good rifleman can do, but they might be a bit wary of giving the nod to a scruffy bunch of prima donnas. We need them on our side, so it's time for a bit of old-fashioned bullshit, to show them we have discipline. We're going to do a bit of drill. We'll march out at shoulder arms, halt, general salute and stand at ease. There'll be no words of command. Watch me. Give it pride and dignity, and give it a bit of swagger. Show them you're professional soldiers who happen to be the great riflemen I know you are. Follow me.'

Directly the four riflemen appeared the pandemonium began to subside. Determined not to let themselves down the three snipers marched behind their sergeant-major like guardsmen, heads up, right arms clamping their rifles at the shoulder arms, left fists swinging in unison, shoulders swaying very slightly with each precise thirty-inch pace, presenting a picture of solid, prideful, self-imposed discipline totally at odds with their blotched and ragged edged clothing. With the sixth sense of professionals they caught the minuscule change in Lappin's stride as he prepared to halt, matching themselves to him, banging their feet in as his own came together at attention. Almost by reflex they followed Lappin's salute, swinging their rifles, moving their feet so that as Lappin's hand reached his forehead their right feet hit the floor in a single solid thump, rifles held vertical in front of them in the classic Present Arms. Again the feet drummed and fists pounded, amid cries of 'Well done, well done' and nods exchanged between old warriors.

Surprised, the general, a former Life Guard himself, jumped to his feet to return their salute, momentarily nonplussed, but not for long. 'It would appear, Sar'nt-Major, that all of my officers wish to be sure of the exact location of you and yours, while you might be within a mile of them. May I congratulate you on your excellent and convincing presentation. May I also congratulate you on catching me out: I had not expected that your riflemen practised rifle drill as part of their training. Well done. There is clearly a consensus: there is a case for the retention of riflemen of ability in the British Army. No doubt in the coming months there will be counter-arguments. They will be listened to. I am most grateful for your contribution. Thank you. Carry on, please.'

Sergeant-Major Jamie Lappin, in the midst of the greatest triumph of his career, fully understood the general, as all those present understood him: the question was still open, but anyone arguing against the retention and possible expansion of the role of long-range riflemen in the British Army had better have a bloody good case, or his own judgement might well be called into question. The general was sold.

Lappin's salute was immaculate, the performance of his riflemen above reproach as they prepared to march off. But then Lappin seemed to hesitate, almost to misstep. He recovered quickly, swung back into his place at the head of the line and led his men away.

Up in the Gods Lieutenant-Colonel Charlotte Aitken closed her eyes and hugged his stumble to her, feeling the hot sexual longing for him, once so familiar, charge through her belly, releasing her from her prison of pent up fear and pain. Lost among hundreds she had not been obvious to him. But as he turned for the last time she had seized her chance, stood up to catch his eye, hesitant, frightened of what she might see there, frightened of a blank uninterested stare, a look that might destroy her. But in that fleeting moment she had seen enough, had watched his eyes turn from pride to agony. He had seen her pride in his achievement, her love of him shine brightly. He would know that she still loved her. She knew that he loved her. It had to be enough.

9 p.m. 24 December 1990
THE IRISH BORDER

'Please get out of the car sir. Open up your bonnet and boot.' The young lieutenant of the Devon and Dorsets was tired, wet and pissed off. Christmas Eve and here he was running around fucking people about, checking out their cars on the Belfast-Dublin road, making them get out into the rain and the reflected blaze of sodium light from the arc lights set up around the permanent vehicle check point, getting nothing but surly looks and verbal from the Paddies shouting down the

227

line at him over the hammering of the generators powering the lights.

The lieutenant didn't blame the Paddies for giving him a hard time. He would have done the same in their position. All day there had been nothing but cars full of half-drunks with Christmas wrapped parcels and dolls and teddy bears all over the place. Any driver trying to get home with a carload of drunks and their gaudily wrapped prezzies would be irritable. Behind the car the young officer was checking others were pulled in to the side of the road, one after the other, a dozen or more. A quick flick of anger passed through the wet infantryman. His own wife of eight months, seven months pregnant with the child he longed and worked for was spending the holiday with her parents, people who believed she had married beneath herself as heiress to one of the biggest arable farms in East Anglia. *Fuck the Paddies. At least they're going home to the wife and kids.*

'Your licence please, sir.' A quick look through the little red book with the photograph inside the front cover: James Kavanagh. 14 St Mark's Park Road, Belfast. Issued 1980. The driver's face was the same as the one in the licence.

'Where are you going sir?' handing the licence to another soldier, who muttered into a microphone as he checked the car type and registration. Just outside Belfast a bored civil servant three months from retirement heard the radioman and fed the details he gave into the P-check computer. All OK. The radioman handed the licence back to the lieutenant. Another one done, or nearly.

'I'm off to Dublin for Christmas with the brother. I hope you get off duty soon, boy. Fucking awful job on Christmas Eve.'

Prick prick in the back of the mind, what is it? 'Yes sir, it is. Who's your passenger, sir?'

'A hitch-hiker, trying to get to Dublin. I picked him up a couple of miles back. I don't know him.'

Prick prick. Go two years back, the last tour in Ireland.

Armagh. South Armagh. A south Armagh voice with a Belfast City driving licence, issued ten years ago? Unusual. Moving round to look in the boot, the driver, a huge man, following.

'OK sir. Soon on your way. No problem here. I envy you. Armagh's a lovely county, the best in Ireland. I spent four months there, working out of Bessbrook mill. Lovely country, lovely people. Lovely girls willing to do a soldier a favour. A few bandits extorting money out of small farmers and planting the odd culvert bomb without taking any risks. Nothing we couldn't handle. The Provos down there are nothing but criminals in it for the money. Still, we've got most of them and we'll soon get the rest. Happy Christmas and on your way sir.' *Yes, a flicker in the eyes. Didn't like the bit about the girls. Didn't like the Provos being called criminals. Definitely south Armagh. What to do? Keep him talking. Watch for a slip. Watch for reaction.*

Calm. Friendly. Relaxed. Shoulders down, weapon pointed at the ground. Walking back along the car. 'You'll be glad to get back home once the holiday's over. Your family will miss you. Going away for long?'

'No. Just going to see the brother.' *An edge of irritation.* 'Back to the farm in a few days.'

'Quite right, sir. I'm a farm boy myself. Couldn't hack it away from the fields if it wasn't for the army.'

Impatience. 'Aye. Never been away much myself. A couple of months in England last year, working on the building sites. I was glad to get home. Hardly been away since.' *Bingo. Got you. A south Armagh boy who says he's never been away from home except to England last year, but with a Belfast city licence issued ten years ago? Doesn't add up.* 'Stand still sir. Stand exactly where you are. Keep your feet together and your arms by your sides. I will shoot you if you move. I believe you to be in possession of a false driving licence. I believe that you are carrying personnel or equipment not conducive to the public good. I say again, I will shoot you if you move.'

At 10.30 on Christmas morning Peter Ewart drove recklessly, bulling his way through the city centre traffic, ignoring the waving fingers and contorted faces of granny-visiting drivers cursing him. He fought hard to keep the exultation from breaking through, resisting the urge to pound the steering wheel and shout with joy. If the identification were wrong or the second man not who he might be the disappointment would be terrible and his depression deep. Pulling into the car park Ewart miscalculated the turn and clipped the kerb, bouncing the car over it in his haste.

Inside the glass-walled observation post overlooking the station entrance two constables exchanged glances. One made a glass-lifting gesture. The other shrugged and said, 'It's Christmas.' His mate lifted his eyebrows. 'Every day is Christmas for that one.' Stung, the other, more senior constable said, 'Don't you criticise senior officers, Mulcahy. I know the chief inspector. I've worked with him. That man's entitled to a drink. He's put more Provo bastards behind bars than all the rest of the CID and Special Branch put together. They've shot him and bombed him and tried to kill him more times than I can think of. You keep your mouth shut and watch out that window.' Constable Mulcahy said no more but watched the tails of Ewart's long black coat disappear through the main door of the station.

Ewart took his eye from the spyhole, grinning hugely. 'Aye, that's him. That's Billy Walsh, Madden's bodyguard. I'm not interested in him for the minute. Where's the other one?'

'In there, sir.' Ewart followed the pointing finger. Ah, that room. The one that had once been painted black, with one white wall. The room Sean McAllister had broken and cried in, calling for the man Ewart hoped might be in there now.

Looking through the one-way glass Ewart studied the man in the interrogation room. Thin, middle height, dirty fair hair falling over his forehead, beginning to thin at the crown. Slightly stooped, face lined and baggy eyed. He looked exhausted, like a doctor with too many patients. Suddenly the man seemed to sense Ewart's presence on the other side of the glass. Turning to face it, he stared at his own reflection. Now Ewart knew for certain. The strange, almost serene fixity in the stare told of a deep cold rage, the killer's rage, the rage that ate away at sanity. Ewart had seen it before in other eyes, the eyes of men who had ordered bombs put in restaurants, who had fired an Armalite rifle through an innocent housewife to get the prison officer, her husband, who happened to be standing behind her at the time. But he had never seen it so intense, so all consuming.

Ewart threw the door open and strode in. He stopped so close that their chests almost touched. Looking down into the eyes of a man who lived in a hell of his own making, Ewart breathed into his face and whispered, 'I am Peter Ewart and you are Gerry Madden. I know you are. And you're never going to see the light of day again. I'm going to put you in a windowless cell six feet square and I'm going to keep you there until you die. Until you die, Madden. And then I'm going to throw you in a hole like a dog. And you'll be no locked-up hero either. I'll see to that. I've been saving up for you, Madden. I know exactly who is in every one of the Belfast ASUs and I know where to put my hands on fourteen of them right now. I'm going to arrest them all and I'll tell them you told me who and where they were. I'll tell them the great Gerry Madden twittered like a budgie when I threatened to put him in among the Loyalist prisoners in the Maze. Your name will be shite, Madden, nothing more than shite. They'll think you're the worst informer of them all. Let that comfort you, you soulless whore's bastard.'

'You've got it wrong, mister. My name's Martin O'Connor and I live at 31 Springfield Place. I'm a Roman Catholic priest. That's all I have to say.'

'You're not Martin O'Connor. I know his people. You're Gerry Madden. Martin O'Connor has been working in Africa with the Jesuits for years. I've got you, Madden. And I'm keeping you.'

'Call me Father. You can't prove I'm Gerry Madden. Or prove I'm not Martin O'Connor.' Madden was laughing at him! Ewart turned on his heel, afraid he might strike the man and give him cause for complaint. Near the door he turned again.

'Not this time. Not with me. I've known you since you were running about the Falls with the arse out of your trousers. You nearly cut my throat in Conway Street. You set people on me and cost me a lung. You bombed me and killed the only friend I ever had. I know you, Madden. I know you know I know you. It's all over, Madden. You're mine, for the rest of your life. I'll visit you, just to remind you. You're finished. I've won. You'll kill nobody more in my province. I hope you die screaming, Madden.'

'What have we got?'

The RUC sergeant looked up sharply at the big man in the black coat, recognised him instantly and jumped to his feet. 'Quite a lot sir. We've got Walsh all right. Positive ID from the files. Possession of a firearm and ammunition. Possession of false documents. Membership of a proscribed organisation. Fifteen years at least. But nothing on the other one.'

'Fuck Walsh! The other one is Gerry Madden. What did he have on him?'

The very mention of Madden's name brought a flush to the sergeant's face. 'Well done sir! Jesus. Gerry Madden. Wait'll I tell the boys! That fucker won't walk without sticks for six months. Well done, sir.'

'You'll tell nobody anything, sergeant. Any harm comes to Madden and I'll have you walking a beat in Ballymurphy, understand? We can't afford to take any chances here. What did he have on him?'

'Yes, sir. Only this, sir.' Crestfallen, the sergeant passed over an old black leather-bound book, heavily embossed with a cross on its front, the words Society of Jesus below the cross. Ewart opened it carefully. Inside the front cover of the old Jesuit breviary was the name *Martin O'Connor* SJ.

'Nothing else?'

'Nothing sir. Nothing except these tablets.' The sergeant held out a flat, plastic-coated tablet packet, silver on one side, gold on the other. On the gold side some of the plastic coating had been ripped away where the tablets had been pushed through, obscuring the name printed there. There were four tablets left in the packet. Ewart carefully pushed back some of the ripped edges, enough to make out GLAXO and ranitidine.

'Get the doctor. I want to know what these are for.'

CHRISTMAS DAY 1990
DUNDALK, THE IRISH REPUBLIC

Siobhan McCaillim was talking on the phone, gesturing in triumph. 'We got them all away. Not one was lifted. It was Gerry's own plan for if he ever got captured. Once he was an hour late we passed the instructions to the ASUs to go to ground in safe houses. Belfast first, then you in Armagh, then Derry, then the border country. The Brits started raiding an hour too late, and only in Belfast. The boys were already away. Gerry made fools of them. Isn't it great?'

The man in Armagh said, 'Aye, it is that. But they still have him, and they'll keep him. We're without a chief of staff. What are we going to do, Siobhan? Dublin will try to put one of their own men in over our heads.'

The first great lie. 'No they won't. I spoke to Padraig Hanna this morning. I told him Gerry had planned for this. I told him Gerry had ordered you to take over until he was released or given a long sentence.'

'Jesus, Siobhan, I can't do that! The other brigade commanders

233

wouldn't accept it. They know I'm too old and thick to be chief. What're you trying to do here? Get me killed?'

Siobhan's voice was soothing, reassuring. *The second great lie.* 'It'll be all right. They know Gerry tells me everything. I'll tell them he appointed you just until the dust settles. You're just a caretaker. I'll tell them he'll appoint a new man from jail as soon as he can, if they find a way of holding him. In the meantime I'll help you. I've the brains and I've learned a lot these last few years. I know how Gerry's mind works. I promise it will be all right. Dublin won't dare interfere. That crowd of burnt-out old dinosaurs are too terrified of Gerry to overrule any plan of his. You're chief of staff until we know what's going to happen to Gerry.' Her voice had changed subtly, varying from reassurance through arrogance to out-and-out command.

'OK, Siobhan. I'll be chief in name only. You'll have to tell me what to do.'

'I've told you. Get down here now. Goodbye.'

Siobhan sat back, well pleased. Her first and strongest supporter had always served her well, but as he said, he was getting old and had never been too bright. Now he could be her stalking horse. Her plan, gently moved forward over the years was nearing fruition. Close cultivation of every ambitious young Provisional IRA activist had enabled her to weed out those too stupid or too crazy to be of real use. The rest, one or two in each brigade, she had cultivated further, prodding Gerry or their bosses into promoting them. Now they were being held back only by the old guard; they were itching to take over, loyal to her and nobody else. When the time came she would seize power in a night of bloody assassination that would see her as *de facto* chief of staff, with her own men in command of the brigades. Then she would quarrel with the Army Council and lead the Cause in forcing out the old men in Dublin at the next *Ard Feis*. She would see herself elected president of a new, Northern-based Army Council and would promote the war with Gerry's ferocity, but without his psychological weaknesses. Even now she could see herself, in five years or less, as the first and female president of the Thirty-two county New Ireland.

But Gerry was still in the way. If he stayed in jail, well and good. But if he got out the first thing he would do would be to order the execution of anyone who had tried to take over in his absence. The brigade commanders knew that, except old Armagh, who believed in her. The other commanders would heave a sigh of relief and let him take command, just in case Gerry did get out of jail. If that happened Siobhan would simply deny that her conversation with Armagh had ever taken place. Gerry respected her brains and would not believe Armagh. He would be found with a hood on his head, and Siobhan would cool her young men, at least until the next chance came.

BELFAST

Peter Ewart was also on the phone, talking to a half-drunk doctor pulled away from his Christmas dinner. 'What does the packet look like? Yes. And the wording on it? Yes. Take one of the tablets out, please. Tell me what it says on it, if anything.'

Ewart popped one of the tablets out of its pocket. 'It's white, about the size of an aspirin. It says, wait a second, I need my glasses, it says Zantac 150. What is it?'

'Does the patient suffer from stress? Does he look tired and depressed? Is he a heavy smoker?'

'I don't think he smokes. But he looks pretty tired. He probably has worries, yes. What are these bloody tablets for?'

'Don't shout at me, Chief Inspector. And don't swear. The tablets are prescribed for peptic ulcers, taken two at a time in 150 gramme tablets. Your boy is not well. Keep him calm and give him lots of rest. Don't interrogate him for too long at a time. Give him lots of fluids, and whatever you do don't feed him out of the canteen. A bellyful of what you people call a decent Ulster fry would have him in agony.'

'Thanks, Doctor. Sorry to have bothered you. Merry Christmas.'

Back in the cell block Ewart called the duty cellkeeper. 'What's Madden eaten today?'

'Nothing, sir. I won't give that bastard a drink of water until he asks for it.'

'Good man. Now send somebody up to the canteen. Get sausages, bacon, fried potato bread, black pudding, fried eggs and a big mug of black coffee. Give it to Madden. He can take it or leave it.'

'He's entitled to food sir, but I don't see why we should feed him like a navvy. Why are you ordering this, sir?'

'Because the man has ulcers, son. That's why. I'll have him screaming before I'm finished. Feed him like I said.'

In his own office Ewart called in every interrogator who could keep up a non-stop interrogation, roughly overriding their Christmas objections. When he had them assembled he told them 'We have Gerry Madden. He'll probably say nothing, but we have to keep him under pressure. The law says he's entitled to eight hours' rest a day. He can have it in one-hour snatches. The rest of the time he's to be under interrogation. Interrogate him about every terrorist incident over the past ten years. Even if he says nothing, keep at him. Every two hours he's entitled to light refreshment. Offer him nothing but strong black coffee. The bastard has ulcers, gentlemen. We're going to take advantage of that. His dinner tonight is to be brought to him between interrogations. The cook has orders. It'll be a hot curry with fried rice. Don't give in to any request for anything else. His breakfast tomorrow is an Ulster fry. Tomorrow night another hot curry. As much black coffee as he likes in between. According to the Prevention of Terrorism Act we have seven days to break him. We're going to do it. Got that?'

When the interrogators had gone Ewart called the duty officer of the Belfast resident battalion. 'This is Chief Inspector
Ewart, Special Branch. There's an old man in Springfield, Frank
O'Connor. I want him lifted and brought to me at the interrogation centre. Be careful. He's an old man and frail, not a
suspect and probably a valuable witness. Bring him in a car, in
comfort.'

Frank O'Connor was at the interrogation centre in under
an hour, brought there by two plain-clothes warrant officers
who had knocked politely on his door and 'invited him to
accompany them to identify a man in custody, to eliminate
him from police enquiries'. The warrant officers had left a pretty
Royal Military Police woman sergeant and a big-chested infantry
corporal, both in plain clothes, in Mr O'Connor's house to make
tea and reassure Mrs O'Connor that her husband would be back
soon. Just routine, they told her, probably a mistake. It wouldn't
take long. Outside the house two four-man foot patrols circulated
the area to discourage Paddy from taking a crack at the soldiers
in the house.

At the interrogation centre Ewart met the old man. 'You know
me, Mr O'Connor. I used to be the sergeant at Springfield. There's
nothing to worry about. I'd just like you to take a look at somebody and tell me if you know him. Then we'll have a quiet cup
of tea and talk about old times in the Springfield. The lads who
brought you will have you back home in time for dinner, OK?'

The old man nodded, his thin legs like sticks under the
baggy trousers, his old cardigan buttoned up close under an
old-fashioned collarless shirt. 'Aye, I know you, Peter Ewart.
You're a good policeman. There wasn't any young hooligans
wrecking telephone boxes and burning buses when you were up
the road. I don't know what it's all about these days. I'm on the
pension now. What can I do for you?'

'Thanks, Mr O'Connor. I'd like you to take a look at somebody
to see if you know him, all right? Would you like a policeman to
help you along?'

The old man stiffened. 'I can walk, Peter Ewart. And there's nothing wrong with my eyes.' He held his head up. 'I don't even need glasses.'

'Of course, Mr O'Connor, I'm sorry. Come this way please.'

In his cell Gerry Madden ceased rocking, arms clamped across his stomach to ease the pain. He forced himself upright, wrenching his face into a bland emptiness as he heard the door bolt drawn, readying himself for interrogation. So far he had said nothing, but didn't know how long he could last out without asking for his tablets. Nothing to eat the night before and the food they had given him lying fat and acid in his stomach.

An old man shuffled into the cell, flanked by Peter Ewart and a police constable, the cellkeeper. Madden recognised the old man immediately, recognised that his identification denial plan, set years ago, might work.

The old man fixed rheumy eyes on him, then immediately fell to his knees, quavering 'Martin! It's been so long . . . Give your oul Da the blessing of God, Father.'

Madden paused just long enough to flick a glance of contempt at Ewart, then advanced to the kneeling old man, placed his right hand on the man's head and said in solemn tones 'In nomine patres, et filius, et spiritus sanctus, amen. Get up, Da. It's good to see you. I was coming home to visit you after Christmas.'

Ewart was staggered, the cellkeeper confused, Madden smiling through his pain. The old man, helped by Madden, was back on his feet, clasping Madden to him. 'Why are you holding my son in your jail? I don't understand.'

Ewart raged. 'I fucking well understand. That's no son of yours. That's Gerry Madden, chief of staff of the Provisional IRA. You're his insurance policy. You're as bad as he is. Fuck you. Fuck you both.'

Six days later, on Sunday, 30 December 1990, Gerry Madden was carried a free man out of Peter Ewart's grasp. At the station gate Madden's lawyer had taken possession of every tape of every interrogation Madden had undergone, every copy of his fingerprints, every copy of every photograph taken of him, complete with their negatives.

In vain Ewart had pleaded, threatened, cajoled the centre authorities to keep back at least one photograph of Madden. But they had said, quite firmly, no. They said Ewart had not one shred of evidence to prove that Father O'Connor was anyone other than he claimed to be. The priest had been positively identified by his own father. It was entirely possible that Ewart might have been sued for inhuman treatment and the withholding of medicines vital to his wellbeing if the priest had not, through his lawyer, signed a letter which 'in the Spirit of Christ, forgave and forgot the transgressions of those who in an excess of zeal have subjected me to inhuman and unChristian treatment, for their efforts, though criminal, have been intended for the public good'. Even the man the priest had been captured with, a man facing fifteen years in jail, still insisted the priest had been nothing more than a hitch hiker unfortunate enough to have been with him at the time of his own capture. Ewart, the authorities said, should be grateful that the innocent man he had twisted the law to break had forgiven him. The law was the law. All copies of anything relating to the priest's incarceration and interrogation must be given up to him.

In the hired ambulance brought to take Madden away Siobhan McCaillim broke open four pockets of a gold and silver foil packet, carefully crushed the white tablets that fell out of the pockets and mixed them with a half-pint of warm milk out of a Thermos flask. She fed the mixture to him through a straw, answering the grateful look in his eyes with tears. As Gerry's pain receded and his mind came into focus she kissed him deeply, lifted his hand to hold it against her face, told him how much she loved him. Then, as his eyes brightened, she seemed to try to pull herself together into some semblance of military order. She wiped her face, devoid of makeup, and briefed him on the treachery of the brigade commander, Armagh, who had tried to seize power less than a day after her beloved's capture.

On the last day of the year a hooded, dead bundle of flesh and clothing was found at the milk collection point of a farm deep in the heart of Armagh. Vengeance against the usurper had been quick and complete. The old man was gone and Gerry was happy. But Siobhan's own man was now in command of the Armagh ASUs.

Chapter Twelve

1 February 1993

LISBURN

Lieutenant-Colonel Charlotte Aitken, almost alone in the ante-room of the officers' mess, HQ Northern Ireland, was also thinking of the future, but not dwelling in the past. She was thinking of her next job, her next promotion. Two years in Lisburn running the G2 (Intelligence) organisation had bored and frustrated her. She hated the little market town with its lumpy farm people and its total lack of the most basic cultural amenities. The town seemed to be a microcosm, a pattern for the whole of Northern Irish society as she had seen it: hard, narrow minds fixed in their prejudices, ignorant of anything beyond the ends of their noses. She hated the place, hated the people, hated the infuriating military bureaucracy of the huge headquarters complex that constrained even the simplest of executive actions. Too many times she had forecast the flow of terrorist activity, predicted the movements of people, weapons and explosives dumps, only to be frustrated by the inaction of the battalions on the ground; too many times told that long-term objectives weighed heavily against her demands for action. She was now thirty-nine, still a lieutenant-colonel, still just ahead of the pack, but had not managed to capitalise on her very early promotion.

Other officers sharing the great barn of a mess often talked of the great sailing to be had at Strangford Lough, the fishing and rough shooting on the farms and parklands all over the province, the great pubs and restaurants to be found in the tiniest of villages, the little theatres everywhere. Charlotte had seen none of these. Obsessed with the need to shine she had spent little time outside the HQ complex at Thiepval barracks, involving herself in the tiniest detail of every Intelligence report, questioning everything, demanding more and more, driving her staff to exhaustion and distraction in her search for a lead into the Big One, the great coup that would lift her out of the grind and into the light of her superiors' view. She needed it.

Two years of the solidly successful but unspectacular had left her in danger of receiving a confidential report that would praise her unstinting effort, mention all her good qualities, but refer to no achievement in particular. Her grading would be Excellent but the vital line which read: Ready for Promotion: Now; In her time; Not yet would see In her time highlighted. She could not accept that. She needed promotion Now if she were to beat off her rivals in the race to the top. She had been a lieutenant-colonel for nearly seven years now, far too long for someone aiming at the highest levels, even if she were still young for her rank. And there were practical considerations. Her grandfather's will had stipulated her loss of the estate if she did not achieve her aim soon. She needed to jump the rank of full colonel, go straight to brigadier, get back into the MoD in London, back to the centre of things: and back to civilisation. She needed a major success, and she needed it soon.

Charlotte turned her thoughts to the Provisional IRA. They were the enemy, her sole means of advancement. Her success must be against them. Watching their activities along the border had been her appointed task, but she had widened this to encompass their activities everywhere, assessing, sifting, looking for the diamonds in the sand, looking for a chance at them. She had had her successes but if she were honest they had not been enough.

The army in Ireland took a long view: there were good reasons for not acting on her every find. The best reason was that her finds had not been significant enough to compromise the army's means of acquiring the information that had led her to them.

But more and more Charlotte had found something edging around the corners of her mind, a woolly thing, but there. Something was happening inside the Provisional IRA, of that she was certain. Patterns were changing, slowly enough, but changing. There seemed to be a slight, but growing, shift in the power balance, away from the brigades toward the centre. That was not like Madden, the Provisional IRA chief of staff. Her psychological profile of him indicated a deeply suspicious nature that preferred to keep his brigades' operations at arm's length, dealing with policy and keeping an overall picture of things, involving himself directly in only the bigger, wider-based operations and then only through his staff. Maybe Madden was changing. Maybe the SAS psyops against him were working, grinding down his capacity to think rationally. Or maybe some other factor was in operation. Maybe both. She didn't know. She did know some sort of youth policy was being followed, with the old and bold, roughneck Provisional IRA activists at all levels being weeded out, replaced by younger, more intelligent, more inventive and less scrupled men, with or without Madden's blessing. Very few as yet in the top posts, though they were well on their way. She suspected that someone somewhere close to Madden was influencing him, or that he was behind the changes himself. Which? So infuriating, so tantalising, so uncertain. If there were a dark horse inside PIRA she wanted to be the one to identify and capture him. He could be her key to everything. She decided to work on that assumption.

1–2 February 1993
ROSCREA, REPUBLIC OF IRELAND

Gerry Madden was a worried man. Nearly thirteen years had passed since he had assumed responsibility for the conduct of the war against the British in Ireland, but the Cause seemed no further forward. He had restructured the Provisional IRA, cut down the incidence of British infiltration, cut down the danger of informers within their own ranks, carried the war into the political field, seen PIRA members elected to the British parliament, seen the development of technology help his bombers thwart British countermeasures, seen the development of compartmentalised ASUs safe from even their own ex-members, seen PIRA become, in British parlance, leaner and meaner. But he was no further forward. Every move he made the British countered, gradually pushing him further and further into the Provo heartlands in the cities and south Armagh, insulting him by withdrawing their troops off the streets, denying him targets, relying on overt and covert Intelligence gathering to bring PIRA to its knees.

Madden had himself predicted PIRA's defeat and scheduled it for the autumn of 1982. Through willpower, ruthlessness and cold intelligence he had fought the war for ten years beyond that point, weeding out the weak, reinforcing the strong. But now, sitting alone – or nearly alone, for Siobhan McCaillim was curled around his feet – he saw defeat stare him in the face. Ten years on and even the most hawkish of his brigade commanders seemed to be leaning more and more towards the abandonment of brute force in favour of political action. Something needed to be done, and quickly, to restore PIRA's confidence in ultimate victory, with himself as its architect. Without it he was done.

'I know what's troubling you, Gerry. It's the war. I know we're losing. And I know why. I know you've thrown everything you have into it, but we're still losing. You have to do something, very soon.'

Startled out of his self-absorption Madden moved a hand to turn Siobhan's face to him, level with his knee. 'Is it a mind reader you are now? How can you tell what I'm thinking?'

'Don't be silly, Gerry. Of course I can't read your mind, but we've been together a long time, through great events and a life on the run. I know you and I've learned to think like you, that's all. I'm your wife in all but name. I just know what's on your mind because it's on mine. You have to do something.'

Madden's face twisted. 'Like what, for instance? And what's the reason we're losing?'

'There's no need to take that attitude, Gerry. I've helped you a lot these last few years. You should listen to me. I think we're losing because we're fighting this war the way the Brits want us to. They can't completely defeat us unless they demoralise us so much that we give up. And they know we will never defeat them, because we can't do enough damage to really hurt them. They're prepared to fight this war for as long as we are, at very little cost to themselves. They're hoping that we will think we can't win and just give up. In the meantime they'll put up with us. Their soldiers don't mean anything to them. We could kill them from now till Doomsday and the Brits would keep mouthing slogans about never giving in to terrorism.

'But you know all that, it's nothing new. I think we think about ourselves in the wrong way, the way we have always thought about ourselves. We've always thought of ourselves as soldiers, fighting a guerrilla war against a huge modern army with every conceivable means of countering us. I think we're wrong. I think we need to change our approach. I think we need to see ourselves differently if we're to break the stalemate. If we don't our people will get demoralised and the Brits will win.'

Madden took his tongue between his teeth, sucking his cheeks in, a sure sign that he was listening carefully. Siobhan decided not to press on but to wait for him to ask. Many minutes later he did, giving her the psychological advantage she sought.

'I'm listening. Do you have any ideas for a new approach?'

Siobhan had very clear ideas, but wanted him to think they came from him. 'I don't have as good a mind as you Gerry. I haven't studied guerrilla war the way you have. I know, everybody knows we can't expect a straight military victory. I know the idea is for us to think long term, do as much damage as we can and avoid a fight we can't win. You've told us that yourself. All we can do is keep torturing the Brits, like fleas on a tiger, until the tiger gets fed up and walks away. But we aren't doing enough damage. We're not biting the right parts of the tiger. The Brits are almost ignoring us, keeping us under control, accepting certain levels of violence and denying they're doing any such thing. They want to stay in Ireland and they're prepared to pay the price. What do they care if they lose a few soldiers or we kill our own people, Irishmen in the RUC and UDR? What do they care if we blow Belfast to dust? They don't care. They lose more soldiers in road accidents than we kill. The EC gives them money to rebuild anyway. We're not hurting them enough: or we're hurting the wrong ones.'

'You're repeating yourself. What do you mean we're not doing enough?'

Siobhan felt exasperated, but hid it well; he was asking the wrong questions, missing her obvious leads. But you could never really tell with Gerry. Many times she had seen him do the same to others while he thought about a single important point they had made.

'We're not fighting hard enough,' she went on. 'We're too busy preserving ourselves. You've given the Cause everything you have. Is anybody else doing the same? The Army Council sit in their big houses in Dublin. Most of our people have wives and kids. Most of them are making money out of the rackets. They're getting soft, not doing enough, they're content to mosey along hitting soft targets and keeping out of trouble. Sometimes I wonder if we should launch a big campaign, do as much damage as possible and be prepared for the Brits to clean them out. They'd not be much of a loss and we could use the campaign to recruit new blood. Those toerags in England for example, the English ASUs. They're a waste of time and money. We'd be better off without them.'

Madden shifted in his seat. Siobhan was telling the truth as she saw it. Maybe she was right. 'Stop talking now. I'm thinking.' She nestled into his legs, content with the planting of her seed, happy to wait for the inevitable plan of campaign Gerry would produce, certain that it could only further her own cause. Madden sat silent for hours, Siobhan asleep, still at his feet. As the night crept towards dawn he accepted her arguments, saw the logic.

Calmly, brutally, Madden formulated a fundamental change in PIRA strategy. In essence it was very simple. He would escalate the war to the point where it was all or nothing. *I will expend every asset Provisional IRA has to strike at the British where it hurts them most. I will attack their men who matter in a personal way. And then I will mount a strike against them, a spectacular that will break their hearts. I will follow the example of Patrick Pearse, poet and leader of the 1916 rising and founder of the IRA. I will rekindle the flames of Yeats's Terrible Beauty, burn the fat off the Provisional IRA. I will drive the Cause to utter destruction or total victory. I will carry the war to the English in a way and intensity never before attempted. I will break the will of the British to go on fighting, sicken them of taking casualties and win the war outright. I will be the man who frees Ireland from British tyranny after 800 years of oppression, or I will be the new Pearse, a shining light to guide the generations yet to come, a symbol of defiance against the might of a crumbling empire. I will rule in my lifetime or live for ever in the annals of Republican history.*

His sense of purpose fired up, Madden turned his mind to the past. Throughout the ages great men had tried to throw off the yoke of England. All had failed. But all were remembered. It would be the same for him: win or lose, he had everything to gain through staking all on one last great effort, one last great throw of the dice.

He shook Siobhan gently, waking her. 'Siobhan, my love, it's time for bed. Come and wrap yourself around me. I have a lot to think of.'

Siobhan, rising stiffly, caught the once in a while urge she had to let herself go, give in to him, for despite herself and her own ambitions she had grown to know him well, seen beyond the day-to-day brutalities, beyond the chill, logical intelligence of the man, beyond even the cold clear rage, sensed his moods and seen the idealist, the personal courage, the pain of the poet in him, sensed the greatness that could have been his had he not been born Irish, that could have been his if he had found a different road to follow.

Poor Gerry. Sometimes she longed for him to find her out, be more of a man in the flesh, wanted him to crush and conquer her. But then again she saw him in his weakness, was able to ease him, bring him peace when the fabled Palestinian he had told her of deserted him. Sometimes her ability pleased her, but mostly it heightened her knowledge of her power over him, weakened him in her eyes, increased her reflex urge to rip him.

She had her own djinn: the fisherman. When she saw weakness she thought of him using a wounded shark as bait for the others. Gerry was a wounded shark; she the leader of the pack come to tear him down. Sometimes, in the dark of the night, as he slept his restless sleep she recognised that she was growing as Gerry diminished. Her time would come the day he fell. The thought excited her. She imagined him gagged and bound, on his knees, and herself in front of him, torturing his mind, telling him of how she had overcome him. The feeling of such power was almost physical. She could hurt him now. But she would wait, enjoy the pleasure day by day, cut into him a little at a time, until she could pull him inside out. In the meantime she had her job to do.

She spoke softly, in the gentle, poetic way he loved. 'I will, Gerry Madden. I'll curl around you and wet your cheeks with my love of you. I'll see you soft asleep with my love your closest blanket. Please tell me when you wake of the thoughts that make you need me.'

2 February 1993
LISBURN

In a corner seat of the mess ante-room a captain of the Parachute Regiment sipped his coffee, rustled through the *Telegraph* and surreptitiously watched the thoughts flicker across the lady lieutenant-colonel's face. *So that's the famous Charlie A., is it? I don't blame Jamie, she certainly is a looker.* The Para smiled at the nickname, a play on her initials, that Jamie Lappin had given her. The Charlie G. was the Carl Gustav, a Swedish-built 84 millimetre anti-tank gun that packed a hell of a punch. Jamie had said that just looking at Charlie A. was enough to knock you over.

Just posted to HQNI the Para, John Harris, was a commissioned warrant officer, the man who had stepped into Jamie Lappin's shoes when Lappin had transferred to the Small Arms School Corps. A spell as company sergeant-major had been followed by a tour as RSM, then commissioning. Harris hadn't seen Jamie since he had left the battalion, but Jamie had been good enough to call him up to congratulate him on his appointment to RSM. John Harris thanked Jamie, for he knew why Jamie had voluntarily given up his own career, a move that had staggered the sergeants' mess and caused much bitter comment about women bloody officers. Privately, more than one of the battalion's more senior commissioned officers had said much the same things, regretting Lappin's loss.

John Harris had often wondered about this mysterious woman, and now here she was, just across the room. The urge to get up and speak to her was strong, but the president of the mess committee, welcoming him to the mess, had briefed him on the mess's more exotic personalities: there was a retired major-general who had the disconcerting habit of dropping off for a minute or two, sometimes in the middle of a sentence, waking up and carrying on as if nothing had occurred. The president had advised him to ignore the general's little weakness; it was the remnant of some tropical disease he had caught on active service. There was an outlandish civilian, a Marconi man, an electronics genius who worked on God knows what who would engage people in manic conversation, wind himself up into a terrible state and then drink until he fell over and had to be put to bed. The Marconi man, Harris had been told, could be good fun in his manic moods, but the rest of the time he stunned your head with long and boring lectures about anything that had caught his butterfly mind. And then there was Charlotte Aitken: a beautiful woman, but to be avoided. She had no small talk, rarely came into the public rooms, never entered the bar and would cut dead any approach made by anyone not useful to her career. The PMC had himself once asked her out to dinner, shortly after she had arrived. She had looked through him, got up and walked out. The Para wondered about that. Jamie had always said she was ambitious, but great to talk to, funny and happy natured. *She's looking at me.*

'Why are you watching me, Captain?' The voice was flat, neutral, but pleasantly modulated, with very clear diction. An educated voice.

'I beg your pardon, Colonel. I was not aware that I was staring. I was thinking about something.'

'I did not say you were staring. I asked you why you were watching me. Explain yourself, Captain.' There was a deliberate emphasis on his rank.

Harris was irritated. She was trying to put him down, using the advantage of her superior rank to force him into an embarrassing position. But he had an advantage he could use. Two could play at the put-down game. A judicious lie was in order here.

'Well, if you must know, Colonel, I was talking to an old friend the other week, in Warminster. He has an odd sense of humour. He gave me a description of a lady he knows is working out here. For a moment I had the stupid idea that you might be the lady. I was wrong of course. I'm sorry.'

And into the trap she fell, a little uncertainty, maybe curiosity creeping into the cut-glass voice. 'What was the woman's name? Who is the officer in Warminster? Is there a message?'

'This is embarrassing, Colonel.' He picked up his coffee cup and held it in both hands, dropping his head to hide his eyes from her. 'My friend is not an officer and he gave me no name. I told you he has an odd sense of humour. The lady apparently answers to Charlie A. Sar'nt-Major Lappin sent no message.'

John Harris instantly regretted his lie. Charlotte Aitken looked stricken, as if he had unexpectedly reached across the room and stabbed her. Her eyes widened in shock, her hands rose to her face, but stopped halfway to flutter aimlessly in front of her, and her mouth opened as if to scream. She seemed to have difficulty breathing. Then she dropped her head into her hands and sat there, vulnerable, as if waiting for another blow but without the strength to ward it off.

Harris jumped up, uncertain what to do or say. He hadn't expected this. 'I'm sorry, I didn't mean—'

But her head was up, she was rising to her feet. Her voice was completely under control, furiously angry but just loud enough to be heard, and her small fists were clamped against her sides. 'You bastard. You absolute bastard. You know exactly who I am. You deliberately set out to trap me and hurt me.'

It was the first time Harris had ever seen such hatred in a woman's eyes and it threw him back a step. But she hadn't finished.

'Never mention Jamie Lappin's name again. You're not fit to wipe his feet. If you ever enter a room I'm in, leave it immediately. Do not speak to me again, now or ever. Get out of my sight.'

Once Harris had gone Charlotte gathered her handbag and gloves together, walked slowly and carefully to her room and let herself go. Hunched in an armchair, the utter misery broke through: she had held it in check so tightly since she had realised Jamie Lappin had been hurt too badly to respond to her unspoken appeal on the day of his Warminster triumph. Now it left her sobbing, shaken and utterly exhausted. Empty, she sat in the dark for a long time, contemplating her life without Jamie. She wanted him and needed him. The long years of constancy, of deliberate celibacy, of telling herself no other man could ever be enough were taking their toll. She wanted Jamie, wanted a home, wanted his children, wanted his love, wanted to know she could be more than she was now, could be free and happy and normal, at peace with herself, sharing herself with the man she loved so much. *I want him back*.

2 February 1993
ROSCREA, THE REPUBLIC OF IRELAND

'Are you really sure this is the way, Gerry? The last time we tried a big campaign in England it was a disaster. It cost us a million, and a lot of lost equipment and men jailed, for very little more than a few bombings. The Brit Special Branch seemed to know everything. Are you sure, Gerry?'

'Yes, I am sure. My first intention was to throw in everything, whatever the cost. But I've learned from the last time. We spent too much money. We hired too many safe houses and used far too many people. You are right about the English ASUs. The way those Saturday night Republicans over there shoot their mouths off in the pubs we were bound to lose out. Siobhan, the answer is obvious. I can't imagine why it has never come to me before. We instigate actions and we claim responsibility for the actions as they occur. Simplicity itself.'

Siobhan McCaillim looked confused. 'So who does the jobs? I don't understand.'

Madden smiled, his eyes burning. He enjoyed doling out his plan in bits and pieces, forcing her to ask the questions. It was over an hour later that he finally told her, 'You said we saw ourselves in the wrong way. You said, quite rightly, that we see ourselves as soldiers. The Brits see us as terrorists. We're going to prove them right. We'll give them a taste of real terror: terror for terror's sake. We will put terror into the heart of every English fat cat who's always thought himself safe from us. And this is how we'll do it: every journalist and so-called terror watcher has been banging on for years about the Terrorist International, ever since Carlos Sanchez pulled a few jobs, the Japs did Lod airport and a few Belgian crazies had a go at NATO hand in hand with Baader-Meinhoff. It's all bollocks. People just do each other a favour now and then, like we did for the Basques last year when we shot that Spanish general taking a fishing holiday on Lough Erne. The Terrorist International doesn't exist. People's aims are too far apart and too hard to pull together for any length of time. But I'm going to create a Terrorist International, just for a month, for a great spectacular.'

'How do we guarantee to get their men out?'

'We don't. They make their own arrangements.'

'It all sounds too good to be true, Gerry. It is a brilliant idea, but we couldn't set it up without somebody getting wind of it. It's impossible.'

Madden's face darkened. 'It is not impossible. And it can be set up. I never said we would set it up. What I'm going to do is see my plan set up as a number of separate actions, apart from setting the English ASUs to run wild. The people carrying out each action will only know about their own operation. After it's all over we announce that it wasn't just us after all. We announce the permanent formation of a worldwide coalition of freedom fighters, led by the Provisional IRA. The Brits will have every government in the world on their backs to do something about us. They'll go crazy. They'll take repressive measures we can exploit in the media for months. They might even say they've had enough and pull out altogether.'

'What are the actions going to be? They'll have to be worthwhile. How are you going to get them set up?'

'They'll be set up for me. I'll tell you how later. I have

a few ideas for targets, but I'm still thinking about it. What do you think of these?' Madden outlined the targets he had in mind.

'Jesus, Gerry. It's tremendous. But that's only four. What are the other three?'

Madden reached behind him and pulled out a copy of the *Daily Mirror*. On page nine was a half page advertisement: THE PORTSMOUTH OPEN DAY. 25TH OF APRIL. THE BIGGEST MILITARY EVENT OF THE YEAR. THE NAVY WILL BE THERE. THE ARMY WILL BE THERE. THE RAF WILL BE THERE. WHY DON'T YOU BE THERE? The ad was spattered with drawings of ships, planes and field guns.

'We will be there, Siobhan. We'll be there all right.'

'It's nearly too much to take in. What are you planning for that?'

'I'm not sure yet. It'll be something special. You can bet on it.'

'I still can't see how you can get it all organised. We'll have to start on the first of April.'

'Quite right, Siobhan. The Brits are going to be made fools of for a month, starting on All Fools' Day. Tomorrow morning I'm flying out of Dublin airport. I'm going to Libya for a few days. You'll have to cover for me. I don't want anybody to know I'm away. I'll have some supper now.'

Siobhan jumped up to feed Madden, glad of the chance to get away from him, her mind racing. She had intended to plant a seed, not grow a tree overnight. She needed time to think.

Chapter Thirteen

1 April 1993

LONDON

On April Fools' Day, at 7.44 a.m., on the morning millions of Britons played practical jokes on one another, Judge Aaron Strausseman opened his front door. He saw a small, slim young man of about seventeen, dressed in slacks and casual windcheater, smile up at him. Beside the boy was a small crush bag of the kind students carried everywhere. The smile was wide and dazzling, the young man's face a smooth olive oval perfectly set to show off his smile and the liquid brown eyes that guilelessly regarded Judge Strausseman. He was, the judge thought, a very beautiful boy indeed.

The young man spoke, in perfect, classical Hebrew. 'You are Mr Strausseman, the great judge? I am Shlomo Baruzinsky, from Kibbutz Taalan in Jaffa. I am honoured to meet you. I have come to see my friend Yitzhak. May I come in?'

The judge was surprised. He had not known his companion knew such a boy. Suspicion flicked through him. Every year Yitzhak took a lone holiday in Israel, travelling around the Holy Land, researching the roots of the Hebrew language. No doubt Yitzhak had had a little fling in Jaffa: no doubt Yitzhak would be as surprised as he to find this beautiful boy at their home so early in the morning; and very probably Yitzhak would be highly embarrassed. Maybe he should send the boy away before Yitzhak saw him. Then Strausseman realised what day it was. He was being had! Yitzhak was playing a joke on him, trying to get him to bite on an obvious lure. This lad was probably one of his Hebrew students, totally unaware of the implications of his early morning visit, primed on what to say. Strausseman decided to play along, use the opportunity to turn the tables by being charming and courteous, fully understanding of how even the most steadfast of friends could be led astray by such beauty.

'Of course, my boy. Yitzhak is just making breakfast. I am sure he will be delighted to see you. Come in, come in.'

Strausseman led the way down the hall, composing his face into the right mixture of consternation and understanding, expecting his companion to appear at any moment. Yitzhak had the ears of a fox and must be just behind the kitchen door, listening, hugging his joke to him, expecting his friend to charge in calm of face but enraged in spirit, to meet a grinning face. But the laugh would be on him.

Yitzhak did not appear. He did have the ears of a fox; and a deep knowledge of Hebrew. He had heard the boy and recognised the voice for what it was, a product of Damascus University, of the tiny coterie of Arab scholars based in Syria who combed the filthy camps of eastern Lebanon, drawing out of the disease-ridden squalor of the Bekaa Valley the best and brightest of the boys and girls they found there, never more than ten years old. The voice was the voice of the Jewish nightmare, the voice of a highly intelligent and able young Arab steeped from birth in hatred of Israel, coached and trained for years on end in the peace of the universities, the savagery of the heat-seared deserts and frozen mountains of eastern Arabia. The voice was the voice of death. It was too late for Aaron, but he might just get away himself.

Strausseman pushed the kitchen door open, saying, 'Yitzhak, a friend for you,' to see his companion halfway out the window, scrabbling for a grip in his effort to throw himself out of the line of fire. For a horrible second he thought his first suspicions had been correct. *Maybe the boy really is from Jaffa! But surely Yitzhak has no need to . . .*

Confused, Strausseman stopped. Standing stock still in the kitchen doorway, he was thrown aside with a force he could not have foreseen from the small figure close behind him.

The Palestinian took in the situation at a glance. He ignored the confused judge, produced a heavy automatic pistol from his bag and adopted the classic handgun marksman's pose. He fired through the window's centre pane, aiming for the head of the escaping Yitzhak, allowing for the deflection to be expected from his special weapon. As the huge recoil passed through him and his body bent forward again, his eyes registered the crazing of the glass obscuring Yitzhak's head from his view. *Not sure! Again.* Adnan al Khali swung on his heels, a fraction, just enough to sight in on the lower chest of Yitzhak Porevsky. He fired as the gun lowered and felt comfortable. The impact of the second bullet lifted Porevsky's upper body and threw it against the window frame, dumping the dead man half in, half out of the window.

In the three seconds in which the beautiful boy killed his friend Judge Strausseman knew that he himself was about to die. He still did not understand what was happening, or why. But he knew he was about to die. He straightened himself against the kitchen wall, fingers twitching, rigid in the certainty of his impending, instant death, trying to come to terms with the shock of what he had seen and what was to come. The Palestinian was merciful; he gave him no time to think. The boy swung quickly to him, smiled his dazzling smile and said quietly, 'Insh'Allah, Ismaeli. Allahu Akbar. Salaam aleikom' and shot him just below the nose, angling the heavy automatic to drive its bullet through his enemy's brain. As the judge's knees gave way Adnan al Khali stepped back, allowing the dead man to fall, muttering in Arabic, 'God is indeed great, son of Israel, but God is merciful. I will pray that the All-knowing receives your ignorant infidel soul.'

At Gatwick airport a wiry little man watched the Air Europe morning flight for Düsseldorf take off. Satisfied that no problems had arisen he made a call to the Syrian Embassy: Adnan Al Khali was on his way home.

At ten o'clock precisely the editor of the *Telegraph* flicked a switch locking his telephone into a tape recorder. A man had called and asked for the editor, quoting a password that galvanised the switchboard girl into action. She said nothing, and immediately put the call through.

'This is the editor. A recording device is in action.'

A west Belfast voice said 'Very good, Mr Editor. I see the system works. At 7.44 this morning an active service unit of the Provisional Irish Republican Army, acting on behalf of the legal government of Ireland, the Provisional Army Council, executed the High Court Judge Mr Aaron Strausseman for his support of the illegal occupation of a part of Ireland by the British Crown. That is all.'

'Wait, wait! Don't hang up! Why Strausseman? He's never made a public statement outside a court in his life. Why murder his house guest? What are you trying to achieve here?'

For a few seconds there was silence. Then; 'Strausseman was a senior member of the repressive British judicial system and a legitimate target.' The phone buzzed, the connection broken.

The editor threw himself into a deep leather armchair with an irritated, explosive puff of air. Gathering himself he said 'The call was genuine. But I do not think he knew about Mr Porevsky.'

The Special Branch officer in the corner of the office closed his notebook, impassive. 'Thank you, sir. I will report your opinion. It may be of value. May I have the tape?'

The editor's instincts as a newspaperman were instantly aroused. 'No. I'll have a copy made and sent round to you. I'll keep the original. Is there anything else?'

'Not really, sir. If there are any further incidents I will be back. If you are contacted again for any reason I expect you to let us know right away. In the meantime I'll wait for a copy of the tape. *Tempus fugit* and all that. The quicker we have information the quicker we can act on it. Good morning, sir.'

On the nineteenth floor of the New Scotland Yard building

the Special Branch sergeant reported to an inspector attached to the Anti-Terrorist Squad.

The inspector listened carefully to the tape, glancing through the sergeant's notes at the same time.

'OK. The clearance squad have two bullets. A constable on the squad thinks one of the bullets is a 9 millimetre DumDum of some kind. That's all we know.'

'A DumDum? They meant business. Not the usual yob off a building site.'

'Yes, we're looking for people who know their business. Professional murderers. Thirty-seven known Provo players have come over to the mainland over the past three weeks. They've stayed away from their usual haunts in London and Birmingham, gone to ground in boarding houses in ones and twos all over the country. A group of eight or nine of them have done this kind of job before. The rest are low-level bomb planters. We've been watching the hard men closely and they know it. I don't think they did this. They're not good enough to slip us, do this kind of thing and expect to get away. A strange thing is that just after the nine o'clock news the whole lot took off, switching lodgings and hotels. I think they're trying to distract us from a team we haven't picked up. It's a possibility.'

'Another team? Provos we don't know? I don't follow you sir. We know them all. At least we know the real hard men.'

'I mean the Provos may have a couple of people we don't have any form on. Long term sleepers or kids from the Republic of Ireland they haven't used before. It happens. They might even have a couple of hard-up ex-soldiers on the payroll. That happens too. We'll have to eliminate the possibilities one by one. If it's new kids we'll have to handle it ourselves. If it's soldiers we'll have to set a thief to catch a thief. I'll get on to the Irish Special Branch. You're co-opted on to the squad as of now. I'll clear it with your boss. Get on to the MoD and ask to borrow the best small arms specialist they've got.'

Reading the Intelligence summary forwarded by secure fax from MoD London Charlotte Aitken felt her certainty grow like a flower as the first day of Madden's campaign died. *Something very big is brewing, and not here in Ireland.* The sudden departure to England of the hardest of PIRA's hard men had alarmed Charlotte as much as it had the UK Special Branch. The IntSum confirmed it. But the strange movements of the Provisional IRA men in England held no surprises for her.

They can't expect to invade the mainland like that and not be noticed. They can't expect to mount a campaign themselves: they don't have the weapons and infrastructure to support them. I think they're a smokescreen, no more, in fact I'm sure of it, it's typical Madden thinking. But what are they covering up? Can't be just an active service unit or two infiltrated earlier, not worth such effort and exposure of their hard men. Maybe a campaign by the English-based ASUs? Hardly. They're a bunch of loudmouthed nobodies. Half of them are Special Branch pretending to be Provisional IRA. The other half are drunks. What then? It has to be something very different. And that's not Madden thinking. I was right. There is someone pulling his strings. I think the SAS psyops have weakened him and someone is propping him up. I must find out who.

This Strausseman thing is interesting. Nothing special, but interesting. It must lead to something more, or be part of something bigger. I'll have to watch it unfold a bit. It's so bloody frustrating. There's nothing I can do ... But maybe there is. I can get to work on identifying whoever is working with Madden. Slow business, thousands and thousands of computer records. Charlotte picked up an intercom and called her chief clerk.

'Chief. Ask Mr Caldwell if he has a moment. Thank you.'

Brian Caldwell was Charlotte's resident computer specialist. He was a former RAOC Ammunition Technician and bomb disposal operator who had lost an arm in a motor accident and turned computer fiend. He was a unique man holding the British Army's highest non-commissioned rank, warrant officer class one. That was not unusual: every battalion had a WOI as its RSM. What made Caldwell different was his appointment: as a Conductor RAOC he could take precedence over the most senior of the Guards RSMs, including the academy sergeant-major at Sandhurst. Different enough, but what made Caldwell unique was that he was the most senior of the RAOC's Conductors. He was therefore the British Army's most senior NCO.

Caldwell rapped on Charlotte's door, walked in and saluted, left armed. 'Evening ma'am, what can I do for the colonel today? A little something special to ease the pain of the day's dreadful grind, a blinding lamp to light the paths of the world's groaning, nightbound masses? Not a problem. You can have it in not more than the ten minutes of our good Lord's bold daylight that remains to us, sinners that we are.'

Charlotte grinned back at him. Caldwell carried his uniqueness with style. Immaculate in dress and bearing he was a very bright man indeed, his weakness a penchant for flowing spirals of sentences delivered in a soft, quick Cork city brogue. Charlotte had liked him at first sight. Caldwell was built like a middleweight prizefighter, with a not very successful prizefighter's face in which deep hazel eyes glowed with the devilment of a man who had never lost his sense of wonder.

'Ten minutes? Too long. You're sacked.'

'Oh dear. I'm a failure. I should hang myself forthwith. Or maybe I can do something, however tinily small, to find favour once again? May I sit down?'

'Oh. Sorry. I'm forgetting my manners. One of these days you'll drown us all in a sea of charm, Mr Caldwell. Please do sit down. I'd like to talk to you about an idea I have. It's a bit woolly but it could be important. Have you got a few minutes now?'

Caldwell's battered face took on a wary look. Colonel Aitken's ideas often generated a hell of a lot of work for small reward. 'Hm. Of course, Colonel. Fire away.'

Charlotte laughed again. 'Stop looking so suspicious. Wait a moment.' She called her chief clerk again, for coffee for Caldwell and herself. 'I have a gut feeling about something. I think you might be able to help verify it or prove it's nonsense. Let me explain.' She told him the essence of her idea that someone was pulling Gerry Madden's strings, or undermining him, or propping him up. 'I want to know who.'

Caldwell was intrigued. 'We'd have to search the records going way back. All known associates. All known PIRA staff. Whereabouts, contact time with Madden, relative influence in Provisional IRA, seniority, personal records, psychological profiles. Over what period?'

'Some years.'

'Years? Difficult. The sheer weight of numbers of reports. How to cross-index. Interesting. I'd have to write a program to sort it all into some semblance of order.'

'How long to write it?'

'Oh, 'bout eight months.' Caldwell held his serious face long enough to convince Charlotte he meant it, then spoke before she could open her mouth. 'On the other hand I might try some wee idea or two of my own. Give me a couple of days to think about it, ma'am.'

'Fine. Thank you, Mr Caldwell. You had me then.'

3 April 1993
LONDON

In a tiny, half-glassed office in the basement of the Ministry of Defence Jamie Lappin went back over the evidence in his mind, making no hurry, ignoring the barely veiled impatience of the young Metropolitan Police forensic scientist sitting across from him, crammed between the table and the wall by the bulk of the Special Branch sergeant who shared his bench seat. Lappin thought his own deliberate time-wasting a bit childish, but in the case of Zache he was prepared to be childish. The man was brilliant; and an extreme pain in the arse. Even forewarned by the Special Branch man's laconic 'Watch this lad, sir. Done a lot of jobs for us. Bit of a prima donna. Full professor; heavy hitter in the brains department. Bit abrasive sometimes.'

Lappin had been surprised by the degree of the scientist's opposition to his presence. Zache was competent enough not to fear being found out: he just took exception to someone being, as he put it, 'brought in over my head' and had made life as difficult as he possibly could.

Two days ago a caller from the Met had asked the MoD for the short-term loan of a small arms specialist, to help in his assessment of the ballistic evidence and weapon-handling abilities of the murderers of Judge Strausseman. MoD clearance had been immediate, Lappin the obvious choice.

Professionally intrigued, Lappin, trailed everywhere by the resentful Zache, had spent a careful half-day at the scene of the shootings, then half a day at the police lab near Camden Lock, north London. He had seen the bodies of the victims in the morgue of the Middlesex Hospital. Zache had unwillingly given him sight of the bullets found at the scene, a copy of the pathologist's report and had shown him colour slides of the dead men's internal injuries, taken during their post-mortem examinations, but had refused to reveal the contents of his own preliminary report, claiming that it was incomplete. Lappin hadn't needed Zache's report. He had seen enough. Now he was ready to give his opinion. Beside him was a Dictaphone-type tape recorder. The Special Branch sergeant crushed the scientist even more as he made room for his elbows, preparing to take notes.

'OK then. I'll give it to you in one lump. Please interrupt me if I say something you do not understand.' Ignoring Zache's bitter twist of the mouth at this, Lappin reached out and flicked on the tape recorder.

'Report of WO2 Rangemaster (Snipers) Lappin J., on detachment from the School of Infantry, Warminster to the Metropolitan Police. Subject of this report is the shooting of two men at a house in Richmond Park, London. Report begins.'

Lappin launched into a detailed description of the scene of the crime, concentrating on ballistic evidence relevant to the extent and nature of the damage inflicted on the dead men. He was constantly interrupted by Professor Zache, who questioned everything he said in rasping, sarcastic tones. The sergeant-major in Lappin had to bite back the urge to show this awkward little shit just how a voice could be used to embarrass and intimidate.

'So, gentlemen, I've given you the technical detail. Now for my conclusions:

'One: the victims were shot with a handgun loaded with doctored rounds, in which standard bullets had been replaced with hollow-point, unjacketed bullets. In addition the propellant load in the rounds had been tampered with to achieve near high-velocity bullet speed. That's very interesting, the nub of this whole business, as far as I'm concerned.

'Two: There aren't many handguns that use 10 millimetre ammunition and are heavily enough built to risk using rounds tampered with in this way. One is the old Russian Nagan, an increasingly rare weapon. I would not risk using such an old gun, no matter how heavily built. The others are the Smith & Wesson gun specially developed for the American FBI and the Austrian-made Glock.

'Three: It seems to me that whoever killed the two men used every technical advantage possible to increase the likelihood of achieving a first round kill, regardless of range, point of impact or damage done to the gun used. The gun was almost certainly intended to be used infrequently or to fire a limited number of rounds.

'Four: One man fired all three rounds. Given the ballistic evidence I would say that he is short but very strong: I say a man because no woman's wrist bones would survive the recoil from such a weapon system. The individual is a very capable marksman, judging by the speed and accuracy of the firing of the first two rounds. He, or whoever doctored the rounds for him, has an exceptional knowledge of small arms ballistics and is technically competent to a very high degree. All three rounds were fired within a six to eight second period, the third round's firing being delayed for not more than three seconds for reasons unknown. I believe that the man in the window was shot first, and that he was shot twice because the firer could not be sure that he had hit with the first round, probably because the crazing of the window glass obscured his view of the victim's head. The standing man was shot a few seconds later.

'The firer is an ex-Special Forces soldier, a Palestinian terrorist or a terrorist supplied by the Palestinians. I lean toward the latter: no professional would use such a readily identifiable weapon system, it's as good as a fingerprint. On balance I would say that the Provisionals have called in a favour from the Palestinians. Only they among terrorist groups have the technical ability to produce the weapon system used. A Palestinian shot your men, or a Provisional IRA activist supplied by a Palestinian. End of report.'

Professor Zache sat silent for a moment, conflicting impulses flickering over his face. Deciding, he reached for his briefcase, which was tucked under the table. Pulling out a buff-coloured A4 folder he addressed Detective-Sergeant Ellis. 'Read this. It's my preliminary report. Look at the highlighted information.'

Lappin sat impassive as Ellis studied the scientist's written opinion, throwing out his usual ungrammatical comments.

'Bullets 10 millimetre or .40 hollow point, unjacketed. Enhanced velocity rounds. Gun a handgun, type unknown but probably heavier in build than most. One assailant, small, 5′ 6″ to 5′ 8″ tall. Very strong, able to control a heavy or medium-heavy handgun at close range and achieve a high degree of accuracy in the firing of the first two rounds. All three rounds fired within eight seconds. First two at man in window, estimated range: eighteen feet. Third round at Judge, range six inches. Assailant probably a professional or a trained terrorist. Weapon system readily identifiable if used again.'

Detective-Sergeant Ellis raised his head and nodded at Lappin. 'Very good, sir. Your assessment is very close to Professor Zache's view. One man it is, then. A highly trained terrorist.'

Lappin inclined his head, satisfied that he had done the job required of him but keeping his professional satisfaction hidden behind as blank a face as he could manage. Then came a surprise.

'I'm sorry, Sergeant-Major. I underestimated you. I thought you were some gunman brought in to question my findings. Please accept my apologies for my treatment of you. I would be grateful if you looked at these.'

Zache grubbed in his jacket pocket and held out three short brass cartridge cases. 'I kept these back. They were found at the scene of the murders. No fingerprints. I haven't had time to check all the records for a positive identification of them. They could be Smith & Wesson shortcase .40 or something else. Your view, please.'

Lappin resisted the immediate urge to take the cartridge cases into his own hand. Five clear striations nicked the barrel end of the cases, where the bullet had once fitted. All three cases were slightly belled out in the same area. A deep gouge a third of the way up each case showed the power of the extraction mechanism which had gripped and thrown it out of the gun. Each firing cap had an oblong dent, smoothed on its impact surface.

Lappin took a deep breath. 'Ten millimetre. The belling of the open ends confirms that a non-standard propellant load was fired out of them. They expanded at the breech end due to back pressure down the gun barrel and locked themselves into the end of the barrel, producing the striations as seen. The striations could not have been caused by the S&W under those conditions. The

S&W uses a rifling pattern of four lands, not five. The Glock uses five. Further, only the Glock extraction mechanism would be strong enough to pull them out and eject them from the gun: the mark caused by the extraction mechanism shows that it was working hard to get the cases out of the breech. The distinctive indentation of the firing cap is conclusive. These rounds were fired from a 10 millimetre Glock.'

Ellis beamed. 'Yes. We've confirmed the gun type. Excellent! What can we learn from that?'

Before Lappin could speak Zache replied. 'The Glock automatic is constructed of non-metallic substances, except for its barrel and magazine. Any determined terrorist could smuggle one through an airport metal detector. All he has to do is carry the barrel and a tube of bullets in his rectum and a magazine in his shoe. When the alarm goes he produces a bunch of keys from his pocket, laughs and apologises to the security men. Then he walks away. Or he uses a non-metallic magazine adapted to fit the Glock and doesn't even have to do that. Whoever used this gun probably carried it through an airport. I think the sergeant-major is right. There's something that hasn't been mentioned: both victims were prominent Jews. I think a Palestinian did it.'

'OK. I'll buy it. But how come Provisional IRA are claiming it sir?'

'It's not unknown for more than one terrorist group to claim an action.'

'That's the problem, sir. Nobody else has claimed it.'

'I can't help you with that. You're the detective. Give us more to work on and we'll tell you more. For the moment we've nothing more to say. Sergeant-Major?'

Jamie grinned, noting the reference to 'we'. 'I think we should be cautious as yet. We are agreed: it was a Palestinian or a Provisional IRA activist supplied by a Palestinian. That's all we can commit ourselves to. Gentlemen, you're not soldiers, please call me Jamie.'

3 April 1993
NEWRY

Gerry Madden settled himself as comfortably as possible, aware that he might be in for a rough ride, as he faced his brigade commanders for the first time in months. Everyone except Siobhan had tried to warn him that these boys were not like their predecessors: they did not take orders blindly; they questioned everything and seemed loyal to nobody but each other. For the first time in his tenure of command Madden felt insecure. The urge to throw up was strong; it had been all day as he prepared for this meeting, trying and failing to bring his nerves and stomach under control. In this last big effort he was going it alone, throwing everything into the ring. He must not allow them to undermine or deflect him. He rapped on the table for attention.

'Our first action in England for a long time has taken place, a High Court judge successfully assassinated. Two days ago and the Brits haven't a clue. Our lads are moving in and out of houses and hotels like yo-yos, reporting Special Branch tails all over the place. None have been arrested yet. Any that do get arrested will have nothing on them and know nothing, except that they were told to keep moving about. All the Brits can do is deport them back to us. The tabloid papers in England are full of it, denouncing us as usual. Nothing too much, but that's to be expected: Strausseman wasn't anybody special to the average Brit factory worker. There's very little in *The Times* or the *Telegraph* other than the basics. That's good. The Brit establishment doesn't squeal when it hurts, so it's hurt. Strike One is complete. We're ready to get the plebs fired up now.'

Around the old kitchen table the six northern brigades' commanders hunched over their beer and cigarettes. Five hours they'd been here, waiting for Madden. When he had finally entered they had not stood up for him, as a mark of their displeasure. But when

Siobhan McCaillim, dressed in a plain dark skirt and pale green blouse had appeared behind him the chairs had scraped as every man got to his feet. Madden had appeared not to notice, or had dismissed it as a courtesy.

It never occurred to Madden that most of these were Siobhan's men, chosen and nurtured by her as the coming generation, brought to power in the bloodletting following Madden's week in the hands of Peter Ewart. Only Tyrone and Monaghan, people he trusted as much as he trusted anybody, were left of Madden's old guard. In the days following his release Madden had court-martialled and executed old Armagh for his short-lived seizure of power. Then he had become suspicious. *Why had none of the rest of the old guard opposed Armagh? Maybe they had secretly supported him.*

Within a month, two were dead. Some of the others saw the way the wind was blowing and applied to the Army Council for permission to retire. At a meeting of the Council in Dublin Madden had forced the issue. The old men went quietly, grateful to be alive, making room for their deputies. They were careful not to comment on Madden's blind spot: the growing power and influence of Siobhan McCaillim. Armagh had warned them and they had laughed at him. But then Armagh himself had come under her spell, to fall when she looked the other way when Madden walked a free man out of Palace Barracks. Tyrone and Monaghan had survived because they had both been in America.

Siobhan's protégés emerged from the shadows and silently took over. One of their number, Martin Slattery of Castlewellan in County Down, spoke now for them all. 'What now, Gerry? I hardly know what you're talking about. None of us know what the hell is going on. You've stripped us of some of our best men without a word of explanation and now they're running about waiting to be arrested. You've started a campaign in England and nobody knows a bloody thing about it. The Cause is not a dictatorship. You have to tell us what's going on.'

'I command here, Slattery. I'll tell you what I want when I

want. In the meantime you do as I order. Got that?' Madden was on his feet, leaning over the table, eyes blazing.

Slattery refused to knuckle under or be drawn. He held Madden's eyes, stayed seated and observed in a detached, almost patronising way, 'I know who commands, Gerry. I have a command myself. We all do. I insist that you tell us what is happening.'

Madden, shocked, saw the writing on his personal wall: he had been right to think his time was nearly done; no man would have dared to speak to him like this a year or two ago. He had to hold on, grip this thing until his campaign was over. Then these bright young men who had known nothing but the war from their days in short trousers would have to follow his lead as others had done before them, or support his bid for the presidency of the Army Council. He had to face them down, impose his will on them, this one last time.

'No. I will not tell you. I've called this meeting to tell you that a campaign has begun and that you will need to keep your heads down for a while. I am running a campaign using outside help to bring the British to the negotiating table or to their knees in Ireland. All you need to know is that throughout my campaign your people are being used for nothing except to confuse the Brit Special Branch. They'll all come back safe enough. The only casualties we will suffer will be among those drink-sodden loudmouths that call themselves the English ASUs. When the Brits give in you'll be happy. But until then keep your heads down and your mouths shut. The campaign will last for just one month. The Brits will negotiate or withdraw, but they might not realise they have to for a couple of weeks after the campaign ends. They might make a last big effort. They'll target you all. The SAS bastards will be hunting you. That's all I have to say.'

Madden leaned back in his chair. 'Siobhan, as head of my planning staff, knows exactly what is happening. She will reassure you. Goodnight to you all.'

With that Madden got up and walked out, forcing himself to

suppress a grimace of pain. Outside the kitchen he leaned against the wall and pulled out his medication, savagely grinding the little white tablets between his teeth. *Bastards. Don't they realise I'm in constant agony since that fuckpig Ewart kept me a week without my pills? I need their support, not their questioning. If God grants me success and leads me to victory I will take great pleasure in personally putting bullets into their ignorant skulls.*

'All right now. Here it is.' Siobhan McCaillim took Madden's vacant seat and quickly explained his campaign in outline, weighing in the balance the certainty of success of at least the early days of Madden's campaign against her own long-term ambitions. Monaghan and Tyrone, Gerry's men, were still present: she would have to choose her words carefully. Watching the men's slack, unbelieving faces she continued.

'Gerry is not well, but his campaign might work. There will be initial successes, but I know some of you may doubt it. I can see it in your faces. Arabs and Basques and Japs and Germans. Palestinian supermen. It's all nonsense, you think. Wait and see. If his campaign works Gerry will be a hero and will move up to take over from Padraig Hanna as president of the Army Council. If the campaign fails, anything could happen. We must just wait and see.'

Chapter Fourteen

7 April 1993

ETON

Angel Baenaste waited patiently outside the open french windows
of the big redbrick house on the outskirts of a town whose name
he felt no need to know. He was somewhere near London, but he
did not really need to know that either. All Baenaste needed to
know was that at 4.31 his target would be sitting at a desk just
inside the windows, with his back to him. At the appointed time
he would do the job, walk back across the lawn to the road, get
into the car and be taken to the airport. He would be back in
Bilbao in time to join his wife and children for dinner. Maybe
later he and his wife would take a stroll together, after her mother
had put the children safely to bed. Baenaste glanced at his watch.
Two minutes. He reached inside his jacket and hefted the heavy
gun given to him in the car. One bullet would be enough, he had
been told. Watch out for the recoil. Return the gun to the man
in the car.

Inside the room with the french windows the headmaster,
scanning some papers, waited for tea to arrive. A discreet knock
on his study door, then the door opened to reveal a black-coated
manservant bearing a silver tray loaded with silver paraphernalia
and a single Spode china cup and saucer. Without a word the
servant placed the tea in front of his master, bowed and retreated.

Outside the windows Angel Baenaste heard the study door
close. He carefully wiped his palm and gripped the big gun in
his right hand, taking a long pace out from the wall to clear the
open window, his right arm hanging loose at his side. He swung
to turn his right side to the interior of the room, clamping the

back of his left forearm tightly across the small of his back, lifting his right arm straight and stiff, pointing the gun as if it were a sword. Directly in front of him the back of his target's head bent forward as he poured his tea. Baenaste sighted carefully at a range of less than four feet and squeezed the trigger. The target threw itself forward over the big desk, arms flinging outward in the death spasm, sending the silver teapot skidding across the desk to the floor. Baenaste nearly dropped the gun as the power of its recoil threw it upwards, sudden pain seizing his right wrist. He stepped quickly into the room, verified his kill, stepped back out, and sprinted across the lawn.

In the car he handed the gun, left handed, to the man in the back seat. The man asked in Spanish, 'Any trouble?' Baenaste shook his head, but held up his right arm. The wrist was swelling rapidly, broken by the fantastic recoil of Adnan Al Khali's gun. The Arab, alarmed, asked, 'The target is dead?' Baenaste again refused to speak Spanish; he knew that the wiry little Arab in the back seat spoke no Basque. A visual report would have to do. Baenaste nodded.

When the murder was announced on the six o'clock news Gerry Madden was ecstatic. He jumped around the old farmhouse living room like a schoolboy.

'Strike Two! It's all working perfectly. Siobhan, get on the phone to London and Birmingham. Leeds can wait until after Strike Three. Tell the English ASUs to get off their arses and start hitting any and every policeman they can find, whenever they like. I want chaos over there. Tell Hanratty to make the call to the *Telegraph* right away. The usual message claiming responsibility. Then the new statement I prepared. It's going to work, I know it!'

Siobhan made her calls as directed, the first tinge of uncertainty slipping its tendrils into her mind. *Maybe Gerry's campaign will work*. All the more imperative that she be ready to remove him at the first opportunity. If he succeeded and lived, the presidency of the Army Council would be his for the asking and he would hold it for ever. She and her young men would grow dry and bitter as Madden sat on a throne of his own making. It must not be allowed to happen; or she must think of a way of removing Madden once the campaign was over.

LONDON

This time the editor was ready, questions prepared, when the call came through. 'At 4.30 this afternoon an active service unit of the Provisional Irish Republican Army, acting on behalf of the legal government of Ireland, the Provisional Army Council, executed the headmaster of Eton College for his support of the British government's illegal occupation of a part of Ireland. That is all.'

The editor waited a few seconds to see if the caller would disconnect immediately. When the line remained open he nodded to Detective-Sergeant Ellis. The caller had more to say, if he were asked. 'Why have you murdered the headmaster of Eton College? It makes even less sense than killing Judge Strausseman.'

'I am empowered to speak on behalf of the chief of staff of the Provisional Irish Republican Army. Do not interrupt.

'For nearly a quarter of a century we have fought a guerrilla campaign against your dying empire. Thousands have lost their lives and still you persist in denying more than a million of our people the freedom that is their birthright. We are tired of killing the brainwashed sons of your working class patrolling our streets in their tanks. We are tired of hearing your rich and powerful mouthing pieties and sending more young men to die while they themselves lie idle in their mansions adding more and more to their millions. We are abandoning the guerrilla campaign in favour of all out war against the men of power and influence. We have selected them with care and we will kill

274

them to a planned schedule. We will continue to kill them until they see the folly of their ways. The day they announce British withdrawal from Ireland we will stop killing them.'

'I ask again, why the headmaster of Eton?'

'Read your history, Mr Editor. Didn't the Duke of Wellington himself, an Irishman I might add, observe that Waterloo was won on the playing fields of Eton? That school has poisoned the minds of generations of your leaders. It filled them with the belief that England has a divine right to impose her will on small nations. Its headmaster died for that.'

'Can you be more clear? Who or what people are you declaring war on?'

'Look to the pillars of your establishment, Mr Editor. Buy a copy of *Who's Who*. We have.'

The editor discarded his list of prepared questions. Things were taking a different course. 'And you are abandoning attacks on anyone else? You are stopping your bombing and sniping?'

'Yes, Mr Editor. Though we reserve the right to protect ourselves. Your soldiers may come and go as they wish, provided they leave us in peace. The RUC and the police forces of England remain legitimate targets because they are harassing our people even as we speak.'

'You say you have already selected the people you intend to murder. Who are they?'

'Don't be silly, Mr Editor. I'm not going to tell you that. In any case, we are going to murder nobody. The only people who have reason to fear execution are the enemies of freedom. Those who think they could be targets probably are. But they can save themselves at any time by calling for the withdrawal of your troops from my country. Something more for you: our target list is not yet complete, Mr Editor. People who attack us in the media and those who publish such attacks may become targets themselves.'

'Are you threatening me personally?'

'How you interpret my statements is a matter for you. But

you should know that our Intelligence network in England is very good. A little example for you. We know Detective-Sergeant Ellis of the Special Branch is with you now. Tell him to be careful as he leaves, though it won't matter much as we know where he lives. Tell him we know who lives at Flat 6 in Harlow House. We also know Sergeant Dorothy Cleaver, Ellis's tart. And by the way Mr Editor, we know where you live too. And we know you stop at the same news-stand in the Cromwell Road every morning to buy your cigarettes. Marlboro, aren't they? Sixty a day. You'll die young, Mr Editor. That is all.' The line buzzed, dead.

The editor was appalled. 'Christ on the cross! The IRA has been tracking me! They could have murdered me at any time. You have to catch these bastards!'

Detective-Sergeant Ellis looked shaken himself. Pale, he said quietly, 'That's exactly the reaction they're hoping for, sir. They're telling the people who wield power in this country that they're going to kill them. A smart move if all their targets react like you just have.'

The editor reached for the cigarette packet on his desk, dropping it as he saw its familiar red and white colouring. Marlboro and a certain news-stand had just lost a customer. 'Yes, I'm sorry. Who lives at Flat Six, Harlow House? You?'

'No, sir. I have a younger brother, a constable in the Met. He lives there.'

The editor shook his head. 'Is there nothing these fucking people will not stoop to?'

'No, sir. Nothing. Change your routine, sir. Try to have no routine. It's the only defence against terrorists. I'll wait for a copy of your tape.'

Inspector Crabtree listened to Ellis's tape, scribbling on a pad beside him. He said nothing at all until he had heard the tape for the fourth time.

'Move out of your house, Sergeant. Get yourself a flat somewhere. Your brother will be moved too. The Met will pay the rents. Are you playing about with Dot Cleaver?' Receiving Ellis's embarrassed nod the inspector continued. 'That stops today. She'll be put on loan to Surrey or somewhere out of the way. You tell her why and tell her to keep quiet about it. We'll bring her back when this is over.'

Crabtree broke off to answer the insistent trilling of a phone. He listened carefully, said 'Fuck', and slammed the receiver down.

'Three uniforms have just been shot dead sitting in their patrol car, scoffing burgers outside McDonald's in Putney High Street. The Provos called Capital Radio and claimed responsibility. Some bastard just stopped a motorbike beside the car and his pillion passenger sprayed it with a machine gun. The station inspector down there says the inside of the car's like an abattoir. The whole road is littered with shell cases, at least fifty. Witnesses say the gunman took time to change magazines and spray the car again before roaring off. Bastard.

'And it gets worse. One of the uniforms in the car was a nineteen-year-old female special constable out for a jolly. Her father is a Member of Parliament, a senior member of the 1922 Committee, for fuck's sake. This is going crazy.'

He picked up his phone and began punching buttons, got the number wrong and had to start over again. Impatiently he waited until his call was answered. Composing himself Crabtree said, 'Good evening, Chief Inspector. Johnny Crabtree. Sorry to disturb you at home, sir. We have a problem growing here. May I come out and see you? Thank you sir.'

By 9 a.m. on the morning of 8 April the chief inspector had passed the buck to his boss, he to his and he to his. At 9.40 the assistant commissioner of the Metropolitan Police was frantically gathering all the facts together, preparing a brief for the commissioner. In less than an hour the commissioner would be standing in 10 Downing Street, explaining to the Prime Minister how the daughter of his closest political ally had been shot to death on the streets of the nation's capital.

At 11 a.m. the first of the midday editions of the big dailies hit the pavements. Headlines were large and all but one asked awkward questions. The odd man out, the *Sun*, asked no questions. For the first time ever a national newspaper used colloquial language in its front-page headline. Sculpted round a computer-enhanced photograph of the blood-soaked interior of the ambushed police car, the *Sun*'s headline filled its front page: BLOODY BASTARDS it screamed. The usual tits and bums on page three were replaced by thick black accusations. We Name The Guilty Men headed a devastating attack on the Metropolitan Police, and the Special Branch in particular. FIND THEM AND KILL THEM roared the centre pages, heading an article ghost-written for an eminent retired general celebrated for his exploits against terrorists in the Colonies, paraphrasing his once-famous *You cannot reason with a mad dog. You find it and kill it.*

By five o'clock Gerry Madden, ulcers forgotten, was dead drunk. His campaign, he was certain, was headed for victory. Siobhan McCaillim made a lot of phone calls.

9 April 1993
LISBURN

Charlotte Aitken reread the Intelligence summary on her desk. Something odd about it was playing in her mind, on the edge of her consciousness. Then she saw it: PIRA had claimed the killing of the police through Capital Radio, not the *Telegraph*, like the others. That was it. Certain proof that two campaigns were running simultaneously, one to kill *prominente*, one to deflect attention. One run by Madden, the other run in England, probably by the English ASUs.

Charlotte, considering, decided to keep this little titbit to herself for the time being. A second oddity suddenly leapt out of the page at her. The name Lappin. One line along the fold of the paper told her the Rangemaster (Snipers) was assisting the Metropolitan Police Forensic Department. Charlotte sat back, thinking. Jamie was directly involved. Maybe she could use this to reach out to him. With a deliberate effort she pulled her mind back to the job in hand. Conductor Caldwell had worked out a method of using several computer programs in conjunction, to speed up the record search, but did not hold out much hope. Madden had been too elusive for too long to pin down his contacts with any precision. Still, he was searching. He had, in a moment of levity, remarked that only Madden's wife could be relied on to be close to him most of the time, if he had a wife, which Charlotte knew he didn't. She was still puzzling when Caldwell knocked on her door. She swung round expectantly. 'Any news?'

'No, ma'am, not really, just something odd. I was running through the system when one of my little macros suddenly seized on something, ran through half a dozen programs and spewed this out. You should look at it.'

Charlotte took the printout from Caldwell and scanned it quickly. 'Wonderful. Brilliant. I see. I see it. Thank you, Mr Caldwell, thank you very much indeed. I must think.'

Caldwell nodded gravely. 'Call me back when you've had a think, ma'am. I've something else, not much, just a hunch. Probably nothing. I'd like to run it past you after you've studied that.'

'OK. I will. Thank you.'

Charlotte's mind was racing. Something Caldwell had done to the computer system had linked together the names of those in contact with Madden, then hunted for their whereabouts past and present, ploughing through a dense jumble of reports detailing their absences from home. Appalled at the likely size of the resulting printout Caldwell had then programmed in a series of random factors as possible indexes. What the computer had seized on was one of these factors. Finding some commonality it had formed a group of names, then looked for other factors that might link them. It had found last night's routine inputs recording the known whereabouts of the terrorists. A very specific group had surfaced.

All were between twenty-five and thirty-five years old. All had visited home and disappeared again within one hour, last night. All were noted as being members of the planning staffs of PIRA brigades or as being known to be second-in-command of some of the PIRA brigades. All were frequent attendees at Provisional IRA gatherings in the Republic, gatherings which Madden only occasionally attended; but which at least some of his planning staff always attended. *I was right. Someone close to Madden, someone on the Provisional IRA planning staff is coordinating the moves of a select group of terrorists close to the top of the fighting brigades, almost certainly without Madden's knowledge.* Charlotte called Caldwell on the intercom.

'This may well lead to something. Please check as far as possible which, if any, members of the PIRA planning staff attended all the gatherings we know about. It will narrow the field. This is brilliant stuff. I can't thank you enough, Mr Caldwell. I'll do some very hard thinking and I'll give you anything I come up with later. Thank you.'

Charlotte called for coffee and lay down on the daybed in her office. *Right. Think. Cover everything.*

First: There is definitely a subgroup within the Provisional IRA, directed by someone on the planning staff, working to their own ends without Madden's knowledge.

Second: The English ASUs are running wild.

Third: The Provisional IRA hard men running around are doing nothing, nor are they likely to.

Fourth: The subgroup have disappeared, at least for the moment.

Fifth: Someone is killing prominente in England, a separate group or groups not connected with the English ASUs. The Provisional IRA subgroup is not involved, at least directly, since they have only just disappeared from view.

Questions:

Who is running the subgroup?

Why is the subgroup in existence?

Who is killing the prominente?

Charlotte gave up on the first question, through lack of information. That person, she was now sure, would be her ticket back to London, if she could nail him. She turned to the second question.

PIRA is going all-out on some complex campaign, using up the English ASUs, who will certainly be caught fairly quickly. The hard men are spinning round, in and out of police hands, doing nothing. They are not killing the prominente. *The subgroup are not killing them.* Charlotte's mind jumped forward. *The English ASUs are not killing the* prominente. *Therefore PIRA is not killing them. Somebody else is, on PIRA's behalf. Oh my God! I SEE IT NOW.*

Charlotte jumped up and paced around. *I have assumed that PIRA is going all-out. PIRA is not going all-out. Madden is. PIRA is not. Gerry Madden is not in real control of events. He thinks he is because he is running this campaign. He is not in control because there is a powerful group inside his organisation that is keeping itself back, letting him run while preparing for something else. It can only be a takeover bid. Madden is fighting for his life without knowing it. He must be running this campaign in a death or glory bid for victory. He doesn't care about losing the English ASUs. He doesn't care about losing the hard men, or thinks we'll have to let them go because they're doing nothing illegal. He is importing killers to work for him. Someone thinks this will backfire on him and they are preparing to succeed him. That's it. That must be it. And whoever is trying to take over will want him and his old guard out of the way. That's my chance. I must find a way to get PIRA's own insiders to work for me. But they must not suspect I know of their existence. I must watch, wait, and seize my chance.*

Charlotte was distracted by her buzzer. Her chief clerk reminded her that Conductor Caldwell was expecting a call from her.

'Yes. No. I won't call him. Ask him to come and see me, please.'

'Mr Caldwell, the stuff you gave me is outstanding. I promised to call you after I'd studied it. This is what I think.' Charlotte outlined her conclusions.

'I thought you might think that. It all fits. I said I had a hunch. I joked that only Madden's wife could be that close all the time. The thought came back to me after I'd seen the printout I gave you. It may seem outlandish, ma'am, but I'm prepared to be embarrassed by this. Have a look at this file. I'll wait here.'

The file was headed SIOBHAN M. MCCAILLIM.

Charlotte studied Caldwell's face, looking for a hint of humour. There was none. 'You're serious. Have some coffee while I read this.'

Charlotte read, reread, thought. Siobhan McCaillim, 30, red-head, small, pretty, Republican background. Father killed the day she was born, in a road accident. Father had been old IRA. Lost home in riots aged seven. Mother known Provisional IRA sympathiser, high in Cumann na mBan herself, Intelligence gatherer, low level. Nurse at Musgrave Park hospital. Access to military wing there? Probably not. Mentioned by several captured terrorists as well known inside PIRA. Not seen in Ulster for years. Captured Provisionals wary of her, not willing to say much under interrogation. Impression is that she's intelligent, vicious. Rumours of her being Gerry Madden's mistress, ten years or so. Always in his entourage. Thought to have been given a non-executive job on PIRA planning staff to cover for her being Madden's mistress. *Yes. It's not a man. It's a bloody woman, whoring her way to power inside PIRA. Yes. Siobhan McCaillim. She's the one.*

Charlotte stared into space, automatically taking the coffee cup that Caldwell passed to her. She sipped at it. It was cold. She chose her words carefully.

'Mr Caldwell, I am not given to extravagant or profane language. You are a genius; we'll have this fucking bitch. Not a word to anyone.'

282

13 April 1993
LONDON

Inspector Crabtree was at his wits' end. Thirty-two policemen and women had been murdered throughout England in the past week, apparently at random and with great brutality. No real leads to the murderers of Judge Strausseman or Eton's headmaster had materialised. Twenty-seven of the thirty-seven known Provos who had infiltrated the mainland had been arrested and interrogated. Nothing had been learned from them. Eighteen Paddies who had been living in England for years had been picked up, four of whom might or might not be brought before the courts on murder or conspiracy to murder charges. Not one had said a word.

The pub Republicans who might know something and who usually spilled in exchange for a few pints and an ear eager to lend credence to their boastings had suddenly become very quiet. Something big, really big, was in the air, something big enough to scare them shitless. One former reliable had even got up and walked out of a pub at first sight of a detective he'd known for years. Collared later he'd just said, 'It isn't worth it. It's too dangerous. I'd get a bullet just for being seen talking to you. The boys you've got in nick know the same. The crazies are out running about with machine guns as if there's no tomorrow. Nobody's going to say a blessed word to you, even if they want to, because nobody knows anything. Let me away from here before anybody sees us, for Jesus' sake. I've got kids.'

The only ray of light on Crabtree's horizon was confirmation from ZL, the Zache-Lappin mutual admiration society, that the gun used to kill the head of Eton was the same as that used to kill Judge Strausseman and his friend. ZL also insisted that the machine guns used to kill police all over the country were

283

Russian AK 47 assault rifles, not more than three of them being passed around between a number of Provisional IRA activists. ZL refused to revise their opinion of the user or users of the Glock automatic and its weird ammunition, but acknowledged that the killer of Eton's head had missed the brain core with an aimed shot. They conceded that a different man might have killed him. But that was all.

The press were going crazy. TV and radio were in on the act, screaming for action. Both Houses of Parliament were up in arms, firing questions for which the Met had no answers. At first the police brass had been eager to jump in, senior officers appearing whenever possible on TV and making carefully prepared, highly quotable 'off the cuff' remarks. But as the slaughter mounted and the questions became harder to answer the brass had melted away, leaving Crabtree alone in the firing line, getting help when he asked for it, but rarely receiving written instructions and never anything with a signature on it. The randomness and intensity of the PIRA murder campaign against the police seemed to have paralysed the various forces' ability to react. As for the men on the beat and cruising the motorways, they were unarmed sitting targets.

LISBURN

Charlotte Aitken was turning her organisation upside down. She had split and reorganised it, leaving most of it on its normal duties, with subtle differences. Instead of looking for patterns of Provisional IRA activity most of her staff were looking at Provisional IRA personnel, not their activities. Her aim was clear: to establish as far as possible who was in command where. Any known PIRA commander aged under thirty-five received special attention. And there was a further question: how often did they come into contact with one another, with Siobhan Maeve McCaillim present, outside known PIRA planning conferences?

All available Intelligence-gathering agencies were carefully, quietly involved, none made aware of the whole of Lieutenant-Colonel Aitken's intentions. All were told that there was a long-term operation in progress to plot the whereabouts of Gerry Madden in the hope that one day his next move could be predicted, that maybe, just maybe, he could be captured alive. None were told that where Madden went, McCaillim went, that Siobhan McCaillim was Charlotte Aitken's real target.

A small, secretly manned army unit based in England but working exclusively in Northern Ireland helped where it could, which was almost everywhere. Its members knew every Provisional IRA activist by name, knew their preferences for breakfast, lunch and dinner, knew their weapon skills, faces, who worked where for whom, who took the dole, who owned multimillion-pound companies, who was fucking who, when and where. They had pictures, tapes, a wealth of received wisdom.

The RUC Special Branch's computer people buried Conductor Caldwell in information, relieved to get rid of it, not bothering to involve their own senior officers in the transaction, grateful that someone was using what they had. The SAS were difficult; they referred Charlotte's people back to Hereford, then to London, then to the small unit Charlotte already knew of.

GCHQ at Cheltenham listened, tapped into just about every telephone conversation carried out over mobile telephones in the whole of Ireland. A branch of the Foreign Office not in White-hall was persuaded to release files they had always claimed were nonexistent. The files were shuttled to Belfast's Aldergrove airport via London's Lambeth North tube station by the Queen's Messengers, faintly military men in their fifties wearing Greyhound ties and steel-lined briefcases chained to their wrists. The Security Service answered questions, only when asked, always with a question in return. Little by little the picture was building up, the threads gathering. Charlotte built a family tree of who was linked to whom in PIRA. Who owed allegiance or favours to whom. Among Conductor Caldwell's select group, identified by computer, the threads grew thicker. Like the strands of a rope they all came together, and the knot at the end was Siobhan Maeve McCaillim.

Charlotte and Caldwell quietly congratulated themselves. What had started as a feeling of hers, a hunch of his, had grown into the Intelligence coup of the war in Ireland. How best to use it?

Outside her main office Charlotte organised a subgroup, headed by Conductor Caldwell, its task to find out all there was to know about Siobhan McCaillim. With the enemy in sight Charlotte Aitken was galvanised. Knowledge that her enemy was a woman drove her to extremes. She slept no more than four hours in twenty-four and expected the same from all around her. Some fell by the wayside, influenced by family or other considerations. Charlotte weeded them out ruthlessly and replaced them with people who could stand the pace. She briefed everyone personally, told them that whatever their preconceptions, whatever briefings they had been given before their arrival were of no importance compared to their current task. With energy and sheer force of personality she brought together people who would do her will, believing it their own.

For the first time in her life Charlotte felt at ease with herself: this was what she was all about, what she had been brought up and trained for. She sensed the stink of battle on the wind and revelled in it, certain she would win.

WAPPING, LONDON

The two Japanese drove straight through the wire mesh gate, snapping the wooden barrier pole reinforcing it. As the red and white striped pole-ends slumped to the ground both men got out of the car and ran back to the guard hut at the gate.

Two security men were on their feet, grinning, preparing to run out and arrest whatever drunken journalist had driven through their gate.

The Japanese forced their way in as the guards tried to get out. The first guard, over fifty, was thrown back against the wall by the opening door. The other took two bullets in the neck and head as he reached for his baton. The older man was still regaining his feet when the soft double *phutt* of the silenced automatics beat through his chest. He groaned as his mind fought to cope with what was happening. One of the Japanese shoved a foot under him, turned him face up and deliberately shot him a third time, through the right eye.

Ourside, a third raider checked his weapon as the Japanese tumbled back into the car. Speed was now vital. The car jerked, stalled, then shot forward, trailing wire and wood as it skidded across the car park and slammed sideways into the wall beside the big double door above the newsprint loading ramp. Out jumped the Japanese, closely followed by the third man. Up on to the ramp, through the doors, across the loading bay and down a short corridor. At the end of the corridor a steel door with a huge ear barred and circled in red stuck on it carried a half-empty row of headphones, Amplivox sound suppressors. To the left a steep flight of bare concrete steps led into the main foyer. Crossing the foyer the three men met a girl with her arms full of research material. Both Japanese stopped dead, took quick aim and shot through the pile of paper, killing her instantly. The receptionist, a plump mumsy woman with blue-rinsed hair, died moments later. Up a flight of wide, carpeted stairs and down a corridor. The Japanese turned off into the main newsroom as the third man threw open a padded door marked EDITOR. KNOCK AND WAIT.

In the editor's office were three men and one woman. The intruder took the heavy pistol in both hands and shot two of the men and the woman in quick succession, one round each, the roar of the gun melding into blasts coming from the newsroom. The editor, shocked immobile, stared open-mouthed at a short, muscular man with a shock of rough black hair and a single thick bar of eyebrow across his forehead. The terrorist smiled pleasantly, showing big white teeth in a dark, Mediterranean face. Humour danced in his eyes.

'Hi there! My name is JoJo. How's this for a headline? "SHOCK HORROR REVENGE MURDERS: JOURNALISTS RIDDLED IN BIZARRE TERROR RAID: DOZENS DIE IN HAIL OF MACHINE GUN BULLETS". Too long? Oh well, no time for editing, I'm afraid.' The terrorist chuckled. 'No time for anything any more. Time to die.' JoJo threw back his head, laughing. Pointing the heavy gun, JoJo's face hardened as he walked towards the stunned newsman. Like a rabbit mesmerised by a snake, all the editor could see was the small black circle at the end of the gun's barrel. Without a further word JoJo shot the editor in the face, watched him fall and shook his head. 'Bye bye, scribbler.'

Outside the office the main newsroom was a pandemonium of noise, the Japanese spraying the big room from two of its corners, blasting computer monitors, pot plants and screaming people alike. On entering the big room the Japanese had swapped their light automatics for much more powerful weapons, Ingram machine pistols, weapons capable of firing 600 rounds a minute. Like automatons the two terrorists stood stiffly, firing constantly, sweeping the newsroom in overlapping arcs of fire, mechanically changing magazines every few seconds, pulling the long black bars of bullets out of canvas bags slung over their shoulders and dropping the spent magazines at their feet. The room was a total shambles: glass and plastic, shredded paper and a nightmare of bloodstained bodies littered the floor and hung across shattered equipment. Blood sprayed up the walls and ran in thick streams across the floor.

JoJo stood in the corridor for a few seconds, ripping bright red tapes from three small black objects. Ready, he started his run down the corridor, throwing the thermite bombs through the main doorway of the newsroom as he passed it without breaking stride.

The Japanese caught sight of the little bombs as they arced between them and bounced off destroyed furniture to be lost from sight on the floor. Their reaction was immediate. Both men stopped firing, dropped their weapons and pulled identical bombs out of their shoulder bags, held them up to show to each other, shouted 'Hai!' and ripped the ignition tapes off.

The running JoJo just made it clear of the end of the corridor as the explosive charges detonated, knocking down the plasterboard wall separating the corridor from the newsroom and covering the floor with white-hot streaks of burning magnesium and phosphorus. The bombs burnt for no more than thirty seconds, but the searing heat they generated turned the upper half of the building and its entire contents into a short-lived, superheated fireball. Paper, plastic and wood bloomed instantly; bodies dead or wounded leapt in the ferocious heat, the still living screaming their way into death. Laughing aloud, JoJo darted back down across the foyer.

In the print room the great machines thundered on, their operators in soundproofed cabins oblivious to the terrible carnage above them. When the fire alarm went off the printing presses ground slowly to a halt. Operators evacuated the print room, flooding out across the flame-lit car park. JoJo moved out, running with the fleeing printers until they slowed near the gate and turned to watch the fire. He watched it himself, checking that the gatehouse door was closed, keeping curious eyes from the hut's contents, as he manoeuvred through the tightening crowd, out the gate and away. Once in the car he grinned at the man in the back seat. 'Went like a dream. In and out in less than four minutes.'

The little Arab grinned back. 'Excellent. Give me the gun.'

JoJo handed the Glock over. 'Sure. You're welcome to it. Fucking thing nearly broke my arms.'

Content for the moment, he turned his head quickly to see

what was happening as the big car accelerated suddenly, throwing him back in his seat. The Arab, prepared for the sudden acceleration, leaned into it, drawing a long, thin-bladed knife, not unlike a flattened meat skewer, out of his sleeve. He chose his point carefully and drove the blade between the base of JoJo's skull and the first vertebra. JoJo jerked convulsively as the blade sank in, cut his spinal cord and drove on into his brain, immobilising then killing him. The Arab drew the blade out, wiped it carefully on the cloth of JoJo's printer's smock and returned it to his sleeve, speaking quietly to the driver in Arabic. 'Achmed. Dump this unbeliever's carcass in the river. Let me out before we cross the river. I will return to the Embassy in the morning.'

'Jesus Christ. I've never seen anything like it. It's a bloody massacre. What kind of animals could do the likes of this?' The chief inspector's face was drawn and haggard, flecks of vomit marring the corners of his mouth.

Inspector Crabtree silently handed him a handkerchief. The older man took it gratefully and wiped his mouth. 'I'm sorry, Crabtree. This is just too . . . too . . .'

'Yes sir, I know. I know.'

Together the chief inspector and Crabtree had toured the site of what had been the offices and printing plant of Britain's bestselling daily newspaper, wading through tangles of firehose and power cables, from the gatehouse to the newsroom full of charred and twisted bodies. Ambulances and fire engines moved slowly about, their revolving blue lights casting a flickering, eerie glow through the wisping smoke, reflecting sickly off the water-drenched tarmac.

Behind the two policemen the sudden bright lights of a television crew burst into life, the concentrated beam bouncing off the wet to set a halo round the reporter. The young ITN man stood slackly as a makeup girl slapped Pan Stik on his face, rubbing it briskly, smoothing it into the skin to cover its sick paleness. The reporter looked worse than ever. A moment later his cameraman signalled: OK.

The reporter straightened and began: 'This is Robert Horsley for ITN. I am standing in the car park of the *Sun* newspaper –' the young man caught a whiff of charred flesh from the smouldering building behind him. 'I, I . . . please forgive me, this is terrible . . . I'll start again. Robert Horsley for ITN. In the car park of the *Sun* newspaper. Tonight the offices of the *Sun* were attacked, it is thought by terrorists. The building you see behind me is almost totally destroyed. So far forty-one bodies, mostly burned beyond recognition, have been recovered. We are told that all of them bore bullet wounds. There may be more –' He gagged again as smoke swirled round him. 'Perhaps many more. This is the most dreadful thing . . . too horrible . . . I'm sorry, I can't –' The reporter lowered his microphone, sick and weeping uncontrollably, thinking he would have to do this all over again, unaware of the camera still following him.

In the control room back at ITN white faces followed the camera, the seven second button seeming to cry out to be pushed, but the news editor had jumped to his feet and jammed a chair under the handle of the soundproof door just in time to prevent the station controller rushing in.

'Keep away from that fucking delay button!' he yelled at a console operator with twitching hands. 'This is great television. Great television. The burning of the Hindenburg all over again. No delay. Keep it rolling, ten seconds more, ten seconds, that's all. Ten seconds!'

Around the country millions of people sat horrified, the full dreadfulness of what had happened brought brutally home to them by the sight of the huddled, sickened, sobbing young man they saw groomed and smiling most other nights, telling them of the doings of the royal family and the blunderings of Whitehall.

The Prime Minister, watching in the sitting room of the flat above his office in 10 Downing Street felt his heart sink.

One more like this and he would have to negotiate, much as he loathed the idea of sitting across a table from people who could commit atrocities like this. He pressed a button on a panel near his elbow.

'Ask the Home Secretary to come to me at once, please. Send for the commissioner of the Metropolitan Police. Require the General Officer Commanding London District to report immediately. Call the Duke of York's barracks and ask for the director of Special Forces. Ask Sir Geoffrey Roling to come over from SIS. Open up COBRA for them. Tell me when all are present.'

An ambulanceman rushed up. Excitedly he grabbed at Crabtree's sleeve. 'Sir, come this way, quick. The guard. He's not dead. Come with me, sir. The doctor wants –' but Crabtree and his chief inspector were already moving.

'He's in a bad way, gentlemen. Severe exsanguination, barely conscious. My fault. I thought he was as dead as the others. But he might just live. I don't know how he's hung on. Insists on seeing a cop. He can just about talk.'

Inside the ambulance the doctor switched the barely alive guard's drip from plasma to whole blood.

'I'm an army doctor on loan to Bart's. He's got a tattoo of his blood group on his wrist. Dodgy to trust it but he'll die if I don't take the chance. Soldiers do it all the time, drunk, forget their group and tell the needleman anything. He's ex-RRF.' The doctor pointed to another tattoo on the guard's arm.

'RRF? What's that?' Crabtree asked quickly.

The doctor replied 'Royal Regiment of Fusiliers. Keep it short, please.'

'I'm a policeman, lad. Don't try to talk yet. Blink once for yes, twice for no. Understand?

One blink.

'You're a Fusilier?'

One blink.

Crabtree slipped a hand into the chest pocket of the young

292

man's shirt, and pulled out a pass card with his name on it. 'Right then Fusilier Sharpe. The medic's had a look at you. You're hit hard but you're going to make it, OK? Hang in there son. We need you. Did you see who shot you?'

The wounded man lifted an arm and scrabbled at the oxygen mask over his face. Crabtree looked at the doctor. The medic nodded. Crabtree lifted the mask.

'Tell us, son. Tell us who shot you.' The young ex-soldier's face was almost frozen by pain, the effort he was making clear in his voice. 'Japs. Two. Nochink. wasn HK. autos. silncd. Fass . . . gooshots.'

Crabtree glanced at his boss. He was scribbling in a notebook like a brand-new constable. Crabtree smiled his thanks. He took the guard's hand. 'Anything else, son?'

The guard blinked yes, too weak to speak. The doctor butted in: 'He served in Hong Kong, knows the difference between Chinese and Japanese. He was shot by two Japanese using silenced automatics. He says they were fast and good shots.' The ex-soldier's eyes moved towards the doctor. Thanks.

'Brilliant, soldier, just brilliant. You're a credit to your regiment. Take your time.' The pain-wracked face contorted with the effort, trying to speak clearly through a torn and blood-clotted throat. 'Offser. Marines. sawm. walked out. JoJo . . . Arthrs.'

'JoJo? Arthurs? There was another man called JoJo Arthurs? You know him? He was an officer in the Marines?'

One blink.

'He walked out?'

One blink.

'Did the Japs leave with him?'

Two blinks.

'Did you see the Japs leave at all?'

Two blinks.

'Anything more, soldier?'

Two blinks, barely perceptible, the eyes closing.

'Just brilliant, soldier. We'll get them. We'll get them for you. You rest and get yourself sorted out. We'll need you in court, OK?' The eyes opened briefly. 'Good lad. Fight.'

Crabtree turned to the doctor. 'Keep him alive. He's a brave man, hanging on to talk to us. Get him to hospital.'

'On our way. There's nobody else alive here to treat.'

'We'll find you at Bart's?'

'No. This lad's going to the Queen Elizabeth Military Hospital in Woolwich. There's a surgeon there, Peter Cross. The best there is for gunshot wounds. Colonel Peter will see this lad through if anybody can.'

'OK. Get him away. And thanks. This is the best lead we've had so far.'

Chapter Fifteen

14 April 1993

LONDON

'I cannot bring myself to listen to your stupid read out message, damn you. Did you perpetrate that inhuman outrage in Wapping?'

'At 11.45 last night an act . . .'

'Fuck you. I will not listen to you.' The editor of the *Telegraph*, white and shaking with fury, slammed the phone down, turning to look at the big policeman sitting in a leather swivel chair.

'I am truly sorry, Sergeant Ellis. I cannot do it. The voice of that filth fills me with disgust. I'm sorry. I will not listen to it.'

'I understand, sir, I heard enough. The Provisional IRA are claiming it. Would you consider this?' Ellis held out a folded A4 sheet of thick creamy vellum. The editor, intrigued, took it and read it, blanching even further as the impact of the letter's contents hit him.

'Am I reading this right? Her Majesty has contacted my paper's owners? She fears that the nation may become demoralised if no newspaper takes up where the *Sun* left off? The *Telegraph* is to continue the *Sun*'s attacks on the IRA? It's too ridiculous for words. Why doesn't *The Times* do it? They have the same owners as the *Sun*.'

Ellis, a convinced Royalist, was deeply offended. 'Her Majesty is never ridiculous, sir. Your owners didn't think so, so why should you? I don't know why she chose the *Telegraph* and I don't wish to question Her Majesty's judgement. Perhaps it is because the terrorists have been using you to speak to us. Whatever her reasons, the Queen has a good finger on the pulse

295

of this country; she knows how well the *Sun* reflected, and sometimes formed, the opinions of working people. She regards it as
essential that the IRA is not seen to have defeated the paper.
Read that letter again. How you achieve Her Majesty's aim is
left open. Her Majesty is offering you a challenge, sir. You realise
the possible consequences if you accept it? And the consequences
if you don't?'

The editor thought quickly. His newspaper's owners backed
the scheme. There could be a knighthood in this if he acted on
it, or the sack if he didn't. Pragmatism seemed wise.

'Of course I accept. This is a royal command. I will do the best
I can until the *Sun*'s owners can get going again. I will move into
rooms in this building. My family will go abroad on an extended
holiday.'

'Very good, sir. In view of your response to that letter I am
directed to inform you that you will be given the most complete
personal protection available. The best rifleman the British Army
possesses will scan this building from every conceivable angle. If
you stay within the areas he recommends no sniper in the world
can possibly hit you from outside. Two former SAS soldiers currently employed by a government department will be within ten
feet of you at all times for close protection. Every floor of this
building will contain certain other soldiers monitoring access to
lifts, stairs and windows. A detachment of the Royal Engineers
Postal & Courier Service will monitor all incoming mail and a
Royal Army Ordnance Corps bomb disposal team will be on
hand at all times.'

'My God. Who authorised all this?'

'The Prime Minister requires that you are kept safe, sir.
Her Majesty will receive you at the Palace at three o'clock.'

The editor slumped into his armchair, thinking.

Detective-Sergeant Ellis almost squirmed in his seat. The commissioner should have had this job. Or a chief superintendent at
least. But chief supers seemed thin on the ground these days.
The chief inspector had collapsed at home, a complete nervous

breakdown resulting from his inspection of Wapping. Inspector Crabtree was busy with Zache and Lappin.

The editor blinked rapidly, still thinking. 'What do I tell Her Majesty?'

'You can tell her that you will attempt to deflect the thrust of this campaign. Tell her you will challenge them. Anything that breaks the pattern of IRA success might give us a chance at them.'

'Very well, Sergeant. I will do just that. Thank you.'

'OK. Tell us what you think.' Inspector Crabtree, his face tired and lined, massaged his forehead as he spoke. The two men sitting in the police issue chairs in his office were tired too. They had been up all night themselves and had been working through the day.

Zache and Lappin had agreed beforehand that the young forensic scientist would speak for them both. Zache cleared his throat and said, 'Plenty of evidence. There were bullets and cartridge cases all over the place. The weapons used in the newsroom were standard Ingram M10 machine pistols. Quite small, light and easy to hide and carry around. Fantastic rate of fire. Change magazines often enough and you have an almost unbroken stream of bullets in standard Ingram cases, 9 millimetre.

'The terrorists just went in there to kill as many people as possible. Probably three attackers. Two in the newsroom and one in the editor's office. The fire was caused by explosive incendiary devices. We think they were probably used to kill off the wounded to prevent identification of the attackers. The people in the editor's office were killed very quickly and accurately where they happened to be standing or sitting when the killer walked in on them.

'Same story as the judge and the headmaster. Killer relatively short, powerful. The same Glock automatic and special ammunition. Could be the same man for all three attacks. Two handguns were used in the gatehouse and the foyer. Beretta M9 automatics, both fitted with some kind of sound suppressor. The suppressors could be from Knight's Armament as they do a special for that gun. Very effective. You'd have to be reasonably close to hear it. Standard ammunition used. That's about it.'

Crabtree was sitting back, eyes closed. 'Thanks. Good work, gentlemen. Some good news. One of the guards survived, an ex-soldier called Sharpe. He saw all three of the attackers. He even recognised one of them. The guard says one of the men is or was an officer in the Marines, called Arthurs. The other two were Japanese, for God's sake. It looks as if the Provos have been running circles round us, murdering cops at random to distract us from the bad boys they've hired in to do the big jobs. You were nearly right the first time, Jamie. I think one man is using the special gun, an ex-professional turned mercenary or terrorist, doesn't matter which. At least we know what to concentrate on.'

16 April 1993
LONDONDERRY

'Can you believe the arrogance of these people? Can you believe it? Can you?' Gerry Madden raging, charged around the farmhouse kitchen. 'They're all out of their bloody minds. Letters of bloody defiance. Who do they think I am? Hitler? I am fighting for my country!'

Siobhan McCaillim sat quietly, saying nothing. Not even she could calm Gerry in this kind of mood. It was pointless even trying to tell him that it was all an obvious ploy to bolster up the British people. But, she thought privately, the Brits must be hurting badly to stoop to this kind of nonsense. The source of Madden's rage lay on a scrubbed pine table, open at its editorial.

Madden, eyes bulging with disbelief, had read the *Telegraph*'s editorial again and again. It was an open letter from the editor addressed to the 'self-styled chief of staff of the Gang of Criminals called the Provisional IRA'. In it the editor attacked the leadership of the PIRA, naming them one by one, with the word murderer following each name. The editor challenged them to sue him for libel in any court in any country, and went on to say that he would spit in the faces of his adversaries from the dock. He said that while Madden and his crew might attack the weak, the unprepared and the unarmed they were afraid to face up to those who were not. He said that Madden was a gutless coward lacking in any kind of personal courage who had salted away several millions of dollars in Switzerland against the day the Irish people finally sickened of him. He went so far as to personally challenge Madden to come to his office at Marsh Wall and kill him, promising that he would capture and hang Madden. 'I am not unprepared. I am not weak. I am not unarmed. I am not afraid. Send your criminals against me. Lead them yourself if you dare. I will hang you from the balustrade of this building and not seek to hide from the Law of this land. I will serve my time for your murder and on the day of my release I will dance on your grave.'

Listening to Madden rage Siobhan had some difficulty in keeping a straight face. The apparent childishness of the Brit response, the impotent fury of it was calculated to enrage Madden, dragging his mind away from the realities. Siobhan had no doubt that the Brits realised by now that it was not the Provisional IRA that was committing the attacks on British *prominente*. They must know that the slaughter of unarmed police was nothing but a smokescreen to distract and horrify the police and the common people. Somebody, somewhere, was sitting back, thinking.

A look through the other papers and a cursory scan of PIRA reports coming out of England proved it. Arrests of PIRA sympathisers had stopped and most of the detainees had been released. *They know these people can tell them nothing.* Surveillance of the PIRA men from Ireland had stopped. *They know that these were only part of our deception plan.* A couple of days of concentrated effort had pulled in five of the remaining English

299

ASU activists, and with them two of the Kalashnikovs they had available. *They're working to stop the attacks on the police, but not throwing everything into it or they'd have had them all by now*. Airport and seaport surveillance had reached levels that had totally disrupted sea and air travel schedules. *They know it's someone from outside and are concentrating on that.*

Siobhan considered her conclusions. Let Madden rage. The destruction of the *Sun* had sealed his fate, whatever he did now. Not even the Army Council could publicly stomach such wanton slaughter taking place in their name. The campaign would go on. Strike Four would probably be successful, but would do no more than enrage the Brits further: it would put their politicians in an awkward position; any who wanted to stop the campaign by negotiating with PIRA would be thrown out of office by the anger of the people. The Brit government couldn't risk it. Therefore Madden's campaign must fail. Those suicidal Japs had done her a favour: they had put the lid on Madden's political coffin. Maniacs, she thought, but useful maniacs. Strike Four would start the nailing process. If Strike Five, the big one, got through it would bang in the final nail. Madden was on his last legs. She must prop him up and defend him in public, to keep the campaign going. She must speak privately to the Army Council. Her own people were ready.

'All right, Gerry, all right. The man's an idiot if he thinks you're going to fall for that shite. You can see to the likes of him anytime, and who cares what the Brits think. Strike Four is coming up. Think of ways of getting more out of it. The Brits are squealing. Make them squeal more. We're winning, Gerry. Your campaign is working.'

Madden stopped almost in mid-stride, his anger too strong for his weakening body, panting with the effort his rage had pulled out of him. 'Squeal. Yes. I'll make them squeal. I'll kill them all, every pinstripe-suited arrogant one I can find. Hang me, would he? I'll see to him after. I'll hook him up like a pig from his fucking balustrade and cut his throat myself.'

'Yes Gerry. Time enough. We have all the time in the world. Why don't you have a drink to calm yourself? Then we'll put our heads together to make the most of Strike Four. Let's use it to really hurt them.'

'Aye. Brandy. That's it, brandy. Then we'll have a think.'

Siobhan smiled inwardly. A couple of large brandies would do nicely. Give it an hour and Madden would be out cold, too weak to resist the liquid Valium she would slip into the drink. Tonight he would be back on his feet, thinking.

LISBURN

'Life is getting rough over there.' Caldwell nodded to the newspapers on Charlotte's desk. He said little, but enough. 'Maybe we could help them. We could help the Special Branch in England.'

Charlotte had been expecting this and was ready to defend her views, but not in her usual combative way. She needed Caldwell. She could not afford to antagonise him. She could, if she chose, simply order him to follow her line, but that would be counterproductive. She felt some sympathy with senior Ordnance Corps officers: it could not be easy managing men of this calibre. Caldwell was too bright and able to fob off. He had to be convinced that her policy, to say nothing to anyone for the time being, was right. Or he had to be made to doubt his own feeling. Either way he had to be handled with care.

'Yes. We should, if we can help. What should we tell them?'

Caldwell looked surprised. 'Everything, of course. It could change the whole way they see things in England.'

'Agreed. It would. But how would it help them? I don't think it would. You've seen the IntSums. They've realised what is happening. They know there are two campaigns running. The English ASUs can't last much longer. They know it isn't the Provisional IRA who are killing the *prominente*. I think the English Special Branch are getting on top. Even if they aren't there is little we can do. If we tell them everything we simply confirm what they already know and then throw a massive spanner into the works. It would distract them from bringing the campaign to a stop. Knowing about McCaillim would not help them, it would hinder them. What McCaillim does or doesn't do is irrelevant to this present battle. She isn't running either campaign in England. Madden is. When Madden has been defeated then it will be time to deal with McCaillim, not before. We will be ready and we will do it. We will do it here.'

Caldwell looked unconvinced. 'McCaillim could do anything. She could assassinate Madden any time now. She could take over and continue the fight.'

'Again I agree. But bear with me for a little. I'll tell you what I really think. Why should McCaillim act now? That woman is very clever, very determined and very patient. She will let Madden burn himself out. She will make sure he is defeated. Then she will take over. She has too much to lose by trying too early. We have an enormous advantage in that we know she's going to do it. Look at it from her point of view. She thinks she's still quietly building herself up and grinding Madden down. She thinks nobody but her own people knows about it. She thinks she has time.' Charlotte got up and walked about the room, thinking aloud.

'Mr Caldwell, I have considered this matter. In my view there are two separate issues here. One is dealing with the battle in England. There is little we can do to influence that. The other issue is how to continue the war against PIRA once this campaign is over, once McCaillim has seized power. I think that no matter how bad it gets in England Madden will not achieve his aim. He will be defeated, if only because McCaillim is undermining him. The second issue must take precedence. The first issue is only a battle, however bad it may seem. The second issue could turn the war. Can you accept that?'

Caldwell considered. 'Yes. People are dying in their dozens over there. A terrible thing. We can justify inaction only if we can prevent McCaillim revitalising PIRA power later. That's the crux of the matter.'

Charlotte nodded. She started walking about again. 'Agreed. But you know there can be no guarantees. We can only do our best. I believe it will be enough. It is a terrible thing, but we must let them fight it out in England without us. Then we take revenge. We accept our casualties from this battle and go on to win the war. Good. We are not far apart on this. Think about these factors.

'There are two ways of dealing with McCaillim. One is to do as we are. We keep quiet and get ready for her, punch her when she leasts expects it, in her moment of triumph. She and her people will have to come North, to show the Provisional IRA footsoldiers they are in control. That's our time. We lift her and every one of her men the moment they set foot in Ulster. We can set the Provisionals back ten years in a single blow.

'The other way to deal with her is to let Madden know what she's up to. There are ways of doing that. He might believe it, kill her and her people. It might stop the campaign in England, while he does it, it might not. Don't forget it is outsiders who are doing the killing for him. Their plans will have been laid. Madden might just concentrate on saving himself while his foreigners fight on in England. We would gain nothing and lose much. Madden is ruthless enough to kill everyone around him and retrench for a while, come at us refreshed. Which is worse, McCaillim or Madden? It's not a choice I think we can make.

'On the other hand he might not believe us. McCaillim has fooled him for a long time. He might have difficulty in accepting a new image for her. He might not want to believe it. She would survive and be forewarned. She might strike before we are ready. Not even the Provisionals' own Army Council could stop her.

She would be in the middle, running the biggest campaign the Provisionals have ever fought. They would have to support her, if she claimed that we had succeeded in turning Madden against his own young commanders, that he was about to start a bloodbath inside the PIRA because of his own paranoia. She would not even have to come North. She would win. We gain nothing and lose every advantage we have built up through our work.

'We must hold our nerve and be ready when the time comes. We must not be deflected in our purpose. Siobhan McCaillim must be defeated before she can defend herself. It is a matter of timing, of seizing opportunities as they present themselves. On no account must we do anything that might give her the slightest inkling that we are aware of her existence, never mind her intentions. Mr Caldwell?'

'I understand. This is not my kind of game. I am out of my depth in this, this . . . this Machiavellian world. I have to trust you in this. We keep quiet.'

LONDON

'We're getting somewhere now, ZL. We've got two of the Kalashes and the headcases that were using them. Thanks to you we know they've only one left, so they'll probably keep it in London. We'll get it in a day or two. All the people we had running round in circles after nobodies have been pulled back in. The air and seaports are tighter than a duck's chuff. We're getting on top. I'm just worried that we're not getting on top quick enough. Whoever organised this is bloody clever. He must have something more up his sleeve.'

Zache and Lappin thought nothing of being addressed as if they were one person. Unalike as chalk and cheese the muscular soldier and the skinny professor who had difficulty keeping his spectacles on his face had forged a link of liking and respect for each other's personalities and professional abilities. It had come together for them when late one night they had shared a half-bottle of whisky after a long, tough day. Zache had suddenly said 'You're not married Jamie. Are you gay?' Lappin had jumped to his feet. 'No I'm bloody well not! What do you mean by that?'

'Don't shout at me. I'm gay. Your being straight doesn't bother me. Does my being gay bother you?'

Lappin, embarrassed by this kind of talk, didn't know what to say and wondered if he was being propositioned.

'I can see what you're thinking, you great hunk of beef. You're not my type. I just wanted to be sure I'm not your type either, clear the air sort of thing.'

A hint of devilment crept into Lappin's eyes. He sat down again, relaxing. 'Don't suppose you are, really. Boobs aren't big enough. Not much of an ass. And those glasses!'

Zache threw his head back, laughing. 'OK soldier! We know where we are. We should make a good team.'

Lappin seemed to consider for a moment. 'Who leads?'

'Nobody, we work together.'

Lappin shook his head. 'That doesn't work. Every team, even if all are equal, needs a leader for when decisions have to be made. You know how cops work. And you're the brains. You lead. I'll support you.'

Zache sat silent, thinking back over the pains of school and college, remembering all the humiliations he had suffered for having a puny body and homosexual tendencies, remembering the bullies and stupid, overweight tough guys who delighted in embarrassing him. All he had ever had to fight with was his mind, and it had never seemed enough. Even his colleagues in the Met still threw him odd glances. Now this plain-speaking sergeant-major with his Para wings and decorations for bravery, a genuine tough guy, was telling him he thought him the better man to lead their team. He decided Lappin could be a good friend to have.

'Thank you. You can't imagine what this means to me, Jamie. I won't let you down.'

'Don't know what you mean, boss. I won't let you let me down. Do you know what they call us?'

'No, what?'

'They call us ZL. Everybody knows we're a team. And everybody knows who the leader is. Otherwise we'd have been LZ. You don't have to be so bloody awkward. You've nothing to prove. Drink?'

Zache held his glass out. 'Thanks. I'll try to be less abrasive.'

Lappin, watching the thin, serious face struggle with a new impression of itself couldn't stop the rumble in his chest, felt it rise up like it used to do when Charlie amused him until it burst out of him in the great bellow Big Jamie had handed down to him. Christ, it had been years!

Zache, confused, joined in, not knowing what he was laughing at but unable to resist the infectiousness of that great rolling roar of unselfconscious humour.

Jamie had stopped laughing as quickly as he had begun, the pain clear on his face. Zache's instincts were aroused, the sensitivity in him telling him exactly what had caused the pain. He rose, walked away from Jamie, turning his back, talking over his shoulder. 'That's the first time I've heard you let go. One of the things a gay learns young is to expect disappointment. You've been hurt. There's nothing I can say to help. Tell me if there's anything I can do.'

Jamie had said nothing, but he drew a clear plastic envelope out of his jacket pocket. When Zache turned round again he held it out. Charlotte Aitken smiled at Zache, the edges of her smile blurred and cracked by years of contact with the inside of a combat smock. 'I carry that everywhere. I love that woman. She's gone, doing other things.'

They talked for most of the night, Zache easing out of Jamie all the pent-up resentment, lancing the boil of Jamie's anger and

306

disappointment. Somehow the little professor seemed to understand, let Jamie talk as and when he felt able to say more. When it was over Zache knew more about Jamie than anyone other than Charlotte Aitken. He tried to help, steer his new friend into a different way of thinking.

'Thanks for letting me inside, Jamie. I had a good friend once. He was married. He went back to his wife and children. I couldn't blame him, but it hurt. I got over it, sort of. I learned not to expect too much of other people. It's hard on them if you do. They can't live up to your expectations and they run away to save themselves. There's been no one else in my life since. Jamie, I'm going to return your friendship. I'm going to tell you something you don't want to hear. But you know it's true.

'You expected a lot of Charlotte, too much. Her career isn't what she wants. It's what she is. What she wanted was you. She wanted you to fight for your career because that's how she measures commitment. She was proud of your achievements and looked forward to you putting on an officer's uniform so you could be with her all the time. She wanted you to be proud of her. She needed you to be there for her. It gave her a reason to achieve her aims. She could point to them and say, "that's how much I love you". You let her down, Jamie. You weren't there for her. All you had to do was say, "I'll be back when I have a commission". That would have been enough. That woman would have fought like a tigress for you if you'd given her a chance. She'd have waited years and been happy doing it. The truth is you let her down, Jamie. Is there any way?'

Jamie Lappin's face was set in stone. 'No. It wasn't like that. I'd have been a poodle on a lead. We have work to do.'

'OK. You don't want to see. Let's get back on the job.'

The newly promoted Chief Inspector Crabtree was talking again. 'A couple of new things. The dental casts you took from the two terrorists found dead in the *Sun* building. They were definitely Japs. We sent copies through an Interpol link to Tokyo. One was unknown. The other was a guy called Samati. Twenty-eight. Professional student. Thought to be a member of a splinter group of the Japanese Red Army, head-bangers who think it helps the cause of world peace if they kill everybody in sight before killing themselves.'

'Sorry to interrupt, Chief Inspector. Why do they commit suicide?'

'I don't know, Professor. The Jap police have a firm grip on the JRA. They think these people kill themselves as an example to inspire others into action and to prevent themselves being captured and interrogated. Something to do with a philosophy of some kind.'

'Yes. Bushido, the code of the warrior. Thanks.'

'The other thing is, we found the body of an ex-army officer called Arthurs floating in the Thames, wearing a printer's jacket. Killed by an icepick through the back of the skull. Bad boy, Arthurs. We thought he was a Marine at first, going by the *Sun* guard's evidence. He wasn't. He was an engineer attached to the Marines for a while. They thought he was a screwball and threw him back at the army, who threw him out for half killing a young subaltern who beat him at snooker in the officers' mess.

'The MoD aren't saying much but it seems Arthurs was at one time a very good soldier who went odd in the head after two tours with some sort of undercover Intelligence outfit in Northern Ireland. In and out of the Army's psychiatric unit over at Woolwich, increasingly violent. The army was looking after him as best it could until he went too far. Turned mercenary when the army finally got rid of him. Last heard of running guns into Sri Lanka for the Tamil Tigers a couple of years ago. My guess is that the Provisionals, or whoever is setting this whole thing up, considered him as dangerous as the Japs, used him and dumped him. That leads to the thought that they only used him once. Which leads on to the thought that several different men killed the judge, the head of Eton and did the job on the *Sun*. They've been flying in and out using the same odd gun to confuse us while we've been chasing our tails after Paddies. Clever, very clever. But the conclusion is inescapable. Whoever is organising it is here. And it's not Madden; we know he's somewhere in Eire. And,' Crabtree grinned broadly, his face filled with glee, 'we have a clue.'

Zache reached for the piece of paper in Crabtree's hand. It was a sheet of headed paper from one of the dozens of small hotels around Earls Court. On it was a name, Abu Horaj. And a number.

'We got that out of the lining of Arthurs' jacket. Abu Horaj is a Palestinian, a founder member of Black September and responsible for the planning of hundreds of terrorist attacks worldwide. His real name is Mohammed Hussein. Nobody knew anything of his whereabouts. Some people thought he was dead, killed by the Israelis. But that number is the number of the cultural office of the Syrian Embassy. Horaj is our man and we know where he is. We can't touch him because he has diplomatic immunity, but we can get rid of him. He'll be declared *persona non grata* and out of the country in 24 hours. But we don't know what he's leaving behind. Any thoughts?'

Zache clasped his hands together, long fingers intertwined, his glasses slipping to the end of his nose. 'A judge. The head of Eton. A national newspaper. The royal family?'

'What are you talking about, Professor? I want to know what Abu Horaj might have left behind.'

'Don't take that tone with me, Crabtree, I'm not one of your plods. I'm talking about a blinding glimpse of the obvious. They've systematically attacked the establishment. I think he may have left enough behind to attack the royal family. I think this isn't over yet.'

Chapter Sixteen

19 April 1993

LONDON

Hans-Jürgen Lippe only became aware of the change of plan at the rendezvous. For nine days he and his comrades had been living in one room of a semi-derelict manor house on the outskirts of Camberley, Surrey, with nothing to do but cook on two double-burner Calor gas stoves, care for their weapons and listen to the news reports of the successes of their comrades on the outside.

Standing around outside Farringdon tube station, Lippe, a city boy from Krefeld in the Ruhr valley, enjoyed the sound and movement, waiting for the Palestinian. It was pleasant to be out in the sun. The room in the old mansion was not large and the group had not moved out of it except to use the adjoining bathroom. The first few days had been a difficult time: being cooped up 24 hours a day with Silke, Tomas and the ever silent Turk had not been so bad, but Heidi had been different, continually raking over the ashes of her dying affair with Tomas. Sniping, bitching and being a debilitating influence on the others, she was endangering the cohesion of the group.

But on the morning of the fifth day the Turk, without any consultation with his comrades, had risen from breakfast, followed Heidi into the bathroom and cut her throat with no more compunction than he would have shown a sheep destined for the table, even though it was Heidi who was to be his helper with the rocket launcher. Lippe and the others, shocked, were prepared to ignore the incident as if it had never happened, glad that Heidi was out of the way. But the Turk had returned from the bathroom to finish his breakfast, shovelling Heidi's portion on to his own plate. Even Silke, the most cold-blooded of women, had shuddered at his deliberate callousness: in his silent way he was warning them all that he would take the life of anyone he thought endangered the success of his mission.

The highly polished black car with the CD plates and darkened windows he had been told to expect pulled in to the kerb beside Lippe and the front passenger door opened. Lippe stepped in quickly, pulling the door closed behind him. Strong arms circled the seat from behind while the driver put a short-barrelled pistol to his head 'Stille, Hans-Jürgen, stille,' barked a voice from the back seat, then switched to English. 'Relax, Hansi, you are among friends. It was just a precaution in case you did not see Abu Horaj and attacked us. Release him, Hassan. Put away your gun, Akim. Turn around, Hansi.'

Lippe turned to see a huge man immediately behind him and a very fat one in the other rear seat. The fat man, speaking above many chins, said, 'Abu Horaj sends greetings. He cannot be here. I am sent to make the delivery.'

'Who are you?'

'I am sent by Abu Horaj. That is all you need to know. There is no change to the plan except the telephone contact number. I will give it to you in a moment. It is the number of the Libyan People's Bureau. Pass the same message as you would have to Abu Horaj. Your exit arrangements are as before. Is there anything you need?'

'We need another helper for the Turk. We had to execute one of our number for disrupting the group. We have buried the body near the house. It will not be found, but now we have no one who knows how to operate the launcher except the Turk.'

'It is not possible to bring in a replacement now. The English have sealed the ports. Abu Horaj foresaw this, and that is why you were brought here many days ago. The Turk must work alone.'

Lippe nodded. The fat man's reply was not unexpected. 'So.

We move as planned. Give the new number to me now.'

Over at Scotland Yard Crabtree was preparing for the future. 'Where's the professor, Jamie?'

'Not available, Chief Inspector. He's working on the Ingram machine pistols the fire brigade dug out of the *Sun* building. The serial numbers were ground off, but he knows a way to use his lab equipment to make them visible.'

'OK. We got the other Kalashnikov at four o'clock this morning. We've got the people who were planning on using it as well. By the way, how did your trip to the Isle of Dogs go the other day?'

'No problem. I looked at the *Telegraph* building from one of your helicopters, to locate possible firing points. Then I used a laser dot sight to help the guys inside the building mark off the limits of how far I could see into the offices.'

'Laser dot sight?'

'Yes. Pretty common in the States. Some of your marksmen have them. I borrowed the one I used from them. They throw a dot of red light on to the target. It lets the firer know he's on target and lets the target know there's a rifle trained on him. The targets usually give up without having to be shot. The guys in the offices just marked where the dots lay on the floor. Anything between the marks and the windows is off limits. Simple.'

'Simple, eh? Yes, well, I'm sure it is. Look Jamie, I'm wondering where we go from here. I know Professor Zache has a bee in his bonnet about an attack on the royal family, but I think we've just about got the lid on this thing. We know we've got the Provisional IRA in England in tatters. We've stopped up the ports against new boys coming in from abroad to make any more trouble. We can give the media some answers and we've had some successes. We've even got rid of the bastard that planned it all. The rest is just plodding police work, tying it all together, getting the names and the countries of origin of the in-and-outers. Secret Intelligence Service is already working on that. All this carry on at the *Telegraph* is bullshit. There's no way the Provisionals are going to have a go at the editor. Not now. Even if they really wanted to they haven't the resources in this country.'

'What about your worries about what Abu Horaj might have left behind?'

'Certain government departments have been monitoring what goes on inside and outside the Syrian Embassy. There's nothing going on. It stopped with the departure of Abu Horaj. It's over, Jamie. You've done great work, but –'

'Yes. I see. Thank you and goodbye, is it?' Lappin stood up to go, smarting under his dismissal with the barest of courtesies. At least they could have given him a drink and a Metropolitan Police plaque to hang on his office wall. The policeman's face was smooth, certain, the kind of face Jamie had seen many times on the type of officer who scented an Other Buggers Efforts in the offing for a task well done; anyone who could possibly claim to have a part in the success had to be disposed of before the brass started looking around for someone to decorate. 'Say goodbye to the professor for me, will you? He's a good man.'

'I'll do that. Come and see us some time, any time you're passing by. Always glad to see you, Jamie.'

Lappin crossed to the door. 'I don't think I will. If we do meet again, Chief Inspector, it will be on my ground. And don't call me Jamie. Goodbybe.'

KNOWLE, WARWICKSHIRE

It was just before midnight that three men, two tall and fair, one short, dark and swarthy moved into the grounds of the big house in Warwickshire, unloaded their heavy equipment and spread out, searching. They made no effort to hide themselves, but moved around freely until one of them, Tomas, called out, 'Hansi, hier ist es.'

Five metres from a track crossing, a thin wand of bamboo was stuck in the soft earth. At exactly 128 degrees from it a second, shorter wand shone in the moonlight. Lippe nodded to his companions. 'Perfekt. Deine Arbeit ist erste Klasse, Tomas. Die Aktion beginnt.'

It took the men less than ten minutes to set up their heavy weapon and prepare it for firing. The centre of the baseplate sat squarely on the spot once marked by the taller of the two bamboo wands. The tube pointed directly towards the lower wand. Behind the baseplate lay six stubby shells, complete with fins, like small bombs. The Turk moved away, his job of carrying and setting the heavy baseplate done. Tomas screwed a knurled knob on the side of one of the steel supporting bars of the tube, until the tube's elevation mark coincided with a pre-cut mark on the knob. 'Alles in Ordnung, Hansi.'

'Sehr gut. Aktion.'

The two Germans worked quickly and smoothly, the job simple. Picking up each of the shells in turn they prepared them for firing, then dropped them one at a time into the tube, clamping their hands over their ears as each bomb hit the end of the tube and exploded back out again, hurtling up into the night sky. Immediately the last was fired they ran out of the grounds of the house on to a side road, abandoning their car where they had left it on the main road. Half-hidden in a horseshoe-shaped layby Silke sat at the wheel of a gaily coloured camping van with Austrian plates. Within minutes of firing the bombs they were moving toward the M5 motorway, heading south-west.

On the brightly lit terrace of a closely guarded house four kilometres from the firing point of the heavy mortar bombs the Secretary of State for Defence shook hands with his most important guest of the evening, bowed sharply from the neck up and stood, feet together, as the car bearing the heir to the throne of England pulled away. He was turning back to walk up the terrace steps to join his remaining guests when the first of the bombs landed. It hit a large ornamental flowerpot, one of two flanking the terrace steps, utterly destroying it and sending shattered concrete flying in all directions to plough through the assembled guests. A lump weighing a pound and a half moving faster than the speed of sound struck the Secretary of State in the centre of the chest. At two-second intervals the bomb's companions arrived, falling in an oblique line across the terrace. The last of them plunged through the roof of the house to explode among the domestic staff clearing up the dining room.

Three hundred yards away one of the patrolling detectives assigned to guard the place stood open-mouthed as the first flames licked hungrily through the shattered end wall of the house. Almost incoherent he stuttered and stammered into his radio that a huge bomb planted under the terrace had wrecked the Secretary of State for Defence's house at the end of a dinner party. The Prince of Wales had been a guest. His car was lying on its side in the driveway.

20 April 1993
LONDON

'You told me it was over. It is not over. They nearly killed the Prince of Wales and killed the Secretary of State for Defence. What are you doing about it?'

Chief Inspector Crabtree looked uncomfortable. The commissioner was furious and he was catching it as the man who had set himself up as the centre point of Special Branch efforts to nail the terrorists. 'We've found the weapon, sir. It's a heavy mortar, 120 millimetre, Russian. It was over three miles away from the minister's house, sir.'

'I don't give a damn what kind of weapon it was. I want these people caught, d'you understand, Crabtree? I want them caught.

They are making fools of us. This has been going on far too long. My God, man, we have had over forty police shot down in the streets, killed or wounded, 107 civilians killed and dozens more injured. These terrorists have successfully attacked every branch of the British establishment with impunity. They've killed a judge, destroyed a national newspaper along with most of its staff, shot the headmaster of Eton in his own study and now they've killed a government minister and most of Warwickshire is in hospital or the morgue. It is beyond tolerance. What are you doing about it?'

The attack on the Secretary of State had been a hammer blow to Crabtree, convinced that he had had the situation under control. Abu Horaj had indeed left something behind. Crabtree fought back the urge to remind the commissioner that there was more to Warwickshire than its county set: every servant in the minister's dining room had been blown to bits.

'We are doing everything possible to track down and eliminate these people, sir. I am confident that we will have them in a week at the most. They must be getting help from somewhere. We will find them sir.'

'You had better find them, Crabtree. God only knows what they will do next. Bomb the cabinet room?'

'They did that two years ago, sir. With a mortar. I don't think they'll try —'

'God Almighty, Crabtree. The question was not put seriously. They have been very ingenious so far. I do not think they have finished yet. Every six days they have committed some new atrocity, each one worse than the last. I think you have about four days. Not a week or ten days. Four days. Get on with it.'

Once Crabtree had gone the commissioner riffled through the midday editions of the national dailies, wincing at their banner headlines. They were calling for his head, the head of the director of the Security Service, the head of every regional chief constable and the head of anyone remotely responsible for the country's defence against this unprecedented assault.

The Home Secretary had already resigned, early this morning.

For nearly a fortnight every time the commissioner had switched on his television or radio strident voices demanded that Something Be Done. In parliament the professional agitators on both Left and Right were having a field day. Prime Minister's Question Time was almost wholly taken up with attacks on the government. Only last night the BBC had featured a major documentary that posed the question *Is Her Majesty Safe?*, going back over the government's record in stamping out IRA-inspired terrorism, claiming that for ten years the terrorists had been allowed to develop and prosper under the government's weak-kneed policies. The documentary answered its own question with a resounding No!

Less than two hours after the BBC documentary the Prince of Wales had escaped death by a hair's breadth, solely because he had left the minister's dinner party a few minutes early. It seemed that this was the last straw and that the people would take no more. The Prime Minister feared for the stability of the government and had privately sounded out the opposition leader's views on covert negotiations with the the Provisionals. The commissioner put his head in his hands and prayed that Crabtree would strike lucky.

LISBURN

The huge wall chart was ready. Conductor Caldwell sat to one side as his colonel took the floor, facing a select group of their staff. Charlotte began to address them.

'Here it is, people. The result of all our work. It is essential that no word of this gets out of this building. It is essential that no one, other than those you see around you, has sight of this or of anything that might lead to it. We, that is you, are going to break the back of the Provisional IRA. You are going to set their war effort back ten years, possibly even defeat them outright.'

There was a shuffling of feet, exchanged glances. This was the first time they had all been permitted to see the results of each others' work, pieced together into a whole. The big chart showed PIRA's command structure in tree form, in black. Superimposed on it was a clear plastic sheet, another tree, in red, twining in and out of the black.

'There are two PIRAs,' Charlotte continued. 'The black is the one we all know. The red is not known outside this room except by its members. Not even the Provisional IRA Army Council know about it. The red is there to rise again if PIRA suffers a major defeat. It is also there for its own ends. Its leaders intend to usurp power from the black at an opportune time, not far away now. They intend to launch a new and vicious campaign, worse than any that has gone before, on the people of this country. You've seen the television, read the papers. All of that is the black PIRA's last great effort. It is only a beginning for the red. Or so they think. We are going to cut it off at the root. Look here.'

Charlotte Aitken turned the wall chart over. On it were names and addresses, linked together in a spider's web of thin lines.

'The red PIRA have set up their own web of safe houses in the North, for when they take over. Careful analysis of which red Provisional IRA leader has visited which houses on reconnaissance has given us this chart. Each leader has a choice of four houses in his home area, with six others in other areas, for emergencies. Should we be prepared, we have the ability to capture more than 90 per cent of those people, because we know that if we miss them in one place we can pick them up in another. This chart stays here. If you need to see it, see Conductor Caldwell. Orders. Prepare a ground plan to hit all the primary safe houses simultaneously. Prepare a ground plan to cover all the secondary safe houses in case we miss someone at his primary. Assume that all military resources in the province will be available. Consult no one other than yourselves. Be ready to run it when I ask it of you. That's all. Any questions?'

Charlotte was staggered when the whole audience rose to their feet, cheering and clapping. Conductor Caldwell ushered her out. 'You've busted these people's asses for nearly two years, Colonel. Now they can see why. They feel trusted. They feel vindicated. You've got them. They'll work like huskies now. If we get our timing right they'll have about 21,000 grunts with rifles on the street, knowing exactly where to go and what to do, all at the same time. They'll strip the IRA to its bones for you.'

CROSSMAGLEN, COUNTY ARMAGH

Gerry Madden was relaxed, calm, content with himself and his world. News of the overwhelming success of Strike Four had reached him in the early hours, leaving him time to crow a bit and get a jar or two down him in the company of Siobhan and two of the Northern brigade commanders. He had slept like a log, Siobhan warm beside him, not seeming to mind that his manhood had, as always since Ewart had captured him, deserted him once again.

Madden had at one time been embarrassed about it and had found ways of spending more and more time away from Siobhan, but she had seen through him, explained that it didn't matter, that it was the strain of leadership and the daily stresses and worries of staving off defeat that had done this to him. She had cried and cried, until her puffed and crumpled face convinced him that she meant it when she said through her tears that to her he was still the best man in Ireland. He had willingly gone back to her, supported and sustained by her belief in him, never guessing that her relief at his return was greater than his own, for it was only through him that her own plans could come to fruition.

'Did you take your tablets when you got up, Gerry?'

'I did, Siobhan. Stop fussing. According to the papers I'm the most bloodthirsty terrorist in the world and here you are asking if I've taken my tablets. You'll be asking if I've washed behind my ears next.'

'Well, have you?' Siobhan was smiling, knowing he enjoyed this sort of banter when he was at ease.

'No I haven't. And I won't until I get some breakfast. I'm hungry. Feed me.'

Siobhan flicked the edge of her apron at him and put a delft bowl of porridge in front of him, thinned down into a milky gruel with plain yoghurt.

Madden flinched at the sight of it. 'Jesus, I'm sick to death of this slop. I wish to God I could eat a big fry.'

Siobhan deftly removed the bowl and replaced it with a covered plate. 'You can't. But the doctor said you could have this if you took your tablets early and were in a good mood. Eat it slowly.'

She lifted the covering plate to reveal a thin-cut steak with all the fat removed, grilled slowly in butter. As the smell of the steak wafted up to him Madden closed his eyes, his lined and pain-wracked face smoothing out in ecstasy. He hadn't had this in years. 'Ah, Siobhan. Do this more often and I'll marry you. You're a wonderful woman, so you are.'

'Shut up and eat your breakfast, slowly mind. If you're well enough tomorrow we'll see about a bit of a fry.' Siobhan sometimes enjoyed playing the housewife and wondered what it would be like to live with a real man who loved her like a man should rather than this burnt-up husk of rage and malice. These moods rarely lasted longer than a day or two, no longer than it took her to think up an excuse to spend a few hours in Dublin, find a couple of likely looking tourists and fulfil their wildest fantasies, driving them on until they could do no more and she brought on her own orgasm in front of them, laughing her contempt in their faces. It had been a while, she thought, as she felt a softness form low in her belly. But it would have to wait.

Breakfast over, Madden relaxed. 'It's time I told you about Strikes Five, Six and Seven, Siobhan. Come and sit down. First, they'll all come together . . .'

Chapter Seventeen

21 April 1993

LONDON

'I don't think we can allow it to go on. The risk is too great. General, talk to your colleagues, please.'

General Sir Hugh Patrick, Chief of the General Staff and Britain's top soldier, shook his head. 'I'm sorry, Minister. I agree with them, not with you. The Combined Services open day at Portsmouth is without doubt the biggest social event the services have ever offered the British public. It has been two years in the planning. It must go on. Otherwise the cancellation of such a great event, advertised for months, will be claimed by the terrorists as directly due to their efforts. It would be handing them an enormously damaging propaganda victory on a plate. The event must proceed as planned.'

The newly appointed Secretary of State for Defence, Bill Marriott, stared unbelievingly at the general. He had expected support from the one man present who had been in London throughout the terrorist campaign. But clearly General Sir Hugh allied himself with the other service chiefs. The stony faces of Admiral of the Fleet Sir Harold Frankland and Marshal of the Royal Air Force Sir David Musgrove held out no hope of compromise. The minister tried again.

'You are all aware that I, as defence minister, can simply order abandonment? I will if I must.'

'And you, Minister, are aware that we as joint chiefs of staff of the Armed Forces have direct access to the Prime Minister on any matter we regard as being of relevance to the security of the realm. This is, and we will, if we must.' The Admiral's voice was as icy and controlled as his face.

'You would defy me? I cannot accept that. Think again, Admiral.'

'There is no circumstance in which the Armed Forces would defy a minister of the Crown, sir, unless that minister were in the act of leading an armed insurrection against the Queen in parliament. You will withdraw your insinuation, sir.'

Bill Marriott had become used, in four years in the cabinet, to carefully worded advice from senior civil servants. He was not used to being bluntly told to withdraw a statement he had made. He considered a moment. These men were not civil servants, they were senior commanders well used to the possession and exercise of great power. They could not be talked down to.

'I regret your interpretation of my statement, Admiral. I will rephrase it. Were I to order the abandonment of your open day, would you abandon it?'

'That is a hypothetical question, Minister. I would have to consult with my colleagues before attempting to answer it. I imagine they, like me, have a distaste for the hypothetical. Your question might well remain unanswered for some time, if it were answered at all.'

Marriott felt trapped by his own inexperience in dealing with these people. If he gave them a direct order they would go over his head, that much was clear. It was unlikely that the PM would fail to support him against them, but he would have to resign in any case: no Minister of Defence could hope to achieve anything if the joint chiefs had made it clear they considered his powers of judgement suspect. He would have to tread carefully.

'We are in danger of getting off on the wrong foot, gentlemen. My prime concern is the safety of those attending the open day –' he paused to glance at a briefing paper – 'all half a million of them. Can you guarantee that?'

Admiral Frankland glanced at General Patrick. Sir Hugh took the question. 'There is no such thing as 100 per cent security, Minister. Nobody can guarantee total security to every person

323

and every place within an area hundreds of acres in extent. What we can do is minimise the risks and provide for maximum response to limit damage. The terrorists know that. It is unlikely in the extreme that they would have a better than even chance of getting away. That is our best defence. No terrorist takes unnecessary risks.'

'I beg to differ, General. There is convincing evidence that at least two of the men involved in the attack at Wapping committed suicide. They knew they would not get away. It did not prevent them from carrying out the attack.'

The general reddened. 'You are as aware as I am, Minister, that this is getting us nowhere. I say again, 100 per cent security is not possible. To defend half a million people against a kamikaze attack we would need at least three soldiers surrounding each person, plus others to cover every possible approach to that person. This discussion is pointless. There are overwhelming reasons for carrying on as planned. It is a matter which directly affects the morale of every serviceman or woman and every paperboy on every street corner. Every thinking person in this country knows we are eyeball to eyeball with these terrorists. We must not be seen to blink first. We must be seen not only to treat these animals with contempt, we must be seen to treat them with indifference. Britain is much diminished, but she is not about to bow the knee to some ignorant wretch with a bomb in his hand. We will take precautions, but we will not scurry into corners. No soldier, while I command the British Army, will suffer the humiliation of having to look a civilian in the eye knowing that civilian is thinking, "what a waste of money *you* are".

'The solution to this terrorist problem lies in your own hands, Minister. My soldiers are without doubt the best trained, most self-disciplined and most frustrated soldiers in the world. Their job is to protect the people of this country from any enemy foolish enough to present his face to them, but you will not let them do it. You will not let them do the job they are trained and paid for. Do away with Rules of Engagement. Let the police identify these terrorists, then let my soldiers see them. Let my soldiers see them and let them kill them. Not capture them. Not jail them. Kill them. That is what the public want. Not some cowardly cancellation of the military event of the decade.'

The furious general sat back, struggling to grip his anger while his military companions sat impassive. In time, his anger under control, General Sir Hugh Patrick said the only thing he could say.

'I am sorry, Minister. I have gone too far. One can think these things but one should not say them. My resignation will be on your desk within the hour.' General Patrick rose to his feet. 'Excuse me, sir.'

'Sit down, General.' Marriott saw his chance to show these hard men his own mettle. 'Write your resignation here, on this table. Now, if you please.'

The Admiral and Air Marshal were on their feet, calling for pen and paper.

Their minister sat, as they once had, impassive while the enraged commanders wrote clearly and briefly. One by one they handed their envelopes to their aides-de-camp for delivery to the minister, rising as he took them.

'You will resume your seats, gentlemen. The business of the day is not finished.' Marriott beckoned over a shoulder and spoke softly in the ear of his parliamentary private secretary, who straightened and immediately ushered every civil servant from the room.

'I have dispensed with my staff, gentlemen, with the exception of my PPS. I would be most grateful if you were to do the same, with the exception of your ADCs.'

As the tall double doors closed behind the last disgruntled staff officer Marriott opened the general's envelope, glanced at it too briefly to have read it and picked up the other two envelopes. Carefully returning the general's letter to its cover he again beckoned to his PPS. 'Destroy these now, in this room, in sight of the ADCs.'

'General, you services to this country are too valuable to dispense with at this time. Your honourable application to resign your commission is rejected. You will complete your tour of duty in your present post. Admiral, Air Marshal: I am impressed by your instant support of a colleague. Gentlemen, I am impressed and convinced by the strength of your feeling in this matter. The open day may yet take place as planned. I trust we now understand in whose hands the decision lies. I remain unconvinced of your security arrangements, but I wish to take advantage of your collective experience. General, you were saying?'

LISBURN

Alone in her room at Lisburn watching the ITN *News at Ten* Lieutenant-Colonel Charlotte Aitken burned. The news went on and on, more and more bodies day by day. Charlotte's mind turned over, watching funeral after funeral. She knew more than the journalists could ever know, but watched the news anyway. It seemed to help, seeing the tearful faces of devastated relatives mourning their dead. The faces built a core of will into her, helped her remain focused. They also built anger, the right kind of anger, the cold kind that turned her inside herself, helped her prepare to act.

Sometimes she was surprised at herself, at the thoughts she thought, as if she were outside herself looking at a stranger, someone capable of things she had never considered a part of her. She knew of this feeling, had hoped it might come to her. It was the feeling her grandfather had taught her every great soldier had to have: the feeling, or sense, of detachment that would allow her to see and interpret the patterns, the flow and counter-flow of events in what seemed to most a senseless, patternless maelstrom of blood and horror. It was the cold detachment that turned a battle into a chess game: move and countermove, carefully conceived, planned, executed with utter ruthlessness. It was what made her certain she could and would win her war when it came. So she watched, waited and burned inside, cultivating her anger.

What bastards you people are! Some time soon some little thing will happen and be reported. Conductor Caldwell's computers will pick it up, run with it and produce the information I need and I will put a stop to this. You will act, McCaillim. You will betray Gerry Madden and betray yourself to me in doing it. I am watching. I am waiting. I am ready for you, McCaillim. Act soon that I may act. Act soon that I may send my soldiers to cut your evil, treacherous heart out. Give battle, McCaillim. I will fight you with every weapon I have to hand. I will hunt you and hunt you until I have you cornered. Are you ready for me, McCaillim?

In his own ponderous way Peter Ewart burned too. Gerry Madden was heavy on his mind, a corrosive presence that not even a bellyful of Jameson's best would dispel. He knew Madden was behind this dreadful peacefulness in his province, behind the slaughter over the water. He believed Madden to be branching out, spreading his wings, soaring out of his grasp. But there was a little time yet: some time, somehow, someone just had to give him a solid lead to Madden. This time there would be no escape. This time Madden would die.

25 April 1993
PORTSMOUTH

It had all gone so beautifully. Half a million people had streamed down the motorways and in specially laid on trains to converge on hundreds of acres of parking space and shuttle buses, people from London, Devizes, Rosyth in Scotland, York and Liverpool and Weston-super-Mare, bent on a long weekend, a great day out, a corporate entertainment opportunity, a weekend away from the wife, a day in the sunshine, a bloody good chance for a laugh and a drink, a long put-off visit to HMS VICTORY, a chance to share in vicarious pleasure the honours and dangers of the victories of Nelson, the battles of the Few and the dusty, muddy tragedies of Rorke's Drift and Passchendaele.

Around them the Challengers rolled, 64 tonnes to the tank, 23 tonnes of armoured turret swinging to the fingers of the milling thousands' sons, the professional crews carefully monitoring the play of their great gun lest it swing too far and cut the tops off the soft-skinned outside broadcast vehicles that were doing their best to show the tanks to best advantage.

'Watch that gun, lad. Watch it and control it. Be careful. It's the most powerful thing you'll ever have a chance at. It'll kill anything put in front of it. Anything. Below you you have the finest fighting machine built anywhere in the world. You're sitting in a Challenger, all Chobham armour and engines eating gallons of top-grade diesel to every mile. That gun you're playing with throws a superheavy bullet so fast it burns the air. Not even a battleship could take the blow it delivers. Watch the monitor, the cross tells you what your gun's aimed at on the screen. Try moving it. Good, you're ready. *Watch the enemy tank running left to right. Watch it! Watch it! Watch the numbers on the sight. Scream them out to your gun layer. Louder! Hit the range button. Hit the firing button. Boom. You've killed an enemy tank!* Great stuff, you'll make a tank gunner yet. *Watch out! Watch out! Another enemy tank has your range!*' The Challenger stops suddenly, rocking on its suspension system. *'We're hit. We can take it. Do something quick before he hits us again! Kill the enemy tank! Swing the gun! Tell the driver which way to go! Lock on. Fire. Boom. You've got it. Great shot. He's done for. Well done!'* Another potential recruit climbed grinning out of the tank.

Above people's heads Harriers gaily waggled their wings. In front of them the frigates in the harbour leapt from dead in the water to 30-odd knots in a solid shock of six Olympus turbines throwing their guts from zero revs to bullet speed in less than the time it takes to tell of it. Big guns fired salvoes out over the Sound, commentators guiding the eyes and binoculars of the huddled masses to the tiny black spot, a shell in flight seen from behind the gun, each shell the price of a well-built car, their taxes flying supersonic.

There were ice creams, hot dogs, burgers by the tens of thousands. There were soldiers, sailors, airmen in their hundreds, dressed in uniforms dating from the June of Waterloo to the Antarctic May of East Falkland, with a scattering from the deserts of Iraq. But the day was dying. Already thousands had boarded the buses, replete, wanting to get away before the rush. But there were many more, hanging on to the bitter end, the grand finale. With them stayed the cameras, the ever open eyes of television awaiting their chance, content to film the commonplace while searching for the odd, the newsworthy.

DUNDALK

Gerry Madden's nerves were screwed up tight, watching the guns and aircraft on TV, listening to the commentator's endless stream of facts and figures. For a moment a long-distance lens had zoomed in on HMS ARK ROYAL, preparing for sea in the bay. Madden jumped up, questioning, 'You're sure that bloody sailor will do the job?'

Mick Rodney, one of Siobhan's young men from the North, answered quickly 'Aye, he will. We have his brothers. He talked to them on the phone last night. He'll do it all right.'

'Good. The rest is up to the Germans.'

PORTSMOUTH

General Sir Hugh Patrick prepared to mount the podium to take the salute on the final march-past of the assembled sailors, soldiers and airmen, proud of how the day had gone. Together with Admiral Frankland and Air Marshal Musgrove he had monitored every aspect of training and rehearsals for the biggest open day ever held by the Armed Forces, using the huge naval base at Portsmouth, HMS NELSON, as its setting. The day had been a roaring success, but now it was coming to a close. A tiny radio transceiver covered by a flesh-coloured sticking plaster behind the general's right ear buzzed softly, calling for attention. The general quietly answered. 'Patrick, send, over.' Again the soft buzz and this time the slightly edgy voice of the officer co-ordinating the final spectacle.

Out in the harbour the frigates had stopped charging about and were wheeling into a double line either side of HMS ARK ROYAL. The big aircraft carrier, her flight decks lined with sailors, turned slowly between the lines, her captain with one eye on her heading and the other on the clock. At five o'clock precisely he had to be in the perfect spot, midway between the lines of frigates and exactly halfway down the line.

The co-ordinating officer winked at a nervous RAF flight lieutenant, giving him the 'thumbs up'. The flight lieutenant spoke urgently into his radio, turning the flight of aircraft wheeling gently out of sight over the Downs above Portsmouth Harbour, bringing them on to their new heading, timed to have them roar over the top of the Downs and into sight and hearing of the vast crowd at exactly one minute and fifteen seconds before five o'clock.

The regimental sergeant-major of the Grenadier Guards called the parade to attention. At exactly one minute and thirty seconds before five o'clock he bawled out. 'Byyy the Leeeft. Quick

MARCH.' At the other end of the column the Commanding Officer, Lt.-Col. the Hon. Simon Quedgly, stepped out smartly from his position at the side of the parade, marching out sword in hand directly across the path of the rapidly approaching column, swinging at the last possible moment to take his place at the head of the parade, exactly nine thirty-inch paces ahead of the first line of troops. The crowd roared and applauded loudly. General Patrick, up on the podium, grinned in pleasure, thinking 'Well done, Simon. *Bloody* well done.'

The general's attention switched rapidly to the skies. Just as Simon Quedgly had joined the parade the thunder of great aircraft engines burst over the crowd. Every neck jerked up and back to follow the path of the aircraft that had appeared over the crest of the Downs. Slow and stately, a single Lancaster bomber, the last of the square-winged four-engined beasts of burden that had pounded Hitler to defeat, droned straight overhead, escorted by a pair of Hurricanes flying just off her wingtips. Above the old aeroplanes a flight of four Harriers, unable to fly slowly enough to keep station with the bomber, wheeled and looped around her.

The voice of the commentator, hugely amplified to be heard above the massed bands and the odd, unsynchronised beat of the Lancaster's four great Merlin engines, called 'Ladies and gentlemen, the pride of the Royal Air Force, symbol of victory over evil, the last Lancaster bomber still flying. The *City Of Lincoln*.' The crowd roared again, applauding, stamping their feet and shouting for all they were worth.

As the head of the parading column approached him General Patrick knew it was all going to work. As the first man passed him he would swing his arm up in salute, just as the *City of Lincoln* passed over the perfectly positioned ARK ROYAL. That would be the grand finale of the day, immediately followed by a huge fireworks display to let the crowd down gently.

He watched the thin white line painted across the road. As the first rank's left feet crossed it he swung his arm up, stopping in mid-swing as he felt a terrible blow and a surging pain in the

331

centre of his chest. He gasped, 'Jesus, a heart attack. I'm having a heart attack', as his legs went from beneath him. As he passed out he was curious and surprised to see the blood spurting from between the clenched fingers of both his hands, pressed tightly to his chest, and thought, 'Heart attacks don't burst . . .'

Up on the Downs the Turk gave himself a second to register the recoil shudder down Hans-Jürgen's back. He had seen the general fall: now it was his turn. He hefted the SAM 7 launcher over his shoulder, settled it and carefully sighted through the optics, centring at the junction of wings and fuselage of the lumbering bomber. Trained to hit fast jets flying only fifty feet up, the Turk had no doubt of his ability to bring the bomber down, but he was concerned about the Harriers swinging around it. The heat from their exhausts might confuse the missile. Ignoring Hansi's excited, 'Feuer, Turk, feuer!' he chose a moment when the Harriers were on the outward curve of their swings and pressed the firing button. There was the familiar *whump* of the discharger as it flung the missile out of the tube, a second's pause and then the heat of the missile's backblast as its rocket motor ignited. The Turk dropped the launcher and grinned at Hansi. The German grinned back, then jumped to his feet, shouting ' 'Raus, Kamerad. 'Raus!' Weapons abandoned, the terrorists sprinted across the cropped grass beside the old redbrick fort, leaping into the back of their van as Silke gunned it into the traffic stream coming up the hill from the dockyard.

Down in HMS NELSON the crowd were suddenly aware that something was wrong. There had been a faraway bang and the general had fallen off the podium. Then a second, much louder bang and they craned their necks to see a thin white trail of smoke streak up from somewhere near Fort Southwick. The smokestream headed straight for the Lancaster bomber, seemed to hesitate a moment and be tempted by one of the Harriers. At the head of the smoke trail the complex electronics in the missile's guidance system sorted out the impulses it was receiving, its heat-seeking homing device aware of ten possible targets.

Programmed to fly as near as possible to its original aiming point and to ignore flares fired to distract it, the missile rejected the hot spot produced by the Harrier, rejected the other Harrier jet streams as decoy flares and concentrated on the six cooler exhausts flying close together. As it got closer the missile centred itself on a spot midway between the four exhausts flying closest. To the horror of the watchers below the missile struck the Lancaster at the root of one wing, its warhead exploding in a bright, black-ringed orange flash. The old bomber lurched in the air as if trying to turn away from its attacker, but the wing that had been hit tore away to spiral down to the sea. The rest of the stricken aeroplane seemed to raise its nose in an attempt to gain height. The fuel in its ruptured tanks exploded in a fireball that caught both its escorting Hurricanes, flinging the little fighters downward. One pulled out of its involuntary dive but the other, its pilot hit by flying debris from the bomber, had no chance. It hit the sea in a welter of foam and fire. The bomber followed quickly, shedding parts as it fell. The dumbstruck crowd saw a flaming engine strike the bridge of ARK ROYAL. The enormous ship shuddered, swung across the line of frigates, and caught the stern of one as it accelerated frantically to get out of the way. The carrier continued its turn, describing a semi-circle before her engines were thrown into reverse, stopping her broadside on to the harbour mouth.

In the uproar in the harbour area hardly anybody noticed the red and yellow helicopter leave HMS NELSON's helipad and fly out to the motionless ship to drop off four men carrying heavy grey suits and helmets with perspex face masks; but the cameras noticed; and with them several million viewers.

One of the viewers, Gerry Madden, slumped in his chair, his eyes shining, trying to get his breathing under control. It had worked! Around him the selected few who had been allowed to watch with him were shouting and bawling, trying to outdo one another in their joy. Glasses banged against bottles as whiskey was sloshed around like mineral water. Siobhan McCaillim sat silent, thinking.

Charlotte Aitken felt almost physically sick. The crippled ship and the smoke still in the sky did not disturb her, but the fact that she could not get directly involved twisted a knife in her. How long would she have to wait? The terrors of uncertainty raged in her. Could she be completely wrong? Could her Red Provisional IRA be something Gerry Madden had put in place himself, knowing that the British would not take this lying down? Was he preparing to let the British destroy the old Provisional IRA so he could rise anew, in total command, answerable to nobody? Should she rush to her general now, tell him everything, prepare for the worst, try to forestall Madden?

Motionless in her chair she fought her private battle, trying to hold her nerve. The telephone rang. Mr Caldwell. Her voice was calm, peaceful. 'Yes, I saw. It's nearly time. If Madden has any further success he will be unassailable. She has to move soon. We must hold ourselves together. We are not wrong. Our time is very near. Tell our people to update the plan. Thank you.'

Peter Ewart caught the first repeat showing and was completely unmoved. He half filled a tooth glass with Jameson's and drank it, grimacing. *Maybe now they'll understand over there what we've been going through for more than twenty years* was his first thought. His second, infinitely more comforting, was that the British could not take this lying down. Maybe they would release more of the Intelligence material they so jealously guarded. Ewart brightened and poured another drink. Some good might come out of that. Maybe he would get another chance at Madden.

The Prime Minister saw only that he would be an ex-Prime Minister unless he did something quickly. Tomorrow was Monday, giving him a breathing space before Question Time on Tuesday afternoon. Heads would have to roll, beginning with the surviving joint chiefs. The commissioner of the Met would have to go, as would the superintendent in charge of the anti-terrorist branch of the Special Branch. The new Home Secretary and

Minister of Defence would survive; neither had been in their jobs long enough to attract the anger of the people. It was his own head they would demand. He had to be seen to be taking action.

As their van rolled quietly along Hans Jürgen, laughing almost uncontrollably, told Silke and Tomas again and again of how it had gone. It was the longest shot he had ever taken, and what a shot! The big gun with its built-in bipod had been perfect. Straight between the shoulder blades, and the missile, whoosh!

Silke and Tomas laughed with Hansi, understanding that it was nerves that made him jabber like this. The Turk sat in the front passenger seat, silent as always.

Once clear of the immediate area and out on to the road to Southampton the Turk looked out through the windscreen, checking his whereabouts. Seeing the motorway sign he had been told to watch out for, he reached under his seat and waited as the van slowed to take the sharply curving motorway entry road. At the van's slowest he pulled the canvas strap under the seat, hard, threw open his door and rolled out of the van, bouncing on to the grass verge. He was up and running toward the long black car with the CD plates long before the ten kilos of Semtex packed into a plastic petrol can below the van's passenger seat exploded, leaving nothing of the van or its contents but a chassis member driven into the road and its engine block bouncing like a stone across water into the trees of a small plantation.

In the car the Turk, who was not a Turk, but a nephew of Abu Horaj himself put into the German team to ensure its success, broke silence for the first time, shouting to the fat man in the back seat as the car moved off. 'Allahu Akbar, it is done, brother!' The fat man smiled back, setting his chins wobbling. 'Indeed, brother Saleem, it is done. Abu Horaj will be proud of you. You have struck a great blow today. You will be a hero in the bazaars of Damascus. Allahu Akbar!'

Chapter Eighteen

27 April 1993

LONDON

The Chamber of the House of Commons was in uproar. Three times the Speaker called for order and was ignored. Both sides of the House were in a fury of a kind not seen since God knows when. For two days the papers, radio and television news had been full of nothing else but what some called the outrage, others the disaster, at Portsmouth. Up and down the country party branches on all sides of the House had met to debate the news with almost unanimous results: they told their MP that unless he made some major and visible contribution to an immediate cessation of terrorism in Britain he faced deselection at the earliest opportunity. The MPs had hoisted in the message: the country was not about to put up with half-measures or sops to its anger. With an eye on the TV cameras roving the mother of parliaments, the MPs were behaving, as one commentator put it, like chimps on Speed. One noted Conservative eccentric went so far as to wrap himself in the Union Flag and declare himself a candidate for the Tory leadership if the Prime Minister was not able to lead the nation. Prime Minister's Question Time promised to be a raucous session.

Peace, or a sort of peace, was restored when the outraged Speaker ordered the TV cameras to be switched off. The MPs calmed down a little, but not much.

The Prime Minister swept in escorted by his advisers and the serjeant-at-arms in person. The Speaker called for the first question to be put to the Right Honourable George Prosser, First Secretary to the Treasury and Prime Minister. Again pandemonium broke out, MPs in their hundreds waving order papers and shouting for attention: the cameras were back in action.

The Speaker, a wily old bird of a parliamentarian, knew full well that the Prime Minister intended to make a major policy speech out of his answer to a carefully phrased and planted question, hoping to deflect others. Discreet pressure had been put on the Speaker to make first call on the Member for Croydon East, an old friend of the Prime Minister and tabler of the planted question. But the Speaker of the House of Commons owed allegiance to nobody and guarded his freedom jealously in the interests of future generations: he had more than once been heard to say that a government that had the Speaker in its pocket had parliament in its pocket, and that was not to be thought of.

'The Honourable Member for Sparkhill, your question.'

Willie Lucas, Member of Parliament for Sparkhill in Birmingham, was the Prime Minister's *bête noire*, as he was the *bête noire* of anybody he saw as not representative of life on the streets. A crossbencher elected on an Independent ticket Lucas enjoyed the solid support of his largely working-class constituency, habitually worked eighteen-hour days, and after twenty-six years in parliament still lived in the two-up two-down Victorian terraced house he had been born in. With a majority of 22,000 at the last four general elections, he feared nobody and was virtually unassailable. A big, blunt, gruff man with a navvy's physique and dress sense he had a mind like a knife and a tongue like a flail. Worst of all, in the light of current events, he was a former petty officer fiercely proud of his still strong connections with the Royal Navy.

The Prime Minister, sensing what was coming, was seen to wince as Lucas stood up. He had read Lucas's tabled question; it seemed innocent enough, but was nothing more than a steel for Lucas to sharpen his blade on. Having had his answer, Lucas would be entitled to ask supplementary questions the Prime Minister had not seen in advance.

Lucas lowered his huge old head, glaring through his eyebrows and rumbling through his beard, a well known technique of his which indicated his belligerent mood.

337

'Prime Minister, can you confirm that HMS ARK ROYAL should be at sea today on her goodwill voyage to Hong Kong?'

The PM cleared his throat. 'Yes. ARK ROYAL was intended to be at sea today, but as the Honourable Member is aware several members of her crew, including her captain, were killed on Sunday.'

But Lucas was merciless. 'Thank you, Prime Minister. I am fully aware of ARK ROYAL's casualties. I am sure that every member of this House joins me in offering our condolences to their families. I was in Portsmouth on Sunday. After she was struck by flying debris ARK ROYAL slewed sharply to port and took up a roughly circular course until her engines were stopped. Any boy sailor could tell that her rudder had been forced to starboard and jammed in that position, damage that could not have been caused by debris from the *City of Lincoln*. I believe that the IRA have made mock of the Royal Navy by disabling our most powerful ship in her home port, before the eyes of the world. Am I right?'

The Prime Minister, cornered, could not lie to the House. 'I regret to tell this House that ARK ROYAL's rudder control room was damaged by a bomb planted by a member of her crew, a rating some of whose family had been kidnapped by the Provisional IRA and threatened with death. The sailor is in detention and undergoing interrogation.'

Even if he had wanted to Lucas could not have gone further. Both sides of the House erupted, shouting, the opposition bawling at the tops of their lungs, accusing the government of hiding the truth from the House and the nation, bellowing for the resignation of the PM, while his own backbenchers were demanding instant action for this unforgivable insult to British national pride.

Harried, the Prime Minister sought the eye of the Speaker, who, realising the terrible mistake he had made in punishing the government for leaning on him, called for order, again and again. But it was too late: the calls seemed to inflame the MPs even further, balled-up papers flew back and forth across the dispatch box while three members openly brawled on the floor of the Chamber. Fearing a riot, the Speaker abruptly stood up and stalked out of the Chamber. Without him parliament could not sit: by walking out he effectively ended all debate.

The government front bench, shocked, immediately stood up and followed the Speaker out: unless he could be persuaded to return immediately there would be a constitutional crisis which could bring down the government. The opposition, equally shocked, was gripped by the temptation to pull George Prosser's administration down, but jibbed at the implications of doing so: to have to go to the country to elect a new government would give the terrorists a stunning victory. The opposition leader wavered until her deputy touched her elbow and guided her out of the Chamber.

It took fifteen minutes of the combined efforts of government and opposition front benches to persuade the outraged Speaker to return to the Chamber. Until he did so Britain was like ARK ROYAL, rudderless, without a government.

The Speaker's first words on returning to an angry, confused and uncertain House were 'Serjeant-at-Arms. Please be so good as to advise Her Majesty the Queen that I beg Her Majesty's indulgence and request that Her Majesty have the Officer Commanding the Queen's Guard, with a suitable escort, wait upon me for the purpose of clearing this House, should I feel it necessary. Parliament is in recess for one hour.'

One hour later a much subdued parliament reassembled, knowing that just outside the ancient oak doors of the Chamber the Right Flank company of the Scots Guards, bayonets fixed, awaited the Speaker's call. Not since Oliver Cromwell had purged parliament had soldiers entered the Chamber and no MP sitting there now wanted to see a repeat of that: one dictatorship is enough in the life of any civilised nation.

The Prime Minister addressed the Speaker. 'Mr Speaker, I ask that Question Time be suspended in favour of an address I wish to make to this House. I further request that the Queen's

Guard be ordered to return to their duties at Buckingham Palace immediately. This House cannot function under military threat.'

The Speaker rose, grave and careful. 'This House is not under military threat. It is under the protection of the Queen's Guard who will ensure, if called upon to do so, that no unruly or intemperate elements prevent the orderly functioning of parliament. Let there be no misunderstanding: I will without hesitation order the Guard to clear this Chamber should there be any repetition of the disgraceful scenes of an hour ago. In the interests of restoring and maintaining orderly procedure Question Time will continue. I call upon the Honourable Member for Croydon East to put his question to the Prime Minister.'

The PM glanced at the opposition front bench. Across from him the Leader of Her Majesty's opposition nodded, a quick jerk of the head: she would keep her side of the House quiet if the Prime Minister did not use the occasion to further his Party's political advantage.

Trembling, the Member for Croydon East rose, question paper in hand.

'Prime Minister, this nation has been assaulted in the most terrible way by the Irish Republican Army, or their agents. What, pray, are you doing about it?'

The PM waited for the question to sink into the House before giving his answer, knowing that every member must realise the importance of the Speaker's calling on an obviously planted question at a time like this. All over the country political commentators waited, tape recorders or pencils at the ready.

In Ireland a delighted Gerry Madden and Siobhan McCaillim watched too. The Prime Minister's political future, and perhaps the British system of government, would live or die by his answer. In Lisburn Charlotte Aitken watched on a portable television she had brought into her office, keeping abreast of events, waiting for her chance, thinking: *He needs to throw a bomb. If he doesn't he'll fall. The Provisionals will have won. I'll never get my chance.*

The PM was more measured and statesmanlike than he had

ever been, conscious of the eyes of the world, thrusting from his mind the incongruous Americanism his tough-talking New Yorker wife had come out with over his breakfast table: 'These terrorists have got your balls to the wall, George. You have to come out punching.' George Prosser intended to do just that, in more formal language.

'I am most grateful to my honourable friend the Member for Croydon East. His question neatly encapsulates the needs of the moment and I am happy to say I can answer it with a degree of confidence. But I must first make the following short statement.

'There are a number of actions I have taken which in more peaceful times would be regarded as an abuse of the power which the people of this land have vested in me. I have taken these actions without consultation with my Cabinet. I have in doing so circumvented the normal process of government and have overridden our tradition of collective responsibility. I am therefore personally responsible for the consequences of these actions. Should this House fail to endorse each and every one of my actions I will resign forthwith in favour of my deputy.'

He has a bomb. He's going to throw it and challenge the opposition to risk a general election that might pull the country apart. Declare war on PIRA, Prosser. Do it. I'll fight it for you.

'This morning I dispensed with the services of the joint chiefs of staff and created a single focus for action in the person of a new appointment, Commander British Armed Forces, in the rank of Field Marshal. To fill this appointment I have recalled from his post in Washington a man who has in his time fought with great success against terrorists in Aden, Malaya, Cyprus, Borneo, the Oman and Northern Ireland. He has until recently commanded the United Kingdom's Land Forces. He is Field Marshal, formerly Lieutenant-General, Sir Harry George. I have tasked the Field Marshal with a single objective which I will make clear in a few moments.'

A political manoeuvre, shifting blame to the Armed Services. You shit, Prosser. You don't need a Field Marshal. You need me.

'Today I have spoken to the Taoiseach of the Republic of Ireland. I have told him that I can no longer accept his territory as being a safe haven for terrorists. I have told him that while the Republic of Ireland is a sovereign state I will not accept that as a reason for hindering the anti-terrorist operations of our Armed Forces. I have told him that our Armed Forces will remove, with utmost force, any hindrance placed in their path by anyone, civilian, police or military, should they feel that hindrance prevents their access to areas in which they believe it necessary to go. In order to impress upon the Irish government my determination in this matter I have this morning ordered the withdrawal of our ambassador, broken off diplomatic relations with the Republic of Ireland and ordered the closure of our Embassy in Dublin.'

Jesus. He's going to go to war! He's going to invade the Republic. He can't do that! We'd never get away with it.

'I have this morning ordered the deployment of the entire 22nd Special Air Service Regiment, inclusive of certain of its reserves, to Northern Ireland with a remit to go where it wills. Carefully selected elements of the 21st and 23rd Special Air Service Regiments are being called up and will deploy in support of the 22nd.' *Yes! Yes! That's all it needs. The entire SAS with freedom of action over the whole bloody island. I could have a big hand in this.*

'I have this morning ordered the formation of an armoured division, to be called the 66th (Ulster) Division. The Ulster Division will, when complete, consist of five battalions of armoured infantry, three non-armoured battalions of infantry, two regiments of heavy artillery and three regiments of main battle tanks. The Belfast, Armagh and Londonderry resident infantry battalions are to be incorporated into the structure of the Ulster Division. The Royal Irish Regiment will secure the cities of Belfast, Londonderry and Armagh in place of their resident battalions. I have ordered to immediate readiness two squadrons of Tornado and two squadrons of Harrier ground-attack aircraft to support our ground forces should they be required.'

Bullshit. Rupert Smith ripped the guts out of his piece of the fourth biggest army in the world with less than that. Ireland is not Iraq. George is good, very good, but no De La Billiere. Who the hell is advising you, Prosser?

'This government's remit to Field Marshal Sir Harry George is that he is to destroy, once and for all, the IRA wherever it is to be found within the British Isles. If necessary he is to destroy the Armed Forces of the Republic of Ireland should they impede his destruction of the IRA. I ask that this House support my actions and that this House hold me and me alone responsible for my enforcement of my will on the territory of a sovereign state, the Republic of Ireland.'

Ah yes, yes. I see it. You're going to use the SAS as a rapier. The Field Marshal and this Ulster Division are a threat, a blunt instrument to hold over the Taoiseach's head if he won't let you run the SAS into the Republic. Very good, Prime Minister. Very good indeed, in parliament. But what if the Taoiseach calls your bluff? You can't invade Ireland and you know it. The Taoiseach knows it. He will call your bluff. You're going down, Prime Minister.

A huge roar of delight echoed through the House as members on all sides poured down to mingle on the floor while journalists fought for speed of exit from the Chamber, punching numbers into their portable telephones as they ran. The PM's intentions were clear: the gloves were off.

Within minutes half-dead generals pulled rudely in from their retirement paddocks, faintly secretive former 'security personnel' and the odd political commentator with his wits about him were being fiercely interviewed by network news channels trying to steal a march on their rivals. Most of what was said was rubbish but one observer saw exactly what she had to do.

I must convince the Taoiseach that our plans are well advanced, that the Ulster Division is no idle threat. I must convince him that Prime Minister Prosser has his back to the political wall and is desperate enough to invade the Republic. I must make him

accept an attack on the Provisional IRA on his territory by the
SAS. And I must convince Prosser that I and only I can lead it.
I must convince him that I can save his political skin. All right,
McCaillim. The waiting is over. I'll have you and Madden both.

LISBURN

Watching the pandemonium in parliament Charlotte Aitken had seen that once in a lifetime chance that comes to those with the courage to grasp it. She had invested her whole life in her career, given up everything to it. Now she was in danger of destroying it in ten minutes, reaching for her personal star. It was suddenly within reach – but only if she stepped off the edge. Her grandfather had seen his chance and failed to take it. Charlotte's jaw firmed. *I will not fail. This is what I've waited and worked for all my life. I will not fail.* She called Conductor Caldwell, had him assemble her staff of insiders.

'The picture has changed. The plan has not. But it will now be part of a bigger plan. We are going to take on both the black and red PIRAs, together. We are going to destroy them all. Get ready.'

Conductor Caldwell was silent, watching her. She crossed the room to him. Caldwell smiled a calm, quiet smile. 'You're about to do something extraordinary, Colonel. Am I included?'

'Only if you're ready to risk your pension. I could be in jail tonight.'

Caldwell beamed. 'It's about time those bastards got what's coming to them. I think you can give it to them. What can I do?'

Within the hour Charlotte strode purposefully into a little theatre her staff had set up for her press conference. Twenty or so journalists, stringers for the big dailies, both tabloid and broadsheet, sat in rows. Two TV cameras were ranged on the desk set up on the tiny stage. A reporter from Ulster Television had been appointed by the assembled hacks to lead the questioning.

Under the TV lamps it was hot, a halo of blinding white light, but a woman from the TV studios had helped Charlotte get ready, using makeup designed by people who knew that even the healthiest of individuals looked like death masks of themselves under the camera lights. The journalist launched in almost before Charlotte could get settled, expecting the usual bland guff the army came out with in press conferences, trying to unsettle her so that he and his colleagues could get a little usable material. Charlotte said absolutely nothing for a full minute, ignoring the question as the cameras rolled.

The journalist smiled to himself and said over his shoulder, 'Sorry, people. I'll start again. Colonel, this time we're live.'

'This is Harry Bellews, reporting from Army HQ, Lisburn. We have Lieutenant-Colonel Charlotte Aitken, head of Army HQ's Intelligence Branch with us. Colonel Aitken will answer our questions on the military response to today's revelations in parliament. Colonel, what is the Prime Minister trying to do?'

Charlotte Aitken looked very composed, very authoritative and stunningly beautiful. 'The Prime Minister is not speaking in diplomatic language. He is saying in plain English that he has had enough. He is saying to the world in general and the British people in particular that he is going to destroy the Provisional IRA, whatever it costs, by whatever means are necessary, regardless of the political consequences, because he knows the British people will depose him if he does not take action of the most severe kind against a terrorist organisation that has attempted to humiliate them in the eyes of the world. The Provisional IRA is going to be destroyed, come what may. It's as simple as that.'

'But we cannot just ignore world opinion. We can't invade the Republic of Ireland. We would be international pariahs and the Irish would be entitled to call on the United Nations to defend them. What would the Americans and the Europeans think?'

'The Prime Minister has no intention of invading Ireland unless he absolutely has to. He is saying that if he is pushed any further he may have no choice. He has to destroy the IRA, by any means. He is offering the Taoiseach a way out: accept the destruction of the Provisionals by the SAS on your territory or I will have no alternative but to do it anyway, even if I have to destroy your country in the process. The Prime Minister knows most world leaders personally and will no doubt be busy on the telephone for the next few hours. World opinion will scourge him in public, but every world leader will be secretly offering encouragement. Everyone is tired of terrorists, including the Russians, and for that matter the Irish themselves.'

A reporter from the *Telegraph* jumped up. 'Robert Jebbison, *Daily Telegraph*. Colonel Aitken, what are the chances of a bloody conflict between the British Army and the Irish Army?'

'I think there is no chance. Just look at the realities. The Prime Minister is not a fool. He knows very well that the idea of throwing a full British armoured division complete with heavy artillery and overwhelming air superiority against the Republic of Ireland is like threatening a peanut with a steam hammer.

'I invite you, and the Irish government, to remember what our 1st Armoured Division did to the Iraqi Republican Guard when it caught at least *three* of their armoured divisions in south Iraq: it mauled them so badly it had to stop in less than 24 hours because it had nobody left to attack. 1st Armoured Division was much smaller than the proposed Ulster Division. The Irish have only a few light infantry battalions, nearly all permanently on UN service in Cyprus and the Middle East. They have no navy, air force or even artillery worth speaking of. Their armour consists of a few ancient armoured cars that might not even make it out of barracks. The whole lot could be destroyed in a few days by a single British infantry battalion equipped with WARRIOR armoured fighting vehicles. I doubt that the Ulster Division will ever take the field. Deploying a reinforced regiment of SAS is a different matter:

they will produce maximum success with the minimum of furore. That is why I am here, to tell you our plan.'

Charlotte locked her fingers, gathering her courage. The journalists said nothing. *Plan? The army never told anybody their plans.* They sat silent, waiting for her to say more, almost skinning their knuckles as they gripped their tape recorders and pencils, knowing a major news event was about to break.

'The SAS will certainly deploy here, in the strength the Prime Minister indicated. If the Irish government has any sense it will make defiant noises but turn a blind eye to SAS operations in the Republic. No harm will be done to anyone but the Provisional IRA. No other troops will be used except in their normal internal security duties. The Ulster Division is a big stick, a statement of intent designed to show the Irish and British people that the Prime Minister means what he says.

'I have said that a single British armoured infantry battalion could cut the guts out of the Irish Army in a few days. A force like the Ulster Division could raze Dublin, Cork and Limerick to the ground in a week. I have said that the Prime Minister is not a fool. I do not believe that the Taoiseach is a fool either. The Taoiseach has little choice. The Provisional IRA have plagued us all, British and Irish, for a quarter of a century. They have just run wild for a month in England, committing the most appalling atrocities. All this must stop. It must stop now. The Taoiseach can either accept that I, a mere lieutenant-colonel, will act for a month in Ireland, with the SAS as my bayonet, rooting out the Provisional IRA once and for all, with no damage to anyone else, or he can face the full weight of a British Field Marshal with an armoured army to hand.

'I say again, I, with a reinforced regiment of SAS, will destroy the Provisional IRA root and branch in a month. That is not a boast, that is a fact. If anyone hinders me the Prime Minister will act. The Taoiseach will have Field Marshal George to deal with. That is not a threat. That is a fact. Be in no doubt of our resolve. The Provisional IRA is on its own, with nowhere to hide.

They are about to get that which they have so richly deserved for so long. The Provisional IRA will be stone dead in a month. No more questions.'

Watching intently, Gerry Madden was aghast, his terror of the SAS rising to choke him, dropping him into an almost catatonic state. But Siobhan McCaillim was exultant. Madden, Siobhan thought, had sown the whirlwind she stood best placed to reap. One quick phone call and her men would be scattered to the four winds, out of play. The germ of a plan came unbidden to her, leading her straight into Charlotte Aitken's trap: this was a golden opportunity to remove all potential opposition within PIRA at a stroke, a chance to get that Brit cow with the film-star looks to do the job for her: when the bitch had destroyed the old Provisional IRA her young guard would rise anew.

Siobhan let her mind run free. She would agitate for elections aimed at bringing down the Irish government, cowards the people had seen knuckle under to British threats of tanks and heavy guns. She would bide her time, preserve her own, seize power in the Republic and force the British to use their tanks and guns. She would force them to invade, force them to occupy the whole of Ireland, a weak and tiny nation struggling for its freedom. Then, prostrate, she would ask the United Nations to send troops to displace the British and enforce peace over the whole island. Ireland would be one again, even if garrisoned by Swedes and Fijians. But first a gesture of defiance, just to stir the pot. Siobhan handed Gerry a glass of milk heavily laced with Valium and his newer medicine, heroin, holding it to his head while he drank it by reflex. Then she ordered out the Provisional IRA hard men, returned from England, to do battle with the SAS.

Second-Lieutenant Alex Menzies had been out of Sandhurst just over five weeks, a bright-faced boy of nineteen just beginning to gain the confidence of his soldiers, when the bullet struck. When the British public saw his face on the Nine O'Clock News he had already been dead for three hours, a gesture of defiance, just to stir the pot.

Charlotte Aitken was in her room in the mess, in close arrest, placed there by an enraged, desperately embarrassed lieutenant-general, the General Officer Commanding Northern Ireland, who was determined to court-martial her and have her commission for her outrageous, totally unauthorised press conference and assumption of authority she did not have. Charlotte was trembling with terror at the enormity of her audacity and its possible consequences. Alone, she longed for her man, cursing him for not being there to support her when she needed him more than ever.

In London the Ministry of Defence public relations officers cursed Charlotte's name as they fought off a deluge of pressmen seeking inside information on exactly who and what she was and how exactly she had come to be running the SAS. They wanted pictures, personal details, human interest angles, the name of her school, what she did to keep fit, who did her hair and was she not just an actress employed to scare the hell out of the Irish government?

The Prime Minister, closeted with Field Marshal George, made a decision. By 10.30 p.m. Charlotte was out of jail and on her way to London.

Chapter Nineteen

11.30 p.m. 27 April 1993

LONDON

The Field Marshal was brief and to the point. 'You have no more than fifteen minutes. If you need more, you will fail. I have read your record. I will listen carefully. If I am convinced I will support you. In here.'

The Prime Minister received Charlotte in a courteous manner, ensured she was comfortably seated, gave her a glass of port and a cup of decent coffee. Before she had a chance to drink either he said, 'That was a remarkable performance this afternoon. It was a fair summation of the situation and my intentions. Your assumption of power you do not have indicates to me that you are either as mad as a hatter or an egomaniac of Herculean proportions. Which are you?'

Charlotte refused to be taken aback: if she showed any doubt or insecurity her cause was lost in her first answer. She smiled and replied, 'If you thought that, Prime Minister, I would not be here. You think I might just be able to deliver on the statements I made this afternoon. I can. The Field Marshal has told me I have fifteen minutes to convince you of that. I cannot afford the time to answer questions with no direct bearing on the matter in hand. You have read my record. You know I mean what I say. What are the areas of doubt in your mind?'

The Prime Minister glanced at the Field Marshal, unused to being told he was wasting his subordinates' time. Sir Harry George remarked, 'Twelve minutes, Prime Minister.' Charlotte cast George a look of thanks.

'I see. You military people are closing ranks on me. Very

well. Colonel Aitken, why should I give you power of a kind no soldier has wielded in this country since Cromwell cut the head off his king?'

'You would be giving me no such power, sir. The army is subordinate to parliament. Parliament gave you the power you describe, with a very clear objective, to destroy the Provisional Irish Republican Army. I and those selected to enforce the will of parliament as expressed by you are not makers or even interpreters of policy, but its instruments. We have no power, other than to obey your orders. Should you order me to destroy the Provisionals, I will. I propose that you do so.'

'How, and why you? Why not A.N. Other?'

'In the way I described this afternoon, sir. I would use the SAS as my weapon. I, because no other has had the will to take up the challenge, the ability to meet it, or, more critically, the knowledge required to make best use of the resources available.'

'Explain.'

'I have studied the Provisional IRA deeply. I have an intimate knowledge of its functioning and structure. I know where and how to hit it hardest. Others have had similar knowledge in the past. But I have it now, up to date.

'The SAS is a specialist unit, with two primary functions. The first is that of Intelligence-gathering under adverse conditions. The second is the application of physical force to carefully selected targets, at times and places equally carefully chosen to inflict terminal damage on our enemies, with the minimum damage to the Regiment itself or our friends. The SAS Regiment can destroy the Provisionals, of that there is no doubt. What has been missing in the past have been the conditions necessary to generate the political will to allow it to do so. Those conditions were brought about by the Provisionals' recent activities. You have demonstrated that the political will is now present.

'I have seen all this develop. I have seized the window of opportunity provided by your willingness to ignore political, social and perhaps even moral considerations from your assessment of how to execute your policy. That window will close soon, as people turn their minds to other pressing problems. We must act now, with determination and skill. I have available to me the means to maximise SAS capabilities. The regiment need waste no time in Intelligence gathering. I have already done that, in the expectation of this opportunity. I know who and where every important Provisional commander is, or will be in the near future. The regiment can concentrate on its other primary function, that of destroying the enemy by selective direct action. I am ready and able to exercise overall command, provide targets and set the regiment's objectives.'

'I see. Colonel, I ask again, why should I accept your proposal?'

'Because, Prime Minister, your alternatives are to invade Ireland or back down. You cannot do either and survive. I made a speech this afternoon designed to convince the Taoiseach that you might just invade his country if pushed hard enough. I think I was successful. He will accept SAS action on his territory. I am offering you an alternative course of action which will achieve your aim without massive loss of civilian lives on the one hand or a devastating loss of face on the other. By tomorrow morning the press will have worked that out for themselves. By midday tomorrow the lunchtime bulletins will be accusing you of dithering. The people will want to see tanks on the move or your resignation on the table. But act now, put out a statement saying that my speech was made at your personal direction. You will be seen as a man who has controlled his anger, thought again and acted to prevent terrible loss of life. By the end of this month you will be seen as a man of your word who delivers on his promises and does so in the quickest, most humane way possible. If I may be blunt, Prime Minister, you have backed yourself into a corner. I am opening a door behind you.'

'Field Marshal?'

George stood silent a moment, then spoke with care. 'Everything the colonel has just said tallies with the assessment of our position we made earlier this evening. She has a clear view of the position we are in and has argued a good case for her proposal. She has, in effect, produced the same way out we saw, but without our inside information. That indicates to me that she has the calibre to see it through. Those we shortlisted to take overall command of SAS operations produced no such assessment. They will have to take a back seat. The emergency Intelligence briefings we had scheduled for them can be cancelled. Aitken needs no such briefing as she is the one who would have been giving them. We need waste no more time. By her foresight and clarity of thought Aitken has staked her claim for command. Her willingness to put her career on the line indicates to me that she knows she cannot allow herself to fail. Her courage in answering our questions in the way she has indicates to me that she has the necessary conviction to act without constant appeals for direction from us. Aitken is the best candidate. I recommend that you put her in command of Operation HALO.'

'Agreed. Colonel Aitken: I hereby order you to destroy the Provisional Irish Republican Army, wherever its agents are to be found. Are there any questions?'

Charlotte, staggered by the discovery that the Prime Minister and the Field Marshal had intended to do exactly as she had, had even shortlisted candidates for the job and given their plan an operational name, felt her insides contract. She could have been laughed out of the army. How could she have been so blind, so grossly arrogant to assume that only she could see the blindingly obvious? But maybe that was it. She had seen it, when no other outside the very highest levels of command had seen it. And she had acted on it. *Now I know for sure. I am fitted for high command.*

'No, Prime Minister. But there is a point I should make. It concerns the legality of my actions. I intend to murder nobody. I ask that you formally declare war on the Provisional IRA.'

'Why? Why should I do so? The Provisional IRA are terrorists. I will not declare war on an illegal organisation.'

353

'In 1972 the Army Council of the Provisional IRA claimed to be the legal government of Ireland,' Charlotte replied. 'The president of PIRA's Army Council claimed that he was head of state of a thirty-two-County Socialist Republic of Ireland. Libya, Iraq, Syria, South Yemen and others recognised him as such. Padraig Hanna, at the *Ard Feis* of that year, formally declared war on the United Kingdom. At the beginning of their latest campaign the Provisionals again declared war on us. If you do not wish to declare war on them you can accept their repeated declarations at face value. You can claim to be making war in defence of the United Kingdom against an illegal government trying to usurp power in a sovereign state, the Republic of Ireland, and which is also conducting an armed insurrection in part of the territory of the United Kingdom.

'The Provisional IRA have always claimed to be soldiers, sir. Let them be. Then they can either surrender and face the courts for their war crimes or be killed in action. The world will see that you have no real quarrel with the government of Ireland. The world will see you using a legal device to try to differentiate between IRA soldiers and Irish civilians. The Provisionals' refusal to wear uniform at all times is not our fault: anyone publicly identified and accused by us of belonging to Provisional IRA can legally be shot on sight. He has the option of avoiding death by walking into any police station and surrendering, or claiming that he is not a member. A court will decide. Anyone identified as a member who does not so surrender will be deemed guilty by his own actions. The world will know that we are doing our best to avoid civilian casualties. It is only a legal device, but it will help our soldiers do their work if they are able to feel that they are soldiers fighting soldiers.'

George broke in. 'A bit convoluted, Prime Minister. But I see value in it. You would be saying to the Provisionals: "All right. You want to be recognised as a political party with a government and an army. You want to be at war. Be so. Take the consequences." '

'Very well,' conceded the Prime Minister. 'I will accept PIRA's declaration of war on us. Anything else?'

Charlotte Aitken looked pointedly at the Field Marshal. He nodded and said, 'It would be difficult for as senior a lieutenant-colonel as Havers of the SAS to accept another lieutenant-colonel having command over him. To promote Lieutenant-Colonel Aitken is the obvious answer. Full colonel would not, I think, be sufficient, since that rank is usually held as a staff rank, not a command rank. Brigadier is more suitable. I recommend that you authorise the MoD to promote Aitken to that rank, in an acting capacity. If she delivers on her promises the rank could be made substantive. If she does not deliver there is a court-martial outstanding against her.'

'You people! I thought politicians were ruthless. Very well. Brigadier it is. Acting, of course. Brigadier, do not fail. Destroy the Provisional IRA. Goodnight.'

Outside 10 Downing Street the Field Marshal took Charlotte by the arm. 'You will not have had time to organise yourself, Brigadier. Have you anywhere to stay in London?'

'I have a flat, sir. I'll get some sleep and get back to Ireland on the first shuttle.'

'Good. I'll send Havers to see you in Lisburn. He could be difficult if he isn't handled right. I'll speak to him first. He was a troop commander under me when I commanded the SAS. He'll take it from me. Well done in there. A piece of advice: don't make any more statements to the press. Don't even let anyone who doesn't have to know discover that you are running Operation HALO. Stay a lieutenant-colonel to all eyes for the time being. I'll speak to the GOC Northern Ireland and tell him to get off your back. All right?'

Advice from a Field Marshal was a direct order. 'Of course, sir. Let the SAS take the flak, sit quiet and thinking. I understand.'

'Excellent. Forget your flat. My housekeeper will feed you and give you a bed. My driver will take you to Heathrow. You've had a hell of a day, Brigadier.'

355

Charlotte smiled. 'Yes sir, a hell of a day.' *Be proud of me, Jamie.*

7–21 May 1993
IRELAND

The storm that Brigadier Charlotte Aitken burst on the heads of the Provisional IRA in the middle two weeks of May received little attention, almost nothing appearing in even the local press. The Irish, as expected, had called on the UN for protection the day after the Prime Minister's threat to invade Ireland and Charlotte Aitken's astounding broadcast but had been brusquely told that their case would be considered if and when invasion of their territory seemed imminent. The bellicosity of Prime Minister Prosser seemed to have receded in the face of wise counsel and the pressing economic problems posed by Britain's deepening recession. There were no new terrorist outrages, no tanks on the move. Nothing seemed to be happening worthy of report and for many, over the first shock and sick of the killing, that was enough. Charlotte Aitken's press conference was forgotten.

A visit by Field Marshal George to 10 Downing Street went unreported, as did the outcome of that meeting. The Prime Minister was determined to take full advantage of the willingness of other national leaders to turn a blind eye to his war on the terrorists in Ireland. The owners of the major news media would co-operate for a time, but he knew that their support and sympathy would quickly be eroded if his war went on too long. Brigadier Aitken had asked for one month. In answer to his Field Marshal's hint that a week or two more might be needed he reacted with irritation. Not more than one month, he said. The Provisional IRA had killed and maimed for a month in England. He could get away with the same in Ireland. The PIRA had to be destroyed and its leaders either dead or in jail by the first of

June. After that he would have to stop the soldiers going into Irish territory and start court proceedings against the captured terrorists. The Field Marshal had balked, but had seen the political priorities. To Charlotte he confirmed the Prime Minister's order. A month she had, no more.

A serious train crash on the main London to Edinburgh line and the announcement of a further rise in mortgage interest rates diverted the attention of the British man in the street. An opinion poll showed that the average householder was still very angry about the Provisional IRA campaign in England but assumed that the government was doing something about the terrorists and was more concerned about keeping his job and home together when redundancies were running at 35,000 a week and mortgage payments seemed to be increasing day by day.

But in Ireland things were far from peaceful. Nothing dramatic seemed to be happening but terrorist activity went into free fall as the SAS launched the British counterattack. All over the country cars were stopped; carefully selected houses raided; telephones tapped; men quietly picked out of airport departure lounges; arms and explosives dumps uncovered with surprising rapidity. The British seemed to know everything about everyone and were using every advantage, from coercion of informers to satellite tracking of the movements of PIRA leaders, to dislocate PIRA's command and communications structures and limit their ability to strike back.

Frightened, sweating young lads of fifteen or sixteen with bombs in the boots of cars and vans were relieved of their deadly cargoes on the way to their targets, a machine pistol pointed at their heads while they were told by terrifyingly calm and quiet men with the thinned-down faces and unconscious grace of athletes to go home and stop playing grown men's games. Their older compatriots were not so fortunate.

A bomb maker in the village of Drumkiln, just outside Cork City, heard something thump against the door of his half-basement.

357

Surprised but not alarmed he left the fragmentation bomb he was building to check the door but was distracted by a rattle behind him. Alarmed now, he jerked round, turning his eyes to the wire mesh covered window at street level. He saw a nightmare hanging there, a gallon can of petrol wired to a quarter-pound of plastic explosive, a cheap and effective device of his own invention, used many times to incinerate innocent people enjoying a drink or a meal out in the pubs and restaurants of the North.

Screaming, the bomb-maker hurled himself at the door; it was jammed solid from the outside. A tapping at the window, then a face appeared beside the fuel can, a hand holding a small blue and white badge, not unlike a little boat in shape, against the window. The face smiled briefly and was gone. Nightmare piled on nightmare: SAS parachute wings and a fuel bomb. White as a bleached sheet he fell to his knees, consigning his soul to God. His body, less than two feet long, was removed by crying ambulancemen not long after. The incident was reported in the Irish press as a horrifying example of the results of careless plumbing of high-pressure gas heating cylinders.

Two hardened men carrying Armalite rifles, accompanied by another man carrying a 10-kilo Semtex bomb packed with six-inch nails in a Tesco carrier bag, walked into a pub in the heart of the Loyalist stronghold of Comber, a pub full of flashing strobe lights and roaring disco music. There they expected to find off-duty squaddies dancing with local girls, and were determined to unload their Armalites and Semtex into the bodies of the dancers. The three men found noise and lights and a pub empty except for four silent men lined along one wall, all four carrying short-barrelled Remington self-loading shotguns. One of the shotgun carriers switched off the music while another, apparently unsure of himself, moved from foot to foot as he softly invited the intruders to surrender.

The bomb carrier, quick of reflex, thought the men were nervous Loyalist paramilitaries. He dropped his bomb and swung towards the door, shouting for covering fire. His companions, uncertain, fell into firing positions. One managed to get a couple of unaimed rounds off before the four soldiers along the wall fired in narrow overlapping arcs, twenty rounds in less than three seconds. The heavy shotguns shredded everything in front of them. Flesh, glass mirrors, wooden pillars, plastic tables, foam-filled imitation leather upholstery and high-tech, low-cost sound and light systems disintegrated into a shambles of blood, spattered ceiling high, and tinkling, tumbling, air-floating bits of powdered glass and cheap dismembered furniture. The local newspaper reports quoted Chief Inspector Peter Ewart of the RUC Special Branch as saying that the remnants of three Provisional IRA activists had been found in a wrecked car a mile outside Comber, killed by their own bomb. A separate report announced that Sammy Maclean, owner of the Step Down Inn disco pub had closed his place 'for extensive refurbishment'. He would reopen in three weeks with a completely new light and sound system.

In the foyer of the Europa Hotel in Belfast city centre a very big man in a beautifully cut pearl grey lounge suit by Glover of Aldershot sat sipping a Wild Turkey, slightly apart from a group of sales reps talking business, but close enough to seem one of them. He waited patiently while the dinner-jacketed and black-tied Paul Flanagan, 52 year old current commander of PIRA's Ardoyne ASU, personal friend of Gerry Madden and managing director of Coldwide Buildings Plc irritably handed his wife's chinchilla coat to a bellboy, tipped the boy and lit a cigarette. The big man watched Flanagan's wife make her way to the powder room. When the woman and bellboy were well clear of Flanagan, the man in the well-cut suit walked up and asked in a cultured English accent, 'Mr Paul Ignatius Flanagan? I'm sorry to disturb you. I have something for you. Mr Prosser sent me.' The man held out a small, heart-shaped box of the kind jewellery is carried in, flat on the palm of his left hand.

Startled, Flanagan jumped, raising his eyes from his own

359

5' 6" to the messenger's 6' 5". 'Who the fuck are you? Who did you say sent you? What are you selling?' He glanced at the little jewellery box. 'What's that?'

The big Englishman looked apologetic, flipped a 9 millimetre Browning Hi-Power into his right hand and said: 'Four questions. Four answers. I'm Captain Bill Holland, Special Air Service. The Prime Minister sent me. I'm not selling anything. The box contains a little something for Gerry Madden. And I have a free gift for you. Goodnight, Mr Flanagan.'

The huge soldier, grave faced, gave the unbelieving Flanagan his free gift: a copper-coated lump of lead, straight between the eyes. He watched Flanagan fall, leaned over to check the shot man's pulse at the carotid artery, judged him to be dead and carefully placed the little box over the entry wound just above the bridge of Flanagan's nose. Then he turned and walked unhurriedly out of the hotel, stepping into a black London taxi at the door.

Flanagan's wife heard the shot and rushed out of the powder room to find herself a widow. A pragmatic woman, she palmed the jewellery box in the confusion. The newspapers reported the death of a prominent businessman shot dead by an unknown terrorist, the latest in a long line of callous murders. The widow Flanagan found an SAS cap badge in the jewellery box. She sent it to Gerry Madden, with a long letter demanding that Madden keep her in the manner to which his lieutenant had accustomed her. Flanagan's second-in-command, one of Siobhan McCaillim's young guard, intercepted both and saw to it that Mrs Flanagan was buried with her husband.

All over Ireland the story was much the same. A flurry of incidents in the second week of May nailed most of Madden's hard men, just returned from England. Mass arrests in Ulster followed as Charlotte switched her attack to Siobhan McCaillim, catching her unprepared, using garrison troops to capture more of Siobhan's young guard than she could afford to lose, trying to provoke her into ordering the rest into the fight. As Siobhan vacillated Charlotte switched the focus of her attack once again, testing Siobhan's ability to switch tactics herself, trying to get a feel for her enemy's level of ability.

Both PIRA organisations suffered, the black more than the red, as increasingly destructive SAS activity built up over the following two weeks, ruthlessly targeted by Charlotte Aitken and Conductor Caldwell. Charlotte slept in four one-hour snatches a day, a four-hour block once every three days. Caldwell worked like a demon, scouring his computers for the best they could offer.

In Dublin the Army Council of the Provisional IRA raged against the British and Irish governments. Amnesty International accused Britain of a selective murder campaign and the instigation of a shoot-to-kill policy. The Irish government, under severe pressure from Westminster, claimed that no British soldier had as yet set foot in the Republic and promised to arrest any who did: the rash of gas explosions and armed murders were explained away as an unfortunate coincidence and the activities of Northern Loyalist paramilitaries taking advantage of the unsettled situation.

Siobhan McCaillim took the first blows well. She had been guilty of underestimating Charlotte Aitken and of underestimating Brit capability, basing her assessment on the assumption that they would act within their own laws, whatever they said in public. She identified and tried to correct her mistakes: she should never have taken on the SAS in a head to head battle, should have been more decisive when it went against her. It was too late to save the Provisional IRA, but not too late to save the best of her own. She issued orders for them to get to ground, well away from anywhere they had prepared, and stay there until recalled, promising herself personal revenge on 'that bloody British cow behind all this'.

The first doubts began to assail Siobhan. Madden was useless; he could not help her. Her people were scattered for the moment. She felt alone and uncertain, unready to cope with Charlotte Aitken's coldly professional assault. She had watched with growing fear as Aitken's tactics had forced her to acknowledge her own limitations as the Brit switched the focus of her attack at will. At first she could not understand how Aitken seemed to be attacking all of PIRA but striking hardest at Siobhan's own men. Then it hit her. *She knows. She's not just fighting the Provisional IRA. She's fighting me too! She knows about me. But how much does she know? This changes everything.*

She decided to back off, to stop fighting the way Aitken wanted her to, watch and wait, go back to her original plan. It was a classic terrorist defensive move, would frustrate her enemy as she ran out of targets, buy time. It was what Gerry would have done had he been able. He had once laid down a golden rule for all operational commanders, culled from his extensive study of guerrilla warfare: 'Never fight when the enemy wants to fight. Always fight when he wants peace. When winning, advance one step less than you might, to avoid being drawn into a battle you cannot win. When losing, retreat one step more than you must, to preserve yourself for the future. Remember, time is a weapon in itself. If you are weak, fight only once a year, but be prepared to fight every year, for ever.'

As she thought more about her long-term future Siobhan consoled herself with Gerry's wisdom. He had taught her well. She would not fight the Brit. She would ignore the fact that Charlotte Aitken was ripping PIRA to pieces, in weeks. She would do as least expected: she would give Gerry's IRA to her enemy, use Aitken to achieve her own aims. Then when the Brit ran out of steam, thought she had won, Siobhan would counterattack with what was left of her own people, a little at a time, until she broke that wicked bitch's heart. In the meantime she would dump Madden and further her political ambitions.

Charlotte had read the books too. Unable to draw McCaillim out into a stand-up fight she went back to Caldwell, back to the slog of picking Intelligence pearls out of thousands of bits of often contradictory information. She decided to harass and intimidate Siobhan's red Provisional IRA as best she could while she dismantled the black Provisional IRA around Madden's ears.

If she could not defeat them simultaneously she would defeat them one at a time, Madden first. Her worry was that Siobhan would not fight at all, but lie low, until next month, next year, with the bulk of her organisation intact. Time was on McCaillim's side. To win she had only to refuse to fight. She must be made to fight.

LONDON

Channel 4 was running a late-night discussion programme: an eminent philosopher, chairman of the Commonwealth Peace through Prayer Committee, posed the questions: 'We think we may be morally justified in executing without trial known terrorists, but are we justified in employing professional murderers? Aren't the SAS committing mass murder in Ireland?'

The studio discussion was brought to an abrupt halt when a grey-faced man in the audience walked on to the podium and declared himself to be a practising Christian, a consultant psychiatrist and the father of a trainee journalist killed at the Wapping massacre. Several millions of people were shocked by the premature ageing evident in his appearance: Dr Adlard Hosking was a well-known television personality, a man who had fought with humour and common sense to bring public consciousness of mental illness out of the Dark Ages.

Standing tired and pale before the cameras Hosking almost whispered that any soldier who felt a doubt about what he might have to do had only to ring him up and he would reassure him. Strengthening a little he stared into the cameras. Terrorists, he said, were not the mad dogs of the popular press: they were clever and ruthless men beyond the reach of reason; for the safety of all they had to be hunted down and killed. Refusing to be interrupted he doggedly carried on, 'Our soldiers act on behalf of us all. Our soldiers are not murderers. Our soldiers are the wielders of weapons we all put into their hands, acting on orders we give them, trusting us not to abuse their trust. It can be no easy thing to walk up to a man and watch him sweat and blink and quiver with fear before you shoot him dead. Our soldiers who do these things will suffer terribly in the years to come, plagued by doubts and awful memories. We must support them, help them. We must not undermine them.'

In tears now the exhausted man fought to make his point. 'The real murderers are those who seek to intellectualise a physical problem, those who are trying to undermine the will and courage of the men who have to go among the wolves. They are the danger, the talkers in the easy chairs, the priests in their cosy parishes. They are the ones who pose the danger to our children. They are the ones we should be questioning, not the men we send to do our dirty work. What right have they to sit in judgement on our soldiers? No right. When they can protect our children let them talk, let them judge. Until then let our elected representatives send our soldiers to protect us with our full support and every aid we have to hand and penny we have to spend. Let us bring our soldiers home when they have done our will and let us then protect them from the horrors they have seen and done in our name.'

The grieving man covered his face with his hands. 'I'm sorry, I'm not doing this right, I'm sorry, sorry,' he sobbed. But as hands helped him from the studio the audience left with him, leaving the pundits to their own devices.

DUBLIN

The PIRA Army Council, meeting daily in the back rooms of Dublin pubs, were severely disturbed: the command and technical structures of the Provisional IRA were being cut down at a frightening rate. Nearly 60 per cent of the best trained and most useful people were either dead or in jail. Every proven sniper in the North was on the run. The bomb-makers had been shocked rigid by the incident in Drumkiln and were lying low, trying to keep out of SAS sight. Even so, two had been picked up and the houses of the rest had been raided in the middle of the night, the usual excited squaddies always accompanied by a hard-faced man who told the wives their husbands were in grave danger, invited them to contact the old man and tell him to walk into any police station and give himself up before it was too late. Worst of all, Gerry Madden refused to attend or explain his strategy for dealing with the situation. His representative, Siobhan McCaillim, shed little light on Madden's intentions, indicating without saying so that Madden had no follow-up plan for dealing with the British reaction to his campaign.

Once euphoric at the success of Madden's campaign in England, the Army Council were now bitterly divided; a couple were for allowing Madden free rein to carry on while others were suspicious, doubtful that he was in real control of the devastated organisation. In three weeks the SAS had crippled the ASUs and cut all real lines of communication with the Republic. Valuable people were disappearing into captivity, or just disappearing. Choosing her moment carefully, Siobhan McCaillim struck.

'I have a report for you. I am sorry to have to tell you that the chief of staff has suffered some sort of nervous breakdown. He's completely incapable of running the fighting forces of the Cause. His condition shouldn't surprise you. He's been sick with ulcers for years. It's not my place to advise you, but I'm very worried about him. His actions are not rational and he keeps talking about using people who just aren't available. Any mention of the SAS puts him in bed for days. He can't fight any longer. He's very sick. The doctor tells me he needs months of peace and quiet if he is to recover. He needs help. My people in the

North tell me the Brits will keep this up until they have him. Every man they pick up they ask the same question: where is Gerry Madden? They seem to be taking this thing personally. They won't rest until they have him. We have to bring him to Dublin and protect him.'

Padraig Hanna closed his eyes in thought, springing them open as his anger mounted. 'Your people in the North? What people? You said you had a report, and tell us that Gerry Madden has a bellyache and bad nerves. Then you tell us what we have to do. I thought you were on the planning staff, not the command staff. Who is talking to you when they should be talking to us? What the hell is going on here? Answer me, girl!'

Siobhan tucked her feet underneath her chair. *This is working beautifully.* 'I said I couldn't advise you. I help Gerry on the planning staff, yes. But I'm nothing more than his girlfriend. Everybody knows that. I love him and I'm worried about him. People talk to me because there's nobody else to talk to. Our whole army is falling to pieces. The SAS are running wild and they're going to kill Gerry. I'm worried sick. You have to help him.'

'We don't have to do anything except preserve the Cause. We've weathered storms before. This will blow over.'

Careful now. Plant the seed. 'Whoever is telling you that is misleading you. This will not blow over. The Brits are determined to destroy the Cause once and for all. They've cowed the government here in Dublin with threats of tanks and they're doing anything they like. They're going to keep on doing it until they're satisfied that we will never trouble them again. Gerry Madden is a symbol of our resistance. It's Gerry that has driven them to this. It's Gerry that has got through to them. They can't claim victory until they have him. He told me so himself. We must protect him.' *That should do it.*

'Don't presume to tell us what we have to do. We'll call you when we're ready to give you a message for the North. Wait outside.'

BELFAST

Peter Ewart was having a field day. The SAS were bringing in more top terrorists than he had ever had a chance at before. But time was tight. He had to nail them down, play one against the other, get as much information as possible while they were still suffering the shock of capture and grateful to be alive. A few days and they would be back to their normal defiant selves.

'Listen Colonel, you're getting the people in but we're not getting through them quick enough. We must have more skilled interrogators brought over from England to take advantage of the situation.'

Lt.-Col. Mike Havers shook his head. 'Sorry Peter, no can do. This has to remain within RUC and SAS control. The less people who know exactly what is happening the less chance of a weeping willie going crying to the press once it's all over. There must be an alternative.'

'The only alternative is to break them mentally or physically. We don't do that, not in my province. The Field Marshal wouldn't stand for it even if I allowed it, which I won't. We need more interrogators.'

'Well, maybe we can get round this. The Americans did a few things in Vietnam that scares the hell out of prisoners, gets them to talk. They claimed that the Vietcong prisoners recovered in a day or two. I'll talk to some people and get back to you.'

Chapter Twenty

LONDON

The waiters finished clearing the table and left the officers to themselves. At a nod from his boss the Field Marshal's aide-de-camp excused himself gracefully, thankful for the chance to nip off and have a small cigar out of the Field Marshal's sight. He didn't get his smoke. The current president of the mess committee at the Royal Army Medical Corps mess in Millbank didn't approve of smoking either, despite the legendary habits of doctors.

'I've read the reports. It's going well. There's something you're not telling me. Tell me now.'

'Sir?'

'Charlotte, I didn't get to be a Field Marshal by not knowing what's going on around me. I read all sorts of things. I even read bits and pieces SIS and the Security Service send round. You've been using them for a while. Something you said on your first Prime Minister's interview tickled my antennae. You said you had prepared for this. I looked into things. I even leaned on a very special gentleman in Lisburn. He's a good man, very loyal to you. Tell me about Siobhan McCaillim.'

Charlotte picked up her handbag and searched for a tissue, to give herself time to think.

'No good, Charlotte. Tell me about Siobhan McCaillim.' The Field Marshal's voice was warm with humour, but a little edge of warning was creeping in.

'Yes sir.' Charlotte told him everything.

'Hm. I agree with you. I think she will not fight. Madden, damn him, knows his business. She will have learned from him.

You're doing far better than I thought you might. You will defeat Madden, it's gone too far for him to recover. When this is over the Provisionals will be effectively dead. Without Madden and his hard men they're just a bunch of juveniles in Belfast and dinosaurs in Dublin. But McCaillim is another matter. She has potential. She has to go.'

The Field Marshal seemed to withdraw into himself. 'I have other priorities. The world is changing. The British Army of the Rhine is a shell. The successors of the Soviets are no threat. I am losing seventeen battalions to the so-called Peace Dividend. I think we'll be up to our arses in alligators as Central and Eastern Europe fall apart: there'll be little wars all over the place. The Argies might even fancy their chances at the Falklands again. I can't afford to employ fifteen battalions in Ireland. Siobhan McCaillim has to go. This world is bigger than she is. Do what you have to do.'

DUBLIN

'Jesus, Padraig, you can't mean it. We can't tout on our own chief of staff. It's out of the question, man.'

Padraig Hanna thumped the table. 'Nothing is out of the question, Mike. We're talking about saving the Cause here. The war was going down the tubes so Madden ran a campaign in England without any kind of sanction from us. He used up the English ASUs, years of training and planning, to massacre know-nothing beat cops just to distract the Special Branch while a bunch of crazy Japs and wogs tried to humiliate the whole British people. It was fucking Germans that shot down that old bomber. Germans, Mike! The worst possible people! And their ship! Since when did we attack fucking aircraft carriers? That was a terrible error of judgement. Jesus Christ, Mike. What else could the Brits do? Madden started a bloodbath over there. He attacked everything the Brits hold holy. The girl is right. They won't stop until they have Madden. If they get him and we declare a ceasefire they might just stop all this. It'll take us years to get over the damage they're doing. We must give Madden to them and we must make sure they kill him. He's done anyway. You heard the girl. This has to stop. Three weeks and we're on our knees. Three months and we're all dead men. The Cause will be finished. For the sake of the Cause we have to sacrifice Gerry Madden.'

BELFAST

'Where are you taking these prisoners, Colonel? I haven't authorised any move.'

'Oh, Peter. Glad we bumped into you. Sorry I missed you earlier, but I knew you'd approve. We're taking action to get them talking. We're taking two groups. Six are going out over the Lough in a chopper. Ten are going up into the hills. Want to come along?'

'Wait a minute! What are you doing to them? I won't have any torture. Just you stop everything until I find out what you're doing.'

Lt.-Col. Mike Havers looked closely at the unkempt Peter Ewart, catching the whiskey on his breath. Jesus. How could the man stand up? 'Come on, Peter, what do you take us for? We're torturing nobody. We're just going to throw a hell of a scare into them. Come on. The chopper first.'

Belted in and flying out over Belfast Lough in a lurching, shaking old Wessex helicopter, Ewart swallowed hard. The movement and vibration of the ancient machine was sickening and the noise and freezing wind coming through the fully open side door pulled the eyes constantly to the yawning gap. Havers noticed his discomfiture and put his head close to Ewart's, shouting.

'Sorry about this, Peter.' He waved at the six hooded men crouching on the floor. 'Need to soften them up, get them worried. They haven't a clue what's going on yet.'

Ewart could sympathise. He knew nothing would happen to him and he was securely belted in but he still felt insecure. The Provisional IRA men sliding loose about the worn aluminium floor, hooded and dragged out of their cells and thrown aboard this roaring, shaking, freezing pig of a thing, must be nearly out of their minds with apprehension. The pilot tilted the aircraft forward, driving part of the rotor thrust into the cabin and giving an impression of huge speed, abruptly went through a series of turning motions, causing the men on the aircraft floor to slide towards the door.

The soldiers allowed a few legs to slide into the doorway, get caught by the slipstream and feel empty space before hauling the screaming terrorists back in. At a nod from Havers the soldiers whipped the hoods off the six men, allowed them to look around, see the sea several hundred feet below them. Cursing and shouting in fear, the men scrabbled with tied hands away from the door. Havers spoke briefly into a microphone. The helicopter bucked and flung itself around the sky, throwing the terrorists now in a heap, now horrifyingly close to the door. Another quick word from Havers and the motion steadied.

Havers unbuckled himself and stood over the cowering men, shouting. 'Right, you bunch of bastards. You've had your chance to talk. We're getting rid of you now. Get the hoods back on them, lads.'

The soldiers leaped on the kicking, struggling terrorists, ignoring their screaming and pleas for mercy. 'Too late, Paddy. Down you go!'

Ewart was fixed in his seat with horror. Surely not . . . but the aircraft bucked around a bit more, swinging under its rotors, disguising a slow downward movement. About ten feet above the water the soldiers suddenly grabbed the hooded, terrified men and flung them out the door. Ewart, bawling incomprehensibly, struggled out of his belt, shouting at the soldiers. Two of them grabbed him and held him secure while Havers pointed out to the sea below. Bobbing gently on freezing water flattened by the helicopter's downwash were three inflatable boats, the men in them hauling two shocked, almost unconscious men into each boat.

Five minutes later Ewart, legs shaking, was back on solid ground. 'Mother of God, Colonel. What the fuck are you doing? This is madness!'

'No problem Peter. Calm down. Here, give me a drink.' Havers reached into Ewart's overcoat pocket and pulled out his hip flask. He took a deep pull on it and handed it to the confused, horrified policeman. Ewart took it automatically, his eyes still wide with shock.

'Don't worry, Peter. The prisoners are safe enough. They're just scared shitless. The men in the boats will keep them hooded until they get them ashore. The prisoners will be brought to police stations, two to each station. Each pair will be told by the men in the boats that there was only one boat. They'll be told that the men heard we were going to kill them and tried to save them all, but the boat was too small. They'll think their mates are drowned. They'll be told we saw the boat and we're hunting for them now. They'll be told to spill their guts so the police can keep them safely locked up and protect them from us. They'll talk. If they don't we'll burst into their cells and drag them out again. Then they'll talk. Any that have the balls to keep silent after all that we'll dump back in a cell here. They will not be hurt. I promise. One of these people must be able to give us a lead to Gerry Madden. I don't mind scaring and wetting them if we get a result on Madden. OK, Peter?'

Ewart seemed to freeze, hip flask halfway to his mouth. 'Gerry Madden? Aye. He's worth having. What's happening to the other ten?'

'They're not hooded. They're being driven up into the hills in a truck with an open back. A couple of them will be able to see where they're going, so they will tell the others. There is, I am told, a deserted farm on the other side of Divis mountain, miles from anywhere. Trees all round it. Do you know it?'

'Yes, I know it. Higgy Black's old place. It never was much. A few pigs, a couple of beef steers. Not much more than a smallholding. The son went to New Zealand after old Higgy died in '87. He still owns it. What's planned for there?'

The colonel lit a cigarette, drew deeply on it and blew smoke down his nose. 'It's simple enough, but nasty. Nobody will get hurt but a few will need a change of clothing. The prisoners will be kept bound hand and foot at first, all in the same empty room. There will be a couple of candle stubs to give them light. They'll hear voices and a few bumps and bangs in the next room. Then they'll be hooded and left to stew for about twenty minutes before they hear a pistol being cocked.

'One of the prisoners will be dragged out into the next room. He will have his legs untied and his hood removed. He will see a kitchen with some soldiers in it, looking a bit nervous. One of them will grab him and push his head over the sink and hold him there. One of the others will shout at him to start talking or he's going to get a bullet in the head. He might talk. If he doesn't two of the other soldiers will gag him, talk quietly to one another for a bit and then walk the prisoner out the back door and throw him in the truck. That's what the other prisoners will be hearing. They will have to assume that the prisoner we took away has agreed to talk. Then nothing happens for a few minutes.

'A second prisoner will be dragged out. Same performance, except that if he doesn't talk the other prisoners will hear a shot after all the threats and shouting, a live round because some of them would be able to identify a blank if we used one. They will hear running water, then a sandbag, the "shot man's body", being dragged out the back door. The prisoner will be quietly carried out to the truck. The next prisoner will be brought in. Same performance, but there will be tiny bits of bone and cattle brains mixed with blood in the sink, roughly

373

washed out. The prisoner will think the second man has been shot over the sink. He will remember that the first man walked out and he'll be told the same as the others; talk or be shot. He will believe that we mean it and he will talk. And so it goes on until all have been through. One or two more "shot" to encourage the others. That's it.'

'I can hardly believe what I'm hearing. Jesus.' Ewart took a long pull at his flask. 'This has always been a dirty war, but I've never heard anything so cold fucking blooded. What kind of people are you?'

The colonel threw the stub of his cigarette to the ground and toed it into the dirt. He kept his face down, eyes hooded. 'You needed quick results. I took it higher. My brigadier planned this personally and takes full responsibility for it. The details I authorised myself. Don't think we enjoy this. Don't stand in judgment. You'll get your results. Goodnight, Chief Inspector.' The colonel turned away, disgusted.

When he was a few steps away Ewart called, 'Colonel! I'm sorry. I apologise. We live in bad times. Here.' He held out his flask. The colonel walked back, took the flask and held it to his mouth. He looked perfectly normal, Ewart thought, perfectly controlled, except for the trembling of his hands.

'Let's hope we get Madden, Colonel. What we're doing is mad. But that filthy animal is not mad. He's bad, evil through and through. I nearly had him once. He won't get away from me again.'

23 May 1993
DUBLIN

'Now listen to me, Siobhan. I have painful things to say to you, and I have orders for you. Are you ready, daughter?'

Padraig Hanna looked old and bear-like, but gentle like a

favourite old uncle. Most of the Army Council were absent; only one, old Mike Jordan, was sitting with Hanna.

Siobhan McCaillim tried to look puzzled. *These people are so obvious. No wonder Madden has run rings round them for years. They're dinosaurs, so far out of touch they'll grasp at anything. But they still have teeth, even if they don't have the guts for treachery. Hanna's calling me daughter as if I'm a little bit of skirt to be humoured. Better play along.* She replied, dutifully.

'Yes, sir. I'm ready.'

'Siobhan, there are times when terrible decisions have to be taken, times when great sacrifices have to be made for the good of the Cause to which we have all devoted our lives. You understand that, don't you?'

My bait's been taken. 'Yes sir. I took my oath. What do you want me to do?'

'Siobhan, I know you're close to the chief of staff, but Gerry Madden has become a danger to the Cause. He is clinging to power when he is unable to exercise it with good judgement. He has brought on our army the most dreadful suffering and damage through his ill-considered campaign in England. He must be removed, Siobhan. But there are people in the North, in the thick of things, people who don't know how far gone he is, people who don't know that he has gone mad. Those people would still obey him, if only because they're afraid of him. Do you understand me?'

I understand you all right, you old bastard. You're afraid of him yourself. 'I think so. I thought Gerry just wasn't very well. He had a lot to do.' She looked at Jordan, her eyes full of worry. 'Is Gerry really mad?'

Jordan nodded 'Yes he is, Siobhan. You've been blinded by your concern for him. He's a very dangerous man. He cannot be allowed to go on wielding power, but he will never give it up while he breathes. You must understand the danger to the Cause, Siobhan.'

Siobhan jumped to her feet, hands flying to her face. 'You're going to murder him! You're going to murder the chief of staff. Jesus, Mary and Joseph! You want to kill my Gerry!'

'Calm down, Siobhan. Don't get hysterical. Sit down, sit down, girl.' Hanna was talking again, placating her. 'Gerry Madden is sick and he's mad and he still has control. If he dies the Brits will stop this insane SAS campaign against us. It's Madden they really want. He's the one that attacked them. He's the one that humiliated them. He has to go, Siobhan. You're the only one that can get to him. Think of your duty to the Cause.'

Now who's hysterical? Careful. Mustn't be convinced too easy. I love Gerry, don't I? Snivel a bit. Siobhan burst into tears, or appeared to, covering her face with her handkerchief, rubbing the edges into her eyes to smudge her mascara and make her eyes run and redden.

'Get a grip on yourself, Siobhan. You're a soldier. You are under orders. So is Madden. In my position he would understand, he would do the same.'

Yes he would. He did it to Sean McAllister, his own right hand man, exactly like you're doing it to him. Like I'll do it to you. 'What do you want me to do?'

'That's better. I want you to arrange a meeting for him somewhere. And I want you to tell the Brits where and when that meeting is. They will do the rest.'

Siobhan seemed to shrink into herself, her voice ragged. 'You want me to tout on my own man? You want me to tout on Gerry? Oh Jesus.' She curled in her chair, weeping.

'It's not touting, Siobhan. You're acting under my personal orders, for the good of the Cause. You have to make the sacrifice. It's on my conscience, not yours. It's a terrible thing I demand of you, and no woman could do more for us. We're fighting for the life of the Cause. You must be brave.'

A small voice. 'All right. God forgive me. All right. You'll never tell anyone, will you? I couldn't stand it.'

'You should be proud Siobhan. You have nothing to be

ashamed of. But I swear to God that no one will ever know except you and me and Mike here. All right?'

'Yes, all right. Can I go and wash my face?' *You're damned right nobody will ever know. You've just signed your own death warrant, Padraig Hanna. You too, Jordan.*

'Of course. Here, drink this up before you go. Come back here and settle yourself. You're a brave girl, Siobhan. The Cause will be indebted to you for ever.'

A quick wash and a quicker phone call and Siobhan was ready: her own men would step out of hiding the moment the SAS stopped their campaign. Her clock of destiny was running.

'I'll need to be able to contact you to tell you what the arrangements are. And I've changed my mind about keeping this secret. I want to see the whole Army Council, except Gerry of course. I want to make sure that this isn't some personal plot of yours against Gerry.'

Padraig Hanna was shocked by Siobhan's matter-of-fact manner and the flatness of her demands. Mike Jordan grinned at him. Forty years of marriage and eight daughters had taught him that women were far more resilient and ruthless than men, once they had accepted the necessity for action. Jordan answered for Hanna. 'The Army Council is due to meet in the top room of the Power Station down at East Wall the day after tomorrow. You come at about three, OK?'

'Yes. Three o'clock on Tuesday. I've not much time. I have to go now. I'll stop into Clonard monastery when I get home and say a prayer for us. Goodbye.'

Driving back to Gerry Madden's latest safe house in the little town of Monasterevin Siobhan went over and over her plan looking for flaws, but found none. She stopped at a public callbox next to a roadside café and dialled a number in the North.

'This is the police Confidential Telephone. Please speak slowly and clearly after the tone.'

'Call me Maeve. I want to talk to Chief Inspector Peter Ewart of the Special Branch. I won't talk to anyone else. It's about Gerry Madden. I'll call back in fifteen minutes.'

Tea and toast later Siobhan called the Confidential Telephone again and listened to the recorded voice. When the time came she said, 'This is Maeve. Put me on to Chief Inspector Ewart.'

'This is Ewart. All right, Maeve. Don't say anything yet. Don't be nervous. If you're in danger tell me where you are and you'll be picked up and taken to a safe place in ten minutes. If you're not in danger that's good. Are you safe?'

Siobhan was taken aback by Ewart's voice. It contradicted everything she had ever heard about him. Ewart had a soft country brogue, very calm and very reassuring. Peter Ewart went up in her estimation. 'I'm safe enough. I'm a secretary. I work for the IRA. I can help you. People were slaughtered in England. People are being killed by the SAS. It's terrible. It has to stop.'

In Belfast Ewart immediately flicked on the internal Tannoy system, something telling him he needed more people to give him instant feedback. 'It's all right, Maeve. You're doing the right thing. We all want the killing to stop. You said something about Gerry Madden. Do you work for him?'

'No. I work for the Army Council. I take down what they say at their meetings. I can help you. I said about Madden to get you to the phone. He hates you and he's afraid of you. You captured him once.'

Everyone in the Confidential Telephone control room quietly swung their swivel chairs towards Ewart, listening in to the voice coming over the Tannoy. Hoax calls came twenty a day: but not many people knew Ewart had once had Madden. Nobody had ever claimed to attend every meeting of the Provisional IRA Army Council. Ewart glanced round quickly to see every right thumb in the room raised, urging him on. If this was genuine and could be maintained it would be the biggest Intelligence breakthrough in nearly twenty-five years.

'All right Maeve. I did capture him once. Do you know where he is?'

'No. But I do know where the rest of the Army Council are going to be on Tuesday afternoon. You won't believe me if I tell you, so what's the point. I can tell you all about where they're trying to hide that anti-tank gun they got from America.'

Dear God. After all these years. The big one. 'Yes, you can tell me that. But other things might be more important. I believe you, Maeve. I believe you know where the Army Council is meeting on Tuesday. I think you're being very brave and you're trying to do the right thing. But I have to convince my superiors. They're suspicious people, Maeve. I have to convince them that we won't be sending policemen into an ambush. Don't get me wrong, I believe you. But there are others who might not. An anti-tank gun wouldn't be enough for them. Can you help me convince them, Maeve?'

Smooth bastard. Suspicious as hell. 'Well, the Monaghan brigade has a safe house in Markethill. Frank Johnson is in there. You can arrest him. He's in room 33 in the Rose Bowl hotel in Chartwell Street. Will that do?'

Ewart clamped the phone under his chin and threw out both arms to silence the hubbub starting around him. 'That'll do lovely, Maeve. I'll arrest him and stop him killing any more people. Let me get him first and let me talk to my bosses. When will you call me back?'

'All right. I'll call you again tonight. Bye bye.'

Twenty-two minutes after Siobhan broke her connection to Ewart a helicopter landed in the middle of Chartwell Street, Markethill. Frank Johnson, commander of PIRA's Monaghan brigade was in the air on his way to Palace barracks in two minutes more. 'Maeve's' bona fides were proven: not even the Provisionals would sacrifice a brigade commander to ambush a few woodentops.

Charlotte Aitken was talking on a secure telephone line between Lisburn and the SAS base at Bessbrook Mill, Armagh. 'Colonel, who told you where to find Frank Johnson? We've nothing on his latest whereabouts here.'

'No problem there, Brigadier. There's a signal on its way to you. We got Johnson on a tipoff from the Belfast Special Branch. Chief Inspector Peter Ewart. He probably got it down the Confidential Telephone or from some Provo gunman who walked into a police station to surrender and tried to ingratiate himself. It's happening more and more frequently. Johnson is a big fish. I didn't want to delay and risk losing him.'

'Fine. I'll talk to Ewart to see if he has anything more up his sleeve. Thank you.'

'Chief Inspector Ewart? Lieutenant-Colonel Charlotte Aitken here. I gather you have just arrested Frank Johnson. Can we talk?'

'I'm very busy here, Colonel. What can I do for you?' Ewart was puzzled, searching through his mental filing cabinet. He had heard of Aitken, some sort of staff officer who kept tabs on the surveillance of border crossings. Sometimes a useful bit of information came out of her office, not much. Oh yes, she was the one who had gone on TV a while ago. A glory hunter. What was her interest in Frank Johnson?

'I know you are busy, Chief Inspector. We all are. I want to know how you located Johnson.'

Irritated by Aitken's peremptory manner Ewart answered in kind. 'I don't see why I should tell you. Why do you want to know?'

'It is my job to know, Chief Inspector. You obviously have an important informer in the border area. I could make use of him. There are gaps in our knowledge about the Monaghan area the informer could fill in. I insist that you give me access to your informer.'

'No. The source is very sensitive. I'm not disposed to disclose it. Anything Johnson says under interrogation that touches on border surveillance I'll let you know. That's all I'll do.'

Charlotte Aitken's shoulders slumped in fatigue and irritation. She longed to tell this bloody policeman that she was the brigadier running this show and that he must tell her anything she wanted to know. She decided to bide her time. Anything Ewart knew would find its way into Conductor Caldwell's computers within twelve hours.

'Not enough. Thanks for nothing, Chief Inspector.' She slammed the handset down and bit her fist. She was tired, very tired. Four hours' sleep would put her right. PIRA was being ripped to pieces and she could lay claim to all of it. She must not get over-tired.

Ewart put down his phone and turned over a page in the transcript of Frank Johnson's first interrogation, Charlotte Aitken instantly dismissed, catalogued in the back of his mind as yet another of the military bureaucrats who seemed to think they had a God-given right to be told everything even when they had no need to know.

BELFAST

It was late, nearly midnight. Ewart was about to give up and go home. The telephone people had patched a line from the Confidential Telephone through to his office and another to his house earlier on, to keep him in constant touch. They could even redirect a call to his car phone. But he wanted to do it here, where he felt in control. He imagined some distraught, emotional woman frightened for her life trying to find a way to call him. He had to be here for her. He opened a drawer and pulled out a bottle. Pouring whiskey into an empty plastic coffee cup he jumped, startled, by an unfamiliar, insistent alarm tone. *Shit! The new phone!*

'Peter Ewart. Hello, Maeve. Are you all right?'

Siobhan McCaillim was in no fear of her life, nor was she emotional or distraught. She was sitting comfortably in an overstuffed armchair in the foyer of a middle-sized hotel in Monasterevin, completely secure.

'Hello. I'm OK, but I'm worried. Did you get Frank Johnson yet? He'll kill me if he finds out I told you where he is.'

'Yes, we got him, Maeve. He is in jail right now. He'll never find out who told me where to find him. I promise that he will be in no position to kill anybody for at least twenty years. Thank you very much, Maeve. Frank Johnson was responsible for some dreadful atrocities. You have done a wonderful thing.'

'Thanks. I feel better now.' *Well, good enough. That's him out of the way. Jonny can take over in Monaghan right away.* 'Do you want to know about Tuesday?'

'Yes, Maeve. Tell me about Tuesday.'

'The Army Council is meeting in the upstairs room of the Power Station pub in East Wall in Dublin. The meeting will be when the pub is closed for the holy hour.'

'Holy hour? Sorry, Maeve. I forgot. Different licensing laws in the Republic. The pub will be closed between one o'clock and three, yes?'

'No. They'll stay shut till four because of the meeting.'

'Thanks. That's perfect. Will they all be there all the time, Maeve?'

'No, they come and go as they're wanted. Some of them will be downstairs in the pub some of the time. But they're getting a report from the North at three, though. They'll all be there for that. I'll have to go soon. Somebody will be looking for me any minute.'

'OK, Maeve. A couple of quick questions. Do you know if Madden will be there? Do you know where he is now? Will there be anybody else in the pub at three o'clock? Is there any way you can avoid being there yourself?'

'The chief of staff is sick. That's why they're having the meeting, to decide what to do until he's better. The bodyguards will be downstairs with the landlord and his son, five or six of them. I'm not going to the meeting. One of the other women will do it. She's one of Mike Jordan's daughters. I'm going up to Drogheda to see my family tomorrow. You're keeping me too long. I have to go. No more questions please.'

'Right Maeve. Don't endanger yourself. Take care of yourself.'

'I'll ring you again if you capture them all. If you don't I'll be done for. I'll have to run for it.'

'Any time you don't feel safe just ring up and say where you are. There'll be a helicopter full of soldiers there in minutes, Maeve. But I'll get them for you, Maeve. I'll get them. Don't worry yourself.'

'All right. Bye bye.'

Ewart was on his feet punching the air and still bellowing in triumph when two alarmed constables dashed into his office.

'Yeeeessss. Yes yes yes yes yes. FUCKIIINGGG YEEEEES! YEEEE . . . What the hell are you gaping at? Fuck off! No . . . wait. You. Get me Colonel Havers on the phone. Yes, now. You. No, not you. You, the girlie one. Stand there a minute. Drink this.'

Ewart handed the half-full cup of whiskey he hadn't had a chance to drink to the young woman constable while her companion punched buttons on the secure phone line to Bessbrook Mill. The pretty girl's face jumped in surprise. 'I don't drink, sir.'

'You do now, girlie. This might be your first and it'll be your best. I've got nearly the whole Provisional Army Council. The whole bloody lot except Madden, and I'll get him soon. Get that down you! We're celebrating tonight!'

Later, in Bessbrook, Havers thought quickly. The brigadier had to know of this. A major action of the kind he had in mind had to have her sanction. Knocking off a bomber in a small town was one thing. Taking out the PIRA Army Council in the centre of Dublin quite another.

'Brigadier? Mike Havers. We have the Provisional IRA Army Council, except Madden. A pub in Dublin, three o'clock Tuesday. What do you say, ma'am?'

'I say brilliant. I assume you want to take positive action. Capture is out of the question?'

' 'Fraid so, ma'am. Too difficult an extraction. Too many people. Too much risk of it backfiring on us. It has to be elimination.'

'Pity. Do it. Ewart again?'

'Yes, ma'am. The Confidential telephone. He has someone very high up or someone with access to very high-grade information. Love to know who it is. Ewart won't say.'

'Wouldn't we all, Colonel, wouldn't we all. I'll try to find out. Thank you.'

Charlotte put the 'phone down, concentrating. *The Provisional IRA traitor is being very selective in whom he betrays: one of the old style hard men, the last but one of Madden's brigade commanders; the Army Council. Not Madden himself. This is McCaillim's work. She's allowing us to decimate the old PIRA. She must be in the process of taking over. The bitch is trying to manipulate me! She's trying to use me to do her dirty work for her. This is becoming personal. Right, you bastard. I'll get you.*

Chapter Twenty-one

25 May 1993

DUBLIN

At 2.30 in the morning of Tuesday, 25 May two men, one of them a very big man, sat astride a wall in Dublin. The smaller man blew softly and intermittently through a thin stainless steel tube, ignoring the drenching rain falling almost vertically out of a cloud-filled, moonless sky, his eyes alert for movement below.

In the yard under the wall two halfbreed Alsatian dogs, huge beasts trained to work as a pair, pricked up their ears and padded out of their kennel into the bouncing rain, searching for the source of the high-pitched peeping only they could hear. Their quarry found, one of them would dance around barking until the other crept silently around and attacked from the rear; then they would go in for the kill.

Near the base of the wall the dogs lost the peeping sound but picked up two solid, widely separated thumps and a powerful scent. Hunting, they split up, one to each thump, each source of scent: nearly a kilo of stinking, half-rotten minced beef offal in kneaded lumps. The dogs fell on the reeking meat, wolfing it down, the whistle forgotten. Up on the wall the men in the sodden black coveralls waited while the liquid anaesthetic in the meat took effect, then dropped lightly down into the yard between the twitching animals. They had an hour before the dogs would regain their feet, a bit sick but none the worse, with nothing about them their owner would notice in the morning. Plenty of time for the task in hand.

At four minutes to three in the afternoon of the same day

the same men, sitting on the roof of an hotel 300 metres from the Power Station, checked their list of photographs against the faces they had seen enter the pub since closing time. All present and correct. All in, none out. One man for whom there was no photograph, no 'face', had left the pub ten minutes ago. Nobody had gone in for whom there wasn't a face, except a woman who had accompanied a pictured man, Mike Sheen.

One of the men on the roof was an enormously powerful SAS warrant officer with a North London accent, known throughout the regiment as the Painless Pole for his unspellable name and his habit of muttering 'I feel no pain' when carrying weapon and explosives loads that would have broken the back of a well-fed camel. The Pole put down his binoculars and said 'Couldn't be better, Boss. Even all the bodyguards have faces. The woman must be Jordan's daughter, up to her neck in it. The lad who went out must be the landlord's son. We have no innocents. Do we have a GO?'

Captain Bill Holland wiped a hand across his mouth. 'We have a GO. You're the demolitions man, Painless, but I want you to give the radio to me, just in case there's somebody in there we don't know about. The recce report was good but it didn't cover the whole place. You have a thing about kids. I want it to be on my conscience, not yours, if there's a sick kiddie in a back bedroom somewhere.'

'OK Boss. Thanks. 'Nuff said.'

Bill Holland took the small radio, switched it on and placed it flat on its back, pulling out the telescopic aerial built into it, tuning the radio to 1500 metres long wave. The little radio was now acting like a rebroadcast station, a backup to the BBC World Service, just in case some local conditions interfered with the arming sequence of the device he and the Pole had hidden under the floor of the Power Station's upstairs room twelve hours ago. A small red light, the stereo acquisition light, popped on. So far so good. Holland switched to FM at 108 Megahertz and switched the radio off, on, off and on again. The red light blinked twice, steadied and shone brightly for two seconds, blinked out and then on again, the electronics inside the radio interrogating and assessing the state of the device in the pub. The light went out and stayed out: the device was listening. Holland had fifteen seconds to complete the sequence or the bomb would ignore him. He switched back to 1500 metres long wave and pulled out the tuning button, locking it with a quick twist to the right, waiting, listening and watching, fists clenched hard.

A woman's voice, cultured, the diction slow and clear, aimed at non-English peoples '. . . now for the world news, with George Newcombe'. A man's voice: 'This is George Newcombe for the BBC World Service. Here is the two o'clock news, Greenwich Mean Time, on Tuesday the 25th of May.' Deep bell sounds, Big Ben in London . . . *Bonggg* . . . One . . . *Bonggg* . . . Two . . . the front of the Power Station disintegrated, flame and brick and glass and plastic advertising signs swirling together into the street, a huge cloud of powdered wood and brick dust rising over a hundred feet into the air even before the thunderclap of the blast wave reached the bombers on the hotel roof.

MONASTEREVIN

Gerry Madden had watched the scenes at East Wall on the news at six o'clock and nine o'clock, and now the news at midnight. To Siobhan his condition seemed almost catatonic. Hour after hour he just sat there, silent, staring at the television, unable to take it in.

'You have to do something, Gerry. You have to do something. You're the only surviving member of the Army Council. You are the legal president of the thirty-two-county Republic. You are the president of *Eire Nua*. You have to do something. We are being defeated. The SAS are running all over us. What the fuck are we going to do? We don't know what to do. Tell us!'

Siobhan McCaillim broke in, attacking the commander of the Tyrone brigade, the last of Gerry's old guard, a man at the end of his tether: he had lost more than half his best men to SAS ambushes, RUC arrests and simple disappearances; his brigade, like all the others, was in tatters. Siobhan's own men, the brigade intelligence officers and seconds in command of all the Northern brigades sat silent around her, taking her lead. They knew where the 'disappeared' lay; not in prisons or unmarked graves: the disappeared were lying low at their orders, awaiting the rising of Siobhan's phoenix from the ashes of Madden's defeat.

'Stop harassing him. He's not well. He'll be his old self in a couple of days. He'll be back fighting soon. He's hurt the Brits badly. They're over-reacting, that's all. There's a car waiting to take you down to a safe house in Kilkenny until all this blows over. As soon as Gerry's well again I'll call you. You have to be patient.'

Martin MacLeese of Tyrone lost his temper, shouting, 'Patience my arse. Who the fuck are you to tell us anything anyway? You're nothing but Gerry's whore. You're nothing. Keep your mouth shut.'

Siobhan lost patience herself. Madden was still sitting silent, letting it all flow around him. She went to him and took his hand. 'Can I sort this out for you, Gerry?'

Madden's eyes moved slowly to her, the British blitz on his finest hour shocking him to his core, the drugs in his food robbing him of mental agility, keeping him slow and profoundly depressed. Tears squeezed out of his eyes as his fingers encircled Siobhan's.

'It will be all right, my love,' she reassured him. 'I'll send them away until you're better. Is that what you want?'

Madden roused himself a little, lifting his head. 'No. No. I'll do it, Siobhan. I command. I command ... Tyrone ... Do what Siobhan says. Go to ground. Go to Kilkenny like Siobhan says.

Safe houses for you. Go.' Madden slumped back into his chair, eyes leaden.

Siobhan took a moment to think. *Gerry is gone, totally mine. The Army Council is gone. The people of the Republic are not listening to nonsense about gas explosions any more. Nothing can hide the fact that the Brits put people into the Republic to butcher the Army Council. Feelings are running high and the government are having trouble pretending they're not bowing to the Brits. There is no way that Brit cow can keep this up without actually invading the Republic. She cannot do that. The UN would prevent it. Give Gerry Madden to her before she has to abandon her campaign against us. Give her Gerry to save her face. Let her think she's won. Then rise again. MY TIME IS NOW.*

Siobhan surprised them all, except Madden, sunk in his own pain and drug-induced despair. She walked up to Martin MacLeese and spat in his face, motioning her own people, including MacLeese's second-in-command to their feet to grab and hold him.

'I declare to all here present that every member of the Provisional Army Council is dead, except for the chief of staff. The chief of staff is through mental and physical illness unable to continue the war against the British or govern the nation in the inevitable event of our victory. Every brigade commander of the Provisional Irish Republican Army is dead or in the hands of the British, except for those present. Those present are not yet fit to lead. I declare that the rightful heirs of Patrick Pearse, first president of *Eire Nua*, are dead or incompetent. As the only available planning officer of the Provisional Irish Republican Army I declare myself to be the heir of Patrick Pearse and legal president of *Eire Nua*. I hereby declare the dissolution of the Provisional Irish Republican Army. I declare myself to be Commander-in-Chief of the army of *Eire Nua*. I appoint Jonathan Rourke, former second-in-command of the Armagh brigade of the Provisional IRA as chief of staff and chief operations officer of the army of *Eire Nua*. From this moment forward I am to be addressed as Madam President. Sit down.'

Boggle eyed, MacLeese shouted, 'You're out of your fucking mind! Madam fucking President! Let go of me, Jonny. What the fuck is going on here? Let go of me.'

Siobhan McCaillim, seating herself, gave her first executive order. 'Jonny, take this piece of shit outside and shoot him. Our time is now.'

Gerry Madden turned his sick, confused eyes to his mistress. She patted his cheek and told him it was time he was in bed. He must rest, she said, in preparation for his journey to the North, to rally the people to him.

The sound of a single pistol shot penetrated the walls of the old farmhouse. When Rourke came back into the house Siobhan told him of her plan to be rid of Madden.

Rourke was puzzled. 'Why not shoot him now?'

Siobhan shook her head. 'No, Jonny. Not us. The British. He deserves that. What's the best route over the border, one the Brits will believe Gerry would use? We'll allow them to ambush him. They'll stop their campaign once they have him, and he will be dead. There can be no talk of murder later. It's the best way for everyone.'

'The old gunrunning route that crosses the border near Forkhill. The Brits had a success against us there a few years ago when they ambushed that carrier party. We haven't used it since.'

'Take a good look at it. See if anybody can remember exactly where the Brits had their men. They'll probably use the same place.'

'I remember it myself. The Brits put a gas pipe in. They built a concrete observation post into the pipeline. They hit us from there. Why do you want to know?'

'Nothing very complicated. There's always an ideal ambush position. Whoever sites the ambush team against Gerry will find it and use it. The Brits are very professional, Jonny.' Siobhan smiled wickedly. 'Listen . . .'

Jonathan Rourke listened. He smiled broadly. 'I like it. Consider it done.'

BELFAST

'You murdered them all. You murdered them. You sent the SAS to kill them! I thought you would capture them. You killed them! I'm not telling you any more, you bastard. Gerry Madden will kill me.'

Peter Ewart came close to panic. The crying woman had launched straight into him, giving him no chance to explain.

'Maeve! I had to do it to protect you. I had to do it, Maeve. They would have realised it was you and got a message out of jail. You must see that. It was them or you. You're a decent woman, Maeve. They were all murderers hundreds of times over. I'm putting a message out for the news. I'm telling the papers that it was the landlord's son who told us. It's him Madden will be looking for, not you. It'll be all right, Maeve. I promise it'll be all right. Do you want me to have you picked up?'

'I hate you. You're as bad as them. Gerry Madden will torture me and kill me. That boy is retarded. He's just a child. Madden will never believe he did it. He'll work it out and he'll torture me and put a hood on me. What am I going to do?'

Jesus Christ. How could I know the landlord's son is simple? Madden will kill her. 'Tell me where you are, Maeve. I promise you'll be safe. Tell me where you are.'

'I'm not telling you. I don't trust you any more. I'm frightened.'

Think. For Christ's sake think! 'Maeve, Maeve. I'm sorry this has happened. But it will be all right. I won't let Madden kill you. You've done too much. Let me protect you. Let me protect you until I find Madden and capture him. He'll never get you, Maeve. You have to trust me.'

'You'll never get him. He's like a snake. Even the Army Council was afraid of him. My mammy is buying me a ticket to Canada. I'm going to try to get out before he gets me.'

'Don't do that, Maeve. If he suspects you he'll have you watched. Let me get you out. Are you still in Drogheda? If you are, tell me where. I promise I'll have the SAS come in helicopters and fetch you out. I'll keep you safe. I'll fly you out of England to Canada if that's what you want.'

'You know I know a lot about the Provisionals. I don't trust you. You would keep me and interrogate me. You would put me into a court.'

'I won't do that. What do I have to say to you? I had Madden before and I'll get him again. It's just a matter of time, Maeve. Can you help me? Can you tell me where Madden is now? I won't capture him, I won't give him a chance to escape. I'll kill him, Maeve. I'll kill him to keep you safe. Can you help me?'

'I don't know. I'm frightened. I'm . . . will you promise you'll kill him? You don't know how terrible he is. If you capture him he'll still find a way to get me.'

'As God is my judge I'll kill him when I find him. I'll shoot him myself if I have to. Can you think of anything to help me get him? Any little thing might help, Maeve.'

'I don't know where he is. I don't know. I only know he's going up to the North some time in the next couple of weeks. He has to meet somebody in Belfast, I don't know who or where. I only know he's taking the old Forkhill route but I don't know when. That's all I know.'

'The old Forkhill gunrunning route? Is that the one, Maeve?'

'Yes. His people told him it was the best because the Brits don't bother to watch it any more. I heard the Army Council talking about it before you had them killed. Madden has to do something up there in Belfast. But he might not even go now.'

'He has to come up here, Maeve. That's what I've been hoping for. With the Northern brigades scattered all over the place he has to come up here and sort them out. That's even more important now the Army Council is out of it. Madden has to come up here. He has to, Maeve. This is all I need to get him. Let me get you out now.'

'No, I don't trust you. I'll hide. If you get him I'll tell you where I am. Do you promise to send me to Canada?'

'I promise. I'll get Madden and I'll get you to Canada. Trust me, Maeve.'

OK. That's enough. He's hooked. He'll kill Gerry. He thinks he still has a chance to 'rescue' Maeve and bleed her white of all she knows. I'm not surprised Gerry hates him. Ewart is dangerous. Jonny will have to see to him. 'All right. Put it on the news when you get him. I'm not listening to you any more until you get him, Bye Bye.'

Jesus that was close! I'll have to get her in somehow. That girlie is too valuable to lose. 'CONSTABLE BAYLIS! IN HERE PLEASE.'

'Yes, sir. What can I do for you?' Baylis, young and pretty, had her pick of the young men on the beat, but rarely bothered. Ewart was her target. By hook and crook she had got into his office and was looking for her chance at him. She wanted an older, proven man, somebody who could retire her and let her spend her time riding horses in the Glens of Antrim and organising dinner parties for the social elite of the province. Ewart had been a prospect since she had drunk his whiskey with him and realised the big old man had a long way to go, despite his fondness of the drink.

'I want you to get Colonel Havers for me. I think I might have Gerry Madden.'

Constable Baylis brightened. *The Provisional IRA Army Council and the dreaded Gerry Madden. They'll have to promote him to chief superintendent at least, maybe commander. The Provisionals are nearly destroyed and the war will soon be over. With his record and my social graces Ewart just has to make commander. And with that behind me I can afford to let him drink himself to death if he wants to. Separate bedrooms after a year or so and the Ulster world my oyster. Ewart is worth a try now. This might be my best chance.*

'Very good sir. I'll get him straight away. If I may be so bold sir, have you any of that whiskey left? The Provo Army Council and now Gerry Madden! That really does call for a drink.' Catching Ewart's surprise she said, 'I think you're tremendous sir. Nobody else has ever got near Gerry Madden even once.'

Ewart could hardly believe his ears. The girl was flattering him, looking at him as if he was some film star! It was ludicrous: his life had been one long war against the Provisionals, a bit of opera and the Jameson's his only relief, and a bit of time with his cleaning woman now and again. Baylis was young enough to be his gran . . . his daughter. Ewart looked at Constable Baylis's shining eyes and the hint of black-stockinged thigh as she perched on the back of a straight office chair. *Don't be so fucking stupid. You're imagining it. You're an old man to the likes of her. You're two stone overweight and you need a bottle a day. Don't be so fucking stupid.*

'Colonel Havers, sir. Do you mind if I stay?' Baylis deftly slipped the bottle out of Ewart's hand. 'I'll get a couple of glasses, sir.'

'Colonel. Peter Ewart. We have a chance at Gerry Madden. He's coming over the border at Forkhill in the next two weeks . . . Yes Colonel, I know your manpower is stretched. But we're talking about Madden, Gerry Madden. He's the man that planned the campaign in England. PIRA's chief of staff, for Christ's sake . . . Who said anything about capturing him? That man is better dead. He has to be dead, I have a source to protect . . . Why are you being so cagey? All I want is a bit of surveillance of well-known ground and a squaddie with a rifle . . . all right, all right . . . What do you mean nothing after the first of June? . . . Jesus wept . . . Why did nobody tell us? . . . It doesn't matter . . . I'll sort this out some other way. Goodnight, Colonel.'

'Problems, sir? Here's your drink.'

'Nothing I can't sort out. Sit down, Constable. What would you do if you knew Gerry Madden was coming over the old Forkhill route in the next couple of weeks?'

Baylis sipped her whiskey carefully. 'Set the SAS on him. Capture him or kill him, it doesn't matter much either way. The Provos are destroyed, thanks to you. I couldn't help overhearing, sir. Are the SAS pulling out on the first of June? Two weeks takes us beyond that date. If that's so I wouldn't waste time capturing Madden. I'd set somebody else to kill him to get him out of the way in case he has a plan to rebuild the IRA. And there's Maeve. I'd get her in and pump her, just to make sure there's nobody else out there who could fill Madden's boots, somebody we don't know about. That's what I'd do, sir.'

Ewart grunted, drinking deep, eyes hidden. 'You've a devious mind, Constable. I never heard such a thing from a young girl. Kill Madden, you say. Break my word to a source, the best we've ever had. Murder and lies. There's the law to think about.'

'The law appears to be suspended as far as the Provisionals are concerned, sir. Gerry Madden is an animal, a filthy animal. Kill him. Get Maeve in and interrogate her. She's having an attack of conscience a wee bit late. How long has she been sitting there listening and writing down plans to destroy our province? Probably for years. We owe her nothing except the rest of her life in Armagh jail.'

Dear God. Even the young ones have no conscience any more.
'Aye, there's that. And who would you get to kill Madden if not the SAS?'

'I don't know, sir. But you must know people in the army with an axe to grind. The SAS have no friends in Lisburn, sir. They just walked in and took over. There's noses out of joint. Who was watching the border before the SAS came?'

'Drink your whiskey, Constable. With a mind like yours you could go far. Have you ever thought of Special Branch?'

Baylis smiled, lowering her eyes. She crossed her legs carefully, carefully enough for Ewart to notice. 'No sir. I'm too inexperienced. But I'd love to assist you in what you're doing. Your glass is empty, sir. May I?'

'Aye. I like a drink, as no doubt you've noticed. Any more bright ideas, Constable?'

Gently now. He's interested but he's not sure. 'You've been fighting this war since before I was born, sir. You've given your life to it. It must be a terrible strain. You're entitled to a drink any time you want one. I'm sorry sir, I don't mean to seem forward, but people like you have kept the Provos from destroying our province. People like you have set the examples. You asked me what I would do and I told you what I thought, sir.'

'I did and you did. Get me Lieutenant-Colonel Charlotte Aitken on the phone. She's the one responsible for border surveillance at Lisburn. I think her nose might be out of joint. She could be useful, Constable. But she might not want to talk to me. I was a bit rough on her the other day.'

'I'm Evelyn, sir, if I'm to work with you. I'll get Colonel Aitken for you. I'll need to know a little more if I'm to get around her. Can I have a wee drop more? I'm acquiring a taste for your whiskey.' *A perfect chance to show him what I can do.* 'And can I use your phone, sir?'

'Colonel Aitken? I'm Evelyn Baylis. I work for Chief Inspector Ewart of the RUC Special Branch. The chief inspector has instructed me to speak to you in the strictest confidence. It concerns the chief of staff of the Provisional IRA. The chief inspector has been under a great deal of pressure of work lately, as you will appreciate. He regrets that he was offhand with you the other day, and thinks there is a requirement to redress the balance. There is a certain amount of information available regarding the likely whereabouts of Gerard Madden . . . Thank you, that's very kind of you, the chief inspector will appreciate it . . . Can I make an appointment for him tomorrow? . . . Thank you. The chief

inspector will confirm that in the morning. Goodnight, Colonel
. . . Goodnight.'

'Well done Constable, — Evelyn. Let's see what Colonel
Aitken can come up with. Probably nothing. But well done. It's
a chance at least. It's late. Time I was in my bed. I'll see you in
the morning, in plain clothes, mind. Get a car from the pool. You
can drive me out to Lisburn.'

Chapter Twenty-two

26 May 1993

LISBURN

Charlotte Aitken's office was plain, spartan except for the racks of files and reports, with no personal touches to indicate the character of the owner. To some that said enough in itself. In a drawer of her desk Charlotte had the scarlet gorgets and badges of her true rank, hidden from view. Ewart had no need to know her rank, any more than he needed to know that she already knew from the Commanding Officer of the SAS the purpose of his visit. Ewart looked around as the colonel and his constable went through the motions of women meeting for the first time, the quick up and down glance that saw and said everything. Aitken was a striking woman, even in the drab green of uniform. Baylis looked just right, a little bit of makeup and a tailored pinstripe suit in charcoal grey, her fair hair up in some sort of braid. Aitken was talking to him.

'Thank you for coming up here, Chief Inspector. It's never easy for me to get away from this.' Aitken pointed at a video unit, no, not a video unit, a VDU with a built-in keyboard. 'I'm a slave to it, I'm afraid. Would you like some coffee?'

Ewart studied Aitken, the first female colonel he had met, with open curiosity. Something special about her or something odd; not in her manner or movements, something in her face, a certainty about herself. He returned her smile. 'No thank you, Colonel. We had some on the way up.'

'Colonel and Chief Inspector are a bit formal, aren't they. I'm Charlotte. I've seen you before.'

'Oh? Peter Ewart. This is Detective-Constable Baylis. She's

not Special Branch but she works for me. We've met before?'

'No, we've not met. I heard you give a lecture in Warminster, years ago. Have you got a picture of Madden now?' Charlotte smiled again, trying to put Ewart at ease.

Ewart's face clouded. 'No I haven't. I did at one time. I even had Madden himself. But I lost him; a question of proof of identity. I'd rather not talk about that. I'd rather talk about the future. Time is short and I want to establish whether or not we have something in common. I'll try not to waste your time, Charlotte. I'm going to talk about a very sensitive matter. I have information, from the same source that helped me get Frank Johnson and the Army Council, that Gerry Madden will be coming up to the North in the next week or two. I want him. I want him very badly. But I can't get him on my own. Perhaps you can help.'

Charlotte sat silent for a long moment, fingers steepled. 'I ought to tell you how very much I want to help. The Provisional IRA is being decimated, Peter, but so is the means of monitoring their activities. The SAS won't get all the terrorists. Those that are left after the SAS go, as they eventually must, will be fully aware of just how we have been working against them. It may take them years, but the Provisionals will rebuild. The capture of Gerry Madden would seriously hinder that. I want to get the hell out of here and I want to do it on a high. The capture of Gerry Madden would be most satisfactory. How can I help?'

'I have no intention of capturing Madden. Do you want to continue this conversation?'

Charlotte blinked, her face carefully registering surprise as she seemed to take in the implications of Ewart's brutal statement. She looked first at Ewart and then at Evelyn Baylis. 'What is the purpose of Detective-Constable Baylis's presence here?'

'Constable Baylis is my assistant. She helped formulate this approach to the problem of dealing with Madden. Nothing you say will be repeated outside this room.'

'Very well. Am I to understand that Madden is not to survive any encounter with whatever force is deployed against him? If that is so, why not simply let the SAS target him?'

'I said time is short. I can tell you that the SAS will withdraw on the first of June, because their political protection ceases on that date. They will not accept any task likely to carry over beyond it, so we must deal with Madden ourselves.'

He's watching closely. Be surprised! Charlotte looked caught out. *Lie in your teeth.* 'So soon! I didn't know. I see. Thank you. How do you think I can help?'

'Madden will be coming across the border at a known point. Our problem is that it could be any time from now until a date unknown but likely to be within ten days or so. We need to put someone in position to intercept him. That someone will have to be prepared to remain in position until Madden attempts his crossing. I expect that the remnants of the Provisionals will real-ise the SAS have gone fairly quickly after they withdraw. I think we have a few days' grace, not much more. Madden is likely to make his attempt soon after that. You must find the means to intercept him. And there is a problem: how will the interceptor identify him?'

'I understand. I need some more basic facts. I also need some coffee. What area are we looking at?' *Jamie! It has to be Jamie. Thank you, Lord. Give Jamie back to me and I'll rid your world of Gerry Madden. And the IRA. Give me Siobhan McCaillim and I'll rid your world of their successors. Give my Jamie back to me! I need time to think.* Charlotte ordered coffee for them all and sat, hands folded, thinking as Ewart talked. Then she acted.

Over a hurriedly but effectively prepared Intelligence map of the Forkhill area Charlotte summed up. 'Requirements: we need a marksman. We need some support for him, not more than six infantrymen equipped with radar and sound sensors, but no night sights because we don't want them to see too much. I am assuming that Madden will come at night.

'Ground: this line on the map indicates the presence of a gas pipeline. The pipeline is genuine. This blue mark indicates the position of a concrete observation post the Royal Engineers installed under cover of the pipeline's construction in 1984. It was from that OP that an IRA gun delivery party was ambushed in August 1986, causing the Provisionals to abandon the route, but they are resurrecting it to get Madden into the North. The OP is in a perfect position, on the forward slope of a spur, with a view out to 1500 metres over an arc of about 220 degrees.

'Outline plan: the marksman can shelter in and attack from the OP. The backup section can set up hides behind and above him. The only real way to do it is simple enough. The backup section warns the marksman of Madden's approach. The marksman hits Madden as he crosses over, at a range of about 600 metres. The story is that Madden somehow got wind of the ambush and fired on the soldiers. The marksman returned fire, killing him. You get to see Madden dead: I get to leave here on a high. That's it. Any questions?'

Ewart pursed his lips. 'Very impressive. But maybe I'm stupid, Charlotte. Maybe I've missed a trick. How does the marksman know it's Madden doing the crossing? Six hundred metres is a hell of a long way, especially at night. How does he guarantee a hit? And it has to be said: this is after all a conspiracy to murder. Where are you going to find somebody willing to do it?'

Charlotte smiled, wide and frank. 'You've been very lucky, Peter. You've come to the only person in this headquarters who could set this up and get away with it. I'm also the only person who knows exactly the right man for the job. The man I know could not only hit Madden at that range in the dark; with a Starlight 'scope he could guarantee to hit him in the head. He also knows Madden by sight. He happens to know you too.'

'How can he know Madden? There aren't any pictures of him. And how does he know me?'

Enjoying herself at Ewart's almost boggle-eyed disbelief Charlotte sat on the edge of the map table. 'You were a beat cop once, Peter. In Springfield Road barracks. Remember Big Jamie Lappin? What's happened to him?'

'How the hell do you know all this? That was twenty-odd years ago!'

'You remember Big Jamie? Tell me what happened to him.'

'Of course I remember. Big Jamie Lappin is a fine man. He took the riots in '69 pretty hard and went on the drink. He came off the booze about five years ago and set up a community centre for kids from both Catholic and Protestant communities. The Provos didn't like what he was doing and kneecapped him for it. I saw him about two months ago. He's still on sticks but he runs a soup kitchen and a recovery centre for alcoholics down in the city centre. What's all this about?'

'Big Jamie Lappin had sons. One of them is also called Jamie. Where is he now?'

'I don't know where he is. He was just a skinny kid ... Jesus! He was Madden's best friend! What are you leading up to?'

'Jamie Lappin joined the army. He was a Para for years, the best of them. He was decorated for gallantry in the Falklands War. He is now what we call the Rangemaster (Snipers) at the School of Infantry in Warminster. He's a highly respected figure and probably the best rifleman in the world. He's the man I have in mind for Madden.'

Ewart sat back into his chair, stunned. 'How do you know all this? What makes you think he'll do it?'

'I know Jamie Lappin very well. He is a very uncomplicated man, very brave and very honourable. He believes that it was the Provisionals that drove his father to drink. He does not know that his father has recovered or that the Provisionals have crippled him. If I can prove to him that it is absolutely essential to kill Madden to prevent him resurrecting the IRA there is nothing in the world that could keep Madden alive. Jamie Lappin will kill him without a qualm. The sooner I meet Big Jamie the better. In the meantime, I want the name of your informant.'

Ewart stalled. 'Informant? Why?'

'I said Gerry Madden would do very nicely to get me out of

here. How would that be so if I could never tell anybody I had him eliminated? You've got the best out of your source, Peter. Give him to me and I'll pump him dry. I'll convince the army that Madden has to go and I'll get him disposed of, maybe not legally but with enough people in the know to get me out of here. Once out I want to write the definitive story on how Madden managed to elude us for so long. It will make my name. No loss to you.'

'No. I promised protection.'

Charlotte shut her notebook with a snap and stood up abruptly. 'No name, no Madden. That's my price.'

Ewart looked defiant, a compound of emotions, anger crossing his face.

Evelyn Baylis watched him. She would help him out and get him further indebted to her.

'He is not a he. The informant's name is Maeve. She is a secretary who worked for the Provisional IRA Army Council.'

Ewart rounded on her. 'How dare you, Constable. I promised that woman —' Baylis interrupted him, 'I'm sorry, sir. I promised nothing. Gerry Madden has to die. I owe Maeve nothing. If giving her name to the colonel is the price we have to pay it's a small price. That bitch listened to them plotting the downfall of our province for years. We owe her nothing, sir.'

Thank you, Constable Baylis. Now I know for sure. Siobhan Maeve McCaillim. I can use Madden to get McCaillim. 'The Constable is right, Peter. Maeve is nothing to you but useful to me. I have work to do, on behalf of us all. Thank you.'

All right you little bitch. Try to manipulate me, would you? My man will kill your man, not for you but for me. Then I'll nail your little whore's hide to my wall. And I promise you I'll find every one of your terror gang and bury them all, after I've buried you. How dare you challenge me?

Sergeant Willie Thorne of the Small Arms School Corps was not happy about his task, but shook himself into readiness, flexed his fingers, knocked briefly on the classroom door and entered immediately, taking two strides into the room and pulling his feet in at attention. Jamie Lappin stopped talking in mid-sentence, turning angrily at Thorne's abrupt entrance.

Thorne got in quickly before Lappin could bounce on him. 'Sorry for the interruption, sir. There's a lieutenant-colonel from Ireland on the phone. It seems to be an urgent matter, sir. I checked your schedule: Theory of Small Arms Fire, as applied to the GPMG in the SF role. I'll take over your class, sir. Where were you, sir?'

Mollified by Thorne's professional preparedness, Lappin looked him over. Every other eye in the room did the same, by reflex. Students arriving at his school learned quickly that the Rangemaster's belief in the value of personal discipline started with bearing and turnout. Nothing but the best was good enough: a sloppy appearance indicated a sloppy mind; sloppy minds made sloppy soldiers; sloppy soldiers were thrown out on their ear with a negative report sent with them to their regiment. Sloppy SASC instructors did not exist.

'Very good, Sar'nt Thorne. We were about to look at the effect of rising or falling ground on the fall of shot, at extreme range. Carry on.'

'Sir!' Thorne advanced to take Lappin's place. 'As you were, class. Ground configuration has an effect on all long-barrelled weapon types, as described in your last lecture. With the General Purpose Machine Gun in the Sustained Fire role these must be planned for. Imagine a 45-degree slope . . .'

Lappin strode down the corridor to his office, keeping his mind open; God knows what this was all about. He picked up the phone and spoke in a controlled, neutral tone. 'Rangemaster. What can I do for you, sir?'

'You can address me as ma'am for a start, Sar'nt-Major. This is Lieutenant-Colonel Aitken. Orders will be arriving by Immediate signal summoning you to HQ Northern Ireland. You are to report to me for briefing. Your Commanding Officer has been advised by signal of your thirty-day detachment to this headquarters. You are to catch the earliest possible shuttle from Heathrow to Aldergrove airport. A car will be waiting for you. You are to be prepared and equipped for a period of field training. You are to bring with you your own rifle. That is all.'

Lappin gripped the edge of his desk, trying to pull himself into reality. Charlotte Aitken, clear and concise, cut through his shock. 'Are you there, Sar'nt-Major?'

'A moment, ma'am.' *Clear your throat.* 'Sar'nt-Major Lappin, ma'am. I have your orders. Is there anything else?'

'Yes, Jamie. There's a lot else. There is a very important and very sensitive task for you here. I met your father last night. He is very well and is looking forward to meeting you.'

'You've met my father? What the hell are you doing, Charlotte? I don't need this. You made your choice. Leave me alone!'

'This is mostly professional, Jamie. There really is a task for you. I saw a chance to bring you and your father together. Don't blame me for that. He sends his love. Come over here as ordered and do the job in hand. Take the chance to meet your father. I've told him how you've done since you left home. I've told him about us. He's very proud of you.'

'I know what you're doing, Charlie. Don't do this to me.'

'Jamie, there really is a job. I can't tell you about it over the phone. I know I hurt you. These last years without you have been awful for me. I'm trying to make amends. I'm trying to give us a new start. There's nothing more I can say until I see you.'

'God damn you, Charlotte. I'll never forgive you if you're using my father like you used me. I'll be there as ordered in the morning.'

'Da? This is Jamie.'

'Hello, son. It's great to hear you. Are you all right?'

'Yes, Da. Are you all right?'

'Aye. I'm fine. Your mother is fine too. Your brothers are both in Australia, doing well. All the girls are married. I'm a grandfather four times over, can you imagine that, Jamie?'

Some of the tension left Jamie Lappin's face as his shoulders and arms relaxed. 'Yes. I don't know what to say, Da. It's been a long time.'

'You did right, Jamie. You got out of Belfast and you made a name for yourself. Your lady friend told me you're a sergeant-major and the chief instructor at the army's top school. I'm proud of you, man. I told your Ma. She sends her love and her prayers.'

'Thanks, Da. I love you. Tell Ma I love her too.'

'I will, Jamie. You're coming to see us?'

'I can't go wandering around the town, Da. Something's being arranged. Do you know why I'm here?'

'No I don't. Miss Aitken wouldn't say much. It's something to do with the Provies. You're hardly on their side, so I suppose you're here to do them some damage. I can't argue with that.'

'Is it true they kneecapped you, Da?'

'Aye. They did. A couple of stupid kids with guns. I can get about all right. I don't hold it against them, son. It's the ones that send them out I don't like. There's been some terrible things going on here, Jamie. The Provies are being shot on sight. But if that's what it takes to rid us of them then they've brought it on themselves. If you're part of it God bless you and keep you.'

'Thanks, Da. I have something to do I can't talk about.'

'You do what you think is right, Jamie. It's you who has to

answer to God, nobody else. If your conscience is clear, whatever it is you're doing do it the best you can. Keep yourself safe and come and see us soon.'

'OK. I'll see you soon.'

Jamie Lappin composed himself and walked into the other office without knocking. Charlotte Aitken and Peter Ewart sat quietly, waiting.

Lappin pulled up a chair and sat astride it, the backrest against his chest. He picked up the dossier on Madden that Ewart had brought along to brief him earlier and flicked through the catalogue of bombing and murder.

'I didn't need to see this. I was working with the Metropolitan Police all through last month. All you had to do was confirm that he was responsible for what happened then. Gerry Madden is not the boy I knew. One question: why can't I or somebody else just capture the bastard and put him into a court of law?'

Ewart took the question. 'You know I have good reason to want Madden out of the way. He's tried for me more than once and he's damn nearly killed me three times. I suppose you could say I think it's him or me and I'm taking advantage of this situation. But we're not planning Madden's death here just because I don't like him or I'm afraid of him, Jamie. Gerry Madden is a very clever and able man. We cannot take the risk of him walking out of a court on a technicality, or escaping back into the Republic. If he is allowed to live he will rebuild the IRA and start the killing all over again. He will certainly torture and murder the brave young woman who has done so much to help us destroy the command structure as it is now. He has to die.'

'OK. I just wanted to be sure. Gerry Madden needs killing. I'll do it. But I want no part of planting a gun on Madden's body. I'll knock him down. After that he's your problem. And this backup section you're talking about: I don't need it. I can sleep in the daytime.'

Charlotte broke in. 'The backup section is there for your protection, Jamie, and to get you out afterwards. We think

Madden will come over alone. But it is possible that he may have support.'

'I see this matter as purely professional, ma'am, a military necessity and not a criminal conspiracy. I think we should observe the military courtesies. Chief Inspector, my rank is sergeant-major. I would be grateful if you took note of that, sir.' Lappin waited as they absorbed his meaning, then continued, 'I regret I am not happy with your plan, ma'am. I don't want anyone to know I'm there, except yourself and the chief inspector.' He turned his eyes on Ewart. 'Sir, I would be very much happier if you told your secretary, or whatever she is, that I turned this task down.'

Ewart nodded. 'I'll do that. What are you intending to do?'

'I intend to make my own way to the place planned. I will kill Madden and then make my own way back to here. Place the backup group if you have to. But tell them they are simply manning a temporary OP. Don't give them radar or sound sensors. Let them carry normal weapons and a couple of night sights for their own protection. Their presence won't bother me. After I've hit Madden I'll take action to avoid them. They will react to the shot as I hit Madden according to Standard Operating Procedures: they'll sit tight and call in help. They'll find Madden's body and nothing else. I will hit Madden with a round not used by the British Army. That way the soldiers in the backup party cannot be accused of having shot him. How you explain away the coincidence of them being in the neighbourhood of the shooting is a matter for you.'

'You can evade six soldiers with rifles and night sights, less than a hundred yards from you?' Ewart looked sceptical.

'I can, sir. I require no further help except the provision of rations, water and two 7.62 high-velocity Glaser Safety Slugs just in case I miss Madden with the first round. It's unlikely, but possible.'

Charlotte broke in again. 'Food and water will be provided, Sar'nt-Major. What are these bullets? Apart from the reason you have given, why do you want them in particular?'

'You'll have to get them from a registered gun club, ma'am. I imagine the garrison has one. Glasers are bullets developed in America for SWAT teams operating in crowded cities. They disintegrate on impact, do not ricochet and will not pass through the target. They're made up of a hundred or so steel balls inside a very thin copper cover with an open top sealed by carnauba wax. On impact the bullet cover breaks up and the steel balls act like shotgun pellets. Kinetic energy release is total, all of it being absorbed by the target. On impact with the body centre of the target all vital organs in the chest and abdomen suffer instant and massive disruption. Madden will not even be aware of having been shot. His death will be instant, painless and guaranteed. He has to be killed to prevent him doing harm: no purpose is served by inflicting suffering on him.'

'I'll get the bullets,' Ewart offered. 'Somebody here might link bullets acquired on this base with Madden's shooting. I have contacts in a few Loyalist gun clubs. They'll probably make the link, but they won't ask questions about it.' Ewart rose heavily to his feet. 'I'm going back to Belfast. I'll bring the bullets up tonight. I'll see you both later. Bye.'

Out in the corridor Ewart leaned against the wall, breathing deeply, reaching for his hip flask. *Thank God that one didn't go bad along with Madden. I'd have been dead years ago if it was him after me.*

Inside the office Charlotte Aitken stared unbelieving at Lappin. 'I'd never have believed you could be so cold, Jamie. You're really going to kill Madden like that?'

'Yes I am. I'm doing what I think is right and I'm doing it without hatred or pleasure or personal advantage. Can you say the same? Don't call me Jamie.'

Charlotte flamed. 'And don't you moralise to me! I see no reason not to profit from something that is going to have to happen anyway. There have been things going on here you couldn't even begin to guess at. Look!'

Charlotte pulled open her desk drawer and pulled out her gorgets and rank slides. 'I'm not a lieutenant-colonel. I'm a brigadier. I had to be involved in this. Madden is only a means to an end, a means of getting to his self-appointed successor, a woman who has set herself up in his place. If I wasn't involved Peter Ewart would find another way and our chance at Siobhan McCaillim would be lost. Don't criticise me for looking after my career. Without you it's all I have. I made a mistake when I was under pressure. I hurt you, and by God you've made me suffer for it. You've ignored me. You deliberately destroyed your own career because you thought you could never be your own man if you followed it through and married me. You prideful bastard! Don't you realise how much I love you? You look at me as if I was a stranger even now, when there's no one to hear or see. I want you back, Jamie. I want you back.'

'What about your career, Brigadier?'

'Stop trying to hurt me. I hate myself for what I did, but I had to do it. You could have stopped it at any time, just by coming back for me. You don't need to say things like that. I want my career because it is what I was brought up and trained for. In the army I'm very good at what I do, I understand my role in life and I have an objective. There's nothing wrong with that. But without you it's all meaningless. I want you to share in my success. I want you to be proud of me like I am of you. You bastard, Jamie Lappin! Look at me!

'Look at me, I said! I've had years to think about this and I'm going to have my say. It's all so easy for you. You destroy one career and rise to the top of another without even trying hard. You're at the top. You were always going to be. I have to throw everything I have into it. You just stroll along on God given talent, doing nothing you don't want to do because nobody would dare contradict you, the one and only Godalmighty Rangemaster. I'm fighting for my only chance for happiness, Jamie. I'm not weeping and I'm not shouting. I'm fighting the only way I can. What do I have to do, Jamie, get down on my knees? I won't, because you would despise me for it. I love you and I need you. Don't ignore me any more. If we try we can find a way to make it work for us. I love you, Jamie Lappin. In a little café in London I said I'd love you for the rest of my life. I meant it. Don't abandon me because I made a mistake. Think of what we had, what we still have. Come back to me, Jamie. Look at what I've achieved for us and be proud of me. I'm proud of you.'

Lappin stood up from his chair and turned away, staring out of the window. Charlotte watched as his back began to shake. She had seen that shake before, a thousand times. Any moment now that great bellowing roar of laughter would burst out of him! Unable to take it she slumped over her desk, letting the tears take over, despair flooding her. At the window Jamie Lappin heard again the words of a thin, gay Professor, the same words he had just heard from a woman he had never ceased to love.

She felt a hand on her shoulder, turning her. Pulling her last vestige of dignity to her Charlotte stood up abruptly, determined to face him. Jamie Lappin was not laughing. He was weeping soundlessly, tears running down his face, holding out his hands. Charlotte threw herself into his arms. They stood a long time, clinging silently to one another, terrified of letting go.

28 May 1993
LISBURN

'You don't have to do this, Jamie.'

Lappin was standing in the doorway of Charlotte's office, dressed for the field, the long rifle bag over his shoulder.

'Yes I do, Charlie. It has to be done and I can do it better than anyone else. It's best if I do it.' Lappin hesitated and looked indecisive for a moment, then his face cleared. 'I've something to tell you, Charlie. I was going to keep it for later, but I want to tell you now.' He came back into the office and sat on the edge of Charlotte's desk.

'I'm due to retire soon. My twenty-two years is just about up. I guess you knew that and I think you're worried about me fitting in as a civilian. Well, forget it. I'm staying in.'

'You're going on extended service?'

'No. The SASC is expanding, Charlie. They're going to have to have two Rangemasters. The army being what it is the chain of command has to be maintained. There's to be a new appointment, to cover both the Rangemasters and to take on advanced weapon training for Warrior crews. The appointment will be as Chief Instructor, Infantry Weapons, in the rank of captain, maybe major later, permanently sited at the School of Infantry. The job was offered to me a fortnight ago. I was going to turn it down. I won't now. You're going to have to do a lot of commuting to quarters in Warminster.' Lappin got up and walked to the door. 'Your mouth is open, Charlie.'

'That's ... fantastic! I ...' Charlotte stopped, thinking, her heart pounding. 'Is that a proposal?'

'I suppose it is. See you later.' Lappin shut the door and sprinted down the corridor, a great burst of his bull-like laughter rolling behind him. Charlotte took a few seconds to react, then cursed as her skirt caught on the corner of her desk. He would get clean away! She wasn't having this. *I want him down on one knee with a ring in his hand!* She ripped the door open. *Too late, he's gone. Shit!*

A little later, sitting on the floor in her rooms, Charlotte hugged herself in happiness. *Charlotte Lappin? No. Charlotte Aitken-Lappin? No. Charlotte Lappin-Aitken? Yes. That sounds right.* Then a thought struck her. *Chief Instructor Infantry Weapons? Two Rangemasters under command? He's still going to be top dog! I'm still going to have to compete. Oh! the PIG.* She jumped up and started looking through her copy of the Army

List, looking for when particular jobs were going to come up for a change of personnel.

An hour later Charlotte had the facts at her fingertips. Jamie was forty-two. About to be commissioned. In four to five years he would be a major. In his sixth year he would be promoted lieutenant-colonel and assume command of the school, simply because there would be no one else of the right age and background to compete. Charlotte's thoughts quickened. Jamie was not good on paper. As CO of the school he would have to do a lot of writing. No problem: the SASC would surround Jamie with Camberley trained staff officers to keep him well briefed and his paperwork decent. He would talk to people and march on to greater glory. If he was lucky and nothing serious happened he could just possibly be promoted brigadier and take over command of his Corps for his last two years of service. With his luck it just had to happen. Charlotte sat back, biting her lip. *I damn well will make major-general. I'll command my Corps and I'll bloody well do it before he gets anywhere near command of that school. I want a whisky.* Sipping her whisky Charlotte leaned back against a cushion, dreaming. *I still have three years. What if I make it in time to keep Tollesbury? I could retire and let Jamie march on, without him thinking I was smoothing his path. I could have his child. I could stay at home at Tollesbury and have as many babies as possible. I must keep Tollesbury for our children.* Charlotte hugged herself. *Jamie's children!* Memories of last night's lovemaking flooded back to her, heating her face. *It was so wonderful* . . . A thought struck her: a parson who knows a duke knows enough. *I know a Prime Minister!* She jumped up, reaching for the telephone.

Chapter Twenty-three

29 May 1993

LONDON

'Thank you for seeing me at such short notice, Prime Minister. Field Marshal George felt that you ought to be personally briefed on current events.'

'I receive a daily brief from the Field Marshal's office. I have been given to understand that we are on the brink of total victory. What is different now? I warn you not to ask me for an extension of operations in Ireland. I have told the Cabinet that SAS operations in the Republic will cease with effect from the first of June. I will not sanction anything beyond that date.' The Prime Minister looked tired and irritable, the country's economic problems foremost in his mind.

'I fully understand that, Prime Minister. But we are not on the brink of victory. We have victory. The Provisional IRA has been destroyed as an effective force, as I promised, in a month. But there are things you should know. Gerry Madden, the Provisionals' chief of staff, the man who planned the attacks in England, is still at large. He is no longer important, except as a symbol of resistance. His elimination would be final proof that the Provisional IRA is defeated. I have information that he will be crossing the border between now and ten days hence. I have acted on that information, without SAS involvement. It will not be possible for operational reasons to capture him. I believe the British people would not want him captured anyway: he would be a focus for a resurgence of terrorism however long he lived in jail. They just want him dead. Accordingly, I have arranged that he will be ambushed and killed, if necessary after the first of June.

No announcement will be made. His death can be confirmed at a later date. Do you concur?'

The Prime Minister waved a hand. 'I don't give a damn what happens to him. I don't want this whole distasteful business dragged through the courts, reminding people of the horror of it all. I want it stopped, dead and buried, forgotten. Do what you must. You didn't come here to tell me about this man Madden. What do you want?'

'I regret to inform you that in the course of Operation HALO we have discovered that there is a group of people led by a woman, one Siobhan McCaillim, which has been operating independently within the Provisional IRA, waiting for Madden to fall. Her group went to ground at the beginning of Operation HALO. I need to have the SAS revert to their other primary role. I need the SAS to gather Intelligence on them. After that we must eliminate them, all at once, if possible.'

The Prime Minister exploded. 'You're telling me that there is a new IRA inside the old? That all this has been for nothing? That the bloodbath will start all over again? Tell me that, Brigadier, and you'll walk out of here a civilian.'

Charlotte glanced at the impassive George, who was standing silent near the door. 'I am telling you no such thing, Prime Minister. I am telling you that these people exist. The possibility of their resurrecting the Provisional IRA or a like organisation exists. Covert surveillance is necessary, then a one-off direct action. Then there will be an end. Without it all this may well have been for nothing.'

The Prime Minister passed a hand over his face. 'Surveillance then. No action not sanctioned by me. That's all.'

'Thank you, sir.'

As Charlotte reached the door the Prime Minister called her back. 'I'm sorry, Brigadier. I'm a bit tetchy today. My congratulations on doing a very fine job. I will report to my cabinet colleagues that the Provisional IRA is dead. The Cabinet Office will leak the end of Operation HALO to the press. It will give our people some joy in these difficult times. I might add that it is a great weight off my own mind. What are your future plans? I would like to show my appreciation.'

Charlotte saw her chance and seized it. 'I have a plan sir, or rather a personal objective. I am aiming at becoming the British Army's first ever woman major-general. Until I achieve that I must just soldier on. After that I will think again.'

'I should have guessed you would pull no punches, Brigadier.' The Prime Minister turned to his papers, then back to her. 'I amend my previous order. You must not use the SAS for anything other than covert surveillance after the first of June, at least until you can be sure that you can damage this new group of terrorists badly enough to prevent its resurrection of the Provisional IRA. You must do that damage in one blow. Should such an opportunity present itself you may act without further reference to me. I will hear no more of this. I want it finished, Brigadier. Finish it and you might just achieve your personal goal. Goodbye.'

0157 hours GMT, 4 June 1993
FORKHILL

Jamie Lappin, Bravo to his friends, blinked moisture off his eyelids. The seventh night was a wet night: not overly cold, but not so warm either, if you were standing around in wet clothes. A little light from the moon and stars fell with the rain, but not much; there was too much cloud too low to earth. Visibility was under ten metres, except through the Starlight 'scope. The time was Zulu 015704Jun93; just coming up to two o'clock in the morning on 4 June 1993, Greenwich Mean Time.

The first six nights had been cool, dry and calm, but a sudden break in the spring weather made the seventh a time of sodden misery; thin rain driven flat by a stiff west wind. Lappin was cold, wet and very tired, but his condition served only to make him feel more determined: twenty-odd years of fighting far from home and training in the wilder parts of Britain had seen to that. He had his hand built 7.62 millimetre L42A1 sniper rifle cradled in his arms, a Starlight 'scope to see through, and a passionless intent to kill lay easy in his heart.

Starlight 'scope to eye then, let's see. Left of arc a gorse bush, 1,200 metres, shining black in the Starlight green. Nothing. Swing right. Swing slow, swing even, breathe steady, elbows clear of the trench edge. Trees black on green, shining. Check base of trees. Nothing. Swing slow, swing even. The barn. Slate roof, one window, no door this side, bright whitewash green in the scope. Nothing. Nobody moving in to offer covering fire, nobody hunkering down with an Armalite. Swing slow, across, down. Thumb safety catch: ON. Finger off trigger; no accidents. Movement! Range 400 metres. Stop swing, rifle steady. Breath stop. Exhale slow, sight 'scope. There. Nothing. There, there, yes. Safety catch OFF. Be sure. Eyes reflecting moonlight. A fox. Not the wolf I'm looking for. Fuck.

Not fuck; no, not fuck. Patience. Watch. Wait. Patience pays off. Breathe deep, slow, relax back, move feet. Safety catch ON. Rifle down. 'Scope off. Watch and wait. Next time maybe. I am here old friend, here in the earth, waiting, till Hell freezes over if I have to. I loved you once, better than my brothers. At least you'll die in Ireland.

Lappin reached for the handset of his radio. It was 2 a.m. precisely, time for his four-hourly report. 'Zero this is Bravo. No change, over.'

The voice of his contact came back almost instantaneously. 'Zero. No change, ou . . .' Then Charlotte was in his ears, telling him she was there if he needed her. He thought a moment. 'Zero this is Bravo. I need you all the time, out.'

'This is the Nine O'Clock News, with Douglas Hodge, on Friday the 4th of June. Northern Ireland. A bomb outrage in Belfast city centre was claimed by an organisation calling itself the Army of *Eire Nua*. No one was injured. An unidentified man was found shot to death early this morning near the border village of Forkhill in County Armagh. An RUC spokesman, Commander Peter Ewart, says the man had a single close-range shotgun wound in his chest. A shotgun was found in undergrowth nearby. Foul play is not suspected. Reports of an explosion in the vicinity of the body have been denied by the army and police in Northern Ireland. Scotland. A boy was savaged by a large dog as he did his paper round this morning. Police are . . .'

'This is the Ten O'Clock News, with Douglas Hodge, on Friday the 4th of June. Northern Ireland. The body of a man found shot to death this morning in Northern Ireland has been identified as that of Gerry Madden, self-styled chief of staff of the Provisional Irish Republican Army. The Prime Minister has expressed the opinion that SAS operations in Ireland drove Madden to suicide. The Prime Minister has also said that Madden's death marks the end of Provisional IRA terrorism in these islands. He has declared the Provisional IRA defeated and Britons avenged for the suffering the Provisional IRA inflicted on us all in recent months . . .'

Charlotte was sitting back, smiling. It was all over. Provisional IRA declared dead and the SAS reporting in that Siobhan McCaillim had called an emergency meeting of her group in the Larkswell hotel, a secluded former country house near the Monaghan border. Colonel Havers was preparing to take positive action. Generalship seemed very near to hand. It was nearer than she thought. The Field Marshal, also briefed by the SAS, had already been to see the Prime Minister.

Charlotte was pouring a cup of coffee, waiting for the first news of Jamie's return, when the telephone rang. It was the Field

Marshal himself. 'Brigadier Aitken,' Charlotte replied. 'What can I do for you sir?'

'Nothing right now. I spoke privately with the Prime Minister earlier this morning. I am directed to inform you that you have been promoted substantive brigadier, backdated to the First of May this year. Expect a visitor. Congratulations, General.'

Charlotte listened to the buzz of a dead line. *General? A slip of the tongue. Would that it hadn't been. Substantive brigadier! Brilliant! There's someone at the door.* 'Come in.'

The so3 gi, a personage rarely seen outside the GOC's headquarters came in.

'What is it, Captain?' Charlotte, eyes shining with happiness, did not even notice that the captain was the same Para she had bidden never to speak to her again.

'A package for you, ma'am.' He saluted, turned on his heel and strode out. Charlotte opened the small box. Inside it were two sets of insignia, the crossed baton and sword plus one star of a major-general. A note fell out, no, not a note, a telegram. It read Herewith a well-earned reward for outstanding achievement. Well done, General. Britain's thanks. George Prosser.

Conductor Caldwell rushed in at her scream, the first she had ever allowed herself. She bounced on him and kissed him. 'I'm a major-general! I'm a major-general! Jamie will be so proud of me! Give me a salute and call me General!'

Caldwell disentangled himself from the new general, grinning all over his face. 'Certainly not. How dare you kiss a conductor, you brazen hussy. My general will hear of this! I've never heard of such conduct. Get away from me or I'll set my wife on you.'

'I am your general, you one armed bloody genius. Give me a salute.'

'No. I couldn't possibly salute an improperly dressed general officer. It would be an insult to my dignity as the British Army's senior senior NCO. Get dressed and I'll go out and come back in again.'

Charlotte, as excited as a schoolgirl, threw her head back

and laughed in unconscious imitation of Jamie Lappin's bawl. 'OK. Give me one minute.'

One minute later Conductor Caldwell knocked smartly on her door. She waited for him to walk in as usual. He didn't. She waited longer. He knocked again. She called out 'Come in.' Conductor Caldwell marched in with his hat on, halted and saluted left-armed. Charlotte waited, excited and enthralled, knowing he would make this memorable for her. He did not let her down. He was frowning fiercely at her.

'A conductor must not be kept waiting, General. In such circumstances he must report you to his next most senior conductor. Since I am the most senior conductor of all I will report you to me.'

'Conductor, I have been kept waiting by my new general. I am insulted. What are you going to do about it?'

'Do, Conductor? I will give her ten extra duties. Will that do?'

'Yes Conductor, it will.'

'Good. I will discipline the general, Conductor. General Aitken, you have been reported to me as having insulted a conductor RAOC by keeping him waiting. I find you guilty since I was privy to the offence. Will you take my award or go for court-martial?'

Charlotte, giggling, tried to look contrite. 'I am guilty. I will take your award, Conductor Caldwell.'

'You will do ten extra duties. At your discretion of course, General!'

'Thank you. You are most merciful, Conductor. I will try harder in future.'

Conductor and general were bouncing round the room together in a paroxysm of fun when there was another knock on the door. Charlotte nearly fell over. 'I know there's another conductor in the GOC's staff. You're trying to catch me out, you old fox. COME IN.'

Peter Ewart lurched through the door, very drunk. Charlotte reacted immediately, jollity forgotten. 'What is the meaning of this? Explain yourself. Mr Caldwell, have one of your staff bring coffee, now please. Thank you.'

'Of course, General. It will be here in just a minute.'

Peter Ewart looked sickly at her. 'General? You're a lieutenant-colonel.'

'Sit down before you fall down. You're in a disgraceful condition, I suppose in celebration of your promotion. I heard it on the news. Congratulations, Commander. For your information I am a general. I was a brigadier when I last saw you. I will explain some other time. Why have you come here in this condition? Explain yourself.'

Ewart thumped himself down into a chair, both hands over his face, pulling it down. He looked up. 'I went to Forkhill. Madden was dead, a Glaser slug in the chest, a hell of a mess. Lappin hit him dead centre. Have you heard the BBC news?'

'Of course I have. I told you so. It's how I learned of your promotion. What are you trying to say?'

'I denied reports of an explosion. You probably heard that on the news. I've just come from Forkhill. I spoke to one of your people there, a Corporal Green. He told me you and Lappin were more than just friends. I'm truly sorry.'

Charlotte felt ice begin to form somewhere deep inside her. 'Sorry? For what?'

'Jamie Lappin is dead, General. The Provos put a bomb under the base of the old observation post, his firing position. Probably sound activated. The high-velocity shot he killed Madden with set it off. There was nothing but a hole in the ground. We were set up. I'm sorry. I'm so very, very sorry.'

Charlotte screamed, a different kind of scream. She was still screaming when Conductor Caldwell burst in, still screaming when the doctor arrived, still screaming, in a curled up ball on the floor, when the doctor pumped a liquid sedative straight into her bloodstream. Six seconds later she was a floppy rag doll being lifted by the doctor on to a wheeled stretcher.

Two days and she was on her feet, out of hospital, cold,

collected, utterly determined that Siobhan McCaillim would pay for her butchery of Jamie in her own blood. Charlotte, possessed of a rage of which she could never have believed herself capable, fully intended to kill Siobhan McCaillim, in person.

7 June 1993
LISBURN

'I told you never to speak to me again, Captain. Get out of this office.'

'My apologies, General. I must speak. You must go to Musgrave Park hospital now.'

Charlotte's face was set and hard, devoid of feeling. 'Why?'

'I hurt you badly once, and I have regretted it ever since. I saw a chance to make amends. I am very pleased to tell you that twenty minutes ago a Royal Greenjacket foot patrol reported by radio. They had found what they thought at first was the body of the Rangemaster, in a collapsed section of a gas pipeline a couple of hundred metres from the site of the explosion two days ago. Apparently he hadn't trusted the old OP and chose his own firing point. It collapsed in on him when the bomb blew in the OP. A medic in the patrol's backup section confirmed the Rangemaster's identity. And reported him alive. He is very badly hurt, unconscious, but not yet dead. He is being flown to –'

The Para captain broke off, for there was no one to listen. The general was gone, running down the corridor, shouting for her car.

10 June 1993
MONAGHAN

Siobhan McCaillim was out of the hotel, walking across the

car park to her car telephone, summoned by her bleeper, when part of the building disintegrated behind her. The blast knocked her off her feet and winded her. She got to her knees, skinned by the tarmac of the car park, and knelt staring at the smoking ruin of her dreams. The hotel itself, solidly built of local stone eighty years ago, seemed undamaged, its walls and roof intact, just a few windows blown in. But the west wing, added just last year, built in plasterboard faced with brick, had completely fallen apart: its roof had caved in and its outer walls collapsed at all angles. Siobhan could even see the remains of the huge old oak table her people had been sitting around when her phone rang: the great central board of the table was split and broken and it leaned drunkenly on two of its six legs.

Of the command force of her army there appeared to be no single man intact. Shattered, dismembered bodies were scattered all over the grass near the building, smaller parts thrown as far as the car park she knelt in. She stood up, took a step towards the destroyed building, tripped and nearly fell over a man's leg. She stared down at it, not thinking, seeing the brown boot on its foot, the silly white-spotted sock turned down over the boot top. Jonny Rourke, her chief of staff, wouldn't miss the leg: the rest of him was embedded in a flowerbed, had dug its own grave with the force of its impact in the soft loam.

Shocked beyond imagining, Siobhan acted by instinct. Walking like a robot, she climbed into her car, started it and rolled it down the drive on to the single-track road away from the hotel, unable to comprehend what had happened. A mile down the road a barrier, blue lights flashing, stopped her. She pulled herself together. *The Gardai. They've seen the explosion. Get out of the car.* Siobhan walked toward a group of dark figures standing in the road. One called softly, 'Siobhan?' She nodded, still too confused to think, to wonder how a country cop could know her name. The figure melted away. Another figure, limned in her car headlamps, moved into view, walking towards her. Ten feet away Siobhan saw the face, recognised it. The figure was in British Army combat uniform.

Charlotte Aitken walked closer. 'You are Siobhan Maeve McCaillim. I am Major-General Charlotte Aitken. The man you put a bomb under at Forkhill was my fiancé. You deliberately set a trap for my man.' The general raised a standard British Army issue 9 millimetre automatic pistol. Siobhan panicked, dropped to her knees, screaming, 'I didn't know! I didn't know who he was! I surrender. I surrender, for Jesus' sake! Don't shoot!'

The general's expression did not change. She held the pistol close to Siobhan's head. 'You didn't care. You bombed my man. You're going to die, McCaillim. Stand up.'

Siobhan crouched down further. Falling back on the only defence left to her, she cried: 'No. I can't. You'll kill my baby. You'll shoot me and kill my baby. I'm pregnant. You can't shoot me. Let me go. Please let me go.'

Charlotte let the pistol's weight take it down until it rested on the head of the sobbing, terrified Siobhan. She squeezed the trigger, watched the hammer rise. *No. I can't. I can't kill her baby.*

Siobhan's head jerked back, blood exploding from its side as the bullet ripped through it. Charlotte jerked back, confused. *Had she . . . ?* But Havers was beside her, taking her pistol from her. He held an identical pistol in his other hand, a thin wisp of smoke curling in the headlamp light.

'She had to die, General. Had to, baby or no baby. And there was no baby.' Havers looked Charlotte full in the face. 'Believe me, General. There was no baby. I saw Madden's post-mortem report. The man was dying by inches, his insides riddled with ulcers. McCaillim must have known. Madden had more heroin in him than a mainlining junkie. And a hell of a lot of depressants. And other tranquillisers. His doctor was probably too afraid of him to tell him. McCaillim just fed him drugs to keep him quiet, keep him going until she could take over. It's unlikely that he could string a sentence together, amazing that he could even talk. It is impossible that he could have fathered a child. McCaillim was not pregnant, General.'

The general nodded silently, bent over to close Siobhan McCaillim's open, sightless eyes. She held back the urge to spit in Siobhan's face. *You heartless bitch. Gerry Madden was a modern savage, a creature from the swamp. He deserved to die for his crimes. But how could you betray your own man? May God forgive you.*

Charlotte turned to Havers, recovered her pistol, holstered it, walked with him down the road. Havers asked, 'What now, General?'

'Go home. This is over.'

10 August 1993
TOLLESBURY

The General sat on a low stone bench beside Jamie's day bed, wheeled out on to the balcony of Tollesbury Manor, enjoying the cool sea breeze that was trying hard to ease the heat of the day. She reached over to take Jamie's hand, waking him gently.

'It's often like this in summer. You'll love it when you're able to be out and about. I have some news. I resigned my commission today.'

Jamie's head turned in its brace. He frowned. 'Why? I'm going to be all right in a few more months. We can soldier on together. Take it back.'

Charlotte looked stubborn. 'No, Jamie. I don't want to. I had an objective. I achieved it. I've seen enough horrors. There are other things to do.' She broke off, then spoke in a rush, leaning over to watch him closely, her face hot. 'Jamie, I want to talk about something else. I don't know how to say this. You remember we made love in Lisburn, the night before you left for

Forkhill? It was wonderful ... After so long alone ...'

Jamie frowned again, raising himself up a little. He tried to reassure her, suffused with embarrassment. 'Don't worry, Charlotte. It was my neck that was broken when that trench fell in on me, nothing else. There'll be more love, sooner than you might think.'

She smiled at him, holding his hand tightly in both of hers. 'Fool. I'm not talking about you. I'm talking about me. I don't feel terribly well just now. I'm not ill, but sometimes I feel awful. Dr Wallten tells me it will pass soon. I hope so.' She caught the fear on his face. 'No, no. Don't be worried, my love. It's nothing serious ... Well it is, really. It's terribly serious ... It's the most important thing that's ever happened to me. Do you mind if it's a girl?'

Notes:

Big Jamie Lappin died suddenly, in July 1994, of a massive coronary, in the act of carrying soup to a very old man suffering the agonies of migraine. Tom McSherry is even older now, in the care of the Sisters of Mercy.

Marion McCaillim suffered an emotional breakdown on learning of the death of her daughter. She is to be found on most Sundays, reading the poetry of Patrick Pearse to uninterested passers-by, outside the General Post Office in O'Connell Street, Dublin.

Commander Peter Baylis-Ewart MBE suffered a minor stroke in 1995 and retired to a small, run-down estate near Waterfoot, County Antrim. Lady Evelyn, much to her surprise, fell in love with her difficult old husband soon after he buried Gerry Madden and took a pledge of abstinence. She has transformed their estate into a place of grace and peace. The Baylis-Ewarts have one child, Sean, and are trying for another.

Major-General (Retd.) Charlotte Lappin-Aitken lives quietly, dividing her time between her job in London and Tollesbury, Essex. Her twin daughters, Alexandra and Jemima, are exceptionally beautiful children gifted in many ways, one of which is a startling natural ability with any kind of sporting gun. The general has high hopes for them. The general's husband, Lt.-Col. James Lappin MM SASC commands the infantry weapons school at Warminster.

A Selected List of Thrillers available from Mandarin

While every effort is made to keep prices low, it is sometimes necessary to increase prices at short notice. Mandarin Paperbacks reserves the right to show new retail prices on covers which may differ from those previously advertised in the text or elsewhere.

The prices shown below were correct at the time of going to press.

☐	7493 0942 3	**Silence of the Lambs**	Thomas Harris	£4.99
☐	7493 1091 X	**Primal Fear**	William Diehl	£4.99
☐	7493 0636 X	**Bones of Coral**	James Hall	£4.99
☐	7493 0249 6	**Squall Line**	James Hall	£4.99
☐	7493 0862 1	**Under Cover of Daylight**	James Hall	£4.99
☐	7493 1441 9	**Before I Wake**	Steve Morgan	£4.99
☐	7493 1396 X	**The Annunciation**	Patrick Lynch	£4.99
☐	7493 1376 5	**Fall When Hit**	Richard Crawford	£4.99
☐	7493 1427 3	**Glass Shot**	Duncan Bush	£4.99
☐	7493 0192 9	**House of Janus**	Donald James	£3.99
☐	7493 1125 8	**House of Eros**	Donald James	£3.99
☐	7493 1252 1	**Running with the Wolves**	Jonathan Kebbe	£4.99
☐	7493 0564 9	**Hyena Dawn**	Christopher Sherlock	£3.99
☐	7493 1323 4	**Eye of the Cobra**	Christopher Sherlock	£4.99

All these books are available at your bookshop or newsagent, or can be ordered direct from the address below. Just tick the titles you want and fill in the form below.

Cash Sales Department, PO Box 5, Rushden, Northants NN10 6YX.
Fax: 0933 410321 : Phone 0933 410511.

Please send cheque, payable to 'Reed Book Services Ltd.', or postal order for purchase price quoted and allow the following for postage and packing:

£1.00 for the first book, 50p for the second; **FREE POSTAGE AND PACKING FOR THREE BOOKS OR MORE PER ORDER.**

NAME (Block letters) ....

ADDRESS...

....

☐ I enclose my remittance for ....

☐ I wish to pay by Access/Visa Card Number ▢▢▢▢▢▢▢▢▢▢▢▢▢▢▢▢

Expiry Date ▢▢▢▢

Signature ....

Please quote our reference: MAND